VERITY GUILD

VERITY GUILD

MAI CORLAND

RED TOWER
BOOKS™

PENGUIN MICHAEL JOSEPH

UK | USA | Canada | Ireland | Australia
India | New Zealand | South Africa

Penguin Michael Joseph is part of the Penguin Random House group of companies
whose addresses can be found at global.penguinrandomhouse.com

Penguin Random House UK,
One Embassy Gardens, 8 Viaduct Gardens, London SW11 7BW

penguin.co.uk

Published by Penguin Michael Joseph, part of the Penguin Random House
group of companies, in association with Red Tower Books,
part of Entangled Publishing LLC 2026
001

Edited by Liz Pelletier
Interior design by Britt Marczak

Printed and bound in Great Britain by Clays Ltd, Elcograf S.p.A.

The authorized representative in the EEA is Penguin Random House Ireland,
Morrison Chambers, 32 Nassau Street, Dublin D02 YH68

A CIP catalogue record for this book is available from the British Library

HARDBACK ISBN: 978–1–911–75037–6
TRADE PAPERBACK ISBN: 978–1–911–75038–3

ALSO BY MAI CORLAND

BROKEN BLADES
Five Broken Blades
Four Ruined Realms
Three Shattered Souls

for JRC and to anyone who has had to hide their real self

CHARACTERS OF NOTE

FROM THE TEMPLE OF TRUTH

Kerasea Vestal... High Priestess

Mirial Bauman... Priestess

Zel... Servant to Kerasea

Osiris Vestal... Former High Priest, Kerasea's father (recently deceased)

FROM THE LEGIONS OF PRYOR

Torren Morvane... Praetorian, the Senate Investigator and Protector

Julian Monroe... Capital Commander of the Sentries

General Hadrian... Leader of the Legions

FROM THE SENATE COUNCIL – REPRESENTATIVES OF THE SEVEN PROVINCES OF PRYOR

Senator Verhardt... Senate Leader, Province I, the capital

Senator Eyo... Senator from Province II

Senator Terrance... Senator from Province III

Senator Foreau... Senator from Province IV

Senator Suh... Senator from Province V

Senator Medea... Senator from Province VI

Senator Paolo... Senator from Province VII

Antinous... Senate Clerk

Verity Guild is a vibrant locked-palace murder mystery full of political intrigue, beautiful liars, and conflicting motives that could bring the republic to its knees. The story includes elements that might not be suitable for all readers, including depictions of violence, death, gore, evisceration, augury, alcohol use, sexual activity, suicidal ideation, self-harm, and suicide. Torture and death of family is described. Readers who may be sensitive to these elements, please take note, and prepare to join the conclave...

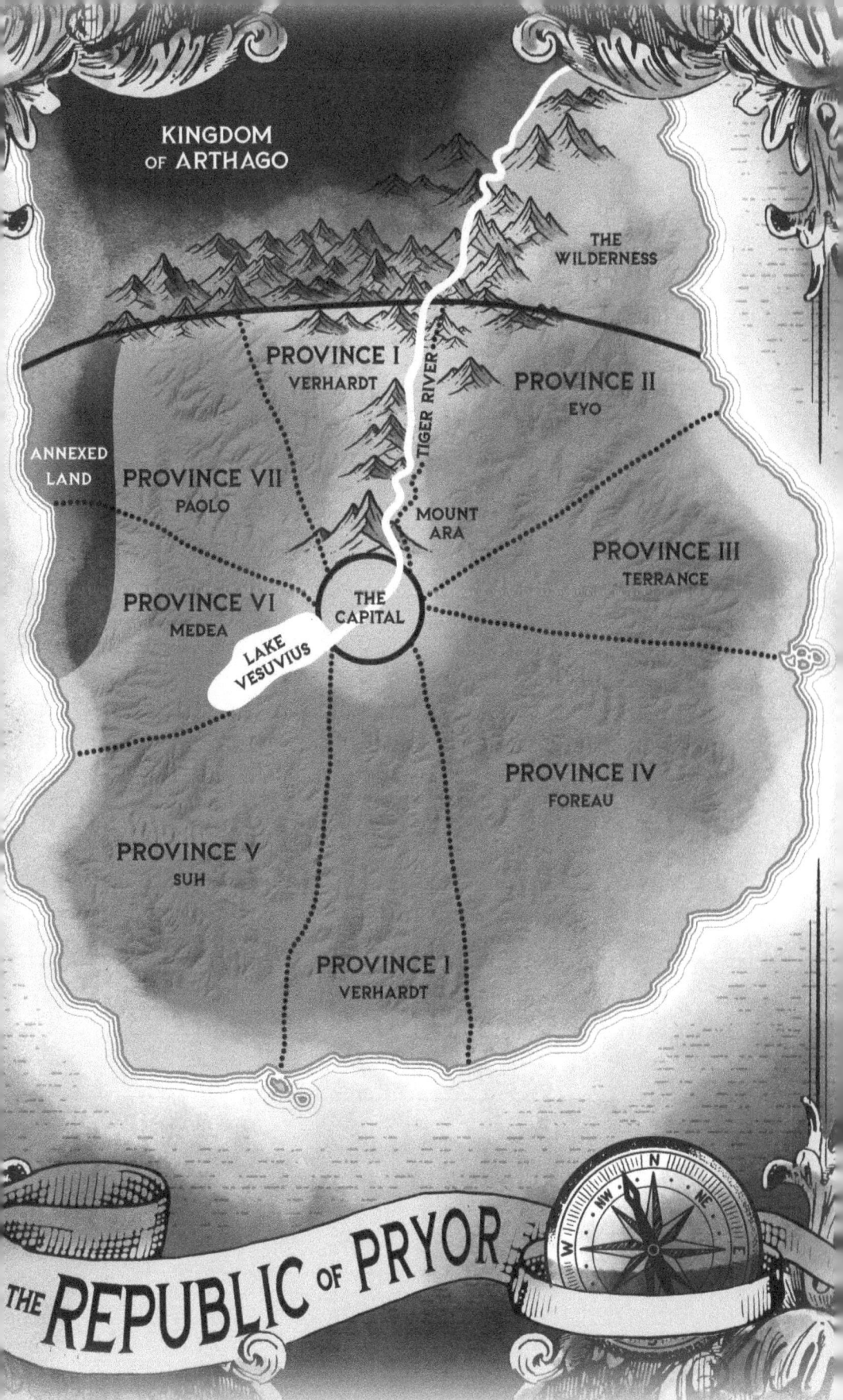

*WE ATONE FOR THE BLOOD THAT HAD TO
BE SHED AND REMEMBER THE SACRIFICES
OF THOSE BRAVE ENOUGH TO OVERTHROW
TYRANNY AND OPPRESSION.*

—the Senate Council on the first Atonement
Day of the Republic of Pryor, twenty years ago

Kerasea

I stand at the feet of a god as a nobleman confesses his latest lie. The colossal statue of the god of truth looms behind me, while the man with blue-black hair whispers details of how he conned a wealthy woman out of her fortune.

I glance to the side.

The same sharp-faced man was on his knees last month when there was snow on the ground. He wore pungent lilac cologne as he confessed to cheating a business partner out of his share. Both the scent and the misdeed felt like ash against my tongue as I smiled and offered forgiveness.

Today, I bite my cheek and try to not react to his latest lie. My father told me to refrain from judgment because confessions are good for the soul. So long as we are honest before the divine, the god of truth forgives us for the frailty of being human. And, of course, the money nobles pay for indulgences allows our temple to thrive not just here in the capital city but throughout the Republic of Pryor.

Still, it's hard not to judge. Judgment is as natural as breathing, as lying.

I'm about to bless the man when a boy runs through the colonnaded great hall. He slips past temple guards and enters the inner area, then stops at the other end of the reflecting pool, breathing hard.

"Sanctuary!" he yells out. His desperation echoes in the white marble space, and I step forward.

He's young, at least ten years less than my twenty-two. Yet his clothes are several sizes too small—inches of his pale wrists and ankles stick out of his worn shirt and pants.

Two sentries rush in and grab his thin arms.

"What is this about?" I raise a hand, and everyone stills.

"Sanctuary, Great One," the boy cries.

"A patron has accused him of stealing a Revelry mask, Excellency," the elder sentry replies in a voice so loud that I hear him clearly from the other end of the room. The guard is old enough to be my father and trying to catch his breath, having lumbered after the boy.

"Northside trash coming over the bridge to pickpocket—that is all, High Priestess," the other sentry adds. He is either a teenager or barely able to grow a patchy mustache. "He ran in here to evade us. Our deepest apologies for the disturbance."

"Whip him at the post and make an example of the boy," the nobleman says from behind me.

I keep myself from sneering at the man who was just confessing to stealing far more than a mask. But he is elite and this child is not.

"A priest will take the remainder of your confession in the silent alcoves," I say, faking a genial smile at the nobleman.

Then I walk to where the sentries hold the boy. My long, gold-embellished robe swooshes as I glide toward them. The two sentries incline their heads as they both take a knee, but the boy just stands staring at me. He's only an inch or two smaller than my five foot three, but he looks up with his mouth agape. His eyes are slightly tipped at the corners like mine, but his hair is far shorter than my waist-length locks.

"Is what they say the truth? Did you steal a mask?" I ask.

His lips quiver. "Yes, Excellency."

"Do you have it now?"

He nods, and a tear falls from his thick lashes as he pulls the item from under his shirt. It's a silver mask—the kind that will be worn this evening by elites as they mark the founding of the republic.

Tonight we will commemorate our senators murdering the Elusian king and his magical bloodline. Through bloodshed, they ended the monarchy and the Hundred Year War. It used to be known as the Crimson Night, but now it's the Revelry. Blood rinsed clearer every year until solemnity became a celebration.

I hold out my palm, and the boy's hands shake as he gives me the mask. I then hand it to the older sentry.

"There. No harm has been done." I smile without showing my teeth. "You may both return to your posts."

"But—" the younger sentry begins.

I raise an eyebrow, and the older sentry shakes his head at the younger soldier. They are part of the legions of Pryor, but I am the High Priestess of this temple. They are only welcome for as long as I permit them to remain. And they wouldn't have dared question my father.

"Yes, Excellency," they say together.

They both bow and withdraw. The boy looks around, now free, but he shifts his weight under my gaze.

"Why did you take the mask?" I ask once we are alone.

"To sell it. My little sister needs tonics from the apothecary and good food to eat, or she won't make it through the spring. I... We can't afford to heal her."

The truth rings out in his voice, and I clench my fists. No more than twelve, and he's already the provider for his family. The capital has changed for the worse in recent years.

Being young and poor, he probably had few options to raise

the money for medicines. Although I am from the Southside of the capital, I know all too well what it's like to not have choices in this world.

"I see," I say. "And that was the sole purpose? Just to heal your sister?"

"And to buy a meal for myself at the taverna." His cheeks color with shame, but doing good doesn't mean you have to be selfless. The weight of a good deed is measured alone.

"You know that stealing from the elite carries heavy punishments?" I ask. "And that it is wrong to steal? The act of stealing is predicated on a lie."

He slowly drops his head in a nod. "I know. But I had to try for Tria."

There's so much love in the two syllables of his sister's name that my heart squeezes.

"I believe you," I say. Then I look past him and gesture to a temple guard.

The guard strides over. He salutes me and stands ready. He must've overheard all of this, but he is expressionless. If I asked him to whip this boy, he would do so without hesitation. The boy stares at the guard's tall frame covered in steel and leather armor, and dread flashes in his eyes.

"Give this boy three gold coins and have the cooks feed him supper," I say. "He is welcome to remain in the temple until we shut the doors at nightfall."

"Great One, I am not worthy," the boy says. But he doesn't hesitate to pocket the money the guard hands him. It will more than cover the tonics.

I reach out and rest a hand on his shoulder. I can feel the hollows between his bones under my palm, and my stomach twists. "You were truthful in this temple, and that is what matters. We are all worthy of forgiveness when our hearts are pure. I hope you can heal your sister."

He falls to his knees in tears, and I bless him, signing over his head with my hand as I saw Father do all my life. The guard escorts him out of the inner hall as the boy praises my name.

"A million thanks to you, Excellency. May all of Pryor see your goodness and know your generosity."

I exhale. I suppose that's better than them knowing the truth.

"Your good heart will be your downfall, Kera," Priestess Mirial says. She stands to my side with her arms folded. I'd startle, but I'm used to her moving on silent feet. Her chin-length gray hair is perfect as always, her lined face in the permanent scowl I adore. "He'll talk, and we will have brats trying for sanctuary from now until the next solstice."

I shrug. "There are worse things."

Mirial harrumphs, but ever since the death of my father and my subsequent elevation to High Priestess a few months ago, she doesn't question me.

"Indeed, there are," she says. "Come with me to the divining room?"

I nod.

"Here I thought you were going to lecture me about not being ready for the Revelry," I say as we walk around the pool and down the narrow hall in the rear.

The afternoon light is already dimming, and I will need to bathe and dress before the celebration begins after sunset.

"That, too, but this takes precedence," she says.

A chill crawls over my shoulders—something is wrong, because little is more important to Mirial than punctuality and decorum.

I discreetly clutch my sleeves in my hands, holding myself together, as I'm always being watched. We pass servants and acolytes in the halls, and they bow to me. Luckily, I have experience hiding how I feel, so no one looks twice as we turn and climb a set of winding stairs.

The inner sanctum of the temple, the holiest place, is the divining room. With an oculus open in the gilded, domed ceiling, we use this space to commune with the gods and foretell the future from the livers of sacrifices. One such sacrifice, a bronze-colored eagle, lies cut open on the marble altar.

When I was younger, I used to hate that my father had to use dead birds for prophecy, but he pointed out that all creatures die, and omens are a divine blessing. We see the future while most of the republic dwells in the past.

But whoever did this sacrifice nearly butchered the animal.

"Is this what you wanted me to see?" I ask Mirial, pointing to the carcass.

She shakes her head and lifts a cloth from the golden offering tray. I glance down and gasp, the sound echoing in the small, stone-walled room.

A mal omen.

I press my hand to my lips and swallow the bile rising in my throat, but my fingers are shaking.

I've never seen a mal omen in person, but it's unmistakable. The pink liver of the eagle has turned as black as my hair and reeks of death. The solid charcoal appearance is the worst harbinger of rot and chaos. My mind races back to the last time one was seen. It was right before the Hundred Year War began, when the nearly immortal king locked us into battle with the Kingdom of Arthago for a century, killing hundreds of thousands of men, women, and children.

The sign means that death is coming to Pryor—and a great deal of it.

My stomach bottoms out as heavy foreboding shatters my composed facade. I scratch at my wrists, wringing my hands.

Bloody lies, what do I do now?

Mirial's pale blue eyes are locked on my green ones. She's as close to a mother as I've ever had, but she's awaiting instruction from me. As High Priestess, it is my role to lead the Faith, my responsibility to know what to do.

But I don't.

I was only a first-year acolyte when my father died and the elder priests pressed me to fill his position. Having grown up in the temple, I've always been considered god-chosen, but my father fell ill quickly and didn't have the time to teach me everything I needed to know. We assumed we'd have time. But time and health are never guaranteed.

For the most part, I've held things together, but I am not Osiris Vestal. I'm not even the person they all think I am.

I swallow hard, forcing down the word that claws up my throat—the truth of what I am—but I can't even *think* it again. My breath comes in shallow sips, and I ball my hands in fists as I try to focus on the mal omen before me. What now? With an omen like this, the Revelry should be canceled and the Senate Council convened on Mount Ara. But...that's not my decision to make.

We divine the truth from the god and share it on earth. The Senate Council worries about the impact on the people. That separation keeps the Faith from ruling the republic. But I have to do something. Maybe I should refuse to start the celebration or—

"It's nearly sunset," Mirial says in a clipped tone.

I eye her. She's not helping, and she knows it.

"I don't...I don't know what to do," I admit. I hate the weakness in the wobble of my voice almost as much as I hate disappointing her.

Mirial sighs. "You need to report the omen to the Senate Clerk and then start the Revelry."

"But..."

"But nothing. It is tradition and your duty, Kera. You must tell the clerk and go take your place on the Revelry dais—unless the *Council* decides otherwise."

Before I can say a word in reply, Mirial is gone, and I'm left with a liver that reeks of blood and rot.

I close my eyes for a long blink as dread courses through me.

And not just from the mal omen.

I try to forget who I'll be seated next to on the dais, as he is the last thing I need to think about right now. But with my elevation to High Priestess, I'll have no choice but to sit next to the dreaded Praetorian. I'll see him tonight, all next week, and after, when the Verity Guild will convene for the first time since my father's passing.

Shaking out my hands, I try to loosen the noose of fear, but it fits my neck like a vise. With one more exhale, I give up. I raise my chin and glide toward my chambers despite the choking feeling. I have acted the part for my entire life — I can do it for another night. Even with the mal omen, even if it's next to Torren Morvane. Even if I am not actually a Vestal, but the last of the magical Elusian bloodline.

Torren

T he roar of the crowd rises in my ears, begging for blood, and I'm happy to oblige.

My opponent sways in front of me, looking but not seeing. He fought well, but this match was over before it began. The man comes from the Southside, the rich end of the capital.

He'd tried to hide his noble status, but it was obvious from his tailoring and bearing. For all the advantages they have south of the Tiger River, they can't fight like the Northside. It's not really their fault—they've never had their lives depend on their hands.

I shift my stance, ready to issue the final blow. Another win. Another knockout. Victory in the fight ring won't change my past, but it's still something.

Sweat stings as it drips down my forehead into my eyes. I blink twice, and then everything slows. The wraps around my hands suddenly don't feel as tight; my heart beats slower. I bounce on the balls of my feet, my legs nearly weightless with each movement. One.

Two. I draw a breath, ready for my fist to collide with the man's cheek. He'll hit the mat with a thud, and I will be declared the champion—as I have dozens of times before.

Nothing can dull this moment.

"Praetorian! Praetorian," a panicked voice shouts from the crowd. I clench my jaw.

Son of a jackal—well, *almost* nothing.

With stiff shoulders, I turn at my title, although I already recognized the voice. It's Antinous, Clerk of the Senate Council, along with a cadre of armor-plated sentries. Antinous is a small man with round spectacles who has never seen the inside of a ring in his life. Judging by the nervous way he shifts around as he waits, I'm not sure he's even been this close to one.

"The Senate is awaiting you, Praetorian. The Revelry will start within the hour."

Which I knew. I had calculated plenty of time for a quick match, but this nobleman surprised me with his refusal to give up. I've knocked him to the mat twice, and he's still fighting.

For a moment, I consider ignoring Antinous long enough to put this nobleman down one final time. But duty makes my fists too heavy to swing.

I sigh as I raise my arm to forfeit the match, even though conceding feels like pushing sand under my skin. Responsibility comes first for the Senate's protector, as it must. The needs of the republic are greater than any one man's pride.

The crowd in the stands gasps because I've never once been beaten or forfeited. They want to jeer, especially those who bet on a knockout, but they don't dare. Not with ten sentries and the Senate Clerk standing here. And certainly not with my reputation.

The referee lifts my opponent's hand in the air. No one applauds.

I shrug on my cotton shirt and button it. The fabric sticks to my sweat and the man's blood speckled across my chest, but I planned to bathe and change before the Revelry anyway.

Antinous smiles up at me. He's around average height for a man, so a head shorter than me, and maybe half my weight when he's soaking wet. I gesture for him to go first as I catch Julian's blond hair in the crowd. He falls in line beside me, and I knock fists with my closest friend.

"It was a good fight, Tor," Julian says.

I glance at him and raise my eyebrows. "Was it?"

I wait for a reply, but he's already smiling to men he knows and women he'd like to. We're opposites, he and I. He's a few inches shorter and less muscular, and he has blond hair where mine is ebony, but it's our personalities that are diametrically opposed. For example, people like him.

"Your fights never are." He laughs, shaking his head. "I don't know how you still manage to con the upper crust out of money and into the ring."

I shrug. There's never a shortage of overconfident men.

Julian is also one of those upper-crust nobles from a storied family in the Southside, but I like him in spite of all that. In spite of myself, I suppose.

I run my hands through my short hair as we walk the paved stone streets past the noisy hawkers in the sprawling market and the quiet, empty arena.

"Are the men ready?" I ask.

He nods, but he's delayed a moment, distracted by a pair of pretty brown eyes and a green sash. I groan. I swear women will be the death of him.

I idle, and two small, dirty children pull at my pants leg. One look and I know they're from the Northside. Beggar children cross over the Palatine Bridge to reach the deeper pockets here. It's a punishable offense, seeking alms across the river, but they appear to be no more than four and six years old. I toss them a few coppers, pretending they fell from my pocket.

Julian catches me, glowing with happiness as he adds silver coins to their little hands. With his money, they'll be fed for a month. There were days I could only wish for that kind of blessing. Memories of hunger pangs stir in my stomach, and I shake them off.

I clear my throat and look away from the children. "Your report, Commander."

"Yes, of course," he says. "All sentries are on duty, Praetorian."

The Capital Commander smirks as he inclines his head at me. He uses my title because he knows the formality annoys me — at least when it's from him. Julian is one of the few who still views me as a person, not just the Senate's fearsome watchdog and brutal investigator.

I keep walking.

"You seem particularly surly today," he says. "Which is no small feat for you."

I stare straight ahead at the towering white marble buildings of the Forum in the distance, each a marvel of civilization, from the towers to the hanging gardens to the shimmering spire. "I am but a ray of sunshine in the dusk."

The corner of his mouth lifts as I quote one of my favorite poets, then he taps his chin. "Let's see, what's bothering you...lately? I know you don't exactly appreciate the upcoming night of sin because to you, it's just more paperwork."

He's right — the Revelry is a headache. What started as a celebration of the end of an eternal war and a magical tyrant has become a night of sin. Most people just drunkenly revel, but some take it too far and think all crime is legal. It is not, but there are always those looking to give in to darker impulses, and it is our job to stop them.

As if proving my point, a man wanders by wearing little more than a fig leaf. Already deep in his cups, he's spilling wine in the street. He almost collides with a dignified couple, but they all just laugh it off.

I shake my head and continue on. "Nothing is bothering me."

"You're the republic's worst liar," Julian says.

I draw a breath and turn to stare daggers at him without breaking stride.

"Oh, those blue pools the ladies love," he says, chuckling.

I roll my eyes. He really is the worst best friend I could have. Sometimes, like right now, I regret protecting him the day we met, but he's also my only real friend. I assume this is what it's like to have a younger brother—to love someone as much as you're irritated by them. The gods blessed me with being an only child. Well, aside from my half sisters, but they're far younger than I am, and we've lived entirely different lives.

"But you hate the Revelry and all of this every year," he continues. "So why grumpier about *tonight*— Oh." He smiles like a cat cornering a broken-winged bird. "Never mind."

"What?" I ask.

"Nothing." He shakes his head, his hazel eyes innocent. He's not innocent at all.

We enter the Forum, and I glance at the clusters of citizens already gathering in the huge, open courtyard. The space is surrounded by every major civic building and temple on all sides, so it's a natural public gathering place on a good day. Tonight, there will be an absolute mob.

I spare a quick glance at Jubilee Palace perched atop the snow-capped Mount Ara, high above us in the distance. It was once the king's pleasure palace, but now we use it to elect the Senate Leader and pass laws each year. Starting tomorrow, I'll be locked in there with the Council and someone far worse than a drunken mob.

My chest tightens, and I pick up my pace. I appreciate Julian's grunt of annoyance as he matches my long strides. We pass the Republic Baths and the Library of Pryor as I head toward the barracks behind the armory.

Four years ago, when I was appointed as Praetorian, I was given the Villa de Armas, but I had no taste for that place. I keep my bed near the Forum, where I'm the most needed, not in a Southside villa like Julian.

Two sentries salute us as they hold open the doors to the barracks.

"Do you have something to tell me or are you just here to torment me?" I ask.

Julian's smile fades. "Actually, I do."

The change in tone catches my attention as we step into the tiled hall. I stop. We don't have to go far—my rooms are first off the entrance. But Julian avoids being serious at all costs. This must be important.

I unlock the door, and we enter my apartment. My quarters are the most luxurious and spacious in the barracks, which isn't saying much. Jules calls it a "grand hovel." But I have a living space, a bedroom, and a private bath, which is all I need. I've lived with far less.

"There's a rumor that the temple of truth received a mal omen today, and we have reports of a potential Arthagian incursion. I'm sure there won't be a war—the Senate will roll over as per usual. Still, some in command are calling for the Revelry to be canceled."

Jules is right. An incursion hardly matters, as we'll cede land to them. Pryor will do anything to avoid another Hundred Year War, and the neighboring kingdom knows it.

Instead, I focus on the omen. Of course it's the temple. Of course it involves *her*. I grip the doorknob in my fist.

"Oh, well, if the bird livers say it, it has to be true," I mutter, flipping the lock.

Corrupt, powerful, and fraudulent, the temple should've been left in the past during the Crimson Night, along with the Elusian king's bloodline, but it was the Faith who legitimized the Senate. The morning after all the magical royals were slain, Osiris Vestal called the people to rally behind the Council.

The High Priest showed the frightened mob a golden liver and said that the god of truth favored a republic of equals. He proclaimed that the Senate would lead the people to prosperity. His actions cemented Pryor's freedom from imperial rule, but ultimately, it was a deal with the underworld. Now the temple holds nearly as much power as the Senate. But while the Senate is the voice of the people, the temple only speaks for themselves.

"I'll be joining you tonight," Julian says, poking at my books near the armchair.

I raise my eyebrows. "You won't be at your father's soiree?"

Julian has had a complicated relationship with his father ever since the war—meaning, nearly his whole life—but Jules can't resist a good party.

He sighs. "Not this year. Uncle Hadrian has ordered twice the guard in the Forum."

Wonderful. Not only will I have to see the absolute last person I want to, but I'll get to watch Julian fall in love with every half-naked woman who parades by. The Capital officers are normally allowed to participate in the Revelry, and Julian's father throws the second-largest celebration in the capital, but apparently, Jules will spend the night complaining about being on duty instead.

"Go get bathed or you'll be late," Julian says. "That's not what you're wearing, is it?"

He points to the armor on my sofa. I've shined the decorated steel to perfection, so I'm not sure why he's frowning.

"What?" I ask. "What's wrong with that?"

"It's the Revelry." He gestures to himself, and I finally notice he's in a white jacket fit for a ball, not service.

I throw up my hands in frustration. "Then fucking pick something. I don't have time for this."

His lips curl into a smile. "Yes, you wouldn't want to keep the lady waiting."

I swallow and look down at the ground before answering. "A thousand curses upon your soul."

I stride out of the room and just barely resist slamming the door to the bath. Julian laughs because he's goaded me into a temper. He's right—about all of it—but there's no need to tell him that. I don't enjoy the Revelry and, for the first time, Kerasea Vestal will be on the dais next to me. Sharing the space with her father was bad enough. She's worse.

A few months ago, Kerasea became the High Priestess of the temple of truth, and thus she is now a member of the Verity Guild—

the three people tasked with deciding cases of high treason. The only other member aside from myself and the temple is Pol Probus, the Chief Judge of the Ministry of Justice. Citizens call us *the Fates* because the Verity Guild is the highest tribunal in the land.

And now Kerasea gets to be a part of that. Next week we will have our first case together—to decide the fate of Trajan Lowe, a high nobleman accused of raising a private army in the sixth province.

I grip the shower's faucet. I've spent years carefully evading any interaction with her, but I can't avoid her any longer.

There isn't a person less deserving than her. Jules teases me because he thinks I'm secretly in love with her beauty, but I'm not. Spoiled, elitist, and heartless, Kerasea might be beautiful, but she's ugly to her core.

Her haughty laugh still rings in my ears the same way her father's scornful look is emblazoned in my mind. I swore on the stars that day that I would ruin them the same way they did my family. And while I know better than anyone how hard it is to topple the elite in Pryor, I *will* find a way to bring her to her knees.

But for now, I have to endure her.

Without waiting for the hot water, I plunge myself into the cold shower.

It's going to be a long night.

III

Kerasea

I try to will this gown to cover more of my skin as bearers carry my palanquin through the crowded Forum. But so far, this dress is just another of my recent missteps.

There's barely room for me to sit up in here. The palanquin was made for one person to recline on pillows, lounging as servants carry their bed-like box atop poles through the busy city. It used to be the way the king traveled in the capital. Still, the people murmur as the golden palanquin passes by. Thousands of citizens have already gathered in the Forum, waiting for the Revelry to begin, but they make way for my grand entrance.

I'd rather just walk.

But feeling ridiculous in a gilded litter is the least of my problems. I keep smelling that mal omen and seeing the charred blackness. I sent a message informing the Senate Clerk, yet the Revelry is still proceeding. And worse, I allowed myself to think of my blood — and that, I never do.

Never, Kera, don't even think it, my father said. *The mouth is a conduit of the mind. If you think it enough, you will voice it, and no one can ever know your truth. Hide and survive.*

Looking for any distraction, I shift the white curtain and peek out the side. Senator Verhardt sits on a golden throne once occupied by the king. Goose bumps coat my skin. I'd know the Senate Leader anywhere. Not from his short gray hair or his large, bulbous nose. It's the cruel shape of his lips—and the way his gaze seems to always follow mine.

Verhardt is the senator who orchestrated the Crimson Night and, with the murder of the royals, he became the most powerful man in the republic. I shift a little farther back, careful not to draw his attention.

Next to him stand Antinous, the Senate Clerk, and Julian Monroe, the Capital Commander of the sentries.

The dais of the Verity Guild lies to the left of the throne. Pol Probus sits in his black robes looking half asleep. He was appointed three years ago, but he has to be eighty years old if he's a day. His eyebrows are completely white, offsetting rich brown skin, and his jowls dip nearly to his shoulders. Next to him is my empty seat—and then there is the Praetorian.

I close the curtain and lean back on my cushion, my heart already pounding. I grip my gown, wishing I were in temple robes and not this golden, nearly see-through dress.

But as the moments pass, curiosity gets the better of me, because I'm not certain that *was* the Praetorian. Torren Morvane should be dressed in armor, and *that* man, although he was tall with broad shoulders, is wearing a finely tailored suit. I can only hope some horrible accident befell Torren today. Otherwise, I have to hope that the Council will refuse to reappoint him at the conclave this week.

But that seems as likely as Verhardt not being reelected as Senate Leader a twentieth time.

I move the curtain just an inch, and the man turns his head, revealing the chiseled features and arrogant forehead I know all too well. Torren is a shade or two darker than my pale white skin, but his features are accentuated by sapphire blue eyes. He's as handsome as he is fearsome, which is no small accomplishment. Being dressed in cloth makes him look like a man instead of a bronze statue.

I'm not sure which I prefer less.

The Praetorian is twenty-five and, like myself, he stands high on the bones of those who came before him. Torren was appointed after he tracked down and dismembered the man who murdered the last Praetorian. I suppose I know better than anyone that no one ever climbs this high with their hands clean.

I leave the curtain closed for the remainder of the short ride to the altar of peace. Too quickly, the bearers come to a stop and set the palanquin on the ground. I take a breath. It's time. I can do this. I can perform my act for the night. It doesn't matter who is here.

The curtains part, and I slip my legs out, my glass-and-silver shoes tapping on the stone. A hand reaches down to help me stand. I place my fingers into the warm, rough palm, and an unexpected calmness washes over me.

As I rise out of the litter, I find that it's not Senator Verhardt holding my hand but the Praetorian. My breath catches. As soon as our eyes meet, he drops his hand and I pull my arm away. His gaze flits to my dress, and he steps to the side, his lip curling.

Gods. I should've stayed in my robes, but my chambermaids convinced me that I should wear something befitting this night of sin.

My hands shake, but I keep my head high and even smile at the Praetorian. He nods and gestures for me to take my seat, as if he's a gentleman.

I suppose we're both acting tonight.

But we do as we must. The Verity Guild needs to present a united front, especially with the tribunal convening soon. The man accused is the nephew of a senator, and the capital has been abuzz about this case for weeks.

Once I am in place, Senator Verhardt glances at me and then stands. Only the tick in his jaw muscle gives away his annoyance at my tardiness. He's wearing an expensive silver suit the same color as his hair, a choice I'm sure was intentional. This man does everything with purpose.

Verhardt walks to the edge of the platform and extends his arms. "Welcome, my people of Pryor!"

His gravelly voice booms, and the capital crowd cheers. Verhardt smiles, soaking it in.

"Tonight, on the twentieth anniversary of the birth of the republic, of the Senate Council risking our very souls to deliver the realm from the tyranny of monarchs, we celebrate!"

The crowd roars. I try to picture him as a younger man, hiding a dagger, sweating and shaking, waiting with six other senators to stab the king in the back on the Senate floor, but I can't imagine it. I've always known him as the most powerful man in Pryor.

"We celebrate an end to rulers who think themselves gods and, instead, revel in the installment of leaders selected from you, by you, who serve *you*, the people. For twenty years, we have prospered, seven provinces coming together as one republic. May Pryor have centuries more freedom than she suffered oppression. May the gods continue to shine their favor on our great nation."

He pauses and glances at the dais. My stomach knots under his stare.

"Justice and truth led us from a tyrannical realm to a free republic of equals. Tonight, we ask the High Priestess of the temple of truth to light the way of the Revelry."

That's my cue. I stand and take my place next to Verhardt, the gold of my dress flowing like water around me. The Senate Leader has known me since I was a baby, but he still eyes my plunging neckline and curves. Ignoring the turn of my stomach, I focus on my role. He remains in the center, a position of unquestioned power, so I'm forced to stand to his left.

The crowd hushes, and I slowly climb down the stairs and then walk to the drained fountain in the center of the Forum. A temple guard holds a torch out for me, and I light the bale of straw in the basin. As it flames to life, I breathe a sigh of relief. My job is done for tonight.

I hand the torch back to the guard but then lock eyes with the boy I helped earlier. His face breaks into a wide smile.

"Hail High Priestess, the heart of our nation!" he yells out.

After a moment of complete silence, the crowd around me erupts in screams and cheers. The mob roars louder than they did for Senator Verhardt as they chant "heart of our nation."

I glance at the altar and catch the Praetorian's stare. He quirks an eyebrow.

Verhardt is also looking at me. I incline my head to the Senate Leader, but I don't miss how his brown eyes narrow, as if he's reevaluating whether I'm a threat. I've heard the stories—ever since the rise of the republic, Verhardt has ruthlessly eliminated all competition. There are even thoughts that he had his own son killed, although I don't believe that. His eldest child merely succumbed to a deadly fever that swept through the capital a dozen years ago.

Verhardt says the senators are chosen of and by the people, but after they killed the king, the Senate appointed themselves for life. There aren't elections unless one dies, so I have to make this right or he will outlast me.

Once I return to the altar, I turn dramatically and gesture to him. I bow at my waist with my leg forward and a hand over my heart. The people cheer again, but this time for him, for the Faith submitting to the Council. Verhardt's thin lips turn up in a grin, and he gives me an almost imperceptible nod.

The tension defused for now, I retake my seat, trying not to tremble. Both Mirial and my father told me to be careful with Verhardt. Father called the Senate Council a pit of vipers and said the role of the temple is that of a snake charmer. I must be on my guard, be friendly but never friends. Trusted but never trusting.

I'm attentive to Verhardt, but as I sit on my cushion, I'm far too conscious of the Praetorian beside me. I feel him the way prey animals sense predators skulking nearby. My skin turns to gooseflesh as he leans closer to me.

"How much did you pay the kid?" he whispers.

Ire rises through my chest, and I clench my teeth until my jaw aches. I shouldn't engage, because I know he's goading me. I shouldn't respond, even if true believers hailing the Faith have been dismissed as a cheap ploy. The temple doesn't shift when a child kicks at its stones. I am above taking the bait from someone like him.

"Shouldn't you be cutting off a man's toes for fun?" I whisper before I can stop myself.

Surprise lights his features, and then he rests his arm on the back of my chair. He keeps his gaze on the crowd as they sing the anthem of Pryor, but his nearness is unsettling. Having avoided each other successfully since we were children, we've never been this close.

"You have your bird signs; I have other means of getting to the truth."

His deep voice rumbles. I inhale and pretend like I don't feel it in the base of my spine. Morbid curiosity fills me, and I want to ask what he means, but then I remember that I don't have casual conversations with this man. And then I recall why.

Torren Morvane became Praetorian at the age of twenty-one—by delivering a man to the Senate in burned pieces. He used tactics so brutal, they changed the rules of engagement after. And looking at him now, I can see that capacity for violence. It's branded into him from the tightness of his jaw to the curve of his fist.

The temple had advised against his appointment because Torren's father was a convicted traitor. Treachery seeps into the blood, my father said, but the Council insisted they would not hold the acts of the father against the son.

Yet, Torren holds it against me. Rather than blame the traitor for his own disloyalty, the Praetorian decided to hate us for my father simply seeing justice done. No matter how harsh the sentence, his father was the one who committed the crimes. Twelve years ago, I swore to what I witnessed, and the Verity Guild rightly convicted him.

I force myself to move away as Verhardt finally sits. The Capital Commander rises, and that draws the Praetorian's attention.

With a population of a million people, the capital city has its own commander of the sentries. Julian Monroe is only twenty-four, but he is a future patron and the nephew of General Hadrian. Which is all to say, the man is connected, elite, and in a position of great power. He is someone to watch.

"Now that the Revelry has officially commenced, I'd like to take a moment to remind the people of this great city that we will be standing guard," Julian says. "It's a night of celebration and sin, but make your celebration large and your sins small or you risk spending the Atonement in a cold jail cell." He pauses, his heavy gaze sweeping across the crowd before a wide smile overtakes his features. "Happy Revelry!"

The crowd cheers, and even the Praetorian smiles slightly.

The citizens of Pryor will now feast and celebrate until predawn. Then, shortly after sunrise, they'll fall on their knees, repenting for Atonement Day.

Senator Verhardt approaches the dais with his sentries.

"Shall we retire to the terrace for refreshments?" Verhardt asks.

Probus nods and stands first—I suppose he was actually awake. Verhardt offers me his arm while barely acknowledging the Praetorian.

"Of course," I say.

Verhardt looks over his shoulder and commands the Praetorian like a dog. "Follow along."

It should feel good to see Torren put in his place, but for some reason, it doesn't. An uneasy sensation tightens my stomach, and I turn and glance at him. He's silent, but there's fire in his expression. Our eyes meet and he looks away, coloring slightly.

I face straight ahead, regret filling me. I shouldn't have turned or felt even a touch of sympathy. The Praetorian would not feel a drop of compassion for me. No, he'd hunt me down and dismember me without mercy if he knew what I am. I've been sure of that for years.

Then I sigh as I remember: the conclave begins tomorrow night. Meaning I'll be locked in with him atop Mount Ara for a week, with no means of escape.

IV.

Torren

The veranda of the Senate Hall is a second-story stone terrace overlooking the Forum. Because it is so close to the altar, sentries make way for us to walk through the crowd.

I keep my eyes sharp, because even though there are a hundred sentries in the Forum, there are thousands of citizens packing the square. Each one could pose a threat, and the mob is the most dangerous of all creatures. It is my duty to protect the Senate — no matter the risk or danger.

And no matter what I may feel about them personally.

I survey the crowd, ignoring the dozens of women clamoring for my attention by waving handkerchiefs and calling my title. Entanglements are a headache I don't need. I have plenty of problems, including the one in front of me.

"What were you two chatting about on the dais?" Julian whispers.

I shoot him a look that says I won't be answering. We are only a few feet behind Verhardt and the High Priestess.

Senator Verhardt comes to an abrupt halt, causing me to put my hand on the hilt of my sword and shift around them. Kerasea smiles at whoever they're facing.

It's just Verhardt's thirteen-year-old son, along with a swarm of tutors, guards, and servants. The Senate Leader kisses him on both cheeks and exchanges some words I can't overhear. The joy on the man's face is genuine as he embraces his only heir.

The boy is the same age I was when my world was stripped away. But unlike me, there's no way this gangly, pampered kid could survive it. I barely did.

An ocean of memories threatens to pull me under, but I push it all to the back of my mind. The woman who caused it hangs on Verhardt's arm like a shining decoration.

I'll admit that Kerasea is different than I expected. As she is the only child of Osiris Vestal, of course I knew her. Everyone does. But we have not been at any of the same events, and thus have never truly spoken. She is more beautiful than I anticipated tonight, but that hardly matters. Disturbingly adored and *that*, everyone noticed.

But there is something off, almost vulnerable about her. She should've been victorious and proud after the crowd worshipped her, but she wasn't. She blanched when I raised an eyebrow, yet shot back when I insulted her. She's a contradiction, but one I can admit I don't know nearly as well as I did her father.

I don't want to get closer to her, but I have to keep an eye on her. Any priest this powerful poses a threat to the republic. And I already know she can deceive.

She and the Senate Leader resume walking, so I follow in stride. I scan for danger as he waves and shakes hands with some of the nobles, but really, I'm focused on the two of them.

"I understand you had a mal omen today," Senator Verhardt says quietly.

"A black liver, charred and misshapen." She matches his low tone. "The god speaks of death and chaos coming to Pryor."

My muscles tense as she details the worst omen imaginable, but

Kerasea is a skilled liar. This could all be a deception—but to what end?

Verhardt pauses or I can't hear him...until I do. "Share the omen at the conclave, though not tonight. I called for additional sentries, but I don't want to spoil the Revelry for our honored guests."

Kerasea stumbles a step, her ruby lips parting. Surprise scrawls across her face, but she quickly makes her expression neutral, as if it never happened.

"As you wish," she says.

Verhardt smiles like a wolf as they continue on, but I exchange glances with Julian. He caught it, too—something is afoot. The Senate Leader has no reason to keep the mal omen a secret, which means he has a hidden motive.

I now have until dawn to figure out what it is.

V

Kerasea

T he party is already in full swing when we arrive at the terrace. Gold-dusted musicians play as half-naked servants rush to refresh the goblets and plates of the glittering guests. Patrons and benefactresses of the elite Southside families wear revealing attire while hiding their faces behind gold and silver masks.

This will turn into an orgy later. I only hope to be long gone by then.

Lady Verhardt rushes over with feathers in her gray hair and her cleavage on display. I quickly cede her husband's arm and gracefully bow to them.

Now free, I have a moment to wonder why he asked me to hide the omen. I couldn't do anything but agree, yet it feels like a trap.

I mindlessly bless people as I pass, walking with purpose, like I have somewhere to be. Only two other senators are present tonight, and they are each holding court with their own entourages.

Senator Eyo has yet another mistress with him; this one looks barely eighteen. She fidgets with her brown ringlet curls and gnaws on her spice-plumped lips. Eyo's pale, noble features gleam in the lamplight as he studies her plunging neckline. With thick black hair and chocolate brown eyes, he has the kind of handsomeness that's striking at first but fades with familiarity. He is younger for a senator at thirty-six, but his position isn't surprising given the massive gold family crest pinned to his white blazer. It's his wife's family with the real money, though. He used her connections to win the seat of the second province and has amassed a fortune since.

On the other side of the veranda is Senator Medea, unmistakable as the only female member of the Council. Medea was one of the original senators who killed the Elusian king. Although she is sixty, her shoulder-length black hair is just turning gray with streaks of silver. Blunt and no-nonsense, she has represented the sixth province from before Pryor was a republic, longer than I've been alive. She has always reminded me of a tactically charming version of Priestess Mirial.

I greet both senators from a distance, with my hand over my heart. The four other senators of Pryor are no doubt in the capital, but they will meet us at Jubilee Palace on Mount Ara tomorrow night.

Servants pass around flutes of ice wine, and I take one just as Senator Verhardt raises his glass. The dignified crowd quiets at the rise of his bejeweled hand, the diamond ring of the republic sparkling on his index finger. It's huge and cut into the same shape as our original borders.

"A toast—to twenty years of the republic and a thousand more to come," he says.

"To the republic!" everyone replies.

The nobility fall over themselves to toast with the Senate Leader. After everyone drinks, Verhardt moves to the edge of the veranda where a black velvet sack has been placed on the ledge of the stone railing. He waves at the masses below us before raining fistfuls of gold coins down on the crowd. Patrons typically entertain the commoners during the Revelry, but rarely are their displays this expensive.

The people are whipped into a frenzy, trying to catch the gold bullions. They chant his name, and the nobility applaud. I turn just in time to catch the hungry gaze of Senator Eyo and the dismissive frown of Senator Medea as they stare at Verhardt.

Not wanting to let my eyes linger on them, I look to the left and meet the Praetorian's stare. I've been looking at them, but he's been staring at me for gods know how long. I want to flee, but instead, I turn away and drain my wine flute, then take another. The golden liquid is sweet, cold, and refreshing.

But it's also strong.

I'm nearly done with my second glass before I realize it. At the same time, Senator Eyo makes his way to me. He has a full flute of ice wine and a glass of red wine. He offers me the flute.

"Thank you, Senator," I say, my skin prickling as he ogles my neckline.

"Excellency." He smiles, revealing straight teeth in his manicured beard.

He casually leans on the column near me. His eyes focus on my face as if I'm the only woman here, his young mistress, like his wife and children, apparently forgotten for now.

"Beautiful night for the Revelry," he says. "The stars favor Pryor." He looks up and then refocuses on me. "And the gods favor you, Excellency. I trust all is well at the temple."

"Of course." I take a long sip to cover the lie, even though I already feel the wine swimming through my head.

"We all miss your honored father, of course, but you have done an admirable job in his stead. It is no small accomplishment to follow in the footsteps of a giant."

"Thank you. I hope to honor his memory," I say.

Eyo looks on either side of us, then leans in closer. It's designed to make me feel special, to hang on his every word. And even knowing it's a game, I lean in, too.

"The Republic of Pryor is changing. Some want to live on past glory." He eyes Verhardt before returning his gaze to me. "I focus on the future. On what Pryor could be—on truly serving the people and being the leadership they need. We are part of the new guard, you and I."

"Oh?"

I try to follow his conversation, to anticipate where he is leading this, but my mind is blurring by the second. I didn't eat supper, and the ice wine makes my pulse beat far too quickly. The night takes on a fuzziness at the edges.

"…change is as inevitable as war," he says.

At least I think he does.

That couldn't be what he said, though. Pryor does everything possible to avoid a war. I blink hard, trying to refocus. I need space to gather myself, because this is not the company nor place to be caught unaware.

"Would you pardon me, please?" I say, gesturing with my empty flute. "I promised the High Priest of the temple of protection that I would speak with him before he leaves."

Senator Eyo frowns but slowly lifts his arm for me to pass. Even though he's not overly tall, when he stands straight, he looms over me. "Of course, High Priestess. I'll have a servant refresh your glass."

Eyo snaps his fingers at the nearest servant and then eyes my body as I move past him.

I make my way through the leering crowd. Stares, perfumes, and laughter feel like they're closing in on me. I focus on my steps, keeping them measured and graceful even as my legs ache to run. Silently, I curse this dress.

My father would never have worn something so ridiculous.

Heat rushes into my cheeks, and tears sting my eyes. My father wouldn't have done any of this. He would've asked Verhardt why he wanted to hide the omen. He wouldn't have drunk too much around Senator Eyo. He wouldn't feel constantly in over his head.

He wouldn't make mistake after mistake after mistake.

I've never missed him more or felt less ready to fill this role.

I break free of the crowd and take the stairs down to the darkened Senate floor.

Once I'm alone, I can breathe and untense my shoulders. Everything is quiet in this space. The colored marble floor is illuminated by a beam of moonlight from the oculus, making the emblem of Pryor glow. The republic is represented by seven blades fanned out with a snake wrapped around the hilts. I stop and stare at the patinaed bronze seal.

I finally manage a deep breath for the first time since I left the temple. I want to go back now. My father would return to the temple well before dawn, but I'm not sure what's expected of me. And I suppose that's the problem—I am supposed to spiritually lead the people, but I don't know what I'm doing. It's only a matter of time before everyone realizes I'm very much not my father.

I blow out a heavy sigh. I'm a fraud.

"They killed him right there, you know," a voice says.

I jump and turn, putting my fingers over my lips to keep from screaming. My heart pounds as I recognize the Praetorian standing in the shadows. He followed—or found—me.

I swallow, forcing my heart out of my throat.

"So I've heard," I say. Somehow my voice comes out as steady, my tone almost bored.

"They stabbed the king a hundred times, terrified of his Elusian-magic blood and his ability to heal himself. After all, he'd lived three hundred years and survived numerous attempts on his life. But all unjust power comes to an end. One way or another."

The Praetorian steps out of the shadows and into the light. His eyes are just deep set enough that they're the last things illuminated on his face. He's attractive the way a knife's gleaming edge begs to be touched.

Even in heels, I have to tip my head up to look him in the eyes. I feel too small, too breakable around him.

"What are you doing here?" he asks.

My limbs itch to flee, but I make myself hold still. I lift an eyebrow. "I could ask you the same."

He smiles as he stops a step too close to me, invading my space, daring me to cede ground. I don't. His lips part as if he's considering telling me a secret, but nothing feels fake about this.

"I'm keeping a close watch on you."

From the way he says it, I'm not sure if he's worried that I'm in danger or that I *am* the danger. A shiver rolls down my spine.

"Why is that?" My pulse leaps in my neck, and I really wish I hadn't finished those wine flutes. I feel his presence, his nearness too much.

His gaze traces slowly down my face to my neck and then up again. "Because you don't belong here."

My breath catches. He can't know that. No, if he knew that, I'd be in Tullanium jail. Or tortured until my death in the arena. I mentally shake the thought away. He must be implying that I shouldn't be High Priestess. My pride responds, steeling my spine.

"What does that mean?" I ask.

"This room is closed." He smiles. "And Senator Verhardt is looking for you. I can make excuses if you're in over your head."

Underworld take me.

I raise my chin and stare at him. "No, thank you, Praetorian."

He smiles to himself before quickly donning his normal emotionless expression. Chiseled marble and nothing more.

I move to return to the terrace, but all six-three of the Praetorian stands in my way. I think about slinking around him, but no—I am the High Priestess of the temple of truth. He's the one who should give way to me. *He* is the one who doesn't belong among civilized people.

With my mind made up, I step to him. He doesn't move, so I brush against him. He stiffens as my dress slides along his suit. I stare him in the eyes. He smells like snowfall in the woods, and unexpected sparks pool in my stomach as time slows. I can feel every beat of my heart, and I can almost hear his pulsing with mine.

His eyes narrow, but he yields, moving just enough for me to pass.

I'm nearly by him when he reaches out and grabs my wrist. He doesn't hurt me, but there's unmistakable power in his grip. My skin burns where he touches it. I inhale sharply, then raise my eyebrows. He immediately releases me and turns away.

I force myself to walk normally as I leave the Senate floor, but my knees and hands shake. What was that? Why did he follow me? And why did I like being caught?

I'm never drinking ice wine again.

VI

Torren

The Revelry ends without me figuring out why Verhardt wanted to hide the mal omen, but it also concludes without the prophesized calamity, so I suppose that's a win.

As I fall into my bed, though, I'm not thinking about the Senate Leader. I'm picturing the flush on the High Priestess's face when I said she didn't belong on the Senate floor. I've yet to understand why she would flee to an empty room. I followed her, thinking she was secretly meeting someone, but as I watched, she seemed...human, like the celebration was too much for her. If I didn't know better, I'd say she was on the verge of panic. But Kerasea Vestal is as elite as any of them—why would the party bother her?

Bird signs and unanswered questions haunt my dreams, but I'm not down for long before someone knocks loudly on a door. An inexperienced sentry must've accidentally locked the barracks' entrance. The watchman will get it.

Groggy, I roll over to return to slumber. My hand spreads over the rough bedsheet, yet I'm not thinking about cotton but a liquid-gold dress. I curl my hand in a fist, pulling.

Two more knocks. I open my eyes. That's not the front door. Someone is at *my* door. Sweet divine, what time is it?

"Praetorian!" a deep voice calls.

I return to reality and release the sheets from my fist, shaking my head. What was I just thinking?

My body aches, but I roll out of bed and toss on a shirt. It's barely dawn, but duty comes first.

Someone bangs on the door again, insistent, as I pad over the cold, tiled floor. I can't imagine anything that could be this urgent, but I answer.

"Yes?" I rub the sleep from my eyes.

Two sentries stand at attention. They salute me together. I give them a half-hearted salute back. It's too early for this.

The hall lamps are still lit, the flames reflecting off the bald heads of the men. They're brothers, twin sons of an olive oil merchant, but between thousands of sentries in the capital and the early hour, I can't recall their names.

The mouser of the barracks hisses at us as he goes by. I have snuck chicken gizzards to that black cat for years now, and he still doesn't like a single soul here. Myself included.

I smile as he slinks down the hallway. I suppose I like that he can't be bought.

"Praetorian, we are sorry to disturb you, but you are needed in the Forum," one of the sentries says.

I return my focus to them. "Why is that?"

"Senator Verhardt may have been found."

I yawn. Julian and a cadre of sentries escorted the Senate Leader back to his villa at the end of the Revelry. "I was unaware he was missing."

The brothers exchange glances. They're not identical, but they have the same mannerisms and the same large, slightly vacant brown eyes.

"Found dead, sir," one explains. "Murdered in the Forum."

His words wake me like falling into a cold plunge pool.

"I'll be with you shortly."

I hurry into my bathroom, splash water on my face, and don the armor of the Praetorian. As I dress, my heart pounds, but I hold out hope they're wrong. It's not possible that the Senate Leader was murdered. No senator has been killed in Pryor in twenty years, and I just saw him a few hours ago. Verhardt has constant security around him—but then again, so had the Elusian king. And *he* was capable of great magic.

No one is untouchable. I know that for a fact.

But the conclave is set to begin at midnight. The seven senators will sequester for a week in the palace on Mount Ara. If Verhardt was murdered or even missing, the timing can't be a coincidence. Someone wanted to affect the laws of our land—to strike at the heart of the republic.

Someone succeeded.

And that means I failed.

My stomach turns as the implications swirl inside my head. But the sentries said "may have been found." Why?

"Where is the body?" I ask as I step out of my quarters.

"On the altar of peace," one of them replies before clearing his throat. "Mostly."

I stride out of the barracks with the twins in tow. It's dawn, but just barely; the sky is lit up in streaks of pinks and purples.

I furrow my brow at the word "mostly." I want clarification, but we're well on our way there, heading through the quiet Forum.

We reach the altar in no time. Julian stands on the steps, speaking with General Hadrian. His uncle is a fair man, honest and hardworking. He's a little shorter than Julian with curly brown hair and a well-trimmed beard. Hadrian is thirty years my senior and a brilliant military strategist. He won key battles as a young general just before the Senate ended the Hundred Year War.

"General, Commander," I say. "Where is the senator?"

Julian points. "Here. Well…what's left of him."

He steps to the side and there, on the sculpted white altar, is the headless body of a man.

River of Death. I now understand why the sentries said he "may have" been found.

The victim is naked and splayed out, robbing him of any dignity in death. He is the correct height and build, but it's impossible to confirm that it is, in fact, Senator Verhardt with the head missing. The torso is cut open, and all of his organs are gone, leaving nothing but an empty, bloody cavity.

He must've been butchered here on the altar. That's the only explanation for the lack of a trail with this much blood. But it would've been incredibly bold to eviscerate the Senate Leader in the Forum during the Revelry.

"That could be anyone," I finally say.

I don't mean it. I'm just hoping against hope that it's someone else.

General Hadrian gestures with his hand out, giving me permission to investigate. While I only report to the Senate Council, as General of the Legions of Pryor, Hadrian has seniority over just about everyone, and my position is technically still in the legions.

If I keep my position.

Cold dread claws at me, but I move closer, inspecting the scene. I focus, my senses sharpening until there's just the body and me. Not the republic, not the ramifications. Just the evidence.

There's no off odor to him, just the copper scent of blood. No discoloration or obvious signs of poisoning on his skin, although his face would tell me more. The cut at the neck is remarkably smooth and clean—meaning his head was taken off in one professional motion with an axe or sword.

The corpse is still slightly warm to the touch. With his chest open like this, that means he was murdered recently—within the last hour, two at maximum.

I catch the gleam of a stone on the man's right hand. I turn his wrist and slowly close my eyes. It's the emerald ring of Pryor, once the king's and now worn by Verhardt on his little finger. The diamond ring of the republic is missing, but there's no doubt that this is Verhardt.

A thousand curses. Someone butchered the Senate Leader on the fucking altar of peace. It's a loud message, but to and from whom?

I stand and inspect the base of the altar, praying for a clue, a lead. There's nothing. No bloody hand- or footprints. No blood splatter aside from the cascade by the neck. And no weapon.

"Send men to Verhardt's villa," I command.

"Already done," Julian says. "He is not at home. Lady Verhardt was the one who reported him missing when she awoke, but nothing was awry at their residence—no sign of struggle or break-in. Initial indications are that he left willingly or he was unconscious at the time."

I raise my eyebrows. "Why wasn't I notified?"

"Because he was immediately found...we think."

I nod. Without the head, we can't fully confirm the identity, but there's enough evidence to say it is the Senate Leader.

I finish my preliminary inspection and stand by the general and Jules. The weight of the murder sits heavily among us, but I try to focus on what needs to be done. I will have to solve this case and deliver the killer to even stand a chance at keeping my position. And I will have to explain how this happened under my watch.

First things first. We need to set up a perimeter and search for witnesses, interview Lady Verhardt and their entire household, and inspect their residence. Something may have been missed by the sentries. The smallest clue can be the largest lead, and I don't trust anyone else to conduct an investigation of this magnitude.

As I consider the fallout, Julian wears his normal pleasant expression, but General Hadrian is off. There are creases in his brow, and they aren't from the state of the body. The murder is unpleasant, but he's seen and done far worse.

We both have.

"What's troubling you, General?" I ask.

The general strokes his beard. "Other than the murder of the Senate Leader?"

I nod, because I know him well enough to be certain there is more.

He gives me a small smile, but then it fades quickly in the mire of this situation. "Last night, the Kingdom of Arthago incurred into our land, taking more of the sixth province. The Council will now decide if we acquiesce or go to war."

Chills ripple against my skin. Julian had mentioned threats from the northern empire yesterday, and now Verhardt is dead. Could this all be the work of our greatest enemy?

"You think they had something to do with this?" Julian asks.

"It's possible, especially considering the timing, but no, I doubt it," Hadrian says. "Their king isn't above assassinations, but we've bloodlessly ceded land every time they've incurred. This is something else. I think someone was seizing an opportunity—or making one."

He stares at Verhardt's chest and strokes his beard. I catch the slight twitch of his left eye.

"What is it?" I ask.

"It looks… I don't know… It almost seems Elusian, with how clean everything is," Hadrian says. "He is completely disemboweled, and those cuts don't appear natural."

We all stare at the body. The Elusians, the royal bloodline, each had different, unnatural powers. The Senate and the sentries loyal to them had to strike in one coordinated massacre at Jubilee Palace and on the Senate floor to prevent them from using that magic, and even then, there were casualties. One Elusian with the right power could topple an empire.

Or so they say.

The lore of Elusian blood magic has grown significantly since the

Crimson Night.

Julian shakes his head. "That's impossible. There are no Elusians left."

General Hadrian frowns. "No, it's not impossible, just improbable. Anything is possible."

I shudder, but it's just the dewy morning—that's all.

"What happens now with the conclave?" Julian asks. "Our province can't elect a new senator in time. Just casting and tabulating a vote in the capital takes weeks, not to mention campaigns and debates."

I rub my forehead. "I suspect that was the point."

We stand silently for the moment. Without Verhardt, the capital's province, the richest and most powerful of the seven, will now lack a voice in this conclave. Someone else will rise to power as Senate Leader. Every senator has ambitions and agendas—could one of them have been behind this murder?

Senators Eyo and Medea were here last night as Verhardt's guests, and the others were no doubt close by, as they all have villas in the Southside.

"General! Praetorian!" a sentry calls out, waving his arm.

Another sentry runs to the steps of the altar. "We found the head of the senator and the...rest of him."

"Well, that was quick," Julian says. "Good job."

"Block this off with work screens—no one goes near the altar," General Hadrian says to the dozen sentries waiting nearby. They salute him and surround the altar as we walk down the stairs.

"Quite a morning," Julian whispers to me. "All of this before you could tell me where you and the High Priestess disappeared to last night."

I stare at him out of the corner of my eye. This isn't the time for humor and certainly not the time to talk about *her*. He straightens his back, heeding the warning shot.

We approach another group of sentries. All ten of them avoid looking at the fountain. The three-tiered structure had been drained and used as a torchier by Kerasea last night. The admiration of the Faith was spoken about all evening—it was mentioned nearly as much as her stunning beauty.

I grind my teeth. Curse Julian for bringing her up. I really don't need to think her name. There's a violent murderer on the loose, the republic is in grave danger, my position is in jeopardy, and I'm focused on a dress and a stare. I'm no better than Jules right now.

One of the twins is among the men standing by the fountain. He's sweating on this chilly morning, and he's turned a vague shade of green. Just as I notice his coloring, he leans forward and vomits, nearly hitting the general's sandals.

"Gods, man," General Hadrian says, jumping back.

"I'm sorry, sir." The man wipes his mouth with the back of his hand.

Some captains would have him whipped at the post for the slight, but General Hadrian sighs. "It's all right. Go get cleaned up and send a replacement."

"Right away, sir. Thank you, sir. I'm sorry, sir." The sentry salutes and runs back to the barracks. I think he's going to be sick again, but something else is wrong. He couldn't get out of here fast enough.

I exchange glances with Julian.

"In here," another sentry says.

Julian extends an arm. "By all means, you first."

I smile but then peer into the upper, bowl-shaped tier of the fountain. I take a step back as Verhardt's vacant eyes stare up at me. His mouth is agape, frozen in an eternal scream. A pile of bloody organs lies beneath his severed head.

Gods.

"We have confirmation," I say slowly.

General Hadrian looks inside the fountain while Julian decides the sky is far more interesting. Jules has always been a little squeamish, but I can't afford that luxury.

I crouch down and search the basin, but there's not a single drop of blood in the rest of the fountain or on the stones around it.

How was this done and, more importantly, why?

I look into the fountain again. It's hard to say if all the organs are accounted for, and I have to know for certain.

I draw a breath and reach in, shifting his head to the side. Under his neck, there is his stomach and heart, two lungs, but there's something else in here. I stand on my toes because I caught a shimmer. It was the glint of something golden.

Could it be the murder weapon? A clue?

I have to reach it.

The bloody, cold viscera is an extremely unpleasant sensation on my wrist, but I push through it. I have to. I reach in until I grab a metal object, then grip it and raise my arm, pulling out a sickle-shaped knife by the handle. I immediately recognize this type of blade with its lapis inlay—it is a ceremonial knife. And these are only used in one place: the temple of truth.

"Bring me the High Priestess," I say.

VII

Torren

My command rings out into the quiet morning, my voice victorious and strong. I try to tamp down my excitement, but I've caught her. This is a misstep she can't come back from. I finally have what I need to bring down Kerasea Vestal.

"No." General Hadrian's veto is gentle but firm.

No one moves.

"I beg your pardon?" I stare at him while clutching the bloody temple knife.

He shakes his head. "You already know that you cannot investigate the High Priestess due to *un exorum.*"

I lock my jaw and stare up at the sky. *Un exorum* is the doctrine that the high priests and senators are above reproach without overwhelming evidence — it literally means self-exoneration. Someone reputable, meaning one of their own, has to witness them committing a serious crime or they have to confess in order to even be questioned. But I have the evidence in my hand.

I open my mouth and sputter, "Th-This is a temple sickle."

General Hadrian doesn't blink. "Which proves nothing."

Nothing?

Words fail to come out as a million retorts race through my mind. I look to Jules for help. Instead of meeting my eyes, he's staring at his fine sandals.

Perfect.

"Don't you find this, along with her mal omen, a little too convenient?" I ask.

General Hadrian shakes his head. "No, I think that's the point of prophecy. She forecast calamity, and she was correct. You can't interrogate the temple, and you know that. You would need to convince the Senate and ultimately get the Verity Guild's approval—meaning Probus's vote."

"Then I will ask him," I say.

I stare at the cylindrical tower of the Ministry of Justice. The temple to the god of justice is seven stories high and doesn't just offer prayers to the divine. The priests are justices who handle all manner of crimes and citizen complaints except for high treason, which is the province of the Verity Guild.

And a member of the guild is now a person of interest.

Hadrian rests a hand on my shoulder. "You will be denied, Torren. Even if you could convince the Senate—which you can't—one high priest is never going to consent to the investigation of another. Let me save you the trouble."

The truth of his statement hits my chest, knocking the wind out of me, but I shake it off. This weapon can't be denied. At the very least, I need to question Kerasea Vestal and find out how many people have access to these blades and the number contained in the temple. And then I need to know her whereabouts after she left the terrace last night, if she has any scars on her body from a struggle.

"We'll see about that," I say.

"No. We won't. Do not go to the Ministry of Justice. This inquiry ends here." The general raises his chin with finality. He is the type of man who speaks softly but always gets his point across.

I freeze, my mouth going dry as Hadrian forbids me from asking Probus. Before I can begin a proper investigation, I've been stymied. I can technically maneuver around the general as he's not in my chain of command, but that would put me in opposition to a powerful man I respect.

Frustration eats at me, but I know better than to show it. I'll have to be more cunning, less by the book, to get to someone like Kerasea Vestal.

"A bet, then?" I suggest. "A friendly wager on whether Probus will agree?"

General Hadrian's brown eyes light up. He has one vice—and it's gambling. We've spent many hours together passing the time by playing dice and cards.

"A vessel of wine?" he asks.

"Torren." Julian sighs.

Sure, now he finds the ability to speak.

"Stop this," he says. "You're about to lose twice, and you're a notoriously sore loser. I refuse to be locked up for a week with you when you're in one of your moods."

I'm not sure what he means by "one of my moods," but Jules is correct that we'll soon be locked in the palace for the conclave, if it goes forward. Still, that only puts a fine point on my need to investigate the High Priestess. By law, we'll spend seven days sequestered on a mountaintop, and I'd rather not have a murderess in our midst.

"Done." I shake hands with General Hadrian. "I'll drink to you."

I don't drink, but that vessel will net me a nice payday when I sell it.

The general smiles slowly. "You won't, my boy, but you are young. Perhaps it's best you learn that for yourself. Come, Julian, we need to handle the senator."

I stride to the Ministry of Justice with the knife in hand. I am right, and I'll prove it. No one is untouchable—not even Kerasea Vestal.

VIII.

Kerasea

A rich patron sets a heavy velvet bag overflowing with gold coins into my hands and then gives his onyx-and-ivory cane to his servant. He slowly lowers himself to his knees at the feet of the colossal statue of the god of truth.

From the break of dawn, the patrons and benefactresses of the elite Southside families have come to the temple to confess their lies and buy clemency for last night's misdeeds. They are, of course, first in line. Lower nobles and merchants will follow, then citizens, and only then, if there is still time, will we hear servants.

As I hold the velvet bag, I wonder if Atonement Day was created just to fill the temple's coffers, but I shake away the doubt and hand the offering to an acolyte.

The line of nobles waiting with their gold suddenly shifts. I look up from anointing the patron's forehead as four steel-clad sentries enter the inner hall. One would be unusual; four Senate sentries standing at the other end of the reflecting pool is remarkable.

"State your purpose," the chief temple guard says, stepping out to meet them. He is a former battle-hardened sentry with a white scar across his brown face.

"The Senate Council requests an audience with the High Priestess," a sentry replies. "We have orders to accompany Her Excellency to the Senate Hall at her first convenience."

An icy feeling settles across my chest, and my stomach twists. Why am I being summoned? My mind flashes to the omen I concealed and then my other, darker secrets. I grip the sleeves of my white robe as I recall the black liver, and the smell of death fills my nose. Was this another misstep? Or did they discover something far worse?

Guilt rises through me, but I swallow it down. They don't know my secrets. They can't.

"For what purpose?" Mirial asks, folding her arms as she appears to my right out of nowhere. Last I saw her, she was taking confessions in one of the silent alcoves far from the inner hall.

"We were not informed, Priestess," the sentry answers.

Sweat gathers on the top of his lip. He can't be more than nineteen, his youthful expression making me feel older than my twenty-two. He shifts his weight as she stares him down like a hawk.

I press my lips together. Whatever this is can't be good. The Senate is well aware that today is a high holy day and the busiest of the temple's year.

I don't want to go, but I also can't refuse without good reason.

"Yes, of course." I hand the blessed oil to Mirial even though her lips are set in a line so thin that her mouth looks like a crease. "I am the Council's servant."

The sentry blows out a breath, looking thoroughly relieved. "Please, this way, Excellency."

As we make our way through the Forum, anyone who crosses my path bows low to me, pressing their fingers to their mouths. I move my hand in blessing, but I tremble as I walk.

The Senate Hall is in the middle of the Forum, so it doesn't take long to reach it. I catch a glimpse of billowing white sheets by the altar of peace just as I'm escorted inside. It's strange for there to be work screens up now, but I don't have time to inquire before I'm brought into the domed room where the Council and Verity Guild convene.

Where the Praetorian found me last night.

Shaking off the memory of him grabbing my wrist, I enter the Senate floor. A ring of seven heavy wooden seats lines the circular space under the dome, and then there are rows for viewing, making it like a political theater. Or…there *should* be seven seats. One is missing.

The room is empty except for six senators. Senators Eyo and Medea stand with Senator Terrance of the third Province, Foreau of the fourth, Suh of the fifth, and Paolo of the seventh. They range in height, age, and skin color, but each of them wears a purple toga, the formal robes of the Council when in session. They all turn as I come in. Senate Leader Verhardt and the clerk are noticeably absent.

I bow to the senators, happy to be in my ceremonial white robe and not that gold dress. "A most blessed Atonement to you all. The Council has requested an audience?"

"Yes, High Priestess," Senator Eyo says, stroking his black beard. Someone must trim it every day because the length never changes. "We are sorry to disturb you on this high holy day, but there has been a development."

He pauses, and silence blankets the room. It's then that I feel the somber, worried aura around me. Their tension pulls my muscles taut as I wait for him to continue.

Eyo parts his lips, but before he can speak, the doors open behind me with a loud thud. My heart leaps as I turn to catch the Praetorian striding in, his breastplate shining in the sunlight of the oculus. In his armor, he looks like a demigod of war.

Torren is the last person I need to see. Heat rises to my face as I think about how I brushed against him mere hours ago.

Curse all ice wine.

He stops beside me and stands at attention. I catch the glimmer of something in his right hand, but it's on his other side, so I can't quite see. And this close to me, his sandalwood-and-snow scent is distracting.

Even the most powerful people in the republic can't help but give him their attention.

Senator Medea worries her hands as she steps forward. Her limbs are thin, but her body is tall and curvy.

"Praetorian, tell us, do we have a suspect in custody?" she asks, direct as ever.

Suspect? I look from side to side. So this is not about me or the omen. I exhale in relief. Perhaps this is about the Verity Guild, but no, Probus is not present. He would have to be, right?

Confusion roils inside me as I bite my tongue. This is the worst place to be unaware.

"Soon. We are working on it," the Praetorian replies.

"Then why are you here?" Senator Terrance's voice booms. At seventy, he is the eldest senator, but he has a tall, athletic frame juxtaposing his shock of white hair. His voice is too loud, though, because he is losing his hearing. But his gaze is still sharp as it spears the man before him.

"I have located the murder weapon," the Praetorian answers.

"Murder?" I blurt out, then I soften my tone. "What murder?"

The senators turn silent, reserved; the shift is palpable. My words seem to hang in the air as no one responds.

Torren holds his chin high, but his eyes drift to mine. I study him, yet he says nothing. The senators exchange glances, and Senator Paolo steps forward. He is the youngest senator at thirty-four and short with a slight build. His wavy brown hair nearly the color of his brown skin and a baby face mean he barely seems his age. Like me, Paolo tried to fill his father's shoes after he died.

"Senator Verhardt was murdered overnight, High Priestess." He speaks softly as he twists the large sapphire ring on his little finger. "I'm so sorry to be the one to give you this most grievous news."

I gasp. The sound echoes in the domed space, and I put my

fingers over my mouth. "Verhardt is dead?" I shake my head as tears immediately sting my eyes. My lip begins to quiver, not out of love for the senator but from shock. And fear of what this might mean for the republic. "But...we just saw him last night. I don't understand."

"It is a difficult crime to comprehend," Eyo says, frowning. "But I am sure the Praetorian will deliver a suspect before dusk. Verhardt's murder will not go unpunished. We will make an example out of the killer."

Eyo holds his chin high as the other senators nod their approval.

"May the River of Death guide him and may the underworld receive him." I incline my head, and the Senate does the same. "May Verhardt's good deeds outweigh his flaws to lighten his soul."

Once I've recited the typical death prayer, I raise my head. "So then the conclave will be delayed until—"

"The conclave will proceed as planned, High Priestess," Senator Terrance says in a loud voice. He straightens his aged shoulders and rubs his fingers and thumbs together, as if physically taking the reins of the Council. "We have unanimously decided to move forward, as the needs of the republic are both pressing and greater than any one man—even our beloved friend. We face enemies both at home and abroad, which brings us to why we called you here. As we will now proceed with an even number of senators, we ask you to serve as the deciding vote in the event of a deadlock at this year's conclave."

My mouth falls open, and I widen my eyes, glancing at the senators. What they're proposing has never been done before. Balance is maintained in part by the fact that the temples and Senate have separation.

Bloody lies, how would my father have handled this request?

My gut response is to decline. The Faith is not supposed to intervene in the political affairs of the republic. But, of course, we have before when we sided with the original Senate after they cut down the royal family. It's how the temple of truth has eclipsed all other faiths.

The Praetorian's eyebrows rise. "The High Priestess is not, nor has she ever been, an elected representative, Senators."

I side-eye him. Of course he'd think I was unqualified. Even though I don't want to vote, I bristle at the implication that I'm unable to.

"It is my suggestion that you allow us to investigate, for the conclave to be delayed, and for everyone to remain in the capital for your own safety," Torren continues.

For our safety? So he believes this is not a single random act but an attack on the republic?

Senator Foreau shakes his head. His scalp is shaved so clean that it shines like varnished wood. He steeples his fingers and says, "We will be safer sequestered on the mountain—unless you and your men cannot properly perform your duties."

Foreau stares at the Praetorian with eyes as dark brown as his skin.

"Of course." A muscle in the Praetorian's jaw ticks. "As you wish."

Senator Medea waves a delicate hand. "We will be perfectly safe. But back to the matter before us: will you vote at the conclave, High Priestess? There is a desperate need left by Verhardt's passing, and we ask that you serve the republic in this trying time, just as your father did before you."

All eyes turn to me.

Underworld, what do I do now? My mind whirls. I need time to decide, to figure out the correct answer, but I feel like I'm in a pit of vipers and one wrong move will mean a venomous strike.

I bite the inside of my cheek. I don't know why they want to hand me this kind of power. I can't shake the feeling that there is more going on than I can sense.

My gaze lands on Foreau's quietly amused expression. My stomach twists. Yes, there's definitely a hidden agenda here.

I eye Medea on his right, but her face is perfectly powdered and expressionless as she waits.

I take in the remaining senators one by one.

Senator Eyo continues to stroke his manicured beard as Suh

leans his large body on his diamond cane. Suh was part of the original council that killed the king. His gray hair is as short as when he was a general, even though he resigned from the legions long ago.

I wait for him to speak, as he was a friend of my father's. He opens his mouth, but he just coughs, his heavy jowls rippling.

An unease settles across my shoulders as I continue to stall. Senator Terrance's mouth is puckered now as if he swallowed a lemon. His patience wears thin.

Finally, I glance to Senator Paolo, but he's not looking at me. He's staring at Senator Medea and spinning the jeweled ring on his left hand. He and Medea have always been kind to me. I hope I can count on them during the conclave.

I startle as I realize I'm already contemplating the senators in terms of allies and enemies.

I turn my gaze back to Senator Foreau's and find his mouth still slightly.

They have all let me take my time because they know I have no choice.

I can't oppose them without a valid reason.

"I am, as always, a servant to the Council." I incline my head and ignore the scream building in my throat. I have a lot of practice with this maneuver. For the past three months, it's felt like I've had to smile while drowning. And now I'm being pushed out into deep water, and I don't know why.

"Excellent." Senator Suh finally looks up and claps his meaty hands together, cane still grasped in one fist. He shifts, his toga pulling taut around his bulging torso, before he goes back to leaning on his cane again. "We will prepare to leave at dusk."

Thus dismissed, I bow again and exit the Senate floor. As I make my way out of the Senate Hall, I do my best to keep my legs from wobbling. Discreetly, I clench and unclench my sleeves in my fists.

I don't see as much as feel the Praetorian following me. His footfall is nearly silent, but his presence is unmistakable, causing the muscles in my back to tense.

"Yes?" I ask without turning around.

He comes up alongside me as we step out into the Forum. I look to the right, toward the altar that had been surrounded by white sheets. But it's exactly how it always is on this crisp spring day. Whatever work they were doing must be complete.

The Praetorian's blue eyes sharpen on me. "Something wrong?"

"The Senate Leader was murdered, and there wasn't a single tear in that room," I mutter. "Men and women who knew him for more than two decades. Could one —"

I cut myself off, remembering that I'm speaking to the Senate protector. I shake my head, trying to pull myself together. He doesn't need to know my thoughts, especially not that I think someone in the hall might be a murderer. "I assume I will see you at the conclave tonight."

"I wouldn't miss it." He drifts closer, and his voice is so low that it rumbles.

I tilt my head. "Even though you have a murder to investigate?"

His gaze flickers from my eyes to my mouth and back again. I hold my breath as he leans close to my ear. "Especially because of the murder."

His lips turn into a small smile. Then he strolls toward the armory. I'm so dazed and dizzy from the past few minutes that I can't even respond. What does the Council want with me? What does *he* want with me?

I suppose I'm about to find out.

IX

Torren

"Genarl Hadrian is going to collect on that vessel of wine as soon as we get back, you know." Julian relaxes, kicking his bare feet up on my sofa.

I harrumph as I pack a bag. The vessel will cost me nearly a week's pay, but I had to try. The general, however, was correct—it was a futile attempt. Chief Judge Probus was thoroughly unimpressed by me dropping a bloody knife on his desk. He was more concerned about me dirtying his papers and interrupting his tea than the fact that I'd found a murder weapon.

Still, I was about to make my case to the Council when the High Priestess asked about Verhardt. I couldn't tell whether she was genuinely surprised or if it was an impressive performance, but her shock made me hesitate.

I was lucky it did.

Evidently, the Council has political plans for Kerasea. They would've instantly sided with her and put an end to my inquiry, so it was better to not reveal the knife for now.

And then she looked directly at the scene of the crime. Not a notable moment except for the fact that no one said he was murdered on the altar. Few people other than the killer know that.

"Let's go," I say. "I need to leave for the conclave."

"This early?" Jules rises from the sofa and peers out the window. "It's not even dusk."

"I am going to ride with the High Priestess to Jubilee."

Or try to.

Julian's eyes widen until they're saucers. "May I ask...why?"

"To get some answers."

Lady Verhardt declined to speak with me, claiming to be too grief-stricken for questions. She also would not let me disturb her son or even question her servants. She literally shooed me from the grounds of her villa. Therefore, I don't have a starting place outside of Kerasea Vestal.

"Hmm, and here I thought that under no circumstances are you to investigate the High Priestess." Julian taps his dimpled chin. "Yes, in fact, I remember Probus saying that quite clearly."

He's not wrong. Jules strolled into my audience with the Chief Judge just in time to hear me be roundly rejected as I urged Probus to reconsider.

I shove a second length of rope into my leather bag.

"There's nothing in the law that says I can't make friendly conversation," I say.

Julian smiles. "The law? No. Your nature, on the other hand..."

I straighten my spine to the challenge. "I can get close to her."

"By making friendly conversation?" He laughs. "Pray tell, when did you develop this new skill?"

I offer a cold stare for a response as I toss my manacles down on the counter.

"Never mind, I stand corrected. This is a beautiful repartee." Julian points between us.

I stare at the ceiling, hating that he's right. "Julian, I am going to strangle you."

"No." He shakes his head and takes a step closer. "You are going to get in over your head with the High Priestess. She has been untouchable her entire life, and you know that. Rumor is she will marry a future patron soon. For some reason, you hate a woman who is protected by the temple, nobility, *and* the Senate—not to mention that she is beloved by the people. You can't win. Hand them someone you know committed other crimes and be done with this."

Of course Julian doesn't understand my hatred for her. By the time he and I met, no one in Pryor believed my father was innocent, so I stopped talking about how the High Priest's daughter falsely swore against him. She, however, knows what she did. She might've been only a child when she testified, but so was I.

I do know I'm on dangerous ground, though. If the Senate were to find out I was investigating the High Priestess without their consent, I'd be censured at a minimum. If she caught me, she could have the Senate strip me of my title. I would fall from a position of power—the highest someone like me could reach, back to being a powerless commoner.

Dread pools in my stomach. No. I won't allow that to happen. I'm not going to lose everything again. Not because of her.

But I'm also tasked with catching Verhardt's killer, and that knife is my only lead. *She* is my only lead. I'll simply have to be cleverer in how I get to her. While friendly conversation isn't my forte, I could tell last night that something in her wants me closer. Like how a moth wants a flame.

I don't bother with messy entanglements for more than a night, but if I play the role of a suitor, maybe I can catch a murderess.

Julian's suggestion that I hand them someone else, while expedient, is untenable. There is no justice, no honor in that. I shake my head. Whoever the murderer is, they cannot get away with this. I just unreasonably hope it is Kerasea because of that knife. I can't fathom what she would hope to gain, but sometimes power becomes an unquenchable thirst.

Still, it doesn't feel quite right for her. What is she hiding?

"Tor, this obsession…"

Julian pauses as I look up and meet his gaze. I'm not sure if he's referring to my obsession with being Praetorian or if he's implying that I'm obsessed with the High Priestess. I grip the metal of the handcuffs as I wait for him to continue.

"I'm going to ask you as your friend one more time to leave her alone, but I suspect you will ignore this warning as well," he says.

I nod.

He sighs, defeated, and we sink into silence.

Julian partially covers his mouth with his hand and stares to the side. He does that when he's trying to conceal a secret.

"You know something," I say.

"Yes, but you didn't hear it from me." His face is serious, his gaze distant.

I wait, bracing myself against the wooden dining table. The thrill of the hunt has started to take hold of me, but I can't be too eager. These investigations always require precision and patience. With the implication of the High Priestess, it will be doubly so. I must stay focused and objective. It was all too easy to lose myself last night.

He draws a long breath and exhales a noisy sigh. "We cannot locate Verhardt's liver."

"What?" My voice carries, too loud for this conversation. Julian grimaces, no doubt already regretting his decision to tell me.

"While you were in the Senate Hall, the healer finished cataloging the body parts we collected from the fountain. Everything was accounted for except his liver."

"That is the prophecy organ, is it not?" I ask.

Julian purses his lips, because there's nothing more to say. "Uncle Hadrian wants this kept quiet."

"Because it also implicates the temple," I say.

"Because it would set you down the wrong path. Torren, this still doesn't equal the High Priestess having any involvement with the murder. You and I both know that the knife was too convenient and the scene too strange. You admitted as much when Probus questioned you. The most likely scenario is that someone is trying to pin the murder on the Faith."

Five gods and yet there is only one worshipped as "the Faith."

"Or she did it to cast the disbelief," I say.

Julian purses his lips. Probus was also unconvinced by that argument. The old man is sharper than people give him credit for. He questioned me until I admitted it could potentially be a setup, and then he promptly denied my request.

Jules sighs. "She couldn't have decapitated him with that knife, and you know it—at a minimum, a sword was used, and we haven't found that yet. And even with the sharpest axe in the world, Kerasea doesn't have the strength to take a man's head off, certainly not in a clean swipe. A last time: leave it be."

We walk out of the barracks, and I admit that his logic is sound. It would take far more muscle and experience than she has to decapitate a grown man in a single motion. I should be more concerned about Julian's warnings, but I can't stop now. Even if she weren't the one to take his head off, conspiracy to commit the murder of a senator is the same as the act. It is high treason, punishable by the foulest death. And that would be a fitting end to her.

"I'll take it under advisement," I say, tossing my rucksack over my shoulder. "I'll see you at the palace."

I knock fists with Julian and walk out. I love him like a brother, but he didn't grow up with me. He didn't live in the filth of the slums, hungry and wanting. Julian can't ever really understand me. What I went through. What the Vestal family put me through.

Alone, I stride toward the massive temple of truth. The colonnaded temple occupies the entire east end of the Forum. It is as large as the public baths, and it is the grandest temple to any god in Pryor.

I bypass an endless line of citizens waiting to confess their lies and buy forgiveness and climb the marble steps of the temple.

As I walk inside the towering bronze-and-gold doors, the scents of lilacs and eucalyptus gently waft through the silent space. Gilded mosaics cover the ground, and sculpted columns reach forty feet into the air, holding up the high-coffered ceiling in the Great Hall. The line of citizens continues into the more austere Inner Hall. The colossal marble statue of the god of truth seated on a throne looms at the end of an enormous reflecting pool.

I genuflect. It is not the gods that trouble me but their use by ambitious men...and women.

A temple guard with a scar on his face approaches me. They all wear steel and leather armor with blue capes, but this one is different, with gold embellishment on his chest. He's a few inches shorter than I am and middle-aged, with grays peppering the black of his short hair. He must be the chief temple guard.

"May I help you, Praetorian?" he asks.

"I am here to bring the High Priestess to the conclave," I say.

He shakes his head. "That's not possible. The High Priestess already left for Jubilee."

"What? It's not yet nightfall." I take a step back, physically thrown by the news.

The guard stares at me, and there is nothing more to say. Either he is lying or she is already gone. Either way, I missed my opportunity.

I turn on my heels and squeeze my rucksack strap. Julian had tried to warn me that Kerasea is cleverer than expected. Perhaps all she was doing in that dress last night was distracting me, and I refuse to be thrown off a scent so easily. The only reason for the knife, the missing liver, and her glancing at the scene of the crime would be her involvement in the murder.

She knows something. And I will stop at nothing until I find it out.

X

Kerasea

W e've nearly reached Jubilee Palace by the time Mirial finishes lecturing me. She hasn't treated me like a High Priestess on this carriage ride and honestly, I've enjoyed it.

"You jeopardized the entire Faith and the very future of Pryor itself," she says.

Well, "enjoyed" is a strong word.

Finally silent, Mirial sits back and folds her arms. My chambermaid, Zel, blows out a relieved breath. Poor Zel. She's not known where to look for the past four hours as we've traveled from the heart of the capital up Mount Ara. Her big brown eyes darted around as Mirial listed out my missteps and foolish mistakes, but Zel has reached into the shadows and bravely squeezed my hand for support. She may only be fourteen, but she often seems wiser than her years. I squeeze her hand back.

It's been a long night, but we're now near the top of the mountain. Jubilee Palace was the former summer imperial residence, built centuries ago by the king so that he could escape the oppressive mid-year heat in the capital.

My father told me that Jubilee Palace is far larger than it seems from the Forum. I tip my head, peering up through the carriage window. The six floors of the residence sit perched on a cliff at the mountaintop—a marvel by itself. And that's not counting the two spiraling towers. As it was the summer palace, there are only thirty guest bedrooms. In a normal year, nearly all of them would be full for the conclave. But this is far from a normal year.

We will hold to the tradition, though, as written in the *lex conclave*. For a week, we will be locked in—the six senators, each with a chosen page and an unarmed sentry; the Senate Clerk; the Praetorian; the Capital Commander; myself with my attendant; and a skeletal staff of ten servants to cook and clean for all of us.

Mirial won't be staying at the conclave. She only accompanied me on these steep winding roads to lecture me about my agreement to serve as the deadlock vote. Apparently, my father never would have consented to such a thing. The balance of power in Pryor keeps the republic from crumbling, and I could unwittingly destroy the entire system—if Mirial is to be believed. She may be right, but I have no idea how to avoid this now.

I scratch the underside of my wrist, an old nervous habit. Mirial frowns. I know. I'm scarring my porcelain skin, and it's already red and agitated, so I stop. I push the sleeves of my white blouse back down.

Instead, I dig my nails into the armrest as the carriage pulls up to the steps of Jubilee—the seat of power for my true bloodline and where they were ultimately eliminated. But they weren't my family. A family is much more than blood and bones.

I release the armrest. The Elusians were nothing to me. I was brought to the temple as a baby and adopted by my father. Osiris saved my life and gave me a new beginning, he and Mirial both. They raised me. *Osiris* was my father, and Mirial is now the only one left who knows the truth about me. Everything else is the past.

I draw a deep breath and push my lineage to the back of my mind.

Despite it being nearly midnight, the inside of the palace is lit up bright as day. The massive, carved mahogany doors are open wide, revealing the Praetorian in the doorway.

Bloody lies, of course he's standing there.

I left out my interactions with him when talking to Mirial, as I still don't know what to make of him. But she scowls.

"Street trash," she whispers under her breath, and I cringe.

It's like my father is still here.

Zel hops out, and then the coachman gives me his hand to help me from the carriage. I'm in riding pants and boots instead of my robes, but I can use all the assistance I can get right now.

As soon as I step outside, the cold mountain air chills me. It was already cooler in the capital today, but the temperature has plummeted on the top of Mount Ara. I have multiple trunks of robes and dresses, along with furs, because it can easily snow on the mountain this time of the year. It feels like it might — the air is heavy and biting around me.

I shiver, my clothes not nearly warm enough.

"May the gods be with you," Mirial says once my trunks are unloaded.

"May the gods bless and keep you." I move my shaking hand in blessing.

She frowns from the carriage window, clear concern in her pale eyes. I suppose she's right to be worried. I have to spend a week locked in with the most powerful people in the republic — including the one in the doorway.

I straighten my spine, push back my shoulders, and take a deep breath. I can do this. I can get through the conclave one minute at a time.

I pretend to casually saunter to the entrance despite fully shaking. I tell myself it's the cold — just the cold.

"High Priestess," Torren says, inclining his head.

"Praetorian."

The Praetorian's full lips curl in a semblance of a smile, but his eyes are on my luggage and the shining carriage pulling away. It must look excessive if you think of everything as belonging to one person, but none of this is mine. As High Priestess, I don't have any personal possessions. Even my undergarments are technically property of the temple. I have a Southside villa that has been in my family for centuries, but aside from that, my sole estate is a simple country house far outside the capital.

Sometimes, I dream of living a quiet life there, but I was chosen by the god long ago. To turn away would be unthinkable.

Once again, Torren stands in my path. At least I haven't had ice wine tonight.

I'm nearly past him and into the warmth of the palace when he leans closer.

"May I offer you a tour, as this is your first time at the conclave?"

I stop short, my mouth falling open. Why is he suddenly interested in me? First, there was that moment in the Senate Hall during the Revelry, then he followed me out into the Forum this morning, and now this. I'm no stranger to drawing the attention of men. Seemingly, every eligible bachelor in Pryor has offered his hand to me, but like my undergarments, it's only due to my position. If I were a chambermaid, they'd try to bed me, not marry me. But that's clearly not what the Praetorian is after. Frankly, he can't stand me, so why the tour?

I want to decline, but perhaps walking with him will help me figure out his motivations.

"I'd be delighted," I say.

He distinctly does not look delighted to hear that, which only deepens the mystery. Something flashes in his eyes—surprise. He expected me to say no.

Torren nods curtly. "Do you need to get settled in your rooms first?"

"No." I turn my attention to Zel. "Please see that my things make it safely to my chamber and take the room to the side of mine."

Zel is a good servant; however, at the moment she's frozen in place by the terrifying beauty of the Praetorian. I doubt she's seen anyone this handsome in her entire life.

It's a few seconds of awkward silence before she shakes her head and bobs a curtsy. "Of course. Right away, Excellency."

"Thank you, Zel."

The Praetorian's eyebrows rise, but he clears his expression. I blink, expectant, as if I am excited for this tour.

He extends his arm. I step forward, but he moves to the side. We wind up face-to-face and far too close. I inhale his scent as time seems to slow like the first drip of candlewax. Then he clears his throat and goes around me.

"This way."

I shake off his nearness, ignoring the feeling of wings fluttering in the center of my chest. It's fear. Just natural fear of prey facing a predator.

"This, of course, is the grand entrance hall," he says.

We both look up at the massive, gilded chandelier. It's larger than any I've ever seen, and the white marble floors and towering windows reflect the light. On the ceiling is a fresco of an Elusian fire king lighting the night half a millennium ago.

"The main staircase is ahead of us, but there are also staircases on either end of the palace. Nearly every room faces north, as the building runs west to east."

That fits with the Elusian belief in the North Star as the guiding light of the kingdom. Under the Elusians, the temple to the skies was first among the faiths.

We walk along the ruby-red-carpeted floors of the eastern hall. Red wallpaper with gold leaf decorates the walls above the wooden panels. All the torchiers and candelabras are gilded. The hallway stretches to a coffered ceiling high above our heads with gilded fleur-de-lis of the Elusians in the center of the ceiling at intervals. It's a fantastic show of wealth, overwhelming to the eye, and my father said the decoration is only half of what used to be here. Much of the gold was taken during the Crimson Night.

"This floor has the main rooms we'll use for the conclave," the Praetorian explains. "Meals will be served in the banquet hall, the former throne room will be used as a Senate Hall, and there are thermal baths on the ground floor. Jubilee was built over a hot spring, at a time before we could pipe in warm water."

He speaks about the lowest level, but he leads me up the stone staircase at the end of the eastern hall. I walk beside him, although he only looks ahead, his pace brisk.

"The second floor was home to the offices and bedrooms of the priests and advisers to the realm. Those, like the drawing and ballrooms downstairs, will be empty this week. The third and fourth levels are guest bedrooms—ten per floor. And the fifth is where the royal apartments were located—the king's bedroom and rooms for his three wives and six favorite children. Those are also now used as guest rooms, except for the king's suite."

The old king had one hundred children during his three-hundred-year reign. I suppose not all of them could be favored.

I nod, trying not to remember how I am the last of those children.

Due to his self-healing magic, he outlived almost all of his wives and offspring, which sounds more like a curse than a power.

I expect that the Praetorian will stop at one of the bedroom floors, but we continue upward. I'm glad to be in riding clothes and not my robes as we ascend another flight of stairs. My chest begins to burn in the thin mountain air, but the Praetorian doesn't break stride, his exercise regime evidently far more rigorous than mine.

The staircase narrows as we enter a tower, leaving me no choice but to follow behind him. I try to ignore his sculpted legs under his leather skirt and broad shoulders barely contained by his armor as we take the stairs, but it's impossible not to notice how his back tapers in, the rise of his blue veins on his muscular arms. I need to focus, though, to figure out why he's doing this, but as we continue, I'm too busy fighting for breath.

Finally, he comes to a stop and opens a door. We must be ten stories high in this tower, and I am officially winded. Perhaps I should start joining Mirial on her predawn runs as she's suggested many times.

My pulse pounds, and I want to lean over gasping, but I sip the air because I refuse to let this man see that I'm struggling.

I glance at him, and he's not even breathing hard.

Jackal. I've never despised him more.

"The western tower features an observatory for the skies, but I thought you'd be more interested in this," he says.

I walk into a room the size of an average bedchamber, but it's circular with an oculus in the domed roof. In the center of the space is a marble altar, and to the right is a brazier containing the purple eternal flame. There is a window with a large basin to burn offerings to the gods.

"A divining room." I run my fingers over the frigid, waist-high marble altar, relishing the familiarity.

The Praetorian watches me with sharp eyes as I move around. Next to the golden offering tray, almost underneath it, is a sickle knife.

"That's odd," I say.

"What is?"

"There's a ceremonial blade on the altar along with the one kept inside the eternal flame. My father must've accidentally left this behind during the last conclave." I stroke the lapis-inlaid handle, and my chest squeezes, the memory crushing. Just last year he was alive, and now he is ashes. I could not miss him more.

"He must've been looking for his knife," the Praetorian says.

There's a tinge of longing in his voice, but not because my father is gone. No, as Praetorian, he has an obsidian-handled sword called a sabine in his scabbard. Razor-sharp, it takes expert craftsmen three years just to make one. Sabines are an honor bestowed by the Senate. But the temple doesn't function the same way with dearly held armaments. The truth, when properly wielded, is a greater weapon than any.

"No, we have two dozen of them in my temple alone, and they're communal. I'm sure he didn't even notice."

I move to place the blade back down, but something in me can't let go of the knife he last touched. I grip it for strength and guidance.

Torren's mouth shifts slightly, and it feels as if he wants to speak.

I arch an eyebrow. "You look like…you're expecting something."

"Just waiting for you to shoot a bird out of the sky." He stares up at the oculus.

It wasn't what he was going to say.

I shift to fully face him, and our eyes meet. As we stare, I realize that I'm alone with him again. I've spent my life surrounded, but this is the second time in as many days that it's been just the two of us in an empty room.

Curiosity has me in a death grip. What does he want with me? I can't win at a game where I don't know the rules, but I also can't seem to stop playing against him.

Bells ring out, and we jump away from each other. My heart thumps as if I were just caught in a lie.

"What are the chimes for?" I ask, attempting to gather myself. I run a hand over my hair, the chignon still perfect thanks to Zel.

He looks around, grabbing at the breastplate of his armor. "The last person must have arrived at Jubilee. All the members of the conclave are now in place, and we will be locked in by priests of the god of protection. We should head back downstairs—they'll be serving midnight supper soon."

I nod. We both have our roles to play. And I need to find a way out of being the tie-breaking vote.

"Shouldn't you leave the knife?" he asks.

I look down at my hand. I have the handle of the sickle gripped tightly in my fist. "Are you worried about me being armed?"

He stares at me. We're close again, since we both moved toward the door. His eyes dart to my mouth. "Terrified."

"I wish that were true," I murmur.

I force myself to leave the blade behind, then I take the stairs first…so he can't see me trembling.

XI

Torren

Kerasea Vestal is guilty.

She couldn't keep her hands off the murder weapon I planted. And we are locked in with her for the next seven days. No one will leave, and the priests from the temple of protection will prevent anyone from traveling on the mountain until the conclusion of the conclave. I swear to the gods, I will have her confession by then.

Her bedroom lies next to mine. I arranged for her to be placed on my floor, between myself and Julian, which wasn't difficult, as the senators had claimed the top two floors with their pages and guards before I even arrived. The senior senators, Terrance, Medea, and Suh, occupy the former imperial bedrooms on the fifth floor. The younger senators, Paolo, Eyo, and Foreau, took up residence on the fourth.

"What an amazing coincidence," Kerasea said when she noticed our rooms were together.

It's not subtle, but sharing a wall will give me the ability to track her easily. I haven't slept soundly since I was a child—I'll be able to follow her day or night.

Right now, though, we're seated across from each other at dinner.

The six senators are also seated at this table. All the pages and sentries dine separately, not allowed in the company of this rarified group. The banquet room can fit hundreds on the divans and settees, but we are alone at the king's table. It's an eerie feeling, eating in this cavernous room. The largest feature is an enormous fresco of an Elusian queen who used her blood magic to feed the hungry during a famine. She kneels in a field, wearing her crown. With a blade, she's cutting her wrist so that her blood could magically grow the crops despite the terrible drought. That was a thousand years ago—long before the opulence and madness of the last king.

Verhardt's chair at the head of the table sits empty, but no one seems grief-stricken by the fact that he's not with us. His chair was also missing from the Senate floor, but furniture is the least of my concerns.

Julian murmurs something I can't hear, and Kerasea laughs, the sound musical. He's seated next to her, and she now wears an elaborate dress as green as her eyes. It's stunning, but I preferred her in riding clothes.

No…not preferred. I suppose I was surprised that she would wear something so common. The elite flaunt their status, not wear common clothes that cling to their curves or call servants by their first names.

Palace servants enter with wine for our golden goblets. I decline, placing my hand over the rim.

Kerasea meets my gaze and blinks. I suppose I was staring.

I turn toward Senator Paolo, who sits to my right. Just as I look at him, he twists his sapphire ring, then pushes back from the table. He stands with his wine goblet in hand.

"I'd like to take this opportunity to wish you all a blessed conclave," he says. "I hope this week will prove fruitful despite these trying times, because, as we know, hardship is what solidifies the will of the strong. Together, we can conquer any obstacle and lead the Republic of Pryor to the greatest of glories."

"Hear, hear," Senator Eyo says, slapping his palm onto the wooden table. His chair is to Paolo's right, and he's already half into his cups.

As Paolo sits and adjusts the wave of his dark hair, Senator Suh rises, using his diamond-studded cane. He's across the table and next to Foreau, but he's one of the original senators. His goatee is grayer than his hair but around the same length. "May I offer a toast to our fallen brother, former Senate Leader Verhardt."

Everyone stands and dutifully raises their glasses. I lift my water; it appears I'm the only one who doesn't drink. It's not that I don't like the taste. I've just never seen the appeal of losing control.

"To our dearly departed colleague, we commend your service to Pryor and honor your memory as one of the founding fathers of our great republic."

The High Priestess took wine, but she draws it in a very small sip between her ruby-red lips.

Everyone retakes their seats except for Senator Terrance, who fixes his dinner jacket. It's nearly as white as his hair. He raises his goblet higher and draws a large breath, as his general tone is just below a shout. "We'd also like to take this opportunity to commend the Praetorian for quickly apprehending the murderer of our great friend."

I look around. This is news to me.

Everyone drinks again, and I will the surprise off my face. I force myself to grin humbly. I've arrested no one...yet.

"Swift justice is the key to reappointment," Senator Eyo says with a smile.

He is correct, but I don't like his tone. I swallow a reply with some water. He's only around ten years my senior, but he's a dangerous man—they all are.

"Where is the murderer now?" Senator Foreau asks. He runs a hand over his bald head.

Great question.

"The prisoner is in Tullanium jail," Julian says before I can speak.

I grit my teeth. So he turned someone in on my behalf. A rush of anger with a twist of betrayal has me strangling the stem of my goblet, but then Julian shoots me a meaningful stare. Perhaps this was the smart play. With a suspect in custody, no one will think that I am investigating the High Priestess. Guards will be down; mistakes will be made. Still, something doesn't sit well about Julian acting on his own under the guise of my authority.

Dinner begins as servants appear with tray after tray of delicious-smelling dishes. The Council remarks on the magnificent spread. Soon there is enough food on this table to feed ten times this many people. Most of the plates contain far-flung delicacies, but the senators only dine on the best.

My stomach turns. All this decadence while the Northside goes hungry, bellies groaning at night. I remember that feeling—my want gnawing at me, keeping me awake. Wishing I had even a crust of stale bread to soak in water. But even if this dinner is wasteful, it is still better than a tyrannical monarchy. Jubilee was created as a pleasure palace, where the king could do whatever he pleased. It's difficult to say how many people were murdered here—dozens, if not hundreds, by the mad king.

"An example must be made of the culprit," Terrance shouts. "Justice in the name of our colleague demands no less."

"One will be made, I assure you," Julian says.

All the senators are evidently satisfied with the promise of a man being hunted, scourged, and dismembered in the arena—that's what they mean by "an example." Prisoners convicted of high treason are the ultimate source of entertainment for the citizens of the capital.

Of course, that means convening the Verity Guild and allowing the woman who may have conspired to kill Verhardt to sit in judgment.

The senators begin to eat. Actually, Suh is nearly finished with his first dish. He was once a general and still eats at legion speed. Only Kerasea Vestal doesn't touch her plate.

"Did he say why he did it?" she asks. "The criminal?" Her eyes are glassy as she turns to Julian.

She seems genuinely concerned, just as she did in the Senate Hall.

I sip more water. Perhaps she feels guilty that someone is taking the fall for her crimes.

Jules shakes his head. "We'll have a full confession when we arrive back at the capital, but the criminal has ties to the Kingdom of Arthago and a violent past, having beaten his wife and young child to death."

At the mention of Arthago, Senator Medea curls her lip and Suh frowns into his goblet. Paolo spins his ring. Pryor lost half of its western seacoast in the Treaty of Everlasting Peace, leaving an enemy right at the border. Sliver by sliver, they've incurred down the coast farther into the sixth province. And now the Council will once again decide whether we go to war or cede more to the kingdom.

I doubt the man in jail has any actual connection to Arthago, though I do believe he killed his family. Having felt the back of his father's hand many times, Julian would have no qualms scourging a man like that.

"You'd think the murderer would've loved Verhardt for giving away all of our land, then," Eyo says.

The senator is well into his wine, but there's truth at the bottom of a glass. Medea and Suh chuckle. Paolo smiles. The laughter and mirth in the room are real.

Perhaps Julian was right. Maybe I have been too focused on the High Priestess. She doesn't have a motive, while every senator benefited far more from the death of the Senate Leader.

But just as I look at him, Julian gazes at Kerasea out of the corner of his eye. I know that stare. He's in lust or love; it's all the same to him. And they do make a stunning couple—elite Southsiders to their core.

My chest tightens, and I grip my napkin in my fist.

He and I have things to discuss after dinner.

XII.

Kerasea

I toss and turn on the massive four-poster bed in my room, trying to quiet my thoughts and get some rest, but it's no use. The senators were so glib at dinner despite Verhardt's murder. No wonder they unanimously voted to move forward with the conclave—they aren't concerned about anything beyond their own ambitions. But was one of them bold enough to eliminate the Senate Leader?

I have to get out of voting.

I fluff the goose-down pillow, but my eyes are open as the night clock chimes two in the morning. It's the worst feeling to know your sleeping hours are dwindling and yet you're nowhere near slumber.

With a groan, I give up and get out of bed. My body aches with exhaustion, but I'm wide awake. It's useless to pretend otherwise. Breakfast will be served in six hours, but I decide to go to the kitchens to make myself a warm glass of cardamom milk. It might not help, but it won't hurt.

Wrapping myself in my silk robe, I grab a candleholder and leave my room on slippered feet.

I pass the Praetorian's bedroom, still unsure why he gave me that tour. But I do know he had nothing to do with the arrest of the murderer. In fact, he thinks the man is innocent. His face was an open book when the senators congratulated him.

The only reason to set up an innocent man would be so that no one looks further into the crime, but why wasn't the Praetorian involved?

I reach the main staircase, and I no longer need my candle. The massive chandelier still burns brightly overhead. I'm not sure how they keep it lit all night, since it's not an eternal flame, but the old king had a reputation for demanding miracles.

Once I get to the base of the stairs, I turn to the western hall. I didn't notice any kitchens in the eastern hall earlier.

Oil lamps light the space, but this late at night, the flames cast sinister shadows. I pull my robe tighter, the silent corridor looming ahead. My candle shakes slightly as I pass darkened drawing rooms and the abandoned ballroom. It's almost like I can hear the music that once played.

I need a heavier robe.

Eventually, I reach the end of the hall and discover the kitchens. I swing through the door and nearly collide with a body in the shadows. I let out a brief scream, and he does the same. We both lift our candles.

I take in the man's small frame and crooked glasses.

"Antinous?" I ask, my mouth dry and my heart pounding. "Underworld, you scared me."

Senate Clerk Antinous adjusts his glasses while also grabbing at his chest, then he issues me a clumsy bow. "I'm so sorry, Excellency. My humblest apologies."

"I didn't think anyone else would be here." I try to stop my hands from shaking. I knew the Senate Clerk would be in attendance at the conclave, but I hadn't seen him this evening, so he slipped my mind.

It's pitch black aside from our candlelight, but the other side of the kitchen is lit by two candelabras. The staff left food on ice from dinner—cold meat, pastas, and vegetables all under glass cloches. I assume that's why he's here. But he's also gotten into the brandy. Antinous reeks of spirits, and I've never known him to drink much.

"You weren't at dinner," I say.

No one remarked on his absence, but he should have been seated next to the Praetorian. I'd noticed his place card.

Antinous shakes his head. Between his receding hairline and glasses, it's hard to tell how old he is. He looks more weathered and exhausted than I've ever seen him, and it's not the lighting. I thought he was in his mid-forties like Senator Foreau, but now I think he's well into his fifties, maybe sixty.

"I couldn't stand to sit there like nothing happened," he explains.

I nod. None of the senators were grieving, and Antinous worked closely with Verhardt. They were longtime friends and allies. Some insinuated they were lovers, but rumored affairs are just a cheap way to diminish someone's importance.

"Are you here for dinner?" Antinous sneaks a look at the leftover food.

I shake my head. "No, please, you go ahead."

He walks over and starts piling food on his plate. I consider returning to my room, but his eyes keep darting over to me. I know that expression—he needs someone to talk to. I see it before the start of every true confession.

I pull a stool up to the counter as he begins to eat.

"I am very sorry for your loss," I say.

"Thank you. You're one of the few." He pushes his glasses up the bridge of his narrow nose and rips off another piece of cold chicken.

I try to find a compliment for the former Senate Leader, but calling Verhardt a great man or esteemed leader would be a lie. He was ruthless and feared far more than adored. But it was Verhardt's idea to overthrow the king and create a republic, and that takes no small amount of genius and gall.

"He was a visionary," I say.

Antinous sighs. "He was a flawed man, especially once he held great power, but he wasn't always the person he became. Absolute power corrupts even the strongest hearts. And even at his worst, he didn't deserve to be butchered like an animal."

Butchered?

An icy chill washes over me.

Despite my shock, I will my face to stay neutral. My father used to say that people innately want to be truthful. It's fear of consequences, of judgment, that creates lies, therefore no matter what the confession, we cannot judge. I remain silent and nod.

Antinous sways as he eats, dropping crumbs on the counter. I'm not sure how much he's had to drink, but it's enough to loosen his tongue.

"No one deserves that," I remark.

Agreement, my father used to preach. Agreement forms a bond between the confessor and the priest. Agreement builds a bridge where the liar can walk themselves to the light of truth.

Antinous sniffles. "It was bound to happen. He knew too much." He pours himself a glass of red wine. "About them."

It takes all of my reserve to appear emotionless. I dig my nails into my palm and clamp my teeth down on the tip of my tongue until it hurts.

"Surely, they…" I trail off because I'm not sure of anything. A pit of vipers can certainly go after their own. But why? Why now when he'd survived for more than twenty years? "What did he know?"

Antinous stares into the distance as if he didn't hear me. "Every one of them lies and conspires."

Underworld, is he just drunk or is he actually accusing the Senate of murder? It's one thing for me to consider the possibility and another for Antinous to say it.

My head spins, and I try to right myself. My father said to let the confessions slide off you and pool their shadows in your memory, that it is our job to act as temporary repositories for the truth. So that is what I attempt to do—to dismiss it for now. But this confession has barbs and burs that cling to me.

"You think they murdered Verhardt like the king?" I ask.

Medea, Terrance, and Suh were among the seven senators who mutilated the Elusian king with their own blades. They stabbed him a hundred times as he lay dying on the Senate floor. Is that what Antinous means?

He shakes his head. "No, they're too clever. The people would not have accepted a public killing. They arranged for the murder."

"By the man in jail?"

"No, the real killer walks free."

He stops eating and stares into the distance. Suddenly, he looks ancient, haunted. Numbing fear spreads its tendrils across my chest. I'm about to ask if he's all right when he speaks again.

"They'll come for me, too, because I know. I know all their secrets, their schemes, and their shames."

My mouth goes dry, and I swallow hard. I try to dismiss it, but Antinous does know everything as the Senate Clerk. None of the senators ever confess to the temple of truth—they don't risk even stepping on holy ground—but Antinous sees all of the messages, the ledgers, and the orders. If he believes they are responsible for Verhardt's murder, they are. And now he fears for his life. I try to tell myself he's just being paranoid. That he's perfectly safe at Jubilee. No one would dare commit murder in a locked palace with the Praetorian here.

I shake my head. "But the Praetorian…"

"No one could investigate the investigator for years." He slurs his words, but his accusation is clear.

My breath catches. He thinks Torren carried out the murder of Senator Verhardt.

The thought is a thunderbolt. I grip my robe, my fingers icy. My father warned me he was a dangerous killer. But is this why the Praetorian is suddenly interested in me? Because he wants to confess, or is it something more sinister?

I pour myself some wine from the bottle in front of Antinous. I take a large gulp, but something doesn't quite fit in what he said. A thought, an inconsistency needles at me. I'm about to ask him to clarify when there's a movement by the door.

We're not alone.

I gasp. Antinous grabs at a steak knife and nearly drops it trying to point the blade, but a few moments later, a household servant comes into the kitchens.

"Good evening," the older woman says with a bow. "Do you have everything you need?"

"Yes, we do." I run my hands over my long hair, ignoring how badly my fingers shake.

This conversation is over, but I will need to ask Antinous more questions once I can process everything.

"I should go back to my chambers," Antinous says, although he looks sad to leave his plate. He moves too quickly and knocks over his glass. Red wine bleeds down the white counter. The servant woman quickly wipes it up, and I realize Antinous is also trembling.

I drain my glass. "I'll walk with you. I'm going to the third floor as well."

He shakes his head. "I'm staying elsewhere. Lock and bar your door, High Priestess. Keep danger at bay. You have a kind heart."

"Thank you—" I begin.

"But a kind heart is nothing more than a meal to wolves."

Antinous rests his hand on my shoulder and then leaves. I stare out through the small kitchen window at the dark night. A few snowflakes fall before I realize I forgot to give him a word of blessing.

XIII.

Torren

I'm still hiding in the drawing room when Antinous stumbles
through the kitchen doors.

The man who just accused me of murder looks both ways, his
movements ferretlike and fearful, before he descends to the ground
floor.

I grip the doorknob. He believes there's danger, and he left the
High Priestess alone.

Coward.

I followed Kerasea after hearing her bedroom door open, then
stood in the shadows by the kitchens. With my ear to the opening, I
heard her pry more information out of Antinous than I could with
fire and sword.

I underestimated her. I should've known she would be a great
interrogator. The Faith never forces the truth; they coax it out. Her
soft voice and kind posturing promised an ease of his burdens,
clemency in exchange for honesty, and he leaped at the chance. Then

he told her that one or all of the senators commissioned the murder of Verhardt—and that I carried it out.

The night clock chimes three, and Kerasea comes out of the doors holding a candle and a glass of red wine. The head-on sight of her is arresting. She's in a silk robe cinched tightly at her small waist. Her long black hair flows around her, down and untamed instead of tightly swept up or perfectly braided. Without makeup, she looks vulnerable, more like a normal person than a High Priestess. Her hands tremble as she holds the glass. She takes a sip, her lips a perfect pink.

I'd escort her back to her room, but the clerk of the Senate just told her I might be a dangerous assassin for hire. I ball my hands into fists. I didn't hear the rest because a servant picked the worst moment to come down the hall. But who knows what else he said.

Rather than take the western staircase, Kerasea proceeds down to the entryway and then up the main stairs. Once she is out of sight, I leave the shadows and exhale.

Antinous, like Julian, believes the High Priestess was not involved in Verhardt's murder. He would never have said all of that if he thought she was part of the scheme to eliminate the Senate Leader.

So, where does that leave me? Are they wrong, or am I? I can't ignore a temple knife at the scene, but she said herself that there are dozens of them. The temple in the capital has a High Priest, eleven standard priests, and gods know how many acolytes and servants at any given time. Plus, there are thirty guards who only serve the temple.

Just as Hadrian and Probus said, the knife is nearly meaningless as proof. But I still need to question Kerasea about her whereabouts, and also what she knows about everyone in her temple. It's impossible to do this during pleasant conversation. I will need permission from the Senate to get answers, but if Antinous spoke the truth, they will want this matter dropped as quickly as possible. My investigation will be halted and I will be in danger for even suggesting it.

I pause on the steps. Maybe, like Julian said several times, I should accept the gift of a solved case, and the easy reappointment, and move on. Continuing to delve into this will only lead to disaster, and to what end? I had no love for Verhardt. He was part of the Senate that denounced my father and destroyed my name. I should drop it.

But I can't.

I hang my head as I reach the third floor. Allowing a killer to walk free goes against everything I believe, and letting things go requires an indifference I lack.

Someone thought they could get away with this, and I have to prove them wrong.

Just as I come out of the staircase, there's a golden blur and then a knife to my throat. I freeze, my body reacting faster than my mind.

"Why are you following me, Praetorian?" Kerasea asks.

She's so small and fragile-looking, but right now she's anything but delicate. Her gaze is homed in on me, and with a quick motion she could slit my throat. Her wineglass and candle are nowhere to be seen, and her dagger is out. She's in a fighting stance, even if she's still in a silk robe.

I raise my hands, although I have daggers strapped to both of my ankles. "I heard a scream earlier."

Her eyes shift. She knows that she screamed when she ran into Antinous. It's plausible that I was simply investigating the sound.

As she thinks, she gets distracted. She has some training with blades, but I bet she's never had to use one when it counted. She takes her eyes off mine for a moment.

It's a mistake.

With one motion, I grab her by her waist and pin her wrist to the wall. The golden dagger falls out of her hand, thudding against the carpet, as our bodies careen against each other. She lets out a stifled moan as her back hits the wall, my knee between her legs.

We're face-to-face, and she's now disarmed. My body completely covers hers, immobilizing her limbs.

"Don't threaten someone with a blade unless you intend to see it through," I say.

"What makes you think I didn't intend to?"

She's trapped, but those lips stay parted, her chin raised in defiance. Her rich perfume of jasmine and spice invades my senses. This close, she is all softness beneath me. I can feel the curves of her body, the silk of her hair. Even with everything I know about her, there's still a pull deep within me.

Son of a jackal, Julian was right—I need to leave her alone. She is one of the most powerful women in the republic, and she will be terrifying once she realizes it. If she's not a suspect, then I need to return to keeping my distance, not admire her spirit.

I release her and step back.

She stares, wary as she crouches down to retrieve her dagger. As if *I* just had a knife to *her* throat.

"Shall we?" I gesture down the hall to break the tension.

She gives a small nod.

We silently walk toward our bedrooms in the middle of the third floor until we reach her door.

"Sleep well, High Priestess." My tone mocks both her and her title. I don't want to needle her, but I can't seem to help it.

"I will...with a locked door."

She stares at me. The fire in her eyes catches me off guard more than her blade. She was so easy to physically overwhelm, yet she refuses to back down. I'd think it was her pampered life, in getting her way all the time, but that makes people cower once they're defeated. This is something different.

She stiffens as I lean closer to her ear, but no matter the circumstances, she doesn't cede.

"If I wanted in, a lock wouldn't stop me," I whisper.

It wasn't the right thing to say, but I also can't help rising to her challenge. It lights something inside me.

She turns her head. We're so close that our breath mingles. She smells like wine and honey.

"I'm glad you don't, then." She keeps her eyelids low, and her full lips curl up into a wicked grin.

Fierce desire courses through me. I want to grab her again. I want her long hair in my hands and her arms around me. I want to feel the vibration of her moans as I—

Good gods, what am I thinking? She literally has a dagger at her side and, even if she's not a murderer, she's hiding something—I sense it in my gut. Not to mention that she is the same girl who ruined my life, my father's.

I need to go the fuck to bed.

I take a step away. "Goodnight, Excellency."

She exhales, and I bow my head. Then I return to my room without looking back. It's harder than it should be.

XIV.

Kerasea

T he gray daylight causes my eyes to ache as I lie in bed. I barely
got any sleep, staring at the ceiling and wondering if Antinous
was right—was the Praetorian the murderer? It didn't *feel* right,
though—which means I'm trapped here with a killer and no idea
who to fear.

Either way, one thing is crystal clear: I have to get out of voting.
It puts me right in a killer's path. I plan to claim that I cannot decide
in the event of a deadlock. And then avoid being alone with anyone
for the next six days. Especially the Praetorian.

I groan and rub my face.

Underworld take me. What a plan.

I still can't believe I held a blade to his throat, but all I knew was
that someone was following me. I didn't know it would be him.

He wasn't at all afraid, though. I close my eyes and remember
how easily he disarmed me. The rush of heat from his body through
his nightclothes made me shiver. There was so much desire radiating

from him when we stood by my door, but then he stepped away like it was all a game.

Maybe it was.

Then why am I falling for it? Why play at attraction when he despises me? It should be easier to get to the truth, since he's such a terrible liar. He knew I screamed, not because he heard it from way up here but because he was already by the kitchens. I can only assume he believes I have some knowledge about Verhardt, but it's Antinous who knows everything.

And he believes Torren is a murderer.

Another chill hits me, this time an unpleasant, blood-draining sensation, as I recall the fear in Antinous's eyes. Poor Antinous. He's an academic, a gentle soul among snakes and blades. But he believes the Praetorian is more dangerous than any of us imagine.

I should heed his warning.

Not because I believe the Praetorian killed Verhardt—I spent the night rolling the thought through my mind and, while Torren is certainly capable, I don't think he did it. He's not a good enough liar to fake concern for the Council after butchering the Senate Leader, and he's too rigidly devoted to his role. But he is still a danger to me. I need to avoid the Praetorian, not lie here thinking about him pressing me against the wall.

A light knock on the door makes me gasp. But it's just Zel. She's always on time.

I placed a chair under the door handle last night. I shift it and smile as I let her in.

"Good morning, High Priestess, did you sleep well?" Her large brown eyes take me in, pausing at my face.

I nod. "The mountain air is quite refreshing."

It is a half-truth. Unlike the Praetorian, I am an exceptional liar.

I skip the morning meal, and Zel spends extra time applying makeup under my eyes, although she says nothing about it. Sometimes, there's a subtle kindness in silence.

I don a simple cotton dress and then my white robe. Like all of my ceremonial robes, this one is embellished with gold and lapis stones. I also slip on four-inch-wide gold bangles and a heavy gold necklace—symbols of being a servant to the god of truth.

Zel braids my hair, her nimble fingers working quickly. Zel's parents are also temple servants, as were her grandparents—a respected position in the capital.

"Are you pleased, High Priestess?" she asks.

"Always." I smile.

She grins brightly, her pale white cheeks turning rosy. "I hope you have a good day today. I'll see you before supper."

With that, I'm ready. I can't help but look toward the Praetorian's chamber as I walk down the hall, but his door is closed.

I arrive at the throne room before ten in the morning, but the Council is already present. Flags of the republic hang over the whitewashed walls except for the northern window bank. The snow continues to fall steadily outside, gathering on the mountaintops and the massive terrace. If this continues, we will be snowed in. Not that it matters for this week—no one is allowed to come or go from the palace during the conclave.

Julian stands by the door in his brown leather armor, his blond hair shining like the gilding around us. He mentioned at dinner that he doesn't do much this week. His function is to organize the sentries, a purely ceremonial role, but twenty years ago, on the Crimson Night, a former Capital Commander protected the Senate, so they wrote his position into the *lex conclave* to honor him.

"Good morning, Excellency." Julian smiles, and his friendliness is genuine and refreshing. He's so different than his friend, like sunshine to a storm cloud.

I smile. "Good morning, Commander Monroe."

The Praetorian is also in the room in his steel, but he stares straight ahead.

There are no longer thrones in Jubilee. The elevated, carved marble apse sits empty aside from a seal of Pryor on the wall. The most prominent feature in the throne room is a large, dark wood table in the center and high-backed chairs around it. No one is sitting, however. They are all conversing together except for the Praetorian.

I take a deep breath and step into the viper pit.

"Good morning, senators, Praetorian," I say.

The senators greet me warmly. It is my duty to open the conclave with a blessing and to foretell the future from a sacrifice at the end of the week. However, even though I am last to arrive, the doors remain open as the sun clock chimes ten.

No one seems to be waiting for me, but as the moments pass, doubt creeps in. Maybe I need to do something to start the event. All my father said was once the conclave begins, we do a blessing.

I keep glancing at the door, so frequently that the Praetorian cranes his neck to see what I'm looking at.

"Are we waiting for someone?" I finally ask.

"Antinous." Senator Terrance sniffs, his voice loud and distaste clear. "He is late."

"He was also not at breakfast or dinner," Senator Medea notes, smoothing her purple toga over her curves. "Are we sure he is even present?"

"I am certain," the Praetorian states.

Everyone turns toward Torren as if they're first noticing him. He meets their gazes but avoids looking at me.

"Well, he is holding up the conclave." Senator Suh raps his cane on the floor. "Commander Monroe, do order the sentries to locate the clerk."

Julian glances at the Praetorian, and Torren nods.

"Certainly." Julian issues a quick bow and leaves.

While we wait, I observe the groupings. Senators Suh and Terrance prefer each other's company—one stocky and broad and the other tall. Foreau and Eyo huddle together, occasionally pausing to preen, as they are both thought of as handsome. Foreau is bald where Eyo has thick hair, so they are another pair of opposites. Medea and Paolo speak briefly—him having to look up to her—but then they return to their respective circles of original senators versus those more recently elected. I realize that's what Eyo meant by us being part of a "new guard." Once Verhardt is replaced, power will shift. There will be more new senators than old for the first time.

One murder has changed the makeup of the Senate Council. The new guard, specifically Eyo, stood to benefit the most from Verhardt's death. And he was speaking of change and war at the Revelry. Was it a confession that I was too intoxicated to process? Or was he simply drunk?

The sun clock continues to move as minute after minute passes.

"Excellency." Senator Paolo smiles, walking toward me.

I incline my head. "Senator."

He brushes his wavy hair away from his forehead. "I want to express again how saddened I was by your great father's passing, but I am happy to see you in the robes and collar of the temple."

He, and all of the senators, attended my father's elaborate funeral procession just a few months ago. But Paolo and I both lost our mothers long before we could remember their faces, and now, we fill our fathers' roles. He understands the loss better than most.

"Thank you," I say. "I will do my best to serve the Council as he did."

"It is a difficult time to be at your first conclave, given the circumstances." He glances around the room. "If there's anything I can do to assist you, please don't hesitate to ask."

His voice is soft but genuine. I'm about to respond when I catch Julian's blond head poking around the doorway. Paolo turns to see what I'm looking at, as does everyone else.

"Praetorian, may I have a word?" Julian asks. There's something off about his tone and his eyes. He's normally so casual and full of life, and he's distinctly neither at the moment.

Torren and Julian exchange quick, hushed words, and then they leave. An unsettling feeling drapes over my shoulders.

"Is this how the first day of the conclave normally proceeds?" I ask.

Paolo spins his sapphire ring and shakes his head. "No, not at all. Verhardt would commence at ten sharp. As the eldest statesman, Terrance intended on opening the conclave this year. But we cannot start without a clerk to document and record the resolutions."

Terrance was going to jump into Verhardt's role? Was there a reason other than age?

"Nothing is normal this year." Senator Foreau walks over with a frown. He rubs his palm along his bald head. "And now we wait on a secretary."

All of them, including Antinous, are from elite families. Senators must be noble, and typically they are patrons or benefactresses, although Medea is the only female senator in the last fifty years. Yet they speak of Antinous as if he's a servant.

It's after ten thirty by the time the Capital Commander and the Praetorian return. The mood is piqued at best with crossed arms, furrowed brows, and sighs. Except for me. The longer the delay, the less time I'll have to potentially serve as a deadlock breaker. I am sure they had difficulty finding Antinous, since he was not staying in an assigned room, but I look past Julian and Torren and don't see him.

"Well, finally!" Senator Terrance's voice booms, and he moves his white head like a swan, staring between the two men. "Where is the Senate Clerk, Commander Monroe? I assumed you'd bring him here so that we could begin."

"He is dead," the Praetorian says.

The throne room is completely silent as a small yelp escapes my lips. The high-pitched sound echoes as I close my eyes and try to breathe. I thought Antinous was being paranoid last night or was just drunk—at least that is what I told myself. I thought that no one would dare harm him at the conclave. But now he is dead.

And since we are locked in, at least one person at Jubilee is responsible.

I look around the room, trying not to shudder as I take in each suspect—the older faces of Terrance, Medea, and Suh and then the younger senators. There are no tears, but also no guilty expressions. They all seem vaguely surprised, with lined brows or narrowed eyes.

Really, they are reacting as if they were told the kitchens have no more orange juice—put out but not weeping. Suh runs a hand over his goatee, and Eyo raises his eyebrows. But I can only read so much truth from people who constantly wear masks.

"We found him drowned in the thermal baths," Julian adds.

Senator Suh twirls his cane. "What an unfortunate accident."

"This certainly is a development," Medea adds.

"It's for the best," Eyo says. "I'm sure he didn't want to live without being attached to Verhardt's teat."

Again, there's mild laughter from Terrance and Foreau. I bite the inside of my lip. Antinous was a faithful servant to the Council for more than twenty years. He risked his own life conspiring to murder the king. My father told me it was Antinous's idea for the Senate to kneel and publicly present their bloody daggers before the god of truth.

There's nothing funny about this.

The Praetorian steps forward. "No one said it was an accident."

That sobers the Council. I grip my robes as my golden necklace feels like lead on my chest. Stares volley around the room, some puzzled, others skeptical.

Senator Foreau looks at Torren and steeples his bejeweled brown hands in front of his lips. "What are you implying, Praetorian?"

"His death is suspicious," Torren replies. "Drowning in a four-foot-deep hot pool is uncommon for an adult."

Senator Paolo spins his sapphire ring. "The pools are five feet deep. Surely that could've been an accident." He looks around for agreement, and Terrance nods.

"It could've been, but it could also have been foul play," Torren says. "I will need to investigate."

"I'm sure there's no argument here." Senator Medea waves her arm, fingers sweeping the air.

The Praetorian waits, eyeing each senator in turn, but when no one objects, he nods. Of course, that doesn't mean he has permission to investigate the senators or me. He can question the sentries, pages, and servants only.

"I think we all are neglecting the bigger issue here." Senator Terrance raps his knuckles on the table. He stands straight and speaks so loudly that his voice echoes.

The Praetorian pauses, and relief flushes through me. Finally, someone will point out that this death on the heels of Verhardt's murder is no coincidence and therefore, there is a killer among us.

"We have no clerk now," Terrance says. "We cannot have the conclave without a clerk. We are in a bind, as fetching someone from the capital will take at least a full day—if we even can agree on the right person to serve us."

I widen my eyes. That's it? That is his sole concern?

"I can do it," Julian says from the doorway.

Torren stares, surprise written on his face. I didn't expect that, either, but Julian did say he has little to do this week.

"Perfect, then it's settled." Senator Suh claps his large hands. "Thank you for your service, Commander. We can now finally begin. Our pages will show you what is necessary for the resolutions, and they will do all the filing. We just need you to tally the votes and sign the laws as acting clerk."

Julian nods and then leaves the room. Torren watches from the corner of his eyes. There's a wrinkle of concern on his brow, and then it vanishes.

"Am I correct in assuming that none of you saw Antinous at Jubilee?" the Praetorian asks.

He knows very well that I did, but he is asking the senators. He has to tread carefully because of *un exorum*. It's bold that Torren even asked the question when they will vote on his reappointment this week.

Senator Eyo frowns as everyone stays silent.

What was that?

Foreau shakes his head. "Of course we didn't."

"Certainly not." Terrance wrinkles his nose as if he smells something foul.

They are lying. The untruth seeps into my skin like oil. Are they covering the truth because they don't want to appear guilty or because they are?

Suh folds his thick fingers. "Praetorian, we have business to attend to. You are certainly not interrogating the Council, am I correct?"

"That is correct," Torren replies. "I was inquiring as to whether anyone knew where he was staying to make it easier for us to locate his chambers."

The group visibly relaxes.

"We do not," Eyo says with finality.

"We'll receive your report at lunch, then," Paolo says softly.

Thus dismissed, the Praetorian turns, but not before locking eyes with me. If he was listening at the kitchens, he heard what Antinous said—the Senate conspires. Whoever murdered Verhardt also wanted him dead, and they acted upon it.

Someone in this room is guilty of double murder, and we are the only ones who seem concerned by this fact.

An invisible string now links me to Torren, but is that a good thing? I suppose it depends on whether both murders were carried out by the Praetorian himself.

XV

Torren

J ulian returns to the throne room while I take the stairs to the thermal baths. I have no idea why he volunteered to play clerk for the Senate Council, but that's an oddity I can settle later.

Right now, I'm dealing with another murder—one made to appear like an accident, a far cry from Verhardt's evisceration.

The different methods would typically suggest a different assailant, but in this case, the timing and the closed nature of Jubilee means it must be the same person.

I do know now that it wasn't Kerasea. She seemed shocked and saddened by Antinous's death, but more than that, Antinous was alive when she saw him last and she didn't leave her bedroom after I walked her back. At least that is one suspect eliminated—that is, of course, assuming she didn't arrange for someone else to do it.

I ponder that possibility as I enter the imperial bathing complex. The baths consist of rushing waterfalls, trickling streams, and multiple rooms all with scenic views of the capital far beneath us. Or there would be a view if it weren't snowing so hard.

The smell of minerals emanates from the water as my footsteps echo past the lagoon-size tepid pool. I continue through the cavernous space to reach the caldarium. We found Antinous face down in one of the hot springs.

As I enter the humid room, a blast of warm air coats my face with dew. I blink, then find two sentries in the water with Antinous's body.

"I said the scene was not to be touched!" My voice thunders in the tiled space, outrage flowing through me.

The men are so startled that they drop Antinous. His body splashes in the pool, making an undignified wave. The two sentries go stock-still and stare at my armor.

"Praetorian," they say, saluting.

"What are your names and which senators do you accompany?" I ask.

The first sentry is tall, with a barrel chest and a vacant expression. "I am Sentry Avarre. I accompanied Senator Terrance."

"Sentry Calais with Senator Eyo," the other replies. The second man looks familiar. He's smaller like Paolo and wiry. I saw his curly black hair and sharp nose during the Revelry. He, like his senator, couldn't keep his eyes off the High Priestess.

"Well, place the body on the bench now that you have disturbed the scene." I point to one of the slatted wooden benches that line the room.

"Yes, sir," they say at the same time.

They lift Antinous out, his muscles completely rigid with death. Based on that, he likely died six to seven hours ago. Which means not long after I saw him leave the kitchens.

Not long after he accused me of murdering Verhardt.

My chest tightens, chills running through me in the heat. That makes me the last person to see him alive—aside from the killer.

"Our apologies, Praetorian," Sentry Avarre says. "But Commander Monroe ordered us to move him so you could examine the body."

I squint. Julian must be rattled. He knows full well not to move a victim before I have a chance to investigate. And now, not only was the area not secured because we had to return to the throne room, but these men were actively in the pool with the body. The scene is nearly useless to me now.

This is the second investigation Julian has interfered with. A thought snakes through my mind, but I dismiss it. Julian is not a conspirator or a murderer; I *know* him. Besides, he's the Capital Commander—one of the youngest ever. Julian is from one of the wealthiest families in the capital, a future patron, and he is loyal to the republic.

But still, the thought persists. *You are the Praetorian. You must investigate* all *suspects.*

"Return to your posts," I say to the men.

They both salute and leave the caldarium.

Antinous's lifeless body lies on the bench, his dead eyes staring up at me. His glasses are gone. Either he left them in his chambers or they're at the bottom of the pool. Possibly they were crushed underfoot by one of the sentries.

I exhale, trying to shake the heavy sense of failure as I crouch down and examine him. It is my duty to protect the Council, and now the Senate Leader and Clerk were murdered under my watch. I did, in fact, fail. But it is also impossible to protect the Senate from themselves.

Like Verhardt was, Antinous is naked. I hold his wrist, but, of course, there's no throbbing of life beneath my fingers. Due to the fact that he was in the hot pool, Antinous is abnormally warm for a corpse. But there are no noticeable marks on his arms. I take my time examining his neck and chest but find no telltale wounds or bruises. Strangulation by garrote or hand leaves clear marks on a dead body. He has no signs of poisoning or suffocation. No, he definitely drowned.

Was it accidental or did someone hold him under?

My gut says he was held, especially because he had no reason to be in the baths at three in the morning. He wouldn't risk coming alone when he thought the senators were after him, and this is a terrible place to hide. Someone must have lured him here.

I exhale, my initial investigation complete.

The Ministry of Justice would rule this an accident, not a murder, but Antinous told Kerasea that he knew too much. What else did he tell her that I didn't overhear? I need to know. But in order to question her, I'd have to admit I was eavesdropping and risk revealing that I was the last to see him alive.

The man he accused of murder.

I stand and shake my head. I need to find another way. Perhaps he had a journal or ledger with him, a file with correspondence, or the like. I'll have to find where he was hiding and get there before the sentries do. They were all handpicked by the senators, and thus I can't trust any of them. One of them works for a killer.

I'm about to exit the caldarium when a shimmer catches my eye. In the pool where Antinous was found, on the step, there's something in the water. These pools are tiled with mosaics of the skies, but there is a blue stone that is out of place in the design.

What is that?

I stop next to the water, shove my sleeve up to my shoulder, and dip my hand in. I was right—it is a loose stone, not a tile. I pull my arm out of the water, and in my palm is a small, polished piece of lapis.

Exactly like the ones on the High Priestess's robe.

XVI

Kerasea

We make it to luncheon without the need for me to serve as the tiebreaking vote. I exhale a long sigh of relief as I plop myself down in a chair. The resolution to send reinforcements to the second province to combat barbarian incursions was approved five to one, and so was the resolution to send naval ships to fight piracy on Lake Vesuvius in Medea's province. Both times, Terrance was the dissenting vote, because he said the republic could not afford these measures.

Because of the late start, those were the only resolutions debated thus far. Strangely, no one has brought up the possible war, and that should've been the first resolution.

Why wasn't it?

Twenty smaller matters, such as renaming the Forum Baths to the Verhardt Baths and measures to clean the Tiger River and improve drainage in the Northside of the capital, passed without controversy.

Yet, every resolution has to be signed by every senator along with

Julian, and every vote must be recorded for the archives.

Gods, no wonder this takes a full week.

Julian has been a surprisingly good clerk, dutifully writing down the results and shuffling through the massive amount of paperwork with the help of the six Senate pages.

Two servants wheel in carts containing meats, cheeses, salads, pastas, and breads. Of course, wine is offered as well, and all the senators drink.

My stomach rumbles, and I eagerly accept a plate, but then I think of Antinous having his last cold meal in the kitchens. The fear in his eyes haunts me. He was terrified of the people in this room. And whether Torren can prove it or not, someone here ordered his death. How can I force the truth from them? How can I get justice for Antinous?

Senator Medea wanders over with a meager plate of a few cheeses. She has been on her feet nearly this entire time, as the senators tend to stand while they debate, but I suppose she's not hungry. Is it guilt weighing her down? Did she have a reason to drown him?

"I'm happy to see another woman at the conclave." She puts her wineglass next to my water. "It's been entirely too long."

Senator Medea is a grandmother and the benefactress of the Medea family, her patron twin brother having died long ago. She's served as a senator for twenty-five years, but she smiles as if we're longtime colleagues while she takes the seat next to me. Her lavender scent is pleasant but strong.

"I'm pleased to serve," I lie.

Women and men supposedly have equal rights in the republic, but that never quite seems to be true. However, Medea argued like a man today, with the same self-assured confidence as she staunchly advocated for her province. So, she is an exception, I suppose.

Medea is from a storied noble family and has a client roll that was second only to Verhardt, but she is often criticized for being vicious and unfeeling. To me, she seems like Mirial—no nonsense or softness, just strength and competence. I don't understand my father's love for one and dislike for the other, except for the fact that traits we admire in our allies, we loathe in our enemies, especially when they are women.

"I find it odd that they chose you," Medea says in a low voice. I blink at her, and she rests her hand near mine. "Not because you're unqualified but because it's a surprise that they believed a young woman would be suitable as a tiebreak vote. I wonder what they want from you…or from the temple."

I've wondered the same. "I thought it was a lack of options with Verhardt's sudden death."

Her full lips curl into a grin. "There are always options."

She is right. There were other elected officials from the capital who would've happily stepped in, including the governor, but I hadn't thought of that until after I'd already accepted. I felt that tradition meant they would only allow the people here enumerated in the *lex conclave*. But perhaps they had another motive.

Yet, Medea mentions this as if she's not aligned with them.

"You didn't agree?" I ask.

"No, I did. Deadlocking at the conclave would mean that millions of people suffer while we sit idle—and that is unacceptable when we are supposed to represent their interests. Even now, as we have lunch, people in my province are dying." She stops and exhales. "But, to be perfectly honest, you were not my first choice, as you have so little experience."

I appreciate her honesty even if I don't like hearing it. I am twenty-two, not a child, but compared to someone like her, I do have very little. Perhaps now is the time to admit I plan to refuse to vote.

The other senators eye us from their conversations and plates, Eyo and Terrance being the least subtle. Eyo strokes his manicured beard, and Terrance sniffs as they watch us.

"We are different, you and I," Medea remarks.

"How so?"

"You are dismissed because you're young and beautiful. I am dismissed because I am no longer those things."

She is still beautiful, but she means the beauty of a young person they want to use. I'm trying to think of how to respond when the Praetorian returns. He looks around the room with a stern expression, but when his gaze lands on me, he doesn't quite meet my eyes. Something has changed. The rich cheese sours in my mouth. He found something.

Suh looks up from his third luncheon plate. The former general has barely said a word to me, but maybe with my father having passed, he feels no alliance to me.

"Have you completed your investigation, Praetorian?" Senator Terrance asks from the chair beside Suh.

Torren nods. "Of the body."

Foreau and Eyo exchange glances.

"What more is there to investigate?" Paolo asks. As the youngest senator, he also sits with the new guard.

"I will continue to investigate the circumstances, as I have found his death to be suspicious," the Praetorian says.

Everyone in the room stops eating, a couple of forks clattering onto plates.

Eyo sighs and tosses down his napkin. "The man drowned in a hot pool—what is suspicious about that?"

Medea sips her wine. "The timing, Eyo. It was a day after Verhardt's murder. Let the man do his job and report his findings."

Terrance shakes his white head. "I don't feel there's a need for a full investigation."

"If I am following the Praetorian," Paolo says slowly, turning his ring, "he believes Antinous might have been killed by someone in the palace. Surely he needs to investigate such a possibility."

"Harass everyone based on an inkling? No." Suh shakes his head and wipes his oily mouth and goatee.

Three of them against an investigation and two for it. If Foreau wants the Praetorian to investigate, I may have to serve as the deadlock vote already. But this isn't a resolution, so perhaps not.

Still, I have to swallow twice to choke down a piece of bread.

I wipe my mouth, then ball the cloth napkin in my fist.

Foreau strokes his square jaw, delaying as he soaks in the attention of the group. He is the most recently elected senator, so the one most often dismissed. "I don't see the harm in letting the Praetorian question the staff and sentries."

I close my eyes for a long blink. They are deadlocked.

"Let's put it to an official vote if we must, so that we can return to our meal." Terrance manages to sound both condescending and put out. His tone is once again a little too loud for the room.

The senators cast an official three to three vote. If this were a resolution, they would revote up to twice after debate and backroom bargaining, but I'm not sure what the protocol is now.

"Well, High Priestess, it looks like you'll need to break our tie for the first time," Eyo points out. "What say you on this matter?"

All of them turn and eye me sharply, except for the Praetorian, who continues to stare straight ahead—the perfect soldier.

Underworld take me.

My pulse flutters in my neck, and I grip the napkin in my hand. I'd love to scratch my wrist again, but the bangles stop me.

"I… This isn't a resolution… I don't think I'm qualified to speak on matters of the Praetorian…"

I suppress a wince. I couldn't sound weaker if I tried. Mirial would faint if she could hear me. Even Medea slightly frowns.

Bloody lies, how do I get out of this?

I sit straighter and try to gather myself with a breath. "Therefore, I leave it up to his expertise."

The room is silent.

Eyo wrinkles his brow. He was a skilled debater and orator, but I shouldn't be surprised, as he's a well-recognized intellectual. But his mind is slower on his third glass of wine. "Is that a vote to proceed?"

"Yes, I believe that is what Verhardt would have wanted," I say.

At his name, the senators blink, skew their faces, or physically recoil. They react as if the Senate Leader was already forgotten or I was bringing up a forbidden topic.

Senator Terrance sniffs. "He is dead, his vote no longer relevant. It is a matter of what you, in your admittedly limited opinion, believe is best for Pryor."

His tone is so loud and condescending that steel rises in my spine. I release the napkin and lift my chin. Whatever they wanted when they appointed me doesn't matter—I'm here now.

"In that case, as a citizen of the capital has died under mysterious circumstances, I vote to let the Praetorian proceed in his inquiry."

XVII

Torren

Terrance, Suh, and Eyo wanted the matter closed, yet Kerasea voted to allow me to investigate. Is one of them the murderer? Terrance's and Eyo's sentries were in the pool with Antinous. Either could have dropped in the lapis. But why frame Kerasea?

When I found the temple knife, I thought she could secretly be a cold-blooded killer, but every time I observe her, she seems genuine. My gut says she isn't a murderess. And if I'm right, then she's in grave danger.

I groan at myself. What difference does it make? She is not my charge. I have no reason to protect her. My duty is first and only to the Senate.

One by one, I interview the ten household servants, six Senate pages, six sentries, and the servant to the High Priestess. The sun lowers in the sky as I scribble codes on my notepad.

Although it takes all afternoon, every single person is predictably useless. No one saw or heard anything, but I had to question them to note personalities, tells, and inconsistencies. I spent extra time with Sentry Avarre and Sentry Calais, the men I found moving Antinous's body, but to no avail. Calais was on duty late last night, and Avarre was asleep. Both of these stories were confirmed by other sentries, so once again, I have no leads.

I now need to locate Antinous's chambers. The problem, of course, is that whoever killed him had hours to find his rooms, but that was true before we discovered his body. Given the choice, I opted to record everyone's stories first. That way, I can question them again if I find evidence.

Somehow, I doubt I will.

Still, I begin my search on the ground floor. Antinous had taken the stairs to this level after talking to Kerasea.

The servant quarters are cramped and sparse compared to the rest of the palace; however, they are dry and temperate, thus better than most of the tenements in the Northside of the capital.

Jubilee once had three hundred servants sharing these fifty bedchambers and communal toilets. Now, there are only ten, but I still have all these rooms to search.

No nobleman would ordinarily choose to stay in this warren, but Antinous might've, since he didn't want to be seen.

Using a skeleton key, I open and close door after door, but either the rooms belong to the servants or they are empty.

I proceed up to the first floor. I doubt he was staying in a ballroom or drawing room, but I have to look.

Nothing—no sign of him.

The second floor won't be used this conclave, and as I unlock the doors, I realize this would be an excellent place to hide.

Seven rooms in, I find Antinous's chambers.

As soon as I push the door open, it is obvious that I am not the first to arrive. The chambers are ransacked, from the feather bed cut open to books and papers strewn over the floor.

His chambers being here and not on the ground floor means he was already heading to the baths when he left the kitchens.

That entirely rules out Kerasea.

With a sigh, I force myself to focus. One thing, one place at a time. I inhale, clear my mind, and begin to inventory the scene. Whoever ransacked this room probably found what they were looking for, but each paper left behind could yield a clue, and each book could contain a hidden secret.

"I thought he was neat and tidy," Julian says from the open doorway.

"How did you find me?" I ask.

He shrugs. "I mean…it's a locked palace. There are only so many places you could be."

I harrumph, but he's correct. It's how I found this room.

Julian walks in and glances around at the knocked-over shelves and floating feathers.

"Still think it was an accidental drowning?" I ask.

"Maybe he had an episode of some sort," Julian says.

I shoot Julian an unamused look as he plays with a paperweight. "Are you going to compromise this scene, too?"

He sighs, eyes praying to the ceiling. "Are we going to go over this again? At the time, I thought it was a simple accident. I believed we should get Antinous's body out of the water so you could confirm it. Obviously, I was wrong."

"Why did you volunteer to serve as Senate Clerk?" I ask.

I study him, but he's not thrown by my sudden change in topic. Either he expected the question or he's used to the way I interrogate people.

He shrugs, his air casual. "To be helpful. There's no one else who can do it. Kerasea, maybe, but they already have her serving as the deadlock vote."

Hearing her name reminds me of the lapis sitting in my pocket. It didn't appear that her robe was missing any stones, so where did it come from?

Julian takes a step forward, crushing some papers under his boot. I frown. I still need to inventory those.

"Torren, stop. I can almost feel you digging your own grave as soon as her name is mentioned. Leave her be."

"You seemed awfully close to her at dinner last night."

I can't hide the bitterness in my tone. It's double jealousy. He's my closest friend, and even if she's not a suspect, I've hated her for a dozen years. There shouldn't be a relationship between them.

His smile fades as he stands straighter. "Are we really going to do this?"

"You've been dead set against my investigating her from the start. Is there a reason for that?"

Julian shoves his hands in his pockets. "Because you don't have permission to break *un exorum*. These people are dangerous—her included. Not because she's a murderer—I don't think either of us really believes that she killed these men. But if she ever realizes how much power she has, she will be a danger to the republic. With Verhardt dead, the senators are trying to court her for her blessing because the Faith follows her like a dog at heel—nobility and commoner alike—with more fervor than they did for her father. You and I both know there are issues with the republic, and it never takes much for holy rule to spread its roots. But most importantly, you are up for reappointment. You have to tread carefully, or you are going to get yourself censured—or worse."

"So you're not trying to bed her?" I ask.

He lets his head fall back, his hands balling into fists and the lump in his throat bobbing. "Did you hear a word I said?"

"That's not a denial." I ignore the tightness in my chest and continue to catalog the papers. Ledgers of the Senate expenses, missives from the frontier, and demands from emissaries from Arthago are all mingled together. Strange this was left behind. Why not take it all and burn it?

"You're obsessed, Tor," Julian says. "You have been obsessed with the Vestals since I've known you, but this thing now with Kerasea is something else. Is it because you can't have her?"

I straighten to my full height as he brings up the real, unspoken difference between us. Julian is a noble from the Southside, the same as

Kerasea. He is free to court whomever he pleases, including someone like her, whereas I could not. But he has never rubbed it in my face.

Not until now.

"Say that again."

He drops his shoulders slightly. "This is madness. I'm not going to stand here and fight with you when I'm trying to protect you. You are letting whatever it is you feel about the High Priestess cloud your judgment. And this is a terrible time to lose objectivity."

"I am not."

He takes a step closer to me. "You are, and I can prove it."

I pause, my silence question enough.

"You haven't even properly conducted an inquiry into Verhardt's murder," he says. "Do you know who the last person was to see him alive?"

I bristle, but Julian is correct. I haven't because I've had no chance to do so. "No. Lady Verhardt was too 'indisposed' to speak with me, and she refused to let me interview her son or household staff. Which speaks to her guilt, not innocence. Perhaps when we get back to the capital—"

"It was me, Torren."

My heart stops. One moment, two, as our eyes meet, and the chamber feels too small and too warm. But Julian calmly holds my gaze.

"I was the last person to see him alive at his villa," he continues. "A group of sentries and I walked Verhardt back, and then I stayed at his request. He and I had a glass of brandy, and then I left at nearly four in the morning. Are you going to investigate me now or just continue to obsess over Kerasea?"

Without waiting for a response, he shakes his head and walks out of the chambers. I remain frozen in his wake. It's the first argument we've ever had, but the suspicion he just cast could end not only our friendship but the republic. Because the nephew of the general and the future patron of the Monroe family just admitted that he had the opportunity to kill the Senate Leader.

XVIII

Kerasea

The only other deadlock I had to break today was whether to increase the grain dole to the poor of Pryor, and that was a fast yes, even if Eyo, Foreau, and Suh argued that full stomachs make people lazy. Terrance had a surprisingly passionate plea to increase the dole, but I'm not sure if that was to help the poor or not, since most of the grain is grown in his province.

I still need a way out of voting again, though. I am not a representative, and my role is already causing a shift in the attitudes of the senators—just as Mirial feared.

Having now opposed Eyo twice, I am clearly not nearly as attractive to him as I was during the Revelry.

Small gift from the gods, I suppose. But I have to keep everyone satisfied. The Faith doesn't need powerful enemies, especially one as intelligent as Eyo.

We mill around the banquet hall before dinner, all of us in formal wear, sipping on sparkling wine. Unlike yesterday's midnight meal, this one will begin at eight. Tomorrow's conclave will start at nine, as the legislative days lengthen through the week. By the end, we will commence at dawn.

The Praetorian and Commander stand close to the doors, although, strangely, I don't think they've spoken to each other since arriving.

Senators Foreau and Paolo stand near me. Foreau continues to talk about his province as Paolo and I pretend to listen, the youngest senator trying and failing to find breaks in the conversation where he can speak. Paolo leans on his toes, spins his ring, but he can't get a word in.

"Of course, with our twin coast provinces, you're already aware of how the god of the earth blesses our shores with abundance," Foreau says to me. "Yet it was kind of you to increase the grain dole today. I hope you will support me in my motion to increase the fishing allowance, as it will also benefit the less fortunate in the republic."

He's not really looking for a response, but I nod politely. Foreau either doesn't notice or care about how Paolo frowns at the mention of a coastline. The seventh province's entire coast was lost under his father's tenure when the Senate gave the land to Arthago to end the Hundred Year War. The annexation and retreat were a complete disaster for the new regime and nearly ended the republic before it began.

Senator Medea walks over to join us. She smells like elderflower this time and smiles gently. "You did well today, High Priestess."

Paolo lights up at the change in topic, rocking on the balls of his feet. I am in heels, so we stand at about the same height. "Yes, you did an admirable job," he says.

I voted on the same side as both of them, but I'll take the compliments. They were the only two senators who seemed genuinely concerned about the people in their provinces.

"Courting the vote of the capital, are we?" Eyo says, strolling over with his wine. He smiles, all charm again. "You'll find, High Priestess, that our two provinces have far more aligned interests than any of the others."

"Because you are the only ones safe from our enemies," Foreau says, frowning.

Eyo raises his black eyebrows and strokes his beard. "A barbarian horde at our border says otherwise."

Foreau laughs. "You mean the people you steal from the wilderness, whom you force to work your lands and brothels?"

Eyo colors red. I've heard that rumor as well—that soldiers form raiding parties to capture women and children. Neither the Senate nor General Hadrian would sanction such a thing, but it's certainly possible in the wilderness. People will always do terrible things for profit and power.

Is that the reason someone killed Verhardt and Antinous? For money or increased power? I've already had the thought that no one rises to high status with their hands clean. And every single person in this room rose to dazzling heights at a young age.

"What enemy does your province border, Foreau?" Medea asks. "Here I thought your province is safely in the east, is it not?"

"Which means my coast is highly valuable to the Kingdom of Arthago," Foreau says, his voice a low rumble.

Conversation comes to a grinding halt at the name of our greatest enemy.

The servants announce dinner, and relief flushes through me.

I take my seat again next to Julian. Of course, Antinous's seat and Verhardt's chair at the head of the table are empty.

The Praetorian sits across from me and finally sets his gaze on mine. He's disturbingly handsome in another tailored suit. He's clean-shaven as always, and his neck looks no worse for having my blade to it last night.

I pull my eyes away from him, trying to forget the feel of his body pressed against mine outside my door, as servants bring in the first course of intricately arranged vegetables and delicacies. I pick up my fork but then recall how some of the Council thought raw grain would be too much of a luxury for others.

"Skies, it is still snowing?" Medea stares at the wall of windows. "The roads will be impassable soon."

"We're locked in for the week, Medea." Terrance chuckles. His chair is angled so that it's nearly on the corner as he continues his bid to quite literally occupy Verhardt's seat. "Don't get hysterical. What is the difference?"

Her mouth slants. "Well, the body of Antinous..."

The room quiets as everyone realizes that having a rotting corpse inside Jubilee Palace is not ideal.

"I sent him down the mountain earlier, and he was received by the priests of the god of protection," the Praetorian says. "They will see Antinous back to his family."

The senators resume eating, no longer concerned about a decaying body.

Most bodies are burned in Pryor, but some of the older families, like Antinous's, have mausoleums where they rest their dead. I've never understood why they pay taxes to keep skeletons in the darkness rather than burn them in the light, but it is an old tradition from before the rise of prominence of the temple of truth. Every one of the Faithful are burned on a pyre.

"Have you completed your investigation, Praetorian?" Suh asks as they clear his empty plate. He claps his hands free of crumbs.

The Praetorian nods. "I found no evidence of foul play."

It takes all my composure to not skew my face. He's lying. And just awful at it. He shakes his head slightly as he delivers a mistruth. However, no one else notices, or at least they don't care enough to.

Torren meets my stare. We both know someone killed Antinous. One of the people in this room gave the order, if not held him under. But he can't investigate any of them.

"Very well. An unfortunate accident, as we stated," Senator Terrance says, projecting his voice down the table. "But at least the other members of the Council will be satisfied now." He sniffs at the frivolous concerns and then quickly composes his face and fakes a genial smile. "We should have music with our meal to lift this somber mood. Medea, your page can play the harp, can he not?"

"The lyre, yes. Go fetch him," Medea says to the nearest servant. A redheaded woman who is around my age takes off running.

But I keep my eyes on Terrance. He is much too happy to sweep Antinous's death aside.

"Commander Monroe, you have done a commendable job as clerk," Suh remarks, shifting his cane. "Perhaps we should make it permanent."

The suggestion is greeted by laughter, as was intended. A man like Julian is far more likely to be elected senator than serve as a clerk.

"I am afraid that, like my uncle, I am more suited for the sword than the pen." Julian smiles.

"Ah yes, here's to General Hadrian." Suh lifts his glass, and everyone joins him. "May the gods ride beside him on his victory chariot."

Everyone drinks.

"Many in the fifth province believe he could finally lead us to victory against the Arthagian bastards," Suh continues, holding Julian's gaze. "If we are bold enough to go to war, we could win back our ceded territories and possibly more."

"The same is said in the seventh province," Paolo adds, spinning his ring at a dizzying speed.

"I will relay your commendations," Julian says with an easy grin. He's far more skilled at politics than the Praetorian or me.

"Some say he should be a warrior king." Foreau frowns into his goblet.

Terrance sniffs and nods in agreement.

"I believe I'll skip that particular recommendation," Julian says to hearty laughter at the table. But Foreau wasn't joking. He exchanges glances with Eyo. The general's popularity is a danger to their power. Perhaps that is why they haven't voted on declaring war yet.

"Some say the same about a holy queen," Eyo says, turning his attention to me. His brown eyes are suddenly sharp instead of dulled with drink.

I choke on my wine as blood rushes into my cheeks. Senator Eyo is voicing a concern that I, specifically, could be a danger to their sovereignty.

"That is what Verhardt believed," he adds with a shrug.

But the accusation is anything but casual. Maybe this is why he cornered me at the Revelry.

Everyone stares at me, including the Praetorian.

Was this why the Council asked me to serve as a deadlock vote, to test where my loyalties and ambitions lie? Mirial hadn't mentioned that in the host of reasons why I needed to decline, but it now seems plausible.

They all wait for my response. I don't have the ability to laugh it off the way Julian does, nor would they accept that from me. The only thing I can do is answer honestly.

"Spiritually leading the Faith and politically ruling the people require far different skills, Senator," I say. "I am loyal to the Council, like my father before me, but my role is ultimately and solely as a servant to the god of truth, from whose light all things are revealed."

They all quickly bow their heads, even the Praetorian. I relax my shoulders slightly, as my claim to no political ambitions seems to release the tension in the room.

"That light could also lead a mob, if you willed it," Terrance adds loudly.

Everyone stops again and waits. They stare at me as if I'm about to declare holy war on the Senate.

"I'd only will the people to the defense of the Senate," I respond. "Just as my father did twenty years ago."

Medea's page finally arrives, thankfully shifting attention away from me.

"Ah yes, you're finally here—play for us," Senator Medea says brightly. The man is around my age, with delicate features. He takes a seat in the corner and begins to strum his lyre.

The musical notes are a relief. As the second course is brought out from the kitchens—a rich pasta with an obscene amount of truffles—I resolve that one way or another, I will find a way out of serving in this conclave.

The third course is roasted game hen trussed with herbs—one for each of us.

I'm cutting into the breast when Foreau's sentry appears at the doorway. He's distinct with light brown skin but fire-red hair. He whispers something to the blond servant girl, who then taps the Praetorian on the shoulder. After hushed words, Torren wipes his mouth and stands. He glances at me before he leaves the dining room.

The senators barely notice as they continue to gossip about nobles in the capital. Talk then turns to the specter of an upcoming execution in the arena. The excitement is palpable except for Medea, as it's her nephew who will stand trial. But even as Julian participates in the conversation, he eyes the Praetorian's empty chair. His brow wrinkles, and then he clears the expression. He didn't know Torren was about to leave, and he's troubled by it.

Gods, what now?

XIX

Kerasea

Dessert lingers on the table, the seven-course dinner complete as we approach our third hour in the banquet hall. The Praetorian's chair is still empty, and something tells me he didn't plan to return.

Curse his good fortune.

I hope that every dinner is not as long and drawn out as this, but dining is an event for the elites, so it follows that it will be. Priests typically break bread in humble, quick repasts with our acolytes and servants. We all sit together at tables in the dining hall and pass around simple yet hearty dishes—the opposite of this.

Julian glances at me and then leans closer. He carries a light scent of leather and citrus. "You look like you're plotting a method of escape."

I nod slightly. "Was it that obvious?"

He grins. "May I give you a piece of unsolicited advice?"

"Of course."

"Don't operate on their schedules. You aren't a senator."

I swallow a sip of dessert wine. That much is true.

"You are above them as leader of the Faith," he whispers. "You can leave when you like—your father did."

Julian's hazel eyes sparkle with good nature. He's so easily disarming.

"How are you friends with the Praetorian?" I ask, then close my mouth. I twist my napkin in my hands. "I'm so sorry, that was careless and rude. You needn't answer."

Warmth fires my cheeks. That was meant to be an internal comparison, and now I just insulted his friendship. Julian and Torren served in the legions together and were friends before that. Everyone knows they are close companions along with being two of the most sought-after bachelors in the capital.

"You aren't the first to wonder," Julian says with a laugh. "He saved me when we were boys. This might come as a shock, but I wasn't always the fine physical specimen you see before you. I was small and scrawny until adulthood, really. But as I turned thirteen, I was overconfident. I believed I could explore the city without guards, tutors, or chaperones. It didn't take long for me to realize that was a mistake—less than a day, in fact. Three older boys followed me as I left the markets. They dragged me into an alley after they stole my coin purse. They would've done worse than beat me, but Tor came in and fought them all off—thank the gods."

Shame and gratitude flash over his face as his hazel eyes take on a distant look, as if he can recall that moment of helplessness like it was yesterday. Elite men in Pryor are not supposed to need saving, which makes the memory that much more humiliating, I'm sure. And yet he's shared it with me.

I don't want anyone to become trapped in past shame, so I decide to slightly change the subject.

"Did you know him then?"

Julian shakes his head and releases the tension in his shoulders. "I'd seen him before because of our fathers, but we didn't piece that together until later. He defended me because it was three against one, because I needed it." Julian pauses and looks me in the eyes. "That is who he is, Kera. He believes in what is right and does it regardless of the consequences. Everyone else I've known has shown me favor because of my father, my position. Tor saved me that day expecting nothing. I've spent my life annoying him in return."

I shift in my seat, the sentiment uncomfortably familiar. Since I can remember, I've been the daughter of the High Priest, and now I am the High Priestess. There are many worse things to be, but I can never be certain of who has ulterior motives to their kindness.

"Was this before his father..." I begin.

I don't know how to end the sentence. After being convicted, his father was given the opportunity to commit suicide to avoid a brutal public execution. He took his own life in Tullanium jail.

"No, it was around a year later."

When someone is convicted by the Verity Guild, everything is stripped from their families. Torren defended Julian when he himself had nothing.

An unsettling feeling grips me. This is not the person I've known—the brutal investigator with hatred in his heart. A man who tortures and punishes and yet still sleeps at night. I can't resolve it.

"Where did he disappear to?" I ask.

Julian scans the doorways. "I'm not sure. But if I had to guess, he's going to get himself in trouble. I should look into it." He sighs and pushes back his chair. "Would you like me to escort you to your chambers?"

He asks the last question in a louder tone, so it could be overheard. Bless him.

"Yes, please," I say. "I'm quite exhausted." That is the truth.

Julian offers me his arm, and I take it.

"I bid the Council a fair evening, and I will see you at breakfast tomorrow." I bow slowly to the senators even though my limbs itch to flee.

They pause their conversations long enough to respond in kind, and then Julian and I leave the banquet room. Senator Eyo is well into his cups and doesn't disguise that he is watching my every move, but I continue to walk gracefully.

I need to do something about him, but I have no idea what.

I take a deep breath when we are in the hall and notice Julian's chest rising as well.

"That lot is suffocating," he murmurs.

It's a grave offense to insult the Senate, but Julian is too powerful and too connected to care.

"I offer no commentary," I respond.

Julian laughs, but then his smile fades. "I am surprised they didn't ask you to vote on a Senate Leader today. I suppose Terrance believes the position naturally falls to him — although why remains a mystery when Eyo is better liked. I expect that it will all come to a head by tomorrow. Be prepared."

My full stomach twists at the thought. No wonder they were all trying to court me today. Terrance expecting the seat makes sense. Only, did he kill to get it?

"Fortune is on my side, I see," I murmur.

Julian snorts, which causes me to laugh. We are both still laughing as we climb the grand staircase. As the distance grows between the Council and me, I feel safer. I can breathe again, and Julian relaxes as well.

All of a sudden, he stops, his back rigid. I follow his line of sight and find the Praetorian standing on the landing between the dual staircases. He's watching us with sharp eyes.

"I see I've missed the end of supper." His stance is stiff, his tone clipped as he looks from Julian to me.

"Was everything all right?" I ask.

He tilts his head, a crease appearing on his brow.

"When you were summoned away?" I add.

"Oh, yes. It was just a report on the road conditions as the snow continues."

He's lying...again.

"I see I'm interrupting," he continues, looking pointedly at my right hand wrapped around Julian's arm.

"I was just escorting the High Priestess back to her room, but now that you're here, you can do the honors." Julian pulls away, but I try to hold on to his arm until he takes another step farther. I drop my hand. The Praetorian continues to stare.

The tension is so thick, it's suffocating, but this obviously has far more to do with them than me. It probably involves the reason for them not speaking earlier.

"No, I appear to be the one interrupting," I say. "Julian wanted to find you, and he has. I will see you both tomorrow, as I require no escort."

"Have a restful sleep, High Priestess," Julian says with a short bow.

Torren's jaw moves, but he says nothing. I see there will be no traditional pleasantries between us, not that there have ever been. I should accept that and walk away.

"A pleasant rest to you, Praetorian," I say.

So much for walking away. Why can't I just leave him alone? I grip my skirts tightly in my left hand.

"Bar your door, High Priestess," he says.

His words send chills down my spine. He is serious in his warning, and his tone makes me want to scream and flee, but instead, I smile.

"I've heard that doesn't work to keep everyone out."

I meet his eyes and then turn.

I take the stairs, hoping to swallow my own tongue.

XX.

Torren

I can't help but watch Kerasea continue up to the next floor. The gray of her dress brings out her eyes and lips... I have to stop. Yes, she's beautiful, but there are plenty of beautiful women in Pryor — ones not framed in two murders. Yet there's something in Kera's spirit, a fire I hadn't expected.

"I was just giving her an excuse to leave the dinner," Julian says. His face is full of innocence. I would believe him if he didn't fall for every woman he sees.

I raise an eyebrow. "I'm sure it was a painful chore for you."

"I stand corrected," Julian says. "You've mastered the art of charming conversation."

Son of a jackal. I should throttle him, but I have more important matters to deal with. He is still my most trusted friend and a brother-in-arms. And I think I've potentially discovered the killer.

"When you instructed the sentries to move the body, which ones did you talk to?" I speak in a low tone because the walls have ears in the palace.

"All of them," Julian says. "Why?" His eyes dart around, and then he draws a breath. "Do I even want to know where you just were?"

I shrug. "Probably not."

He groans, looking at the servants walking the halls below us. "Let's go."

"Where?"

"The baths, of course," Julian says.

I stare at him for a moment but then realize that between the shape of the baths and the running water, we won't be able to be overheard. It's one of the reasons the senators negotiate their backroom deals there.

We silently take the stairs down until we reach the baths. This time of night, they have an eerie quality the naive would mistake for being peaceful. The mist rising off the water makes it look like the River of Death, and I'm sure that's fitting. Given the history of this place, I'm certain Antinous was not the only soul lost in here.

I follow Julian into the frigidarium. This room is for cold plunges. Icy spring melt flows down a waterfall and into the various interconnected pools. People believe that diving into freezing waters is good for their health. I'm not sure why.

Julian and I stop next to each other. I watch the water run while waiting to see if we were followed.

"You found something," he says after a minute passes.

I rub my forehead. "I found a lot. After I cataloged Antinous's papers and ledgers, there was evidence to implicate both Senator Eyo and Senator Terrance in the murders."

"Implicate? Tor...don't tell me you left dinner to search their chambers..." He closes his eyes for a pained blink, but I don't bother to deny it. I asked a sentry to interrupt my meal at nine sharp, without telling him why. I excused him back to his own meal and then headed upstairs as the senators remained in the banquet hall.

"All right, what did you find?" Jules asks.

"Verhardt was blackmailing both senators."

Julian raises his eyebrows, not shocked so much as mildly surprised. "Based upon what acts?"

"That was what I was trying to determine. For Terrance, it's obvious. Antinous had numerous complaints from merchants he extorted, but he was also embezzling money from the treasury of the republic. The tax ledgers were off, and Terrance, who oversees the vaults, was the cause. Terrance has books recording payments made to Verhardt's accounts, and they match the private books Antinous kept. It looks like Terrance was paying Verhardt a quarter of what he stole. But there are also payments from Eyo, and I'm not sure why. I haven't gotten through all the papers, but he wasn't embezzling money as far as I could tell."

Julian takes on a thoughtful look. "It could be something else. I heard a rumor about him a while ago."

Of course he did. The upper class loves nothing more than to gossip about each other as if they are not all guilty of similar acts.

"Which was?" I ask.

"One of his mistresses disappeared five years ago—two or three years after he was elected," Jules continues. "I can't remember her name… It doesn't matter. She was found dead, washed up downriver from the capital, her body weighted with rocks. It was ruled a suicide by the previous Praetorian, but the suspicion was that she was pregnant, and Eyo killed her."

It feels true, but maybe that's because I am looking for a reason. Suicides are awfully convenient, and I know for a fact that the former Praetorian was not above corruption.

Still, rumors are not enough.

"That sounds like speculation," I say.

"It is, but it's rather surprising that Eyo has no illegitimate children; I've always thought that, given his staggering number of mistresses. The only offspring he has are his three children with his wife. But she is the one who comes from the established line and real money, not him. Although he's accumulated quite a bit serving in the Senate."

I consider the possibilities as I stare at the rushing water.

"Did his wife kill the mistress?" I ask.

Julian shrugs. "It's one and the same as far as blackmail is concerned. Plus, Eyo's fortunes rise and fall with his wife, since his family was newer nobility. The Eyos didn't curry favor until after the Crimson Night. She is the benefactress."

As much as they hated the Elusian monarchy, the republic still puts faith in the families who held power for centuries.

I think through the possibilities of Eyo or Terrance being the killer. It was their sentries who moved the body before I investigated it. Eyo was Verhardt's guest at the Revelry party, but Terrance's sentry is strong enough to decapitate a man. Antinous said the Senate conspires, but who did he mean?

Or did he mean both?

But something doesn't sit well about this.

"The drowning of Antinous fits the senators' styles, but why disembowel Verhardt?" I say, thinking aloud. "Why the scene? The safest play was to make it look like an accident."

"It could have been someone losing control," Julian posits.

I shake my head. "This wasn't an act of passion; it was a ritualistic slaughter. Why take the time and the risk, unless it was all designed to implicate the Faith—the knife and the organs where she lit the flame, the missing liver, and the body on the altar..."

Julian and I exchange glances, and he pales slightly.

"Kera is alone here," Julian says. "She is away from her guards, servants, and priests. They could murder her easily if they wanted to, could claim Arthago killed her. No one would look too deeply if we go to war, and the Council would gain the full support of the Faith as well as the republic."

I remember the way both Terrance and Eyo looked at Kerasea, how condescending they were despite asking her to vote in the conclave.

While I have disdain for the temple, even I can admit that it's the only balance to the Senate's power. Without her, the Faith would be rudderless, and the Senate could step in.

Perhaps the murderer had planned to frame her for the crimes. But now that it hasn't worked, what would they do next to topple her?

Without another word, we race out of the baths and up to the third floor.

XXI

Kerasea

I rub my face, glad Zel removed my makeup and jewelry before the Praetorian and Commander showed up, banging on my door. I thought there might be a fire—turns out it was worse.

"I'm going to need you to repeat all of that," I say. I'm seated on one of the armchairs in my silk robe, and my head is spinning.

Torren paces in front of me, his expression darkened with newfound care for my well-being. He pauses just long enough to frown at me.

"We think it best, as you don't have a temple guard here, for one of us to escort you during the remainder of the conclave—that is all," Julian says.

"I understand that much, but why? Why the sudden obsession with my safety when you ruled Antinous's death to be an accidental drowning?"

"Because you know that wasn't the case." The Praetorian stops again and stares at me like I'm painfully naive.

Maybe I am.

Ice slides along my veins, and I grip the upholstery. I suspected; I didn't know for certain. The undeniable truth sinks in, and my stomach drops.

He was murdered.

My eyes sting as tears well in them and my pulse throbs until it hurts. This isn't the time to mourn, but still, a tear slides down my cheek for Antinous. He was never anything but kind to my father and me, and he was murdered by someone here, someone who believed they could get away with it.

I hastily wipe my tear and sniffle as discreetly as possible, but it's silent in the room, and Julian and the Praetorian are both staring at me. Of course they notice.

Sympathy flashes in Torren's eyes. I have just a moment to notice it before he blinks the emotion away.

I swallow back any other tears—now isn't the time.

"Who ordered his death?" My voice shakes, but I push my shoulders back and manage the words. Discovering the truth is more important than sadness or anger right now.

"We aren't certain—" Julian begins.

"Senators Eyo and Terrance are implicated," the Praetorian says.

Julian sighs in a long-suffering way. The Praetorian must be looking into them despite *un exorum*. In the history of the republic, there has only been one exception to the law protecting the leaders of the Senate and temples, and the High Priestess to the skies conveniently died before charges could be brought twenty years ago.

But Torren stands on rocky ground. I could report him. He would be dismissed from the conclave and not reappointed—just the thing I wanted before I left the capital.

Yet he's risking his career to trust me.

I look from one to the other as the strangeness of this situation takes hold. He's despised me for a dozen years. Why hand me a means to bring him down? "Why are you concerned about me, though? What aren't you telling me?"

Julian and the Praetorian exchange the guiltiest looks I've ever seen. I sigh. They wouldn't last a day in the shoes of a woman who has to lie for her own survival. Julian needs to get better at this, as he's a future patron. The Praetorian is a lost cause.

"You were selected to replace Verhardt in the conclave," Torren says. "It's incongruous with tradition, and the Council asked you for a reason. It's not beyond imagination that if someone was so bold as to murder Verhardt in the Forum and Antinous here, they are settling all affairs this week."

He thinks someone might want me dead. I shudder but push down the fear, because something is still off.

He's telling the truth, but not all of it, which leaves more questions than answers.

"But you didn't know any of this last night when you were following me," I say.

Julian's eyes dart to his friend. He didn't know.

The Praetorian stares directly at me. "I found it suspicious that you were leaving your chambers in the middle of the night."

"So you were, in fact, following me. And then you hid to listen in on my conversation with Antinous." I state it as a fact, not a question.

Julian turns and pinches the bridge of his nose.

"That is correct," Torren answers.

"I need to be...elsewhere." Julian raises his hands. "I literally cannot hear this, Tor. Plausible deniability. Peaceful slumber, High Priestess."

Julian bows to me before exiting the room.

As he shuts the door, I realize that once again I'm alone with the Praetorian and, this time, we're in my bedchamber. The heat of his gaze burns when it's just the two of us. Whatever roils under the surface in public erupts when we're alone together.

My dagger sits in my nightstand, but, of course, it wouldn't be much use if he wanted to harm me. He disarmed me last night so easily. My wrist burns with the memory.

He keeps his distance, though, staying on the opposite side of the room. However, there's no sense of ease.

"Why were you following me, really?" I ask.

His gaze dips to my lips and then drifts to where my heart pounds. "Because your actions were suspicious."

It's the truth, mostly.

"Why should I trust you?" I ask. "If you were listening at the door to the kitchens, you heard that Antinous thought you carried out the murder of Verhardt. You'd have the motive to kill a clerk who suspected you. Especially when no one could investigate you."

I hold my ground as Torren's cheeks take on a reddish hue. He's either embarrassed or angry—maybe both—but there's no guilt in his expression.

"I didn't kill Verhardt or Antinous," the Praetorian says through his teeth. "If you'd like to consult your bird signs, feel free, but do me a favor and ask the eagles who actually commissioned the murders so I can bring charges against an elite."

I spring to my feet, outrage flowing through me as I ball my hands into fists. He just insulted my entire Faith. "You mock the gods at your own risk, Praetorian."

He strides closer. "You are the one at risk here. And rather than realize it and accept my protection, you accuse me?"

My heart leaps as he stops just a step too close. We're face-to-face, and it's like I can feel the heat radiating from his chest. I keep my chin high as we stare at each other. "I'm only at risk if you continue to fail at your job."

He flinches, wounded for a moment. Regret floods me, but he clears his expression and squares his shoulders.

"As you wish, Your Excellency. Consider it my order for you to be escorted at all times. Ignore that and pray your god will protect you or, better yet, that you learn some skill with that blade."

He bows with a flourish and leaves the room. My legs shake, and then I tumble back into the armchair once the door is shut.

Bloody lies, what have I gotten myself into?

More questions than answers swim in my mind, but I do know one thing: he was telling the truth. He didn't kill Verhardt or Antinous. So who did?

XXII

Torren

I pace in my room like a tiger in an arena cage, glancing over at my bed from time to time, but there's no chance of rest. It is a good thing that in my service to the legions, I got used to operating on little to no sleep. This conclave will not be the boring respite it has been in the past. Then again, it never was going to be with her here.

Her.

Kera cried when I confirmed that Antinous was murdered, and it caught me off guard. I hadn't expected her to show that amount of compassion. I didn't think she had any at all, yet that tear that rolled down her cheek…

I stop and shake my head. What am I even doing? I can't allow her to pull at my heart.

I don't know why the gods have cursed me with thinking about this woman. Maybe it was the dead bird comments. But I offered her my protection and went beyond my duty, as she is the High Priestess, not a member of the Senate. If she ignores my warning and gets killed, my conscience will be clear. If the temple has complaints about her death, so be it.

I run my hands down my face. Son of a jackal. It's one thing to lie; it's another to lie to myself. If what I just thought was true at all, then I'd be fast asleep, getting the rest I sorely need. It's been an hour since I left Kerasea, after arguing with her yet again, and I'm wide awake.

Enough of this.

I leave my room and stride past hers down to Julian's door. It takes three knocks for him to answer. He finally opens the door with his hair mussed from bed. Evidently, he had no problem getting to sleep.

"Leave your door ajar and listen for anyone coming or going down the hall," I say.

He rubs his eyes with a yawn. "Yes, sir. Wait, where are you going?"

"To patrol for an hour."

Julian lets out a long sigh, his shoulders slumping. "Should I ask where you're really going?"

He left Kerasea's room earlier because, as Capital Commander, he is supposed to report all breaches of protocol to Hadrian — even mine. Following Kerasea after being specifically instructed multiple times by multiple people not to investigate her counts as a breach, I suppose. But this time I have nothing to hide. He doesn't hold the authority to inquire, but that hardly matters between us.

"You may ask."

"Where, then?" Jules has all the enthusiasm for questioning me that a war dog has for a bath.

"The armory. I can't sleep. I'm going to work out and then I'll be back, but you need to stand guard until then."

He sighs and leans on the doorframe. "You know, normal men who were this frustrated would just bed a servant girl."

I curl my lip. Somehow, seducing a girl who is mildly willing but mostly unable to refuse doesn't sound appealing. And Julian knows this, because it's not appealing to him, either.

"I leave that to the esteemed nobility." I bow and walk down the hall.

The armory is on the same floor as the baths and servant quarters. The weapons were removed from the palace after the Crimson Night, but the space still retains exercise and training equipment.

I light the torchiers in the darkened gymnasium until the sparring ring is illuminated. Every piece of equipment is the finest in the world—the Elusians demanded no less.

I spit at the memory of the magic bloods. At first, they were viewed as demigods, saviors who brought order and united seven city-states into one kingdom thousands of years ago. But all of that power corrupted the Elusians. The last king, being nearly immortal, was by far the worst. No atrocity or indulgence was out of reach by the end of his three-hundred-year reign. But it was really the endless war that left the Senate with no choice.

What was it Antinous said? *Absolute power corrupts even the strongest hearts.* There are times I wonder how much better we are with lifetime senators than the former monarchy. Then I shake off the thought. Of course it's better.

With no one else in the massive armory, I strip down to my underwear and then jump rope to warm up my muscles in the cold room. I brought wraps for my hands, and I tie them. I take my time, focusing on my breathing, as I usually do when I prepare for a fight. It feels good to follow my routine, at least in this one respect. A shred of normalcy here.

I square up and hit a sand-filled leather heavy bag. I strike again and again, bouncing on my feet, pushing myself faster and harder until sweat starts to drip down my face. I deliver knockout blows, jabs, crosses, then I turn and roundhouse the bag.

I work out my frustration about everything from being

stymied in my investigation into the murder of Verhardt to my failure to protect Antinous. He wasn't a senator, but he should have been safe here. Kerasea was kind enough to pour salt in that particular wound tonight.

And then there's her, generally. And that's too much frustration to work out in a lifetime.

Still, I shouldn't have said those things about the Faith. In truth, I shouldn't have interacted with Kerasea at all. It's a stupid, fatal mistake to get entangled with her. She is in danger, but maybe all that means is that she'll finally get what she deserves. The temple is a rotten institution, fitting for someone like her.

I punch the bag ten times in a row as I remember her pointing to my father, saying she witnessed him start the fire that burned down half the warehouse district and killed thirty people.

After my father was found guilty by the Verity Guild, I appeared before them and begged for clemency. Osiris Vestal sat in the center of the tribunal dais, looking down his nose at me as he flatly refused. Even at thirteen, I could tell that it was hopeless — I wasn't going to change anyone's heart or mind on a corrupt tribunal.

My voice shook with tears, and I begged them to punish me in his stead. Someone in the room gasped, and then Kerasea, who'd been sitting in the gallery, let out ringing laughter. Everyone else joined in. The sound still plays in my nightmares.

My lungs and muscles burn, and I realize I wasn't breathing. I stop and catch my breath as I lean against the bag.

That is who Kerasea Vestal is — who she really is. Even if she fully believed her own lie, there's no excuse for mocking me. I cannot allow myself to forget that she's poisonous — and like most poisonous things, she is also tempting.

With too much energy left, I move on to a battery of other exercises until I'm exhausted and coated in sweat. Until I can finally think straight. The High Priestess may not have had anything to do with the murders, but she is not worth saving. No, I have to discover why someone is setting up the Faith and expose them. That way, they won't be able to act on their plan, but I won't have to interact with her anymore.

I finish my last circuit and relax now that I have a clear objective. I'll go back to my room and closely review Antinous's papers. Maybe there's something in there pertaining to the temple or other clues I missed earlier. Once that is complete, I'll finally get some rest.

I toss on my pants but carry my shirt over my shoulder. I turn out the oil lamps and snuff the gilded torchiers, not at all thinking about the golden dagger I pressed out of her hand.

XXIII

Kerasea

When Zel knocks in the morning, I have to push the entire armoire out of the way of the door. She stares at me, no doubt puzzled as to why it took me so long to answer, but she doesn't question me. It's not her place to.

"I trust you slept well, Excellency," she says.

"Yes, did you?"

I'm still trying to slow my heart from moving that heavy wardrobe. I can't tell whether it was foolish or wise to let the Praetorian get into my head, but I didn't feel safe with just a chair blocking the door last night.

Zel's eyes dart around. "Well, I kept my door locked as you said. There were two knocks, and someone tried the handle, so I wedged a nightstand under it, but then it was difficult to get back to sleep." She pauses and then forces a smile. "Otherwise, I slept just fine. Thank you for inquiring."

Two knocks and someone tried to get into her chambers? My

cheeks tingle as blood leaves my face. Did someone mistake her room for mine? Or were they simply looking for a young girl to prey upon?

"When was this?" I ask, as casually as I can. She's already frightened, and I don't want to worry her even more.

"Around an hour after you told me not to answer to anything but your voice."

I exhale, relieved I told her that much.

Immediately, I think to inform the Praetorian, but he insulted my entire Faith last night. I won't speak a word to him again without an apology. I swear it.

Zel readies me for another day of the conclave. It's best not to think about how many more there are.

As she rests the golden collar of the temple on my neck, it feels like hands choking me. And the Praetorian thinks someone here wants me dead. I struggle to breathe, but then I remember that my father wore the same necklace. I'm sure the Senate wanted to eliminate him at points. I just have to be smarter, make fewer mistakes.

I sigh as I walk down the hall. I miss my father so much that there's an actual pain in my chest.

As I enter the banquet room, I brace myself like someone will attack me in broad daylight. Instead, everyone is present, helping themselves to a sumptuous breakfast spread. We won't break for luncheon for five hours, so I should eat something. However, the thought of deviled eggs, smoked fish, or charred steak is nauseating. I take a pastry and some fruit.

Even though all the food is already laid out, servants stand ready to pour our drinks and fix our plates. A blond servant stands holding an orange juice carafe.

Suh raps his cane to get her attention. She begins to pour a glass but accidentally overflows it. Suh curses, and she mutters apologies.

The senator remains red-faced, but as I sit, I have bigger problems than some juice on a toga. If what Julian said was correct, the Council will want to elect a Senate Leader today, which means I may have to choose who will ultimately be in control of the republic.

And if the Praetorian is correct, I will have to decide between the two men who may have killed Antinous and Verhardt.

I place my half-eaten pastry back on my plate, my appetite gone. I can't be the one to hand them more power, but what is even the protocol for this? Verhardt was the only Senate Leader since Pryor became a republic. This vote should be up to the people, or at least an elected representative of the first province. The objection makes logical sense in my head, but I doubt their ambitions will accept it.

The whole conclave feels like a game of bock—the black-and-white board game of strategy where you think multiple moves ahead. And I am sorely lagging behind.

Eyo stands and raises his wine goblet. "May I offer a toast?"

Everyone stops talking. Terrance seems put out, and closer than ever to Verhardt's empty chair. The arms of his seat touch the head of the table, and I'm sure he was planning on giving the toast.

"To the Senate's continued health and to the success of this year's conclave," Eyo says. "Already we have bridged our differences and made strides toward a better republic. Although we mourn the loss of our dear Verhardt, we will continue our reforms and service to the people of Pryor in his great memory."

Eyo pauses and lowers his head dramatically.

"Today, with the guidance of the gods, we will elect a new Senate Leader to fill the cavernous void left behind by the senseless, horrific murder of our colleague. May our hearts and minds select a leader who will fulfill the legacy he established, further the interests of not themselves but of the republic as a whole, and bring glory to all of Pryor. May we each embrace the future over the past."

I try not to look at anything in particular, but I meet the Praetorian's gaze. His face is neutral, but his eyes betray his thoughts. He thinks Eyo may be a murderer.

"Hear, hear," Foreau says. He bangs on the table, the white jewels of his bracelets contrasting with his rich brown skin.

Paolo taps his glass on the table while Suh continues to eat, eggs clinging to the sides of his goatee. Medea simply raises an eyebrow and goes back to her cheeses.

Terrance seems the least amused, sniffing as he frowns.

Eyo retakes his seat, and conversation resumes. He is drinking red wine despite the early hour. Everyone else is drinking water or orange juice, but they stop as a servant wheels in coffee.

The aroma is incredible as the servant distributes the drink in delicate porcelain cups with sweetened milk.

We import thousands of pounds of coffee beans from a faraway kingdom. Most is kept by the nobility, but some is rationed out to citizens on high holy days. The best is kept for the Senate and High Priests.

I'm enjoying my second cup when Senator Eyo begins to cough.

"Excuse me," he chokes out.

Suh stares over his fork and Medea wrinkles her nose as his fit continues. Both have long-standing grievances with him.

Conversation stops as his cough worsens. Eyo's arm shakes as he reaches for his water, but instead of grasping the glass, he knocks it over. Suh and Foreau both stand as water spills along the mahogany, but they merely brush off their togas. Suh looks particularly vexed, as he has now been spilled on twice.

"Get ahold of yourself," Suh says.

But Eyo's face is turning dark red, his breathing staggered.

Foreau and Suh exchange glances as my wrists and head begin to throb. Something is very wrong here.

Paolo pauses from cutting his steak to look at the senator. "Is he choking?"

"Not if he can cough," Terrance says, waving his hand. "Really, Eyo—show proper decorum or excuse yourself."

But Eyo continues to gasp and sputter as the room goes silent. He drops his wine goblet. It clangs onto the mosaicked floor, bleeding onto the tiles. Eyo clutches at his own throat as he leans forward and claws at the table, convulsing.

I rise from my seat, horror propelling me. He's dying.

"Someone get a healer!" I yell out.

"We are locked in, High Priestess," Julian says, also standing. He's paler than I've ever seen him. "There are no healers in the palace."

"There must be someone who can do something," I say. "Please."

Stares volley around the table.

"Fetch the sentries!" the Praetorian yells out.

His voice reverberates in the room as Eyo falls to his knees. The senator's face is so dark red, it's nearly purple.

The Praetorian leaves his seat and races over as Eyo collapses, but everyone realized the problem too late. Whatever is happening is killing him. Death wraps its tendrils around his body—I can see it. The room begins to spin, my head feeling too light, my pulse too heavy. He is dead even if he still clings to life. I grip the table, trying to remain in place. This can't be happening.

Torren leans his ear close to Eyo's purple lips. "He isn't breathing."

I stand frozen like a statue, as still as everyone else, while the Praetorian tries to clear Eyo's airway. He sticks his fingers into the senator's mouth and pounds on his chest. But in seconds, the sounds of struggle fade, and both men go quiet.

The Praetorian sits back on his knees. Senator Eyo lies stiffly on the ground. The air is knocked from my lungs as my hands and face go numb.

"Senator Eyo is dead," he says.

XXIV

Torren

Romlock poisoning has distinct hallmarks, and Eyo has all of them, from the way he collapsed to the purple marks now spidering on his cheeks and his engorged tongue.

Someone poisoned him, but who?

I stay next to the body as my suspicions immediately turn to Terrance. He and Eyo were both being blackmailed by Verhardt with payments recorded by Antinous and now, Terrance is the sole survivor.

The eldest senator looks shaken, collapsing into his chair, his eyes wide. It's either an impressive acting performance or it's genuine shock, because the color has left his lips and cheeks, giving him a ghastly appearance.

"What just happened?" Senator Medea asks. Her hands shake, her jewels shimmering. She pats her silver-streaked hair and takes a deep breath as she looks around. Her concern seems genuine, but I can't rule out that it could all be for show.

"Did he have a stroke?" Senator Foreau asks, blinking rapidly. He's standing near me, gripping his toga in his fists as he looks down at Eyo. The sky is gray with snow, but the lights of the room reflect off his bald head.

"Or a fit of some kind?" Paolo nervously brushes his wavy hair away from his forehead and spins his ring.

"It looks like poison," Senator Suh says.

He is one of the only people in the room who is completely calm right now as he stays seated in his chair. Suh was a general before he became a senator, and he saw death regularly under the old king, but is his placid demeanor just because of the legions?

Terrance shakes his head, his hands still trembling. "It couldn't be poison. He looked…he looked like my son Emilius when he died of an allergic fit. It must have been allergies."

Terrance's eldest son died in his thirties. From my understanding, he was a rising star who choked at a dinner party thrown by Verhardt. Medea and Suh were also at the soiree during the celebration of the ten-year founding of the republic. Many tried to assist Emilius, but he died in his father's arms.

The death, of course, was never ruled as anything other than a tragic accident—an unknown allergy—but it's more than a coincidence if they died in the same manner.

Medea looks from Suh to Terrance to Eyo's body.

"Praetorian, what happened here?" she asks.

"He might have died of an allergy of some kind, but I can't rule out foul play," I say.

It was certainly not an allergy, but I must tread carefully. Someone was bold enough to act in the daylight, to murder a senator in front of us all. Poisoning is clever, as it is notoriously difficult to trace. Romlock takes between fifteen minutes to an hour to kill a grown man, depending on the dosage and the victim's health. Eyo could have been poisoned by anyone in here or even before he came down for breakfast. Yet given the acuity of his death, it was likely done here.

"Close the doors, Commander," I order. "No one comes or goes from this room."

Julian rubs his knuckles, his old worried habit, but he shuts the doors. The sentries had arrived in the hall.

Now that I've said that it could be foul play, the senators have the good sense to look shaken. They laughed at Antinous's death, and none seemed fazed by Verhardt's grisly murder, but this is different. This was one of their own dying in front of them.

"Praetorian, are you saying you believe someone in this palace may have…poisoned him?" Paolo asks, his mouth agape.

"Under your watch?" Medea adds.

I'm certain of it. Eyo didn't have any known intolerances, and there was nothing in his airway, but if I tell them that, I admit to failing to keep Eyo safe. But it's notable that Medea is pointing out my responsibility.

"You also mentioned allergic fits," Foreau says before I can reply. "Isn't it possible he had a condition we weren't privy to?"

I take in Foreau's smooth brow and steady voice. He, like Suh, is calm considering the death of his ally.

I bite my tongue. "It's certainly possible, as Terrance said. I will need his body examined by a healer to be certain. Of course, that will prove difficult with this storm."

Everyone slowly turns toward the windows where snow still falls. It's not a whiteout, but it's not far from a blizzard. The storm that started yesterday has caused steady, accumulating snow. And we can't even see the capital below us. The roads are now impassable.

We are all trapped inside the palace with a killer.

The room is silent, the five remaining senators in various states of disbelief. Julian and Kera are simply quiet, looking around at intervals. But they already knew we had a murderer here.

I must solve this, but for now I have to deal with another dead body. I can't send Eyo down the mountain like I did with Antinous, but I need to preserve his corpse. I stare out the windows. If I bury him in the snow, that will hold him until we can leave.

"Hopefully the storm will subside tonight, and then we'll depart at dawn," I say.

"We...we must proceed with the conclave," Terrance says. His lips are still colorless, and his spotted hands shake, but his white head is high, determined as he stands.

Everyone looks at him. The High Priestess's eyes widen. I can feel the ridges in my own brow as Julian's head tilts. What did he just say?

"I beg your pardon, Senator," Kerasea says slowly, "but there is no one to vote for the province of Cortana now. Surely we must conclude."

It's the first words she's spoken since Eyo died.

Her eyes are glassy, and her skin is another shade paler. She's rubbed her temples several times and clutched at her golden bangles. She's the only one who is reacting like a murder took place, and she was also the first to suggest we do anything to save him.

"Terrance is right," Suh says. He uses his cane to rise from his seat. "We cannot conclude the conclave under any circumstance. Even this." He pauses and looks down at Eyo with the same regard he gave to the orange juice earlier. "Not when we are on the precipice of war. Now, more than ever, is the time to act with valor. We must vote upon the Arthagian aggression before we conclude."

He bangs his cane on the floor.

Terrance nods eagerly, wetting his lips. "All Senate sentries and pages are from our home provinces. Due to the critical nature of this year's conclave, I propose that one of the staff from the second province stands in Eyo's stead."

Paolo waves his hand, physically brushing away the suggestion. "We cannot allow a commoner to vote on matters before the Senate just because it is expedient. We must conclude the conclave and allow the provinces to hold elections. We can convene a special assembly in the Senate Hall regarding Arthago after the new senators have taken their seats."

Suh shakes his head. "That will be months too late. Today is already a tardy response if we want our nation to be respected. If we want to uphold the dignity of this republic."

"Eyo's sentry, Lucius Calais, is the son of a man I made noble decades ago," Medea says. "He is young, as he is serving his legion time, but he is no younger than the High Priestess. He could step in if necessary."

Foreau shakes his bald head. "He is not elected."

"Neither is the High Priestess," Terrance urges.

Conversation swirls around Kerasea Vestal like sharks circling blood. She stays silent but seems increasingly agitated, twisting the bangles on her wrists and clutching her necklace. Her chest rises and falls rapidly, and then her eyes dart over to Eyo's body on the floor.

"Commander, bring in Sentry Calais," Suh says. "We will interview him and then hold a vote on whether he is suitable."

I step forward. "Senators, I have ordered that no one is to come or go."

They cast incredulous glances my way. No one restricts the movement of the Senate. But in this case, I must. After three murders, this is my first opportunity to take in the scene before anyone can tamper with it.

"You *ordered*?" Foreau repeats.

The senators variously express their outrage with being trapped in here "like a bunch of commoners." I focus on my steady breathing to keep frustration at bay. They just watched Eyo die in front of them; either they are blinded by their ambitions or they are being led by the murderer.

"I am sure you want me to determine whether anything else might be tainted," I add casually. "If, as Senator Suh posited, it was poison."

That sobers them. Each one looks around, casting suspicious glances at their own goblets and plates and then at one another.

"I can divine the truth," Kerasea says.

Everyone turns and stares at her, including me. A fork clatters to the ground. Someone gasps, and color returns to the High Priestess's cheeks as she blushes.

"As to whether it was a natural death or a murder," she adds in a quieter voice.

Son of a jackal. She is going to get herself killed.

XXV.

Kerasea

As soon as the words leave my mouth, it's like I can feel my father turning over on his funeral pyre. It was the very worst thing to say, in front of the worst people, at the worst time. But I just watched a man die. I witnessed a murder, and everyone is pretending like it didn't happen. The truth clawed its way free from my lips.

This is exactly why my father told me to never even think about my blood. Because I'd give myself away—and I have.

Underworld, what do I do now?

I have to hide and survive.

The senators stare at me with wrinkled brows. Suh's jaw literally hangs open, and Paolo tilts his head sideways while spinning his ring like a discus. Medea blinks rapidly three times.

Obviously, I should not have said that. But I couldn't believe they'd still push forward with the conclave even with Eyo's body still warm on the floor. I didn't expect tears and lamenting—that is a show put on for funeral processions—but I thought they'd be mildly concerned.

"I wasn't aware that omens can reveal the past," Foreau says. He and Paolo exchange wary looks.

Actually, every single one of them seems horrified at the thought that I can discover past crimes.

Terrance's brown eyes narrow on me. "This was not in the temple powers your father enumerated to the Senate."

When Pryor became a republic, the High Priests all listed the powers they possessed and how they used them. But this, of course, was not on that list.

I need a way out. Now.

"It is possible, but I… Of course, the only way would be… That is to say… I would need his liver as an offering. It's my theory that the divine would share the sacred truth as to the senator's demise."

I make it sound like I am reluctant to speak the details, instead of inventing a fiction.

Sounds of grievance turn into outrage that I would "cut a senator open like an animal." Paolo looks faint and Medea wrinkles her nose in disgust. I lower myself back into my seat. Eyo's body will be burned eventually, but no one will let me have his liver. That should put an end to my foolish confession.

But what did I just tell myself about making mistakes? Someone in this room committed multiple murders. I look from senator to senator. Any of them are capable. Terrance has bottomless ambition and little time left. Suh was a warrior who headhunted Arthagians in his youth. Foreau is suspected as an Arthagian spy, and Medea is known as a ruthless she-wolf. Even Paolo, who has a kind face, is rumored to have hastened his own father's demise.

And any of them could have a motive, if that motive was to delay the conclave or take Eyo's place as the heir apparent Senate Leader.

I do know one thing: the killer is growing emboldened by not being caught, by *un exorum*, and the others can't sense it.

Torren stares at me with a hard gaze. My muscles tense as he looks right through me. I try to hold still, but why is he eyeing me like that?

"Back to the matter at hand, Praetorian, as we will clearly not allow our dear friend to be eviscerated." Terrance pauses and issues me a second disgusted look. "We do not consent to being held in here when we have important decisions to debate for the good of the nation. However, you may conduct your investigation by questioning the staff and servants as you see fit."

The four other senators nod.

Suh claps his hands together. "Very well, with that settled, we should proceed to the throne room for the conclave."

I stare at the Praetorian. Surely he'll stop them. I could read on his face that he knew it was poison. But Torren bows his head as Senator Terrance opens the door and leaves. The Praetorian doesn't offer another objection. He is, of course, up for reappointment. He and Julian exchange quick hand signs I can't decipher before Julian departs with the senators.

Torren's gaze then falls on me. His brow wrinkles slightly with concern. My lips part, but I don't know what to say. We seem to be the only people who realize there is a murderer on the loose—one who is striking freely now.

The ever-present scream in my throat begs to be released, but I swallow it down once more.

"High Priestess, you will be joining us, correct?" Paolo says from the doorway. "If not to vote, then at least for your divine presence."

I shudder, surprised by his voice, but he's looking down at my feet. I glance at the floor. I've come to a stop right near Eyo's body.

Paolo frowns in sympathy. "I am certain you don't wish to remain here."

I nod and draw a breath.

The Senate conspires—that's what Antinous said. But which senator?

A thought freezes me in place: did Antinous mean that all five are in on this together? Even Paolo?

I force myself to smile at the senator.

"Of course," I say.

I need to know what happened and, like the Praetorian, I have my own ways of getting to the truth.

XXVI

Torren

Alone in the banquet hall, I blow out a sigh and run a hand down my face. The High Priestess just admitted that she could use Eyo's liver as an offering to the gods. Verhardt's same organ went missing. Have we…have *I* been falling for an act this entire time? The knife in the fountain, the lapis in the pool, and now the poisoning— was it all her?

I draw a deep breath. No. I've already established that someone is framing her. This is not the time to rethink what's already settled.

My training kicks in, and I begin my search of the banquet hall. I start with the body, rummaging through and around his purple toga, but I find nothing. There is also nothing unusual on the table or under it, nothing odd on the buffet itself.

I stare down at Eyo and stroke my chin—why not? If someone was trying to pin these crimes on the High Priestess, why not leave evidence here?

I catch my reflection in the polished gold of the goblet, including the deep line between my eyebrows. Maybe there are answers in the poisoning itself.

Red wine has pooled next to the corpse, but there is still some left in Eyo's cup. I pick up the goblet and then use a clean glass to pour out the remains. Wine flows first, but then tannins and a thicker substance slide out into the glass. A powder turned wet. I dip a spoon in the powder and then light it on fire. It burns green—the color of romlock fumes.

The confirmation somehow makes everything worse. In the back of my mind, I was holding out hope that it could have been an allergic fit.

The sentries still wait in the hallway, and I look at each of them through the open doorway. All are suspects, because all of the men were handpicked by the senators. Again, I need to handle this with care. It's better that the killer believes I haven't caught on yet.

"You may all return to your posts," I say. "Sentry Avarre?"

He's just turned, but he halts. There's no guilt in his expression, only vague cluelessness from Terrance's sentry. "Praetorian?"

"Bring me all of the household staff, then return to your position."

"Yes, sir."

I study him, but he also doesn't look relieved by being dismissed. It's curious.

Minutes later, the ten household servants enter the banquet hall. They come to a halt when they notice the senator on the ground.

"A senator of Pryor has died, and someone in Jubilee may have poisoned him," I say. "The Council demands inquiry and swift justice. Burn all the food in the fire, throw all the drinks into the snow, then boil all of the place settings. I will question you one by one."

The servants do exactly as I ordered. I keep Eyo's plate and the bottle of wine to examine, but I doubt the food and bottle were poisoned as well. The more thorough the poisoning, the more likely someone could get caught.

As the servants carry out the place settings, I lift Eyo's body onto the table. Then I set up two chairs.

I am sitting beside the corpse when the first servant walks in for questioning.

"Have a seat." I point to the chair that I placed next to Eyo's face.

Normally, I'd move a body to a discreet location, but I want the servants to sit near the victim as they answer me, in the event one of them colluded on the murder. Romlock has caused the veins on his face to become purple webs and his tongue to swell to the point that his mouth is open. It's grotesque, but it should help me elicit the truth.

"Did you do this?" I ask.

"Gods, no." The blond woman holds my stare as I look for a tell. Then she examines her hands. "Is this an interrogation?"

Fear flashes in her brown eyes as my reputation precedes me. Dismember, burn, and variously torture men under interrogation and you earn the mantle of brutal investigator, I suppose.

"Not at the moment," I say. "Did any of the sentries or pages enter this room as you set up breakfast?"

She shakes her head but then pauses. "Sentry Avarre came in, but he was just looking for milk. He was only here for a moment."

Which would be long enough to plant poison in a goblet.

"No one else?" I ask.

She shakes her head and bites her lip to keep from trembling. Then she glances at Eyo. "Why is his face like that?"

"Effects of godless death," I say.

Unlike truth and justice, death doesn't have a god recognized in Pryor.

She stares at her lap, but she has nothing more to tell me.

"You may return to your duties," I say. "Send in the cook."

As I wait for the next servant, I consider the fact that Sentry Avarre was in this room for no real reason. He was in the pool with Antinous, too, and Senator Terrance does not hide how much he wants to be Senate Leader. Verhardt's and Antinous's murders gave him freedom from blackmail, and with Eyo dead, he has a path to absolute power.

But what about Kera's assertion that she can divine whether this was a murder? The only reason she would make that claim and then backtrack away would be because she doesn't want them to know how much power she has. But if she can divine the truth about past crimes, perhaps she can aid me in hunting the suspect, in toppling a senator.

I hang my head.

I may need to work with her.

The gods have cursed me. I really shouldn't have made those comments about the dead birds.

XXVII.

Kerasca

I sit in the throne room, scratching at my wrists under my bangles as the Council begins to vote on whether or not to conclude the conclave.

"Now is the time for action," Suh says, banging his fist on the table. "Now is the time for bravery, in honor of our dearly departed colleagues. We must save this republic from her enemies. I, along with every patriot, will vote to proceed."

"I agree," Terrance says loudly. "It is the moment for action, for resolve. The loss of Senator Eyo should galvanize us. Thus, to fulfill my duties as senator and champion the republic, I, too, vote to proceed."

"Meaningless bravado aside," Foreau says, waving his opal-encrusted hand, "because we are a *republic*, the first and second provinces must have elected representatives in any conclave. I vote to conclude until new senators are chosen *by* the people, *for* the people."

Terrance narrows his eyes, his cheeks coloring at the slight.

Paolo stands and turns his ring. "I vote to conclude, although I motion that with concluding, we hold elections with great haste. I further add that we convene a special session on Arthago within a month's time."

Terrance and Suh both sputter as Paolo retakes his seat, his light brown cheeks assuming a cherry hue.

"Which will be far too late for the people of my province," Medea says from her chair. "And because of that simple logic, I vote to proceed."

My stomach sinks. With the majority vote, the Council has decided to stay.

I stare at the five remaining senators. Is it possible? Could they have truly colluded together when they can't agree on simple resolutions?

Senator Paolo leaps to his feet. "The High Priestess must vote for the first province."

Terrance shakes his head. "We are not tied."

Foreau looks from Paolo to Terrance, his brown eyes lighting up. "On a matter of this level of importance, all provinces need a voice."

Before anyone else can speak, I stand. "I vote to conclude."

Terrance, Suh, and Medea all sit back in their chairs with varying levels of annoyance as the room falls silent. Then their gazes sharpen like knives on me. Chills careen over my shoulders, but I hold still, gripping the sleeves of my robe.

The six of us revote, but everyone holds the same positions. We are deadlocked, and because we are six, there is no solution in sight.

"Commander Monroe, fetch Sentry Calais, please," Terrance says, rubbing the bridge of his long nose. "As he is from the second province, he can vote to break this deadlock."

I'd marvel at how quickly Terrance found an answer in his own favor, if it didn't mean us staying trapped with a murderer.

Foreau stands before Julian can respond. "We cannot allow a man who will benefit from continuance of the conclave to have the final say, when we have not even voted on his acceptability."

Paolo murmurs his agreement.

Suh raps his cane on the floor. "If every province is to have a voice, as you just asserted, the second province must have one."

Medea keeps her chair but shifts her arm enough to draw everyone's attention. "While I agree with you in theory, Suh, Foreau is correct that the sentry would have a vested interest in the outcome of the vote. We cannot allow him a voice before we decide on his suitability."

At Medea's words, Terrance's eyes widen, and sweat breaks out along his white hairline. If Suh and Medea fail to support him, he will likely never be the Senate Leader. He frantically looks around the room, and his eyes fall on Julian.

"Very well, what say you, Commander Monroe?" Terrance asks. "You, like the Praetorian, are responsible for our safety, and you come from a noble house with a storied tradition of leading the republic. Pryor depends upon us for law and order. As unprecedented as these times are, they call for leadership. Do the needs of the republic demand we proceed or do they not?"

"He is also from the capital, and one province should not have two votes," Suh says.

Terrance sighs. "I am open to suggestions, but we are hopelessly deadlocked. If we remain this way, we will not be able to vote on another resolution, and we will all lose."

Suh eventually nods. "I withdraw my objection for this vote only."

I turn toward Julian, shocked that they would choose him, but as he stands, I loosen my grip on my sleeves. I exhale, welcome relief easing the pressure in my chest. Foreau and Paolo both relax their postures as well. Julian and the Praetorian were both worried for my safety last night. They know these are murders, not accidental deaths. Julian will vote to conclude, and this nightmare will be over. We can all return to the capital at dawn if the mountain is passable.

"I vote to proceed," he says.

His voice sends shock waves through my chest and ripples through the room. My mouth falls open, and I shut it so quickly, my teeth click. I blink twice and shake my head. I must have misheard him.

Terrance smiles while Foreau and Paolo throw up their hands in frustration. I glance at Julian. What is happening right now?

"My vote may come as a surprise to some," Julian begins. "But grave assaults have occurred on our republic. A violent madman has murdered our Senate Leader while our greatest enemy has once again violated the peace treaty honored by us to the letter for the last nineteen years. The passing of Senator Eyo was indeed tragic, but laws must be made here for the other three million citizens of Pryor."

He gently paces, commanding the eyes and ears of everyone in the room.

"As nobles, we enjoy the pleasures of our elevated births, but ultimately, we are servants to the people," he says. "We are shepherds of the flock, and we cannot shrink from our duties in the face of wolves. Not if we dare call ourselves elite."

Suh raps his cane, seconding Julian's thoughts.

"I have full confidence that the Praetorian will get to the bottom of Senator Eyo's demise and if, gods forbid, someone is to blame, I swear that justice will be swift and merciless," Julian continues. "In the meantime, I will conduct the sentries in full daily watches to ensure that the Council remains safe through the conclusion of the conclave. May the gods guide the Senate and may they bless and save Pryor."

Julian sits after sounding every inch a polished politician. I glance at the others, and even Paolo and Foreau look swayed, slowly nodding. But his words only cause more doubt to swirl inside me.

Whose side is Julian Monroe on? What does he truly want?

My stomach twists when I consider what I really know about him—not distracted by the charm or the disarming nature. Julian was born powerful, a future patron of one of the wealthiest families in Pryor. He is General Hadrian's nephew and the youngest Capital Commander ever. But due to both, he was close to Verhardt. Antinous would have trusted Julian, as he was not part of the Senate. And Torren would hesitate to even look sideways at his best friend.

Is his affable nature the perfect cover?

Julian smiles, and a shadow crosses his face, distorting his features. His teeth look sharper, his eyes darker. I dig my nails into my palms, my wrists itching so badly, I want to take off my bangles.

Could he be a killer? Is he murdering his way to a seat on the Senate Council? Or worse?

"Given the vote and eloquence of Commander Monroe, we will proceed shortly with the next resolutions," Terrance says. He smiles with his yellowed teeth to their gums, unable to hide his glee.

"Very well." Julian picks up his reed pen and motions to the Senate pages.

He has just dipped his pen in ink when Torren steps into the doorway.

"Commander, a word, if you please," the Praetorian says.

Julian turns and looks at his friend. "Of course." Then he stands and bows to the Council. "I will bring in Sentry Calais upon my return."

The Commander and Praetorian both disappear as the Senate muses over the bright future of Julian Monroe. But if he is who I think he might be, none of us are safe now.

XXVIII.

Torren

I don't know that I've ever been this furious. Even when I dismembered that criminal, I wasn't angry like this. That was cold vengeance. This is molten...annoyance.

"That was an interesting vote," I say as we walk down the hall.

He smiles. "Wasn't it, though?" He lowers his voice, leaning closer. "Kera voted to conclude, for what it's worth."

I straighten my spine, but I continue to walk briskly to the frigidarium.

We enter the baths and stand by the waterfall of the cold plunge room for the requisite amount of time to be sure we weren't followed.

"So, when were you going to tell me about your political ambitions?" I ask.

He laughs. "I don't have any, Tor. You know better than anyone that I would never risk making my father proud."

He smiles like it's a joke, but it isn't. He is the eldest son, but his father has called him a disappointment more times than I can count—even in the presence of others.

"Why the fuck did you vote to proceed?" I ask through my teeth.

He stares at me, his humor vanishing. "Because it's our best chance of catching who did this."

Julian's face is sincere, but it feels like there is more to the story. Voting to proceed wasn't just foolish; it was reckless. Best practice would have been to conclude and remove everyone from potential harm. Julian is by the book the way I am, so what convinced him to deviate?

"You mean it's the best chance of the murderer trying to kill again?" I ask.

He shrugs. "I mean, maybe, but there won't be another time you'd be able to watch the Senate this closely. We are snowed in. We can keep a constant eye on them and together, we can solve this. And we need to. Otherwise, Torren, they will blame you." He pauses and takes a step closer, lowering his voice even further. "I'm surprised it hasn't been mentioned yet, but that's because they believe Antinous's death to be accidental and they are not convinced Eyo was poisoned. Once a healer looks at him, and they absorb the fact that there was a second murder under your watch, they will start to challenge your competency and...your innocence. They have brought treason charges for far less."

My heart stops, and my skin prickles in goose bumps. He is correct about all of it. I withheld my knowledge from them not only because I think it's the best way to catch a killer, but for the sake of my position. If I am not Praetorian, then I will be powerless in the face of the elite or...executed as a traitor in the arena.

Still, is that the only reason Julian voted to continue?

He was the last man to see Verhardt alive. He was also the first to find Antinous's body. And he was first into the banquet hall this morning. He volunteered to be clerk, putting himself into the Senate's orbit. It would all make sense if...

Then I look into his eyes. No, my best friend isn't a killer. I've known his gentle nature for more than a decade.

Julian frowns. "Tor, whatever you're thinking, I voted to proceed for you. You have to figure out who is behind all of this—it's the only way for you to survive."

I exhale, annoyed that he's correct. "What do you propose, Commander?"

He rubs his knuckles. "Our greatest issue will be keeping the High Priestess safe while we investigate, since she is being framed. Did you find anything to implicate the Faith this time?"

"No."

He raises his eyebrows in a way that makes me feel like I missed something, but I checked thoroughly.

Julian stares at the cold pools, his hazel eyes moving rapidly.

"Nothing from the servant interviews, either?" he asks.

I grit my teeth. I suppose it is time to show my hand.

"The worst possible outcome: one of them confessed."

He sighs at a scapegoat being preselected for us. "Who?"

"The cook. He was the second servant I interviewed. I asked if he knew who poisoned the senator, and he fell to his knees and confessed that he did it. Which means he didn't."

Julian's lips slant. "Naturally. Who got to him?"

"He wouldn't say."

Not under my threats to him or his family—the thing he claimed to care most about. I haven't yet inflicted physical pain, although I was angry enough to try. Instead, after I took his full confession, I forced myself to walk away and seek out Julian. Only, I arrived at the throne room just in time to watch his grand political speech.

Jules strokes his clean-shaven jaw. "What was his reason for using romlock?"

I knit my eyebrows. "It's fast acting, hard to trace, and has no cure. Why do you look like that?"

He stares at me and tips his head. "Romlock comes from Arthago originally. It's grown here now, but it was the traditional means to put traitors to death in their kingdom."

Of course Julian knows this. Along with regular instructors, he had tutors from the Kingdom of Arthago. He is fluent in both languages and has taught me some, but it is not the same as being bilingual from birth. When my father led the merchant council, my family could afford a tutor from Pryor, but that ended when I was thirteen. Everything else I've learned on my feet. I study constantly, far more than Julian, but his level of knowledge still eludes me.

Silence flows between Julian and me, steady as the waterfall.

"Do you now think Arthago is involved in this?" I ask.

I hold my breath. If the answer is yes, everything becomes far worse.

Julian runs his hands through his hair. "Not particularly, but I don't think we can rule it out. It would be convenient to strike at the heart of the republic just as they break the peace treaty."

"Why those two senators, though?" I ask. "Why the clerk? Especially when Verhardt was the one who insisted we cede land."

"I'm not sure. Maybe there is something in Antinous's papers? The Council will debate the war today. I can keep track of how they vote, and maybe that will provide us with a lead."

A lead?

"You're suggesting that one of the senators could be in league with Tyronne?"

He shrugs a shoulder. "Ever since the annexations on the western coast, there has been a thought that at least one senator has been bought by Arthago—most thought it was Verhardt, but maybe it was one of the others. Foreau has also been mentioned."

Julian breezily speaks about the deepest possible treachery to our republic—short of someone harboring an Elusian. I shake my head, but the suspicion sticks. The senators are not above taking bribes. Why wouldn't they line their pockets from the richest treasure chest? It was exactly what they accused my father of. And Terrance has bottomless greed—enough to steal from our treasury.

"I have to go fetch them the snake Lucius Calais," Jules says, interrupting my thoughts.

"Why is that?"

"They want him to vote for the second province."

I remember finding Calais moving Antinous's body, and now he stands to directly benefit from Eyo's murder. The coincidence gnaws at me. If they approve him, there will be two unelected people voting on the Council. This all feels like a grand design, but for what purpose?

"What do I do about the cook?" I muse aloud.

Julian blinks at me. "You already know what to do. Lock him away somewhere for interrogation and use whatever means necessary to get to the bottom of this. Make him more afraid of you than he is of them."

He's right. Violence is often the answer in Pryor.

I nod, ready to do my duty. Although I begin to wonder what I am really protecting.

XXIX

Torren

S on of a jackal, I am this close to snapping. The cook has blubbered and wheezed his way up five flights of steps, muttering prayers to the gods to watch over his family.

I look up. We have too many stairs left.

Although the man is obviously in lousy physical health, it's fear taking his breath away. He was bold in his confession, but now a coward in the face of torture. This is the worst showing of dignity I have seen in a while, and that's a high bar.

We stop again on the first landing in the tower, as he's red-faced and hyperventilating. I'm now worried about him dying before I can even question him.

I stand with my arms folded as he catches his breath. The man leans down with his hands on his knees. His whole body is shaking like a wet dog, and he smells like onions.

"I'm sorry. I just need a moment, sir," he wheezes.

I wait.

Finally, he nods and we continue. We climb even though he's still crying. We have to stop twice more, but eventually, we reach the door. I open it with the skeleton key.

The room is empty, of course—no one will use the western tower this week. This far up, he shouldn't be heard or located by the Senate. It was the best place to stow him away.

I step inside the domed space. Gold constellations shine in the cobalt-blue ceiling. The tower has an abundance of windows, and there are a variety of instruments to measure the stars atop a marble altar. Like the tower on the other side of the palace, there is a basin for sacrifices, but this is a celestial room for the temple of the skies. Since the Crimson Night, worship of the god has been nearly abandoned.

I toss a pair of manacles onto the altar, but I doubt I'll need them. I could overpower this man with a paper fan.

The cook looks around with his knees quaking. "Why am I here, sir? I have already told you that I was the one who poisoned the senator."

I lean against the altar and cross my arms. "That's exactly why you're here—for interrogation under pressure."

He swallows hard and takes four rapid breaths.

"Let's begin, shall we? Did you act alone?" I ask.

He mops the sweat off his brow with his meaty hand. "Entirely."

"What poison did you use?"

He hesitates, his brown eyes circling. Gods, he isn't even certain. I stay silent and let him squirm. Maybe he'll rethink whatever bargain he made. I'll certainly give him plenty of time to think about it up here.

"Romlock. It was romlock, sir." His round face is hopeful that he landed on the correct answer.

"I know you're lying," I say. "Because that was not the poison used."

It's a bluff, but it's effective. His face was sweaty and red, and now he's paling and stammering.

"I thought…that it… I… Maybe I grabbed the wrong vial." His eyebrows rise. The assertion is ridiculous, but he doesn't seem the type to think well on his feet.

If it had been even partially his idea, he would know what he used. But of course, he was only paid to take the fall.

"I'm sure whoever you made a deal with didn't bother to explain what poison it was, nor how it worked." I wave my hand like it's irrelevant. "How did you use it?"

"I put it in his food."

It's also a lie, but that means he wasn't the one who put the poison in at all. If he'd poisoned a senator, I'd argue to put him to death, even though he wasn't the mastermind, but he didn't even do that much.

River of Death.

"You know, it's funny, I burned his food myself and didn't find any trace fumes from poison — romlock or otherwise."

"He…he must've eaten the poison part." His voice rises at the end like a question.

I sigh, closing my eyes for a long blink. Why is *this* man my best chance at solving the Senate murders?

"Do you understand how you will be executed in the arena?" I take a seat on the padded window bench. "They try to make an afternoon out of it — allow you to battle wild animals to entertain the masses, then if you survive, you will be roasted inside of a brass bull, your screams turned into a melody. They will pull you out while still alive, and then the real torture will begin."

He stares at me with mournful brown eyes. "It is what I deserve."

I don't entirely disagree at the moment.

"Why did you kill Eyo, then? You forgot to state your reason."

"I…I accepted coin from Arthago in exchange for the poisoning."

A loud sigh escapes my lips. This man has to be the worst liar in the seven provinces.

But his lies could accidentally add up to the truth. If he is implicating Arthago, either it is true or, more likely, someone wants to make certain we go to war. And that is exactly the Verity Guild case ahead of us—a nobleman from the sixth province wanted to make his own army for battle.

"Any idea why the Kingdom of Arthago wanted Eyo dead? His province is pretty far from their border."

He shakes his head.

"How much did they give you?" I ask.

A spark of life returns to the cook's eyes.

"One hundred gold bullions, sir," he says.

Finally, something true. That is exactly how much he was given. It is an easy sum for any senator to pay, but it would change a servant's life and the life of his family. The amount, invested wisely in the right shop, could elevate them from servants to the merchant, citizen class. He knows that he will die, but he is willing to do all of this to better the lives of his wife and daughters. He spoke of them lovingly during his confession.

It's honorable, in a way, and there's a pull of sympathy in my chest. But of course, he's forgetting that his family won't be able to keep that money or anything else. He will doom them, not save them.

Perhaps he is simply ignorant of the reality. Maybe the truth will be enough for him to disclose who paid him.

I bring my leg across my knee, my leather skirt shifting. "Do you know what happens when the Verity Guild finds someone guilty of treason?"

He blinks. "They are killed."

"Obviously, but do you know what happens to their families? What will happen to your family if I submit your confession?"

He stills and looks around, but then he shakes his head. "No, sir."

It's not a surprise. It's not often spoken about.

"They are thrown out onto the streets—their home and every single thing they own are all confiscated by the republic. Because your family isn't noble, they will strip them naked first. Hopefully the sentries who conduct this are honorable—many aren't, not to traitors, anyhow. Your wife and daughters will have no home, no food, not even clothing. Then the Senate will issue a decree to shun them, to not offer them shelter or work."

I pause and let my words sink in. The easiest part is that everything I said was true. The only detail I exaggerated was stripping them naked. That law changed fifteen years ago. My mother and I had the clothes on our backs, but that was all. The sentries even had me turn my pockets inside out to prove I was taking nothing else. Then they searched my mother's dress for anything we might've tried to hide. The sentry enjoyed groping under my mother's skirts while I was held back by two others.

But then Hadrian caught him. At that time, Hadrian was the Capital Commander. He immediately, without pomp or circumstance, tied the man to the post and whipped his back.

Hadrian was the reason I enlisted as a sentry at sixteen. I had few other opportunities, but I saw what power could do when used for good. It's why I must keep my position.

No matter what.

I lean forward and stare the cook in the eye. "What do you think will become of your wife and young daughters on the street? They are fourteen and eleven, right? Feel free to actually give it some thought—the three of them with no food, no work, and no shelter."

He begins to cry again. "Please. Please, gentle gods, no."

"You were played for a fool," I say.

I slowly stand and stroll to the door. I will leave him in here to ponder his family's future. If that is not enough, I will have to resort to violence, and I don't relish torturing an innocent man.

Yet, if it is necessary, I will do what needs to be done for the republic.

I pause with my palm on the door handle. "I will give you until sunrise to recant your confession, but remember that whoever gave you gold to take the fall won't feel an ounce of concern as your wife and daughters have to work on their backs for copper coins."

The cook falls on his knees, wailing. I open my mouth, compassion getting the better of me, but I force myself to walk out. I lock the door behind me.

XXX

Kerasea

Sentry Lucius Calais is twenty-three years old with seemingly no achievements or commendations. His four years of service in the legions have resulted in a censure for cowardly desertion and an allegation of rape. The allegation was later withdrawn—meaning the girl's family was paid off.

I glance to the side. I've never seen a man as simultaneously overconfident and underqualified as Lucius Calais.

"Thank you, Sentry Calais," Terrance says. "You may return to your post."

Calais bows while undressing me with his eyes. I suppress a shudder.

"He will be a fine representative for the second province," Terrance urges.

I vote no along with Foreau and Suh. Medea, Paolo, and Terrance vote yes.

We deadlock, but interestingly, the vote isn't split between old and new guard.

Senator Terrance stares at me with a cold expression as Julian announces the deadlock. Disdain and anger flash through his brown eyes as he sniffs.

"May I remind everyone that we can resolve this deadlock if the High Priestess is not permitted a vote," Terrance says loudly.

My mouth goes dry. He is correct, and I am not sure what to say in response, but I hold my ground because Calais seems like the worst person to hand power.

Medea looks from me to the senator and then stands between us, facing him. "We have already resolved the importance of the first province having a voice in this conclave. Equal representation is why we are considering Calais."

The tension in my shoulders eases slightly as Medea comes to my defense. Is she able to go toe to toe with them because of experience or is she simply a different type of woman—one who doesn't wear power as much as emit it? She seems to know everyone, from Eyo's sentry to her treasonous nephew, and they all seek her favor. Whatever the answer, I'm glad she's on my side.

"Agreed," Suh says.

Terrance retakes his seat with a huff, knowing he won't win.

However, the sun clock strikes noon, and we are still deadlocked. The Council has not heard any new resolutions, and Julian had mentioned that there are hundreds of laws to still be decided, along with the declaration of war. People are undeniably suffering while we sit here and do nothing. I feel the same pressure Medea mentioned, to do something, anything but stay idle.

Suh runs a hand down his goatee. "May I present a new resolution in regard to the vacant seat?" He pauses and stands, leaning on his diamond cane. "I propose that we log Eyo as abstaining so that we can continue. I propose that this resolution hold until a later vote on Calais."

This new suggestion garners nods from all of the senators, but it now needs to be debated according to the laws of the conclave.

Suh then stands and also gives a glowing tribute to Eyo, which is curious, as he hated him. He blames him for his eldest daughter's death years ago.

"...a man of great honor, enviable talent, and remarkable compassion for his fellow man," Suh says.

I keep my expression neutral.

As Suh speaks, I remember the story my father told me about him. Decades ago, when he was General of the Legions of Pryor, Suh fell in love with a beautiful woman who was already the wife of a young sentry. That soldier's entire battalion was slaughtered during a skirmish in the Hundred Year War. Suh married the young widow a few months later, and she has been Lady Suh ever since.

The whispers were that Suh knew the battalion was walking into an ambush. Other versions said he purposefully sent five hundred men to their deaths just to dispose of his rival. Both would've been war crimes, but he was never prosecuted. He returned to the fifth province with his new bride, resigned from the legions, and ran for the Senate seat. At that point, the Senate was elected every six years, not members for life. But he amassed a fortune crafting arms for the legions until the war ended.

Suh finally stops speaking, and the new resolution passes. Julian records the votes.

We can now hear the other resolutions today, and the first is a motion to declare war on the Kingdom of Arthago. General Hadrian makes all decisions in a war, but the Council decides on the declaration.

Suh slams his large fist on the table. "We have rolled over for far too long. We must send a message to the scourge of Arthago: stay within your borders or there will be consequences. If we keep allowing them to take our land piece by piece, soon there will be no republic left."

Foreau shakes his head. "And risk another Hundred Year War? No. Sending our army to the sixth province will only result in a full-scale conflict. They will take your coast and then come for the whole nation!"

"We mustn't engage in another costly war. Not when we killed a magical tyrant to end the last one." Terrance sniffs, once again worried about our treasury. "Give them the land they took and be done with this."

"The land they took contains the homes, livelihoods, and bodies of my people, Terrance," Medea says. "Sliver by sliver, they are bleeding this republic to death. You have convened the Verity Guild on my nephew, who took matters into his own hands to raise an army to fight the Arthagians, but such an action would not have been necessary if this Council actually acted to protect its citizens. We must hold the line. It is beyond time to defend ourselves."

"They have proven time and time again that they will take as much as we allow," Paolo says softly while turning his ring. "I stand with Suh and Medea. It is time to declare war and meet strength with strength."

The Senate is split between those on the west who want a war and those on the east who oppose. By a three-to-two vote, the motion will carry.

Terrance's eyes land on me again, and I shrink under the hostile gaze. I've unintentionally made an enemy out of him today.

"As you have insisted that the High Priestess vote on important matters, surely she must vote on this," Terrance says. "What say you for the first province?"

No one objects, even though I thought the resolution already passed.

Bloody lies, am I to vote on all of these matters now? What have I done?

The senators stare at me, waiting. I glance at Medea, but she is not intervening on my behalf this time. She studies me, more curious than anything else.

What do I do?

Over the past twenty years, we've given Arthago land to maintain peace, so it feels like I should follow suit. But was Verhardt's nonengagement because it was best for the republic, because of how many men we lost in battle, or because he feared General Hadrian becoming unstoppable if he won a war against our greatest enemy? He'd already won decisive victories as a young general before the Senate pulled him from the front.

I am about to oppose the resolution and deadlock the conclave, but a feeling of wrongness drapes over me. The truth is that I don't know enough about politics to vote intelligently, and ignorance is dangerous. Especially on something where so many innocent lives hang in the balance. I shouldn't be voting in this matter, or any of the laws, just as Mirial said during her four-hour lecture, because it isn't the role of the High Priestess.

My pulse pounds and my wrists burn. I try to breathe, but I only manage shallow sips of air. Heat rises to my temples as the walls close in, but then I spot Julian out of the corner of my eye. He said that I am not one of the Senate at dinner—that I don't need their permission.

Maybe he's right.

A calm washes over me as a way out crystallizes. An exit has been here this whole time—I just didn't see it. They cannot force me to vote. They can pressure me, but I am ultimately the one who has to yield.

I know what I have to do.

I rise from my seat. "Senators, I find that I am unqualified to speak on foreign affairs and, therefore, I am unable to properly protect the interests of the first province. As I agreed to only vote in the event of deadlock and that is not possible with five senators, I will abstain from voting at this conclave."

Senator Terrance's brown eyes gleam like amber. Foreau shakes his head, looking disgusted. Medea raises her eyebrows. Everyone is silent, though. I suppose there is nothing they can say.

I return to my seat feeling lighter than I have in days.

"In that case, the motion to declare war on Arthago passes on a three-two basis," Suh says.

Suh smiles at me, and it's the first time I've seen him grin. It looks odd and ghastly on his face. He cannot contain his glee that we will once again be at war.

Was all of this just to return to battle? The deaths of Verhardt and Eyo meant that the resolution would pass. Suh will now be able to arm the legions again, lining his own pockets with the profits.

Did he kill his way to war?

Julian records the vote, and the three senators sign the resolution bill. He then pours wax and seals it with the stamp of Pryor.

"Now, may I present a motion to elect a Senate Leader?" Terrance says while the ink is still wet. "The untimely death of Verhardt has left the Council rudderless. The needs of Pryor demand a leader, a first among equals, and I resolve we now bring this to a vote."

Paolo gets to his feet so quickly that the wave of his hair bobs. "No. We must vote on Lucius Calais first."

Terrance shakes his head. "I currently have a pending resolution. You may bring your motion afterward."

Foreau's normally calm features contort. He stands and points a finger at Terrance. "You'd elect yourself leader without the voice of half the people? This is a republic! And you are not a king."

Foreau bangs on the table so hard that I shudder.

Suh stands without using his cane. "I support Terrance as Senate Leader."

"Seconded," Medea adds from her seat.

Terrance puts his hand over his heart. "I humbly accept and cast the vote of the third province for myself as leader."

The coup happens so quickly that I am still looking between the two factions when it's over. Paolo and Foreau both open their mouths, but neither speaks. They have been outvoted according to the laws of the conclave and outplayed by the old guard.

As the three senators sign the resolution, both Paolo and Foreau walk out of the throne room in protest.

My stomach twists as dread flows through me. What have I done? By giving up my right to vote, my voice, I gave Terrance the republic.

I exchange quick glances with Julian, but there is nothing either of us can do now. Julian pours molten wax on the paper and presses the seal of Pryor on top.

"May I now bring forward a second vote on the acceptability of Lucius Calais as a temporary replacement for Eyo's Senate seat?" Terrance says.

"Denied," Suh says.

"Denied," Medea adds.

Terrance nods. "The motion is denied on the basis of a three-to-nil vote. Eyo will thus vote to abstain going forward in this conclave, as there is no suitable replacement."

They vote so quickly, striking as one, that Julian is still lifting the seal from the first vote. He turns, surprise written on his face, but he dutifully picks up the new resolution from Terrance's Senate page.

I feel like I'm sinking in wet sand as I grip the arms of my chair. I was looking at Suh, but Terrance and Medea flipped their votes in a way that means they never were in favor of Calais. So why did she suggest him? I've never felt more in over my head, trying to figure out each senator's motivations.

That mystery aside, the old guard is now in full control. With a three-two majority, they don't even need Foreau and Paolo in this room. Their agendas will pass without objection.

Was it enough that I silenced my own voice? Or have I now put myself in even worse danger?

XXXI

Torren

Julian briefs me on the Senate as I change from my armor to a suit. I have to pause several times to absorb the information.

Terrance has seized full control of the republic. After Paolo and Foreau walked out in protest, the old guard decided dozens of resolutions, including moving half of the republic's treasury to Terrance's province.

"On the plus side, the conclave is ahead of schedule," Julian says.

I draw a breath and adjust the collar of my dress shirt. This is not the time for his humor.

"Where did you put the cook?" Julian whispers.

"Somewhere safe."

I gesture to the walls around us, but the truth is, I'm not going to disclose to anyone, even Julian, where I put him—it's too risky. The cook is now my best and only hope for evidence. If he turns on the person who paid him, I can persuade the others to let me investigate. And the person with the most to gain was Terrance.

I slip on my suit jacket, and Julian and I leave the room. He stops and knocks on Kera's door. I pretend not to look, but I can't help glancing at the handle.

There is no answer.

He tries the door, and it's locked.

Julian looks at me, and in his eyes there's the same dull panic that's gripping me. She likely just left without an escort, but it's also possible that someone got to her. Terrance has made no secret of his disdain for Kerasea.

I use my skeleton key and open the door—her room is empty. Was she taken or is she simply at dinner? The tightening in my chest is uncomfortable...and unwelcome.

We quickly descend to the banquet hall, and there she is. I feel my breath return in a whoosh, but surely it's only relief that she is well, and not because tonight, she's wearing a backless, wine-red dress. Her long hair is swept up, and her green eyes shine like gems.

Relief and anger flood me at the same time. She's alive. Seemingly by accident, as she can't follow a simple instruction.

She turns, and our eyes meet. When she looks at me like that, there's a pull in my chest, but I know better than to give in to it. I look away.

We take our seats for dinner, her directly across from me. Senator Terrance slides into Verhardt's chair at the head of the table, spreading out to fully occupy the seat. The room is rather empty with Eyo, Verhardt, and Antinous dead and Paolo and Foreau not attending dinner in protest. But no one seems devastated by their absence.

Any of their absences, really. Was the old guard colluding together?

Servants place down cold salad and platters of cured meats and cheeses. With the cook up in the tower, someone else had to cobble together tonight's meal, and this is more of a luncheon.

No one remarks on their plates, though. Actually, no one is touching their food.

Terrance stands and lifts his wine goblet. His face is aglow with victory, making him appear years younger. "Here's to a historic day of the conclave, one where the true spirit of the republic led us to make Pryor great again. I am humbled by your confidence in my abilities and recognize the weight of the office bestowed upon me. I will endeavor every day to deserve the trust and faith placed in me by the people of Pryor."

He takes a gulp of wine, obviously not afraid of being poisoned. Is it hubris, or is it because he never had a reason to be afraid?

"Hear, hear," Suh says. He also takes a large swallow of wine.

Medea drinks to Terrance and then fixes her gaze on me. "Tell us, Praetorian, what have you found today about our dear friend Senator Eyo?"

She gestures to his empty chair.

"I need a healer to examine the body, but I have completed my interviews," I say. "While an allergic fit is likely, if there was wrongdoing, trust that I will deliver a suspect shortly."

Suh nods and picks up his fork. "Should it have been poison, we expect a confession sealed with blood."

He means that literally. Confessions are "sealed" with the bloody thumbprint of the perpetrator. But why does Suh suddenly expect a confession?

Worry creeps up my spine. I will have to check on the cook sooner rather than later.

As desserts are being served, Kera excuses herself. She, of course, leaves without an escort. Julian's brows rise in concern, but I have another person to attend to.

A few minutes later, I stand.

"I bid the Council a good rest. I will now continue my inquest, but I will join you at the conclave tomorrow." I bow and exit the banquet hall before anyone can object.

Julian posted two sentries at the doorways to the banquet room — Medea's and Foreau's. They salute me as I go to the kitchens.

I place a dinner plate, a small bottle of wine, and water into a basket and then jog up the western tower steps. After a day's fast, the cook should be close to breaking. I'd planned to leave him stewing overnight, but a bribe of food and wine may be all it takes for him to confess that Terrance paid him to take the fall. Especially since he now knows the truth about what will happen to his family.

Energy surges in my limbs as if I'm in a fight ring. I always feel this when the hunt closes in: the knowledge of a knockout coming. I can end this tonight if I break the cook. I hope reason and bribes will work, but I'm always prepared to do what is necessary.

I reach the top of the celestial tower and, on instinct, try the door. The handle turns.

No.

I withdraw my hand, then slowly place it back.

River of Death. I'm certain I locked it, and I have the only key. But these are not complex locks—they can be opened with enough trial and error, and the man had hours.

My chest fills as I draw a long, steadying breath. If the cook picked the lock and fled, I will have to hunt him. And then it will be difficult to get the truth from him because I'll be busy strangling him myself.

I push open the door and there, in the middle of the room, is the cook. He's lying on his back on the floor. A surprising amount of relief floods through me as I remove my suit jacket and place the basket on the ground.

"Well, have you had enough time to reconsider your confession?" I ask. The room is cold, but I begin to roll up my sleeves in case this leads to bloodshed.

Silence greets me. Perhaps my relief was premature.

As the quiet continues, dread begins to settle on my shoulders, weighing them down. Something is wrong.

I light the oil lamps and take another step toward him. It's only then that I notice his head is lying in a pool of blood. A celestial measuring instrument protrudes from the side of his neck.

My limbs react before my mind, and I dive down next to the cook, searching for life at his wrist. Puncture wounds line his throat, but even a slight amount of consciousness will give me something—a name, a clue.

"Stay with me, stay," I say. "Who did this?"

There's no reply.

"Give me a name! Just a name!"

I slap his cheek, careful to avoid the gash in his neck. Still nothing. I go quiet, aside from the pounding of my heart, and hold his wrist. Nothing—no pulse. He is dead and yet still warm. He was killed recently—sometime in the past hour.

I drop his arm and ball my hands into fists. Rage flames under my skin. Someone found and murdered my only lead while I sat at dinner.

A thousand curses on Jubilee.

I tip my head all the way back, staring at the inlaid ceiling as I struggle to breathe. Another victim. This one dead because he was trying to better the lives of his loved ones.

But I was the one who left him alone. I should've tortured him this morning when I had the chance. He would've screamed as I removed his fingers and toes, but he was weak: he would've revealed who paid him. I let my own history get in the way. I hesitated because he was innocent.

Frustration fills my chest at my failing. I'll never make this mistake again. I can't afford the cost of mercy.

I get off my knees and trip over the dinner basket, letting out a humorless laugh. Minutes ago, I was so certain that I wouldn't have to resort to violence that I selected a bottle of wine. Barely able to see for the pounding rage in my head, I grab the basket and hurl it against the wall. Meat and shards of glass rain down on the stone.

Violence is the only answer in Pryor—I've known this for years. And yet.

All I'm left with is a false confession and a dead scapegoat. I'm trying to bring down a senator—the most elite person in the capital— with nothing more than my hunch that he's guilty. I might as well try to dismantle a temple with my bare hands.

Chief Justice Probus, General Hadrian, even Julian would tell me to leave this alone. Everyone would…aside from the High Priestess.

I stand straighter as thoughts race through my mind. Terrance was particularly horrified that she might be able to reveal past crimes, and if he is behind the murders, he's also the one framing her. If I can follow through on my earlier idea and form an alliance with Kerasea, I may just be able to bring a would-be king to justice, prevent any more murders, and save my position.

I stare at the dead body of the cook. Kerasea Vestal may be my only hope.

Fuck my life.

XXXII.

Kerasea

I close and lock the door behind me and stand in the center of the tower, trying to catch my breath. My exhales make little clouds of mist in the frigid room.

Curse those flights of stairs.

Finally, my breathing returns to normal and I can speak to the divine with dignity.

"God of truth, I pray you hear your servant, your vessel here on earth."

I stand next to the brazier and prick my hand with my hairpin. It hurts, but the truth often does. I push the pad of my finger until a drop of blood falls. It lands, sizzling into the eternal flame.

There are other ways to call the god, like how most priests use lapis, but this is the most direct.

When my blood hits the fire, it causes swirling red smoke to rise and float through the oculus of the domed roof. I tilt my head back, watching as the crimson plume enters the night's sky. The storm has stopped, and millions of stars twinkle in the blackness, but the cold bites and lingers. I shiver. I'm in my red dinner dress, not temple robes or furs, but this won't take long.

"All-seeing divine, I call upon thee to answer my prayer and guide your humble servant toward the light."

I bow my head and, moments later, a bronze eagle falls through the oculus. It gracefully descends until it lands on its back, dead in the center of the altar.

I give thanks for the sacrifice, signing a circle in the air with my drying blood. Then I take the sickle knife and make the primary vertical incision. The innards steam into the cold air, but the preternatural liver is exactly where it belongs. It's at least a positive beginning. The organ also has the correct feel and smell.

Maybe the omen will be positive. Maybe the killing is over.

I place the liver on the golden offering tray and sprinkle it with holy oil and blessed salts. I ask the god for an omen of the future. Then I place the tray into the center of the eternal flame.

Black smoke pours out of the brazier, surrounding me in a billowing circle. Darkness closes in, but there's something amiss. The swirl of smoke is broken, and there can be only one cause for that—a disbeliever in my midst. And that can only be one man.

I sigh at Torren following me once again. I thought I locked the door, but I'll deal with that later. I have to continue or the life of the eagle will have been wasted. I raise my arms and chant.

"In the dark of night, the truth will be revealed.
In the dark of night, all will be revealed."

The heavy weight of the divine enters the room and extinguishes all the lights, the last being the eternal flame. The whispers of truth fill my bones as the god accepts the sacrifice. Then the light returns and the pressure fades as I lower my arms.

I reach into the eternal flame—a fire of intense heat that will not burn the faithful. Placing an arm into the fire is the final test for acolytes hoping to become priests, but I've never had anything to fear. I walked through the flame as a child.

I take the tray out and set it on the altar, then I stare at the liver. Confusion roils my stomach. I don't understand this, but I have called and the god has answered—even that much is a blessing. Humankind is not owed anything more. The truth must be a comfort in itself; however, in this case, it is not.

Bloody lies, what now?

My face tingles and my chest tightens. I hang my head and wash my hands clean in the water bowl.

"I'm sure you want to see the prophecy," I say aloud.

The Praetorian fully opens the door he was hiding behind. His jacket from dinner is gone, leaving him in a fitted white shirt and dress pants. His sleeves are rolled up, revealing his muscular forearms. Somehow, he looks more dangerous in cloth than he does in armor.

"That was quite a show," he says.

I arch an eyebrow at him, but I refuse to take the bait. "You know, for an investigator, you're not terribly discreet."

He shrugs his broad shoulders as he strolls fully into the room. "I don't need to be—typically."

No, I suppose violence isn't subtle.

I tear my eyes from him and look at the tray again. The liver is partially black—bisected in the middle. One side is healthy pink and the other charred. A line of gold divides the two. What is this?

The Praetorian's eyes search my face, not the organ. "What does that mean?"

I sigh, because I am not sure. The pink is natural, signaling a return to order and peace, but the black means rot and death. How can it be both? How can our future contain a duality? And how can glory separate the two?

Stalling, I cradle the dead eagle in my arms and carry it over to the sacrificial basin by the window. Then I light the fire and say the prayers to the five gods of Pryor to watch over us and accept this offering.

"It means that either blood will continue to be spilled at this conclave," I say, "or that the republic will return to normalcy."

He moves closer to me. "Which is it?"

I grip the basin as the carcass burns. I don't know.

"It is almost like diverging paths. I've never seen this kind of omen, but any amount of blackening is death and disaster. However, I am not sure which side we are on."

His brow wrinkles as he stares at me. "Isn't it your job to know?"

I feel my temper flaring, but he is right—I am supposed to know. The problem is, and remains, that I am not my father. He would've known.

"What does it matter?" I shrug a shoulder. "You don't believe in my 'bird signs.'"

I glare at him. Mirrored back in his eyes is the same anger I feel. What happened to make him so full of frustration?

He looks away and then clears his expression, trying to fake a genial smile. "I think we have gotten off to a bad start. I'd like to begin anew, if you're agreeable."

A bad start? Does he mean our whole lives or just this week?

I stare at him. He must want something, but I can't think of anything he'd need from me this badly. I have a feeling it's related to the blood dappling his sleeve, though.

"Let's start with honesty, then—why are you following me?" I ask.

He gives me another shrug. "I instructed you to have an escort. You know there is danger here."

It's the truth, but it's not.

"I see that," I say.

His eyes dart around. "What do you mean?"

Using small steps, I move closer to him. His breathing hitches as I reach out. I let my fingers graze the white cotton of his shirt by his elbow. He flinches, clearly repulsed by my touch, but he holds still as I raise his right hand.

"There's blood on your sleeve," I say.

He yanks his arm away, looking anywhere but at my face. He's hiding something—shame, maybe, but that doesn't make sense. The Praetorian isn't ashamed of being brutal. His gaze flickers to me, and there's just a hint of vulnerability in his face.

It's completely unnerving.

"You seem... What happened?" I soften my stance, because something is actually wrong.

When I push aside what I know about Torren and force myself to not judge, it's easy to sense the turmoil wafting off him. I feel the weight as if it's pressing down on my own shoulders. It's failure of some sort. I would think it was related to the deaths of the senators, but no, this feels like something else.

He clasps his hands behind his back and stares at the wall. "Nothing I didn't expect."

That much is true, but he's shaken nonetheless. He's not going to confess and cleanse his soul, though. Not to me.

"Why are you really here? What is it you need?"

"The truth," he says. "But if you can't understand your own bird signs, then perhaps I have reached a dead end."

Fire rushes through me, and I clamp my teeth down to keep my insults to myself. Then I force a smile. The smile will irritate him more.

"This is an amazing new beginning," I say. "A fresh start, yet it feels the same."

His lips curl into a smile as he hangs his head. Then he draws a breath and unclasps his hands. "It's more difficult than I expected to break old habits. But you're right—I do need you."

He lingers on the word "need," and a shiver runs through me.

"Why?" I ask, holding my breath.

"You and I seem to be the only people who understand what is happening here," he continues in a low voice. "Someone at Jubilee has murdered two senators and the Senate Clerk, and they believe they can get away with it."

I exhale a cloud of fog. Of course I knew that, but it's different falling from his mouth. After today's events, I no longer think Julian or the Praetorian was involved. Most likely it was Terrance, either acting alone or with Suh and Medea. If I'm right, we, along with the republic, are in terrible danger now.

"What are you proposing?" I ask.

He draws a breath. "That we form an alliance. Whoever is behind the murders won't want you to discern the truth, and my position, if not my life, is in jeopardy. We both have a vested interest in bringing the murderer to justice. Our goals are aligned for now."

I swallow hard and grip the altar as the truth of his words settles on me. "What exactly do you need from me?"

He opens his mouth and then closes it. He's hesitating.

"For now, just stay alive," he says, "and when your time comes, I'll tell you. Let me escort you back to your chambers."

I don't want to accept an open-ended agreement, but if he's willing to put aside his dislike for me, I should accept. It's the only way for me to survive.

"All right, Praetorian," I say. "Allies, then."

I extend my hand. He glances down, keeping his arms at his sides, but then slowly he meets my palm.

As he touches me, the heat from his hand warms my whole body in the cold room, and the same feeling of calm grips me.

Our eyes meet, and a spark lights in my core. The same is reflected in his eyes. Silence drags its feet, making the moment too important, but I don't know what to say. Torren's breathing gets faster, and then I realize we are still holding hands. We both pull back.

He flexes his hand and then balls it in a fist. Then he steps to the side. "Allies, then," he repeats.

He strides to the door but then stops and gestures for me to leave first. I take a shaky step. I tell myself that aligning with Torren is a good thing. It will enable me to survive the next few days. And maybe, just maybe, together we can catch the killer and save the republic. Most everything about working with him is good for me.

That is, of course, unless he uncovers that I am Elusian.

XXXIII.

Torren

Allies for now.

Kera's hair smelled like winter rose oil, and her hand was so slight in mine. But it was the way she looked at me when we agreed that haunts me. That pull I feel when our eyes meet became a chain binding me to her.

She is the very last thing I need, but in order to get to the bottom of these murders, I have to align with her.

It's a deal with the underworld, and I now understand the choice the Senate made all those years ago.

Shaking my head at myself, I take the stairs behind her. It's ridiculous to dwell on a handshake, even if heat flushed through my body when I took her hand.

The most important thing is that I will be able to work with her and Julian to counterbalance the power of the Senate Leader.

But what did that omen mean? Even the sight of it caused unease to settle in my gut. And the fact that Kerasea didn't know is a different kind of troubling. Unless she did understand it and chose not to share. I can't expect her to instantly trust me when I don't fully trust her.

I can't completely trust anyone.

She and I wordlessly descend, but I'm all too aware of how close she is to me. I shouldn't feel anything besides reluctance, but as I watch her naked back shift in her dress, other feelings stir inside me.

I grip the railing and try to focus on something else. Anything else. I stare down at the blood specks she noticed, and it's a sobering reminder of where we are and what the senators are capable of. I've been behind in this chess game, and I need to get a step ahead. Are Paolo and Foreau in danger now? Or is it enough that Terrance is the Senate Leader and the scapegoat is dead?

Uncertainty makes my chest feel leaden as we reach the third floor. We walk down the hall, Kera brushing her hand against mine and then correcting, pulling farther away, her steps unsteady.

I don't want to look, but my gaze is drawn to her. She trembles, her skin coated in goose bumps.

"You're shaking," I say.

"I'm cold."

I move to give her my jacket, but then I remember I'm only wearing a dress shirt. I left my suit jacket in the other tower.

Son of a jackal. I have another dead body to handle. And then tomorrow, I will need to tell the Senate something about the cook. Anything but the truth.

I'll report that the cook took his own life. The killer will, of course, know I'm lying, but they can hardly admit that. I will omit his confession.

We reach Kera's chamber, and her hands shake so much that she can't get her key in the door. She tries again.

I place my hand over hers and she stills, holding her breath. I guide her key and she doesn't let go, so we unlock it together.

She pushes open the door and takes two steps inside, then turns and faces me. Her lips part as she grips the doorknob. Kera seems like she wants to say something, but no words come out.

Is she going to invite me inside? Do I want her to?

"Good rest, High Priestess," I say hastily. "Bar your door and don't leave tonight."

Whatever she was going to say dies on her lips, and her expression changes.

"Good night, Praetorian."

She shuts the door, and I linger in front of it, regret flooding my chest. I spoke too soon.

I have to get ahold of myself. Allies. We are allies because she will help me prevent any more harm coming to the Council. That is what I need her for. That is all I need her for.

I force myself away from her doorway and walk briskly down the hall. I knock on Julian's door. He answers, but he's dressed for bed. He runs a hand over his blond hair, sleep still in his eyes. He's about to speak, but I beat him to it.

"I need help moving a body," I say.

His mouth opens, but then he exhales and nods. "All right, let me put on shoes."

XXXIV.

Torren

I t's easier to move a body with two people, but not down this many
steps in a narrow space. And Julian is struggling. I pause when we
get to the bottom of the tower to give him a breather.

"You know, sometimes it's really hard to be your friend, Tor."
Julian smiles while shaking out his arms.

"I'm aware."

I put a pillowcase around the cook's neck wound and then
wrapped and tied him into bedsheets from one of the spare rooms.
He lies on the ground while I wipe sweat from my forehead. I carried
the body's heavier torso, and it was no picnic to move him around
the winding staircases. We're only lucky that rigor mortis hasn't
completely set in yet.

"Any idea who killed him?" Julian asks.

We're in a staircase where anyone can overhear us, so I shake
my head no. I combed the entire celestial tower while waiting
for Julian and found nothing. Whoever killed him knew to cover

their tracks.

After a brief rest, Julian and I take the stairs until we reach the kitchens. Only the front door is chained. We'll bring him out the delivery door.

There aren't any deliveries during the conclave, since no one comes or goes, but as we pass the pantry, the lights are on, and it's still fully stocked.

We stop again by the grain sacks, and then Julian nods for us to proceed outside.

He walks backward, making deep indentations in the snow, as we step into the cold night. We pass the woodshed and stop behind it. It's a good place to store a body, as there isn't food nearby and it's decently far from the palace.

I've already used it once today.

My stomach bottoms out as I clear another depression in the snow, and then we lay the cook next to the mound that contains Eyo's body.

Julian catches his breath quickly and then helps me cover the cook with tightly packed snow.

"If you'd told me he was in the tower, I would've posted a sentry at the door," he says.

"I'm sure the sentry would have conveniently seen nothing."

He shrugs. "Possibly, but then we'd know which sentries are in league with them."

I pause. "Them? You think it's more than one senator?"

Ice grips me, and I stomp my feet. I've had the same thought myself, but Julian giving it voice makes it feel even truer.

Julian shakes his head. "It's possible, but conspiring requires trust. I don't see any of them giving one another that kind of leverage. At least not for long."

I stare up at the moon—so he's had the same thoughts and come to a similar conclusion. Everyone remains a suspect.

My hands are red and painful by the time we're finished burying the cook, but I barely noticed, lost in my thoughts.

Julian and I both blow into our hands. Eyo's body is undisturbed, so we are done here.

"Let's get back inside," I say.

"Wait." He walks two steps closer to me. "*Why* didn't you tell me where you put the cook?"

I glance at the snow mounds. "We can have this conversation inside."

Now that we've stopped moving, the cold seeps into my bones. I put my suit jacket on when I was searching the tower, but I'm not in furs, and Jules is in nightclothes and boots.

Julian shakes his head and folds his arms, remaining in place. "I'd rather have it here and now. Do you not trust me?"

Before the conclave, my answer might have been different, but too much suspicion has been cast on everyone here. I have to keep my thoughts to myself, as toppling an elite is a nearly impossible task. I don't need to worry about anyone else breaking under pressure.

"I don't trust anyone."

Julian flinches, and then his eyes search mine. "We've been through a lot for you to say something like that. Too much for you to mean it—and yet you do."

"Jules…" I don't know what to say because he's right, but this isn't about me or my friendships. "I trust you with my life, but my investigation, this role, has to come before anything else—even you. I am impartial and unfeeling because I have to be. Because the republic is more important than my individual feelings or allegiances."

"No, you *choose* to be unfeeling." He points to the two bodies buried in snow. "Because this is the republic, Torren—the scheming, the bloody grabs for power, the corruption, extortion, and violence, the lechery and selfish desires, all of it. This is what you're defending. This is what you're putting first."

It's a treasonous insult to Pryor and one I never thought he'd utter. The worst thing is that he means it.

I straighten my spine. "Say that again?"

Julian sighs, and his shoulders slump. "Let's go. We can have this fight somewhere with a fireplace and brandy."

He walks away, and as he goes, I realize that I need to settle this in my mind once and for all. I've already aligned with Kera. Can I fully trust Julian, enough to work with him?

My stomach turns at the thought of him betraying everything we hold dear. As different as we are, we became friends because we have the same values. As young men, we both bled and killed for this republic. He has literally fought at my side in the wilderness. Would he ever turn traitor?

No, it's not possible.

I know for a fact that killing a man stains his soul. He couldn't sleep after he killed, even in defending this republic, and when I asked why, he said it was because the men he hurt haunt his nightmares. He couldn't shake murder even when it was in self-defense.

And he's been sleeping just fine despite three murders.

I hurry after Jules and find him outside by the kitchen door. My breath makes fog in the air as I come to a stop.

"I don't think you killed him," I say. "The cook...or any of them."

A line forms on his forehead as Julian stares at me. "Well, at least there's that, I guess."

He rubs his arms, holding himself tightly. Then he stomps his feet to warm them.

"Why are you still out here?" I ask.

"The door is locked."

"That's not possible."

He raises his eyebrows. "I beg to differ."

I try the handle, and the door doesn't budge. It *is* locked, but these doors don't lock on their own. Luckily, I have the skeleton key in my pocket.

I put it in and the lock turns. I push the door, but it doesn't open.

Julian and I exchange glances. It could be an accident—a servant who was going about their nightly routine and barred the door—a coincidence of timing. But it doesn't feel like that.

Someone locked us out.

I glance at the palace; there is a kitchen window just large enough to fit through. However, it's too high up to reach from where we're standing, even if I lift Julian.

"I'll kick in the door," I say.

If it's barred with thick metal or heavy furniture, I won't be able to, but something smaller could break. It beats trudging through this snow trying to find another way. And the longer we stay out here, underdressed for the cold, the more dangerous it is.

Julian steps out of the way as I stand in front of the entrance, ready to try. I plant my left foot, swing around, and extend my leg, channeling my strength into a single strike. I kick straight into the center of the wooden door. It flies open and bangs into the wall, the wood waving back and forth from the force. But nothing breaks.

Julian and I stare at the opening and then at each other.

"Maybe it was frozen shut," he says. But he rubs his knuckles. He doesn't believe his own words because we had no issue getting the door open before.

No, someone was holding it shut, then heard that we were about to kick it in.

I grab my dagger from under my pants leg and hand it to Julian, then I pull out the long blade hidden in the breast of my dinner jacket.

I motion my head for Julian to fall in after me. Wordlessly, he follows. I regret not changing into armor before I moved the body, but my blade will have to be enough.

As we walk inside, the kitchen is darker than when we left. No light comes from the pantry.

That's not a coincidence, either.

I'm about to tell Julian to get back when something flies at my face. I dive against the wall, taking Julian with me. We fall back just as a dagger clatters onto the ground.

It missed me by an inch.

Heart pounding, I check Julian, but he taps three times on my thigh, giving me the all-clear signal.

We recover just as the door to the kitchens swings open. In the sliver of light, I catch the edge of a white robe fleeing down the hallway. A ceremonial robe from the temple of truth.

XXXV

Kerasea

I am doomed. I turn on my side, unable to get to sleep yet again. It's been hours since Torren walked me to my room, but I keep replaying everything we said in the tower. I don't know why he wants an alliance, and my ignorance here is a recurring problem. I don't know who is committing murder. And I also don't know what the omen means.

I have racked my mind trying to recall my father's teachings on unusual signs. I wish Mirial were here because she'd know. As High Priestess, I'm supposed to be the font of knowledge, but my father couldn't teach me every single thing about politics, leading the temple, *and* divining from the god in my short time as an acolyte. And we're far from the Forum, where there are books and scrolls to help me.

Wait.

We passed a library when the Praetorian gave me a tour of the palace. There could be a copy of *The Compendium of Signs*.

Technically, an almanac of omens is never supposed to leave the temple, but the king might've had one, as there is a divining room in Jubilee.

With no time to lose, I spring from bed and throw a velvet robe over my black nightgown. Then I hike up the hem and strap my dagger to my thigh. Torren told me not to leave my room, but I have to. I have to find the meaning.

I lock my door, then knock on his, but there's no answer. I pause. Either he's a sound sleeper or he's not in there.

I hesitate, torn between proceeding and going back to my room, but I need that book. There's no decision to be made—I have to go alone.

The palace is silent as I take the main staircase to the first floor.

Although the east and west hallways are lit, individual rooms are dark, and the shadows are vicious. Walking these halls is far worse than the first night because now I know that there is, undeniably, a killer among us.

My skin prickles, my muscles tensed. I breathe in shallow inhales, listening for the telltale sound of being followed.

Jubilee is full of death. Paintings and busts are missing at intervals, destroyed during the Crimson Night. All that remains are indentations and smudges of what used to be. The empty spaces are reminders of power lost, warnings that everyone, even those at the top, can fall.

Each of my steps echoes like a whisper to turn around and go back to my room. To lock and bar my door. The only thing Torren asked of me was to stay alive. And this is inviting the opposite.

I freeze, unable to push myself any farther, the danger making my limbs leaden. Someone could be hiding in any one of these darkened rooms.

I tip my head back and groan, running a hand down my hair. Torren has completely invaded my mind. I'm just going to the library.

Because I need to be useful in this alliance. I have to find answers.

Shaking off my fear, I force my feet to work until I reach the towering doors. I pull on the cold, gilded handle, then enter the library and light every oil lamp I can find.

Now brightened, the space is far larger than I thought it would be. The room is ornate with carved molding and gold everywhere, the ceiling painted blue with a fleur-de-lis in every coffer. I sigh. It's beautiful, but this is massive. An entire wall is covered in a fresco of an Elusian whose dreams foretold the future.

Gods, I could use that power right about now, since it could take hours to locate the book—if it's here at all.

I tamp down my panic and start to search the central bookcases to my left. *The Compendium of Signs* is gold plated, and thus should stand out, but that's not necessarily the case for a copy.

I scan the shelves looking for the title. The freestanding bookcases are so tall that I can't see over them. Each holds well over three hundred tomes. I move quickly, but there are thousands upon thousands of spines to read, and some are unmarked.

My temple has a library, but it is nothing compared to this. The only repository I've been in that's larger is the Great Library of Pryor in the Forum. It sits across from the Senate Hall, but it serves all the people of the republic. This served one man, the last Elusian king.

I walk down a row filled with books on the history of the kingdom, running my fingers along the old leather bindings. These were written centuries ago, the actors and scribes long dead, but the knowledge remains. There's something both sad and comforting in that.

Each volume in this section is filled with the works of the Elusians. The original rulers used their abilities for good, but as so often happens, the monarchy descended into selfish desires, murder, and madness. I'm surprised the books weren't dumped into the Tiger the way the Elusians' bodies were sent down the river.

The heads of the royal family were kept and placed on pikes atop the Tullanium jail. Mine should've been there as well.

I shake off the thought, but it's far more difficult to avoid my blood in this palace. Every painting, every room is a remnant of them. Of who I really am.

When I come to the end of the aisle, the Praetorian stands there, his muscular body blocking my way.

My heart leaps into my throat as I scream. Then I cover my mouth as the sound echoes.

He's still in a suit, with his jacket on this time, but he could be mistaken for a chiseled statue. I'm not sure how long he was watching me, but it doesn't look like he just arrived.

"What are you doing here, High Priestess?" His voice rumbles with anger.

I point to my own chest and blink. "What am *I* doing here? What are *you* doing here? Aside from scaring me to death?"

He shrugs. "I saw the light."

I stare at him. He's standing in a shadow so I can't read his eyes, but his voice rings true. It's just not the whole truth.

I try to will my heart to slow, but it doesn't help that I was just thinking about the Elusian slaughter. I was wrong about the Praetorian not being discreet. Apparently, he can move soundlessly if he wants to.

"Is that so?" I ask.

The Praetorian shakes his head. "You didn't answer my question. It's rude to continue to ask your own."

I look around, trying to remember what he asked, but it's difficult to recall while trying not to faint. "What didn't I answer?"

"What you're doing here. I seem to remember asking you to stay in your room when I saw you last."

I sigh and decide to tell him the truth, although I'm loath to admit it. "I thought there might be a *Compendium of Signs* here. I need to find out what the split omen means before the conclave begins tomorrow. I can't tell the Senate about it without being able to explain the meaning."

His eyes stay locked on mine, his mouth still. I hold his gaze but then notice that he's standing oddly. His arm is bent, hiding something behind his back.

"What do you have?" I ask.

He pulls out a crumpled white robe lined with gold. It's balled in his fist, but it's clearly from my temple. "I found this."

I tilt my head as I touch the edge, confusion crashing into me. "Where?"

"By the kitchens."

That makes no sense. I shake my head. "What was it doing there?"

"I was hoping you knew."

So he did seek me out. He noticed the light in the library because he was already looking for me. But I have larger issues than him stalking me. Why was there a temple robe anywhere near the kitchens? And why does he have it?

Now that he's out of the shadows, I can see his eyes. They're troubled. We're allegedly allies now, yet he keeps me at arm's length.

"What aren't you telling me?" I ask.

He parts his lips, but then his expression closes off and he shrugs. "I just found it highly unusual for one of your robes to be lying on the floor. I thought I'd return it, since I'm sure you need it."

"I appreciate the thought, but it's not one of mine," I say.

Surprise flashes on his face, and he tips his chin. "This is a robe from the temple of truth, is it not?"

We wear white, justices sit in black, and the temple of protection is cloaked in bloodred. There's no chance of mistaking robes.

"It looks to be, but it's not a High Priestess robe. Mine are embroidered with the eternal flame and the sword of knowledge. This is plain." I point to the solid gold of the hem. "It's a standard priest's robe."

His jaw moves like he's physically chewing over my words, his gaze tight on me. He's dancing around something.

"Did you actually find it by the kitchens?" I ask.

He nods. "I did."

"I don't... I don't understand why it would even be at Jubilee. Maybe former priests left it behind. Or I can ask Zel if she accidentally packed the wrong robe, but I don't know why she would and then how it would get there..."

I trail off because once again it feels like I'm far behind in a game of bock. And I'm so tired of this feeling. First the murders, then the Senate coup, and now this.

"Swear it, Kerasea," the Praetorian says.

What? I blink.

He leans closer to me. "Swear on your god that the robe isn't yours and you don't know why it's here at the conclave."

I narrow my eyes because I don't know why he needs this, but he looks desperate for my oath. His gaze is intense, and the veins on his neck pulse. Still, I hesitate. I don't take swearing on the god lightly because using the divine's name in vain is a good way to get burned.

"I need to know it's real," the Praetorian says, stepping toward me. "If we are to remain allies."

It's a striking admission—he can't tell when I'm lying. But it's difficult to focus on anything aside from how near he is. Warmth radiates from his chest even though he smells like snow. His sapphire eyes shine as they stare at only me. His gaze is like a beam of moonlight.

I swallow hard, but I raise two fingers and sign in the air. "I swear on the god of truth that this robe is not mine and that I have no idea why it is at Jubilee."

He holds still but then slowly nods. Instead of looking relieved, he only seems more troubled.

"Are you going to tell me what it is you suspect I did?" I ask.

His eyes flash with respect, then he presses his lips together. "I was attacked tonight. By someone wearing this."

"What?" The word carries, echoing in the enormous library. I lower my voice. "What do you mean, 'attacked'? When?"

I scan him for wounds, cuts, but it's hard to tell with him wearing a black suit. I don't see any bleeding, though. My heart pounds, but it's only because I'm so shocked.

"A few minutes ago. So, imagine my surprise at finding you out of your room."

I can't stop shaking my head. A few minutes ago? That means he was searching for his assailant and found me here. That explains why he looked at me the way he did, but why would someone wear this? Who would dare attack him to begin with?

An icy feeling grips me. The only reason someone would leave this behind would be to frame me. Whoever it was simply didn't realize my robes are embellished.

Or they thought I'd be dead before he could notice.

"Why would someone frame me?" I ask aloud.

He nods and leans closer to me. "That is exactly what we need to discover."

XXXVI.

Torren

Kerasea stares out of the window of my bedroom, trying not to watch me undress. Every now and then, she blushes.

It's unexpected.

After the attack, I sent Julian to the ground floor to search for the assailant while I took the first floor, but I doubt he'll find them. The person likely went into hiding. And I didn't want to let Kerasea out of my sight.

I slip my armor over my undershirt and pull the leather bindings as I replay the exchange in the library. Kera's keeping a secret—I'm sure of it—but she swore on her god that it wasn't her robe, and no priest takes that lightly. So where does that leave me?

Someone is still trying to frame the High Priestess, but their purpose remains unclear. Terrance is the main suspect, but striking at me and framing Kera makes little sense when he is now Senate Leader and she has recused herself. If he suspects we know the truth, that could be reason enough, but it feels like I'm missing a vital piece of information. It sits right at the edge of my mind, but I can't get there yet.

I place my sabine at my hip. Dressed and now armored, I grab my manacles. Kerasea eyes them when they scrape on the wood of the bureau, but she stays silent as I slip them onto my belt.

Thinking through the assault kept me from noticing how her long black hair hangs down to her waist. How she touches her full lips when she's worried. But it's hard not to look now.

I step to the door, but she moves at the same time. She brushes against me, her velvet robe soft as rabbit fur against my bare arm.

"Sorry," she says.

"My fault."

And it is. I'm allowing her to draw too much of my attention. My duty requires me to focus on my role as investigator. Regardless of what Julian thinks of this nation, the republic is better than the alternatives. I have been outside of Pryor. I fought in the wilderness where there is no law, no justice, no elections, where might equals right. The Senate is far from perfect, but the institution ended Elusian oppression and keeps worse at bay. It is worth saving.

I take a steadying breath as I lock my door. At least we won't have to go far. My first interview is with Kerasea's servant.

Earlier today and yesterday, I questioned the girl, but I only asked a few surface inquiries because she is, in fact, a child. But now I need to find out who had access to this robe. Unlike Kerasea, her servant girl doesn't lie well, so it will be easier to get to the truth.

Kera knocks on her door. She already agreed to assist me with this.

"Zel, it is me," she says.

"Just a moment." The voice behind the door sounds odd, panicked, and very awake.

Kerasea's brow knits, and her eyes dart over to me.

"Does your servant normally instruct you to wait?" I ask.

She shakes her head. "No, but this has been a frightening time for her. I've told her to bar her door and only answer to me."

The door opens, but only enough for Zel to stick her face out. Her eyes are so large and wide-set that they remind me of stags I've hunted.

"Yes, Excellency?" Zel is in nightclothes, dressed for bed.

"We need to speak," Kerasea says.

Everything in the High Priestess's voice and manner acknowledges the strangeness of this interaction.

Zel nods. "I'll be right in."

I raise a hand, looking at Zel. "In your chambers, please."

Kera looks over her shoulder at me. "The wardrobe is in mine."

"But the trunks are in hers."

I didn't see any in the room when Kerasea had her door open earlier. And I have to figure out what the girl is hiding.

Zel's eyes go even wider. "My room is… It's quite messy."

"That's all right, Zel," Kerasea says.

The girl takes a deep breath and nods a couple of times. "Hold on just a moment. I need to move the chair and some other things out of the way so that I can open the door."

She shuts the door, and I wonder if this girl could have worn the robe and thrown the dagger. It would explain her obvious guilt and strange behavior. She had the time to flee up the stairs and change. But surely she doesn't have the strength to hold the door closed on two grown men.

"You ask her." I hand the robe to Kerasea.

Her eyes flash with surprise, but she nods and tucks the fabric under her arm.

Again, I'm taken aback by her willingness. Perhaps she meant it when she agreed to align with me. But looking at Kera in a new light has its own problems. The draw I've been feeling becomes an undeniable magnet, and that's a distraction. Even if she's not the same girl she once was, she still caused the ruin of my family.

This is a temporary alliance. Nothing more.

I take a step away and stand at attention.

A few moments later, a chair scrapes the floor, then the door opens. The room is, in fact, a mess. In the legions, everything we carry must be folded and put in place. This girl has never heard of the concept.

Or maybe the whole point is chaos so that it's harder to find something amiss.

Her room is as large as mine, as they are all guest bedrooms of the old king, but hers is cramped. Makeup, a clothes press, books, and linens are strewn around the room as if it were hit by a windstorm. The window is open, but that wasn't the cause.

There is an en suite bathroom to the left. I step toward it.

"What are you doing, sir?" she asks.

"Investigating," I say.

She doesn't say anything in return. I open the door and look around. The bathroom is also messy, but it all seems like the normal items a teenage girl would have. The tub is empty—no weapons or obvious vials of poison in here, although there are plenty of terra-cotta pots and glass jars. I could toss the room and conduct a thorough search, but it appears unlikely I'd find anything of interest, and Kerasea would likely object anyway. Right now we are in accord. It's best to keep it that way.

I walk back into the bedchamber. Kerasea sits in an armchair across from Zel, who perches on the side of the bed, looking embarrassed but not guilty. She is patting Zel's hand. Kerasea looks at me and stops. Then she leans closer to her servant.

"Zel, this was found by the kitchens," Kerasea says. "Have you seen it before?"

She shows her servant the robe I found, but interestingly, she doesn't mention that I was attacked. It's the same way I questioned her earlier.

"That is a priest's robe, Excellency." Zel looks completely confused as to why Kerasea would ask.

"Did you bring this to Jubilee?" Kerasea asks.

Zel shakes her head. "No."

I watch her closely. She's being honest, but she's also hiding something. Her shoulders curve in, her fingers fidgeting.

"Were you in this room all night?" I ask.

The girl starts breathing like a rabbit, completely undone by one question. She shakes terribly, and notably, she wasn't this nervous when I questioned her about Antinous or Eyo.

Kerasea reaches out and rests a hand on the girl's arm again. "It's all right, Zel. Just respond honestly and everything will be fine."

Zel nods but still fidgets, not looking at me. "I left for dinner and to undress the High Priestess. That is all."

My mind shifts at the words "undress" and "High Priestess" in the same sentence. But I push aside thoughts of Kerasea naked.

"Do you have other robes in this room?" I ask. "High Priestess's or otherwise?"

Zel shakes her head. "All the ones we have are hanging in the High Priestess's wardrobe."

I look at each of them in turn. If they are both telling the truth, then this is yet another attempt to frame Kerasea for murder.

But why go to the lengths of attacking me just to frame her? An attack on the Praetorian is an attack on the Senate. It is treason and attempted murder. Someone would need a compelling reason to take that risk.

Suddenly, my mind races. Unless *I* wasn't the target.

The memory of standing outside in the snow, arguing with Julian plays in my mind. He was in even thinner clothes than I was, and likely would have succumbed to the frost first.

Was he the real target?

Molten panic pours down my back as I think it through.

Julian is well liked, but he voted in a single resolution and that was to proceed with the conclave. His vote, like Kerasea's abstention, ultimately robbed Senators Paolo and Foreau of power. What if the dagger wasn't aimed at me? Did one of them try to kill Julian and frame Kerasea?

Something about the idea sinks its claws into me. A blade thrown, Julian dead or wounded, and I'd find the temple robe. Instead of continuing in my alliance with the High Priestess, I'd pursue her relentlessly and follow the clues left for the other murders as well.

Maybe the High Priestess isn't the only one in danger. Maybe Julian is, too.

And he's alone now, searching for the assailant.

"Excuse me, please," I say, standing.

Both Kerasea and Zel stare at me.

"Lock up the remaining robes, then bar your doors — and this time actually stay in your rooms until breakfast," I add. "Do not leave under any circumstances."

I wait, looking at Kera, who slowly drops her head into a nod, then I grab the doorknob, nearly knocking over a variety of items on the bureau in my rush to leave. Julian is alone on the ground floor because I sent him there. I have to find him.

I only pray he's still alive when I do.

XXXVII

Kerasea

T he door slams shut and Zel shudders—as well she should. She
just lied to the Praetorian, and I need to know why. Wherever
she was, whatever she was doing, she was not in her room all night.
But I wasn't about to give her lie away in front of Torren.

Once he put on his armor, any softness in his features vanished,
and he became the dreaded Praetorian once more. As we walked
into Zel's room, his gaze sharpened on her. She became a suspect.
While I could shield her from investigation at the temple, I can't here.
If he found evidence at Jubilee, he could torture her, even over my
objections.

And then, just as he was closing in on her, he left, fleeing so
quickly that a sea of questions built in his wake.

I stare at the teacup he almost knocked over. It sits innocuously
on the corner of her dresser, next to some used plates and silverware,
in a terra-cotta mug.

"Since when did you begin drinking tea, Zel?" I ask.

She has wrinkled her nose, calling it "leaf water," whenever her parents urged her to take a cup at our communal meals.

"Oh…um, we have to rise so early for the conclave." She rubs her finger and thumb together, and it's all I can do not to sigh at such an obvious tell. It's how I knew she was lying about staying in her room.

"I see," I say, walking up to it and placing my fingers around its rim. "But the water inside is hot."

Her eyes dart around. "It's a nighttime tea."

I nod—at least that much is true. It smells like honey and lavender in here. But the fact that it's hot sends alarm bells ringing in my head. The tea and boiling water would've been procured from the kitchens. Recently. Around the same time I was in the library.

The same time someone attacked the Praetorian.

I lean closer to her. "You truly don't know anything about the robe? Or the attack on the Praetorian?"

Her mouth falls open. "He was attacked?"

Her voice is full of genuine surprise, which means that whomever she is covering for didn't tell her the truth. It's best to let her sit with that. Silence can force out confessions like a cold press.

I rise from my seat. "I'm sure he will interview you again tomorrow, but tell no one about the attack in the meantime. That is my order." I pause and stare her in the eyes.

She squirms, but she nods.

"Swear your silence, Zel. On the god of truth." I take a page from Torren's book, because it was clever.

"I…I swear," she says.

"You should get some rest," I say.

"Yes, Excellency."

I glance at the tea once more as I leave her room, suspicions building in me, then I shut the door and stop in the hall.

My shoulders droop. My young servant just lied to me several times. She knows who had the robe, but more than that—there had been someone else in her room. Who? And why would she lie for them? Money, perhaps, but her family has been loyal to the temple for decades and does well enough. First love? But there is no one here her age. Not that age matters to a young heart…or to some men.

As I unlock my door, I wonder if I should disclose what I know to the Praetorian. It's what a true ally would do, and he'd have theories on why Zel would lie and who she would cover for that we could discuss together. But I shake my head at myself. Until I'm certain he won't brutalize her, I won't have her harmed over a lie, especially because she wasn't the one who attacked him. Her surprise was genuine—she didn't know.

I slip inside my chambers and bar my door. I take off my velvet robe, lie down again, and smother the light. The candle is still smoking when I realize I forgot all about *The Compendium of Signs*—the whole reason I left my room to begin with. I still need to find the meaning of the omen, but the Praetorian said under no circumstances should we leave our rooms. The only choice left is to continue to hide the omen until I can decipher its meaning.

My stomach turns. At this rate, I'm not even sure we will all still be alive tomorrow morning. Someone wants me dead or in chains, and that someone was bold enough to attack the Praetorian to do it.

But where did Torren run off to? He looked so pale, so *human* as he fled. What could have been so important?

I lie awake with my eyes closed, but sleep won't come. Nearly half an hour later, I'm still listening for the sound of the Praetorian returning safely to his room. And then I sit up and hold my breath because I did just catch something. It was the murmur of a hushed voice.

A grown woman's voice.

I think it came from Zel's room, but it could've also come from the Praetorian's. Yet I know he hasn't returned to it.

And then I don't hear anything else. Did I imagine it, or does one of them have a woman in their bedchamber?

XXXVIII.

Torren

I run down to the ground floor and call out for Julian.
No response.

Fear slickens my palms, but I need to keep calm. This palace has a massive footprint; he may not have heard me. But I sent him alone after a dangerous assailant. There is another possibility for his lack of response.

I swallow the lump in my throat and brace myself. If the worst happened to him, it would be all my fault, but I have to know. Now is not the time for cowardice or hesitation.

I begin to search.

Lamps illuminate the halls at intervals, but it's far darker down here than on the upper floors. I grab a torch and walk with it in case his body is on the ground.

Gods...he could be on the floor.

My pulse pounds in my throat, but I force myself to breathe, to lose all emotion. I lean on my training. I am nothing more than the

Praetorian, searching for a missing person.

I sweep the halls from right to left, looking for the sheen of a blood trail.

"Julian!" I sharply whisper.

No signs of blood or struggle. Nothing at all.

I follow the hall into the thermal baths. As I open the door, I keep my back to the wall and proceed slowly, walking through the entry room, the changing room, and into the tepidarium.

Then my heart stops. I see him.

There, across the lake-like pool, is Julian. Not drowned or stabbed, just searching with his back to the wall, like me.

Relief floods through me, making my chest numb. He's alive. He's unharmed.

My heart hammers in my rib cage, and I rush over to him. "Thank the gods."

"Nice to see you, too." He laughs. Then he looks me over. "You seem...surprised to see me." He pauses, his smile fading. "Well, that's not good."

I shake my head at his levity, but now that I found him, I'm trembling.

"I finished sweeping the armory, the servants' quarters, and the smaller rooms of the baths," he says. "Did you find her?"

I nod. "Kerasea was in the library. It wasn't her, though."

His eyebrows rise as high as they can go.

"She swore on her god," I say. "And the robe belonged to a standard priest—it wasn't one of hers."

Julian's eyes narrow as he stares at me. "And you believe that—despite finding her on the first floor?"

Slowly, I nod because it sounds remarkably foolish. But I have interrogated people for years. I felt her honesty and shock. It was real.

"I never saw who did it." I sigh.

Julian shakes his head like he's clearing water from his ears. "Tor, what is going on? You have hated the Vestals for as long as I've known you. And now, suddenly, you doubt yourself? You trust her?"

"I am conducting an investigation. It's too convenient the robe was left there — the same as the weapon in the fountain. She is many things, but she's not sloppy."

I try to sound logical, not defensive. His questions are valid and nothing I haven't asked myself.

"It's rather convenient it *wasn't* a High Priestess robe," he counters. "Just as the sickle knife was too convenient. And whatever else you found that you haven't disclosed to me."

I look away. At times, Julian knows me too well.

He sighs loudly, and it echoes in the space.

"All right, let's say it wasn't Kerasea," he continues. "If not her, then who?"

"I'm not sure yet. It could've been any of the senators' sentries, and I think her servant is hiding something. No...I'm certain of it."

Julian quirks an eyebrow. "The teenage girl?"

"That one."

He sighs again like I'm a fool to believe Kera, which puts me in the terrible position of defending her.

"River of Death, Julian. You were the one trying to convince me of Kerasea's innocence!"

"In that she didn't kill Verhardt or Antinous. Don't make the mistake of trusting her, Tor. You'll end up discharged or with a blade in your back."

I shake my head. "I'm not the one who needs to worry."

Julian tilts his head, and then he pales.

"Think about it," I say. "Foreau and Paolo have reason to bring you both down. Your vote made the conclave continue, and her abstention gave Terrance control of the Senate. Revenge is a great motivator."

Julian runs both palms over his face, but he pauses to consider my theory with his hand over his mouth. "They believe I'll run for Verhardt's empty seat, though. If elected, I'd be new guard like them, and they have always been able to overlook vendettas when it suits their interests. Medea hates Terrance, and yet they're aligned — which is suspicious behavior in and of itself." He stares into the distance. "I suppose it would actually make a certain amount of sense for Foreau to get rid of me."

"Interesting," I say. I've never heard him say anything negative about Senator Foreau. But we need to consider every possible angle.

"There's a rumor Foreau, like his father, is taking bribes from Arthago. If that's true, he would not want the general's nephew on the Council."

Foreau is taking money from our greatest enemy? Julian said it so casually that I'm slow to react. He's accusing Senator Foreau of the deepest treason with nothing more than a shrug.

"Is this only conjecture?" I ask.

Julian nods. "It was just whispers and rumor until he opposed the declaration of war today. It's an odd vote for someone worried about them advancing on his own coast."

Foreau has been a senator for two years. He is a nobleman from a family who owns half of the fourth province, but unlike Suh, Eyo, and even Paolo, he never served as a sentry. Instead, his renown came from sending his private merchant ships to Hadrian's aid during a battle in the Hundred Year War.

Foreau was hailed as a patriot for shouldering the cost and swept into office after the death of the last senator, but he never bled for the republic. Could Arthagian silver have tempted him? He certainly has the strength to drown Antinous, but then again, so do my half sisters.

"Why would he have killed Eyo, though?" Julian asks. "They were allies."

I blink at him. "Who says it's the same person?"

Julian closes his eyes, and his whole body appears to deflate. "So what do we do now?"

I look around, but there's nothing to do. The trail has long gone cold.

"We get some sleep," I say.

He gives me a quizzical look because he doesn't believe I'll give up this easily—and he is correct. But we need to regroup, and I need to go back to Antinous's papers.

It's time to examine the affairs of Foreau.

XXXIX

Kerasea

The five senators are still alive for the start of the conclave this morning, which makes this the best of the last three days. That is, if you don't consider the fact that someone in this room tried to kill the Praetorian and frame me.

I shift in my chair in the throne room.

"A word, please, before the start of the conclave," Torren says.

He strides to the center of the room, his armor shining in the sun. Now that we are on the same side, he seems much more human, but that's also a type of danger for me. He is perilously attractive, and the last thing I need is to be one of his broken-hearted one-night stands. We can work together, but I need to keep my distance for a great number of reasons.

"An unfortunate event took place last night," Tor begins.

I try not to react, but is he really going to disclose the attack by the kitchens and how he found the robe?

I grip the arms of my chair, regretting that I didn't question Zel this morning. I wanted to put her at ease and make her think I'm unaware of her lies. But because of that, I don't have additional knowledge as to what she was hiding or who wore the temple robe.

"What was that, Praetorian?" Terrance asks. He now tries to be the first to speak at every opportunity, although his volume is more reasonable.

"The cook took his own life."

The senators murmur their surprise and questions, but they're not nearly as confused as I feel. The cook at Jubilee? Torren never said anything about this.

"Was he a person of interest in Eyo's potential poisoning?" Foreau asks, steepling his jeweled fingers in front of his lips.

I was surprised to see him and Paolo back in the throne room, but I suppose a day of protest was enough to make their point.

Torren nods. "Indeed, he was. But I did not have the opportunity to interrogate him before death took him."

"Still, an act like that surely speaks to his guilt." Suh rubs his goatee and taps his cane.

The Praetorian tips his head, neither agreeing nor disagreeing. "Unfortunately, we'll never know for certain. I will continue my investigation; however, I wanted to alert you all to this turn of events."

"If the cook did poison our dear fallen colleague, further investigation will be futile," Terrance says. "We will simply have to wait for a healer to confirm whether or not there was foul play." Terrance folds his hands like that is the end of the inquiry.

Terrance has now urged us to drop the matter twice. Surely he must know how guilty that makes him appear.

Torren sets his gaze on the new Senate Leader. "If it were poison, and I must proceed as if it were, murdering a senator was an action so bold that he might well have had coconspirators at Jubilee."

The senators exchange glances, the thought striking a chord.

"Gather your evidence, Praetorian," Medea says, waving her fingers. "I motion that we convene the Verity Guild on the cook's guilt as soon as we return to the capital."

"You mean after the tribunal on your nephew's rebellion," Terrance corrects her.

Medea moves her mouth just slightly before she shakes the expression. "Obviously."

That's right, Trajan Lowe is Medea's favorite nephew. The Council voting to convene the Verity Guild on his guilt sent shock waves through the capital.

Suh stands. "I second the motion."

"I support," Foreau says.

"Supported," Paolo says.

"The motion passes unanimously," Terrance concludes.

All of a sudden, the Council now believes it was poison, and yet they all remain calm because the suspect is dead?

My head is spinning. I will now have to try a dead man for the second tribunal? That can't be right. It's not even possible.

"Forgive me," I say, "but with the cook already deceased, who stands trial?"

The accused is the one who stands before the Verity Guild for questioning. The Praetorian will present the case, the Chief Judge will ask questions, and it is my job as High Priestess to call to the god of truth, whose heavy presence coerces honesty.

Terrance sniffs. "There will be no accused to stand, but the Praetorian will present his case, and the guild will deliver its finding to the people."

Suh nods. "A verdict is necessary for Senator Eyo's memory, the Council, as well as for the cook's lineage."

Because they strip everything from the families convicted of high treason.

An expression flashes on the Praetorian's face, and I remember this all happened to him because of his father's treachery. It was, of course, my testimony that led to the conviction, but there is only so much guilt I can feel when I spoke the truth.

His gaze finds mine, trouble in his eyes, and my chest squeezes with true sorrow for what he must've endured. It's a harsh sentence, imposed so that citizens are not tempted to commit treason to better their families' lives. Yet looking at him now, I'm not sure it was just. He was only a child and innocent of the crimes he paid the price for.

"As you will it." Torren swallows hard and then bows to the Council.

I twist the bangle on my wrist, reliving the day Torren appeared before the guild. It all happened so long ago that I'd pushed it to the back of my mind, but he came before them to beg for his father's life. I'd gasped at his brave offer to take his father's place—to be tortured and die in the arena—but my father heard me. My gasp drew his attention as well as his ire. I covered my gasp with a laugh and then, to my horror, others joined in.

My father was satisfied, but Torren had just stood there with his chin raised until he glared up at me. I never got the chance to explain it or apologize, and now it is so far in the past that it doesn't seem worthwhile to pick at old scabs. But perhaps I owe him an explanation.

I'll seek him out after this.

I've just resolved the matter in my mind when I notice Senator Foreau eyeing both of us. Goose bumps coat my skin. He says nothing, but from the slight raise of his chin, I can tell he knows there's a connection between us. His eyes shine like a wolf's at night as a smile plays on his lips.

I'm left with one thought: has our tentative alliance already been viewed as a threat?

XL

Torren

Fifty resolutions are voted upon in ten hours as I stand guard. I've casually watched the Senate while trying to figure out a way to exonerate the cook.

If the Verity Guild is convened, he will be found guilty. As Praetorian, I am supposed to vote in favor of every high treason conviction unless there is insurmountable evidence to the contrary.

In this case, there won't be. The healer will confirm Eyo was poisoned, and because I said the cook took his own life, that will be the end of the inquiry. The Senate wants to tarnish his memory and punish his family in order to hide their own crimes.

I cannot stand for it. This isn't justice.

But it is too late to claim the cook's death was foul play. And it's not like corpses can talk.

My eyes fall on the High Priestess. She can divine whether or not a person was murdered.

That is my way out. *She* is my way out.

She catches me staring at her, and a blush creeps up her neck. The corner of my lips rises involuntarily, but then Foreau slams his fist on the table.

I didn't find anything in Antinous's papers on him accepting bribes from Arthago, but that information wouldn't be in the Senate's ledgers. I'd need to search Foreau's personal accounts, and for that, I'd need unfettered access to his room.

"This is an outrage," he says.

They've been debating this year's fishing regulations—specifically, the size of the catch to be turned over to the republic. Not normally a hotbed topic, so this must be about more than fish.

"Already our fishermen must forfeit the most lucrative part of their daily catch." Foreau's voice reverberates through the room as the sunlight reflects off his bald head. "They are met at the docks, their boats searched by the sentries as if they're criminals."

He, of course, owns most of those boats.

"Now, if this regulation passes, my fishermen will soon be as poor as the farmers in the third province."

Terrance stands, his face reddening. "Have a care for who you insult, sir."

"I would never insult the man who crowned himself King of Pryor." Foreau smiles and then stares at Terrance, daring him to react.

Terrance skirts around the table, the end of his toga over his arm as he closes the distance to Foreau. The Senate Leader is taller and athletic for his age, but Foreau is twenty-five years younger and the fittest of the senators. What he loses to Terrance in height, he makes up for in muscle.

"Bold speech from a man who takes money from an enemy king." Terrance wags his finger in Foreau's face.

I think Foreau may strike the Senate Leader—as I would, given the insult. I place my hand on my sabine, but it's not like I can cut down a senator. I cannot protect them from each other.

Foreau softly chuckles, and then he stares at Terrance. "That's all you have? Debunked rumors of my family's wealth? You are the one who needs to watch your back, Terrance, lest you meet the same end as the Elusians. Pryor has a specific way of dealing with tyrants."

There's not a sound in the throne room. Julian stares from the clerk's desk, and Kerasea sits frozen with her eyes wide as saucers. Suh casually leans back and takes in the argument while Paolo nervously spins his ring. Medea smiles to herself and then clears the expression.

What was that? Why was she amused?

I can't remember the last time senators threatened each other's lives directly. Certainly not during my time at the conclave, although, historically, they have attacked and even killed one another in the Forum. That was decades ago, though, when they were squabbling over crumbs from the imperial table. There hasn't been violence inside the Senate in twenty years.

Just when I think this might come to blows, though, Foreau turns on his heels and walks out, laughing.

"I move to censure Senator Foreau," Terrance says once the man is gone.

It's an empty gesture when senators are elected for life, but it used to mean something. When Pryor was a kingdom, three censures by the Council would lead to a recommendation of removal by the king.

"Seconded," Suh says.

Paolo draws a breath. "Opposed."

The two elder statesmen look at Paolo in disgust, and he shrinks slightly in his chair. Then all three of them turn toward Medea. If she opposes the censure, they will deadlock. But she stares at the doorway.

"Medea, are you with us?" Terrance's voice is laced with annoyance and condescension.

She doesn't move her head, although her mouth shifts slightly. "The motion passes three to one."

There's something in her eyes when she stares at Terrance. Something sharp with teeth. But when I look again, it's gone. Just like her smile earlier.

"That brings our day to a close," Julian says.

The senators all variously stretch or slump in their seats. Kerasea releases a long breath.

Now they will bathe, change for supper, and then dine together for three hours as if they didn't antagonize one another all day. As if they don't truly despise one another.

The senators move to leave—Terrance and Suh first. I catch Kerasea as she rises from her chair.

"A moment, if you would, Excellency," I say.

She smiles, this time in a genuine way. I can't help but notice how it lights up her face, like she glows from within. "Of course, Praetorian."

But I also don't miss how Paolo and Medea both watch us as they speak to their pages. Julian also eyes us as he files paperwork. I suppose we are standing half a step too close.

"I'd like to show you something in the baths, if you'd follow me," I say.

This time of day, there won't be anyone using them.

Kerasea blinks, confused, and then clears her throat. "Certainly."

Medea stares at Kerasea and then me before she finally exits the throne room. Suspicion creeps along the edges of my mind. Why would she be interested in our conversation at all? I suppose an alliance between members of the Verity Guild is notable to all the senators.

Of course, there's another alternative: she thought we would be enemies by today.

XLI.

Kerasea

The baths are a marvel of Elusian magic, drawing hot, cold, and temperate from a time long before we understood engineering. But that's not why Torren wanted me to come down here. We stand in the frigidarium by the rushing water so that we can't be overheard.

Not compared to the way I noticed a woman's hushed voice in his room last night.

My stomach twists, and I look away. I'm being ridiculous. What difference does it make if he had someone waiting for him in his bed? Why would I even care?

"Are you all right?" the Praetorian asks.

"I... Were you speaking to someone in your room last night?" I ask.

Confusion clouds his face, and I already know it wasn't him. My heart sinks, because then it was Zel, and somehow that's worse. Who could she have been talking with? The only other woman here is

Medea, though there are also servants. Maybe it was innocuous—just her asking for more tea. But I doubt it.

"What did you hear?" he asks.

We stand next to the waterfall, and mist gathers on his armor and in his raven hair. He glistens as he leans closer to me.

"A woman's voice. But only for a moment and then not again for the rest of the night, so maybe I didn't even hear it."

"I assure you there was no woman in my bed last night," he says with a laugh.

Heat flushes my cheeks, and I stare at the waterfall. Curse my face. I might save the Senate some trouble and die of embarrassment right here.

"Kera..." he says.

The last thing I want to do is look at him, because I'm sure I am red as a rose. But the silence lingers.

Reluctantly, I look up. Amusement decorates his lips. He stares down at me, his features softer than I've ever seen. His full attention with that little smile is intoxicating.

Just a glance feels so intimate—like he's only ever looked at *me* this way. Like he's only ever been kind with me. And unlike with Senator Eyo, this isn't calculated. Tor's gaze shifts to my lips, his eyes mesmerizing. The draw to him is a siren call, and my limbs itch to obey.

I hold still.

He had a reason for asking me here, and it wasn't for this.

"What did you want to speak to me about?" I ask, clearing my throat. It's a rather pathetic attempt to regain some footing.

His brow wrinkles in confusion. Could he have been caught up in the moment as well? Just as I think it, he inhales and stands straighter. "If I gave you the cook's liver, could you divine whether he was murdered or took his own life?"

"What?"

My head hurts from the sudden change in topics and the jarring change in tone. I stare at him like it's a joke, but, of course, he is serious.

"After Senator Eyo died, you said that you could divine whether he was murdered," Torren adds.

Bloody lies. What do I say to this? I can't admit that I fabricated it to cover up my admission. I have no choice but to continue with the charade.

"I would need the whole body—not just the liver." I say a silent prayer that he doesn't have it.

He nods. "I can give that to you."

Of course he can.

I am doomed. It's like I can feel the rope around my neck, but it's just the collar of the temple. I grip my robe and force my breathing to stay steady as I think it through. The Praetorian is a disbeliever. If I put the cook's liver into the eternal flame, nothing will happen, but Torren won't know that. He doesn't understand how I interpret signs from the god.

I take a deep breath. I can play along, but why does he even want this?

"You suspect the cook was murdered even though you said he took his own life?" I ask.

He frowns slightly. "I know he was killed."

'But then why…"

"Someone paid him to take the fall. If I reported that he was murdered after confessing, the Council would've convened the Verity Guild to convict him of high treason."

That is the real story? My heart pounds. So this must be the reason for the blood on his sleeve and why he seemed off when he was in the divining room. And also possibly why he pulled away from me when I touched him. Did he align with me just so he could discern what happened to the cook?

"Why do you care so much about a servant?" I ask. It doesn't match up with his brutal image, that's for sure. "What if he did put the poison in?"

"He didn't. And justice is never served by letting an innocent man take the fall."

In his eyes, there are a million unspoken words. He still believes his father was innocent. I won't be able to change his mind, because it would require changing his heart.

Still, the cook is already dead—there's no worse the Senate can do to him. But maybe that's not who Torren is ultimately worried about.

"You want to protect the cook's family," I whisper.

Torren swallows hard. "Yes."

My heart squeezes. This is a completely different man than the one I thought I knew. This is who Julian is friends with, who the sentries admire and Hadrian respects. I see it now.

I see him.

This is the moment to tell him that I never intended for him to lose everything, but what do I even say? *I'm sorry for what happened* doesn't quite cut it. Not this many years later. *I understand* might work, but I *don't* truly understand—I'll never be able to get my mind around having everything taken from you overnight when you did nothing wrong. *I didn't mean to laugh* seems far beyond the point.

I bite my lip at having nothing good to say.

"I could have you removed for lying to the Senate, you know," I murmur.

Well, that wasn't on the list, yet he looks relieved. Perhaps he also wants to let the past lie.

Tor shrugs. "You won't. We have an alliance, remember?"

There's that smile again. He stares at me and shifts closer, or maybe I moved in—it's hard to tell. The draw to him is undeniable. I stare down at the pools of the frigidarium, finding them suddenly very interesting. I need to do anything other than look at him.

Tor reaches out and places his thumb under my chin. Gently, he raises my face so I have no choice.

Why does something light up inside me when he touches me? Why do I want him closer when it's the worst thing for me?

He stares into my eyes and then at my mouth. My lips part. He's going to kiss me, and I think I might want it. But then, as my eyes drift closed, he backs away. "I'll get you the body after supper."

Thrown by how he cooled off, I'm about to ask what happened. I open my mouth, but then a movement catches my eye. I whip my head to the side. He turns to see what I'm looking at just as the shadow shifts.

Someone was listening in. We were so lost in whatever this is between us that we didn't notice.

Underworld.

He and I exchange glances, and then he runs.

XLII.

Torren

I'd hang whoever designed this palace by their ankles if they weren't long dead. There's no clean line of sight as I run out of the frigidarium. I race through the changing room and then the entry hall of the baths, but the door swings open to the palace before I can get a look at who it was.

Curse the Elusians' grave.

Someone was eavesdropping on Kera and me. Someone may have heard that I suspect the Senate murdered the cook, could have seen how close I was to taking the High Priestess in my arms and kissing her.

I need to find them and silence them—no matter who it was.

My sword bangs against my hip as I enter the hallway off the baths. I look to the left and to the right, but there is no one. The halls are empty.

Son of a jackal.

Someone is either hiding in one of the servant rooms, the armory, or they made it to the stairs.

Footsteps sound around the corner. I back up a step as I grab my sabine, silently pull my sword, and hope the person mistimed their reappearance. I swing back to strike just as an old servant woman comes around the corner. She grabs her chest and falls against the wall, dropping a basket of knitting as I halt my motion.

I stop the sword just in time.

"Where are you coming from?" I ask.

"The kitchens...s-sir," she stammers.

Kerasea comes out of the baths. She freezes, taking in the scene of me with my sword out and the servant I nearly killed.

I place my weapon back in its scabbard. "You are dismissed."

"Thank you, sire. Excuse me, sir," the old woman says, breathing hard.

Kerasea helps her pick up the yarn and then waits until the woman hobbles back into her quarters. With one leg slightly shorter than the other, and being probably seventy, there is no way that woman outran me.

Kerasea shifts closer and leans in.

"Should we search the rooms?" she whispers.

We? Kera stares at me, her eyes earnest, and I'm right back to when I nearly kissed her by the waterfall. I was so drawn to her, but then she seemed uncertain and I stopped myself—just barely. I imagine us sweeping the rooms together, me kicking in the doors and her with her dagger out, but she is not Julian. I would have to protect both her and myself.

No, I need to get her to safety. Someone was bold enough to follow us. I have to protect her first.

"Let me get you back to your room," I say.

It physically pains me to abandon a hunt, but I have higher priorities. I tell myself that no damage was done even if someone managed to overhear the entire conversation. There is no way to prove that the cook confessed. It would be my word against theirs. And I didn't actually kiss the High Priestess; I was only tempted.

But who was it?

It had to be someone fast enough that I couldn't outrun them. That means it wasn't Suh, Terrance, or Medea. It could've been Julian, as he's beaten me in a footrace before, but he'd have no reason to flee.

I highly doubt Paolo is faster than I am, but it could've been Foreau. He left the conclave, and if he's setting up the Faith and attacking Julian, he would have a motive to follow us. If he is bought by Arthago, he'd have a reason to eliminate us all.

As we take the stairs, I realize that now, more than ever, I have to find a way to access his rooms. I'll get the opportunity to search his chambers during dinner tonight or the conclave tomorrow.

Kerasea and I reach the third floor, and although I keep a sharp eye, there's no sign of danger.

"I'll need to speak to Zel again after dinner," I say.

I'd like to interview her now, but we don't have long before we need to appear at supper. And it's imperative I pretend everything is still fine.

Kera shakes her head. "She couldn't have outrun you…"

Her eyes move in a way that reveals she doesn't trust her servant. I tuck away her suspicion in the back of my mind.

"I know, but something was amiss with her last night, and you know it," I whisper.

She bites her lower lip as she grips the embellished sleeves of her robe. "I know, but don't…hurt her."

Sweet divine. That's what she's afraid of—me dismantling a teenage girl?

"I'm not the monster you think I am," I say.

"I don't think you're a monster."

Kerasea speaks plainly, and something about it strikes at my heart. Probably because I am, in fact, a monster. I'd just rather not be.

She stops at her door, and again, we're far too close. I shouldn't have reached out and touched her in the baths, but I couldn't seem to help it. I got so distracted that I didn't notice the shadow until it was too late, and this is the worst place to be caught unaware.

I need to keep my distance for both of our safety.

She opens her door and walks in. Kera hesitates just for a second and then closes the door behind her.

After waiting a moment, I force myself to go to my room and strip off my armor. I don't dwell at all on how she waited before shutting the door. As if she was thinking about inviting me in.

No, I need to stop.

I take a bath at legion speed, and the cold water focuses me. Then, once I'm dry, I dab on sandalwood cologne, glad I already shaved this morning.

I've just put on my suit pants when someone knocks five times in rapid succession. It's Julian. I open my door, still shirtless.

"Ready to face the wolves?" He smiles. Then his grin disappears as he realizes I'm not dressed yet.

"Always," I say.

He steps into the room in yet another white jacket. They're all cut differently but immaculately tailored. He has a full room of expensive clothes in his villa.

Jules closes the door behind himself. I shrug on a white dress shirt, still wondering who was listening in the baths. Foreau does make a certain amount of sense, yet it doesn't ring true.

"I know that face," Julian says. "What's wrong?"

"Someone followed me earlier, and I didn't catch them."

I finish the buttons and grab my blue suit jacket. I had to bring six suits to the mountain because the elite would be scandalized by me repeating an outfit. The suspicious deaths of the clerk and senator are just fine, but gods save fashion.

"That's...unlike you," Jules says slowly. "Followed you where?"

"To the baths."

He raises his eyebrows. "Someone followed you while you were following Kerasea?"

I frown at him. "Talking with her. You heard me ask for a word before we left the throne room. Did you see anyone leave after us?"

"All of the pages, but the conclave was done for the day, so that's hardly incriminating. Medea, but she couldn't have outrun you."

Medea. Her sentry might have been fast enough, but the same could be said for the other sentries.

For now, I have other matters to discuss with Julian. "I'll need your help tonight after dinner," I say.

Julian smiles. "You need my help…moving another body?"

I purse my lips. He won't like having to haul the cook back up ten floors. I wonder if Kerasea can do her divining outside, but then I remember that she needs the eternal flame.

Ten floors it is.

At the look on my face, he groans. "Gods, I was joking! Who this time?"

"The same."

He slowly closes his eyes and sighs. I don't blame him, as moving a frozen corpse isn't anyone's idea of a good time.

"I need a new best friend," he mutters. "Do I even want to know?"

"No."

He groans. "No is right. At least I'll enjoy dinner first. Let's go."

XLIII.

Torren

Dinner is served, and I am glad I didn't make an excuse to search Foreau's chambers tonight. His chair is vacant, his absence a protest. Given how the conclave ended today, I'm not surprised, but the senators ordinarily pretend that nothing said or done in lawmaking affects their friendships. So, it's something to note.

The light purple of Kerasea's dress catches my eye. The color makes the green of hers as vivid as a spring meadow. She is stunning as per usual, but softer, more like candlelight this evening.

I look away from her. This is exactly what caused a lapse in my judgment earlier. I should be thinking about what her servant girl was hiding last night. Zel's secrets are far more important than the way Kera closes her eyes slowly when she tastes something delicious.

Right, Zel.

For some reason, I keep linking the girl to whoever followed us earlier, and gut feelings shouldn't be ignored. Does someone want to make the Faith, the High Priestess, too obvious of a suspect, so that I have to rule her out? It's a puzzle inside of a game, but I will be victorious.

As has become customary, Terrance gives the dinner toast, and Medea's page plays the lyre in the corner. With only four senators, Julian, Kerasea, and myself at dinner, the music fills in the empty spaces.

We are nearly done with the second course when servants and two sentries sprint down the hall.

I turn in my seat.

Medea holds up a hand for her page to stop playing. The music ceases instantaneously.

"What was that?" she asks.

All of the senators, Julian, and Kerasea turn and stare.

I rise out of my chair and walk to the doorway. "What is the meaning of all of this?"

The older woman I nearly killed today stops, catching her breath.

"There is a fire, Praetorian," she says.

"Where?" I look up, but there is no smoke. Nor can I see any fire from the windows.

"The woodshed," the woman clarifies. "We are trying to put it out now."

Julian catches my eye as my heart stops. That's where we buried the bodies.

He rises from his chair and meets me by the door.

"What is happening, Commander?" Senator Paolo asks, spinning his ring.

"Apparently, there is a fire outside. I will go offer my assistance." Julian pauses as he takes in their expressions. "Not to worry—the fire cannot spread to the palace, but it is best to put it out."

Julian walks straight past me, and I fall in line beside him. His family, like many nobles, made their money in fire insurance and fire brigades. His is second largest in the capital behind Verhardt's.

"Guard the senators and the High Priestess. No one in or out," Julian says to the sentries.

"Yes, Commander," they say.

"I don't suppose this fire is accidental," I say as we race down the hall.

He raises his eyebrows. Certainly not with the recent snow.

We break into a jog until we reach the kitchens. As soon as we are out of the delivery door, the scent of burning wood hits us. The woodshed is fifty yards away and engulfed in an unnaturally bright blaze.

"Definitely not accidental," Julian murmurs.

The servants stand around, occasionally tossing a bucket of water onto the blazing fire before they run all the way back to the kitchens for more. The water smokes and sizzles but does nothing in such small quantities.

"Form a line," Julian says. The authority in his voice carries over the crackling blaze and the panicked sounds from the servants. "Someone stand by the sink to fill the buckets, another by the door, and so forth until you're near to the shed. Constantly move full buckets down the line and pass the empty ones back. The strongest man should stand closest to the fire. Do it now."

As Julian organizes the servants into a makeshift brigade, I run to where we buried the bodies. I raise my arm to shield my face as I pass close to the fire. The heat from the inferno is immense, the dry wood inside fueling the blaze.

I cough, the thick smoke sticking in my nose and throat. Embers float high into the night's sky.

I scan the area. The two mounds where we put Eyo and the cook are gone. All that's left is trampled wet grass.

Impossible.

I continue around the shed, hoping I had the wrong side, but no, all I find is green grass. The fire superheated the ground around the shed, either by design or accidentally.

But where are the bodies? Two corpses didn't just disappear.

I stop and stare at the blaze, chilled even in the heat. I can't see inside the shed, but I know that the bodies are burning right now.

That's why the air smells like charred flesh.

River of Death.

I turn and narrow my eyes at the palace. Someone in there set this fire; someone wanted to destroy the evidence of Eyo's poisoning. That person knew where I put the bodies and knew that Kerasea could divine a murder. They have been watching me, watching *us* this entire time.

My stomach turns as my resolve cements. I need to finish this before they finish us.

XLIV

Kerasea

The Praetorian smells like a bonfire as I follow closely on his heels. His anger is obvious from his posture and tensed muscles, but more than that—he won't even look at me. Instead, he careens straight ahead.

When he came back into the banquet hall, he was dressed in armor. He stood at attention and reported that Senator Eyo's body was lost in the blaze. This news was met with great consternation by the Council. They were displeased with him keeping the body in the woodshed, but I'm not sure where they wanted the corpse. It's not like he could've been kept on ice in the banquet room.

We reach the third floor, and the Praetorian continues past his room and mine. His strides are so long and quick that I nearly have to jog to keep up. But he stops in front of Zel's door and knocks twice.

There is no answer.

"She is probably still down at dinner," I say.

"Just as well."

He takes a skeleton key from his pocket, and I stare at the ridges as he puts it into the lock. I'm not sure why I haven't thought of the fact that he would have access to every room in this palace—including mine—this whole time. It's how he spied on me in the divining room. Has he been in my bedchamber without my knowledge?

No. He wouldn't abuse his power. He's not that type of person.

Just as before, the room is a mess. I don't go into Zel's private quarters at the temple, so I'm not sure if she always lives this way. I can't imagine so, but she is only fourteen—maybe her parents clean up after her.

"Do you want to tell me what you are looking for?" I ask.

"Evidence," he says.

That's a no.

The window is open, giving the room a chill. It was also open last night. I would think more of it, but her room doesn't have a balcony, and we are three stories up.

The Praetorian performs a general sweep of her bedroom and bathroom and then a more focused check of every corner of her chambers. He's locked in like a hound on the scent of a fox, but he moves items to the side gently, disturbing little despite the chaos. I'm still not sure what he's looking for, but he's almost done when Zel opens the door.

"Excellency," she says, bobbing a curtsy. She freezes with her eyes wide on the Praetorian. "Sir. What are you... Why are you... How can I help you both?"

She had no idea we were in here. I must've put her mind at ease before dinner when I pretended like everything was fine.

"I have more questions for you," Torren says to Zel. "Take a seat, please."

"Yes, sir." She circles wide around him but trips over a stepstool before righting herself and sitting on the bed. She swallows hard and folds her shaking hands on her lap, cheeks coloring and looking like she's on the verge of tears.

He hasn't asked a single question yet.

"Did you bring any blades to the conclave? For the High Priestess or otherwise?" he asks.

She shakes her head. "No, sir."

I study her, and she's telling the truth. No one is supposed to bring weapons aside from him, but he saw my golden dagger, of course, at his throat.

Heat rushes through me as I remember him pinning me against the wall. I look away and focus on Zel.

"In that case, please explain this." He takes out a blade from behind the dresser and holds it with a handkerchief. It's fairly plain, but around a foot long and razor-sharp.

Zel's eyes go wide. "I can't... That's not mine. I didn't bring it, sir."

That is also the truth.

Torren frowns. "It was in your things—hidden in this mess. It is quite similar to the one thrown at me last night." He shrugs and then continues. "I also want to inquire about your book on poisons."

"I don't have a book on poisons," she says.

I wait for a tell, but she is speaking the truth.

He holds up a leather-bound book titled *Toxic Horticulture and Herb Science*. Just like with the tea last night, I've never known Zel to be interested in science, either. What is that book doing in her bedchamber?

Tears of confusion swim in her eyes as she shakes her head, causing a few drops to splash onto her skirts. I'm positive she's never seen that book or the dagger before.

"Have you stayed alone in your room this whole time?" I ask.

I can feel Torren's gaze on me, but I keep my focus on Zel.

"I...I... Yes, yes, I have." She rubs her thumb and forefinger together at a rapid rate.

I suppress a sigh.

"I will need to question you further," the Praetorian says.

The words are like a knife to the heart, sending shock waves through my chest. I know that tone. I said I didn't think he was a monster, but he is going to torture Zel—a girl who is only a child.

She gets so pale and breathes so rapidly that I worry she'll faint.

"No. You won't." I physically step in between her and Torren.

He slowly shakes his head. "High Priestess, you do not have authority here."

His tone sounds more resigned than anything else, and he is correct. If we were in the temple of truth, I could order him out. But this is Jubilee, not my temple. Still, I hold my ground. I don't care what the laws are; I won't stand idly by.

"She is a child and my responsibility," I say.

"She is an incriminated suspect."

"Based on a book? A plain blade that wasn't used in any murder?" I ask. That amount of evidence wouldn't be enough to justify him disturbing my teatime, but the standard is different for a servant. "If you insist on proceeding, I will go to the Council and request a halt to your investigation."

He slowly opens the book, then extends it toward me. Inside the pages is a pair of small crushed spectacles. I gasp. Those were Antinous's.

"You may, but you won't win," he says. "Not in my investigation of a servant."

"How... I don't understand," I say. Then I turn my head toward Zel.

"I've never seen those before—I swear!" Her eyes are large and panicked as she looks from us to the glasses and back again. "Who do they belong to?"

I stare at her, but she has no idea who wore them. Someone placed all this here—possibly the person she is covering for, the one who might've murdered Antinous.

But to admit I know that much would result in an inquisition.

"This is all far too convenient, and you know it," I say to the Praetorian.

"I can't assume that, Kerasea," Torren says.

A tinge of regret in his tone sends spikes of fear into my stomach. I thought he'd be vicious and victorious, but instead, he's resigned to do his duty. And that makes him so much more dangerous. He is correct—with the poison book and the glasses, the Senate would allow him to interrogate her over my objections. I'll have to stand by simply because we aren't in my temple.

Because I brought her here.

"I understand," I say.

I step closer to Zel. She looks up at me, hopeful that I can intercede, but I can't. Not here. I lean down to kiss her forehead, and then I linger with my lips near her ear.

"Run," I say. "Don't stop until you get to the divining tower. Shut yourself inside and wait for me."

I drop my key into her skirts. She hesitates, and for a second it looks like she won't save herself. But then she takes off out of the room. I remain, staring at the Praetorian, daring him to make a move.

I just broke our alliance, but it wasn't going to last forever.

XLV

Torren

Zel is gone, but I have bigger issues than a servant girl right now. I'm busy facing off with the High Priestess of the temple of truth.

All five-three of her is draped in a silk-and-crepe dinner dress, but she is anything other than soft and delicate. Kerasea stares at me, the embodiment of power and resolve.

"You just impeded my investigation." I state the obvious to break the silence in the chamber.

"Bring me before the Senate, then," she says.

She doesn't shrug, but the sentiment is in her voice. She has no regret, no nerves or shyness. I am staring at a woman who is very much a leader in the republic—not the girl she played at being during this conclave with her blushes and sighs.

I don't know whether to respect her or be furious, but I'm glad we have dropped the pretenses.

I glance at the door. I could run after Zel and still overtake her, but the truth is, I don't want to. I wasn't looking forward to questioning her under pressure. However, the evidence I found was too much to ignore. I would've done my duty despite my reservations, but now I have to handle the High Priestess.

A rush of excitement flows through me, and I recognize the rare feeling—it's meeting a worthy opponent in the ring.

I decide to shift into a more conversational stance, letting my shoulders relax while I choose my next move.

"The priests to the god of protection will intercept the girl and bring her back," I say. "No one is to come or go from the conclave."

"I didn't send her to the capital," the High Priestess responds.

"Where did you…"

I trail off and think about where else she would've told Zel to go. It would have to be somewhere out of my reach, somewhere Kerasea holds sway. There are multiple temples of truth in every province, but Zel would still run into the same issue of leaving the conclave… unless she didn't leave.

"The divining room," I say.

She nods, respect glimmering in her eyes.

The tower is technically an offshoot of her temple. It's based on a thin reasoning, but the Senate and the Ministry of Justice would side with her if I tried to take the girl from holy ground.

Let it never be said that Kerasea Vestal isn't clever.

Amusement fills my chest, and the corners of my lips rise. I force the smile from my face. I shouldn't feel this. I shouldn't be anything other than furious that she stymied my investigation and broke our alliance over a servant girl.

"Who is Zel to you?" I ask.

This time she does shrug. "An innocent girl."

I have no choice but to respect that. It's the same as I feel about the cook, only I didn't expect Kerasea to have a sense of justice and certainly not feel a sense of obligation to a servant. I don't know many nobles who would. But *is* Zel innocent? I still have the book in my hand. Kerasea is correct in that all of this is too much evidence to have in one room. If Zel were actually responsible, these items should've been burned, disposed of, like the bodies. They were saved specifically to implicate a suspect, but it is still my duty to investigate.

"One could assume these effects to be yours, if that is the case," I say.

Kerasea arches an eyebrow. "Go to the Senate with that, Praetorian."

She knows that this is not nearly enough—even if I found these items on her person, the Senate would not break *un exorum*. There's no proof anymore that Eyo was even poisoned, and I said Antinous had died accidentally. No, they'd censure me for looking into her affairs without permission.

"Someone else was staying here," Kerasea says. She turns hesitant as she glances around the room.

I nod. "Undoubtedly."

Kerasea's brow knits. "You know that, yet you were going to torture her?"

She can't hide the disdain in her voice. But there are those who get their hands dirty and those who can wring their hands over the manner in which they are kept clean.

"I was going to lock her up with minimal food until she gave me the identity. Call it torture if you like, but plenty of citizens in the Northside live worse than what I'd subject her to for a short amount of time."

The High Priestess stares at me and then shakes her head. "Your reputation is deserved."

Her condescending tone makes something inside me snap. How dare she sit swaddled in luxury and judge me.

She holds still, even as I storm closer. Anger propels me, molten in my chest.

"It must be so easy to cast judgments down from your golden palanquin." My voice rumbles through my locked jaw.

Her mouth opens in outrage, and then she shuts it and breathes out a laugh. "You think it's easy for me?"

"I think you've never known a hard day in your life. Nor would you know what to do with one."

"You don't know a thing about me." She holds her body rigid, her chin high even as I stand a breath away from her.

"I do know you, Kerasea. I have for years. Cross me again and, innocent or not, I'll bring you down from on high. I swear it on the five gods."

She narrows her eyes slightly. "You won't ever see me on my knees, Praetorian."

That smug mouth.

She's too close, and the image she painted in my mind is too vivid. I look at her face, and all I see are her perfect lips. All I can think about is how I want to taste her.

I reach out and grab the side of her face. This time not the gentle way I lifted her chin before, but something else entirely. Surprise lights her eyes, but then they grow heavy-lidded in desire.

"I will see you on your knees, Kerasea," I say.

Her eyes widen, and then she smirks. "You first."

The pull toward her feels as natural as falling. I lean down and press my lips against hers.

XLVI

Torren

The second our mouths meet, it's like a thunderbolt striking through me. All my muscles tense as fire dances inside my bones. A kiss has never felt like this. I'm not even sure why I have this connection with her, but I just want more.

Our lips part at the same time. It's hard to say where we begin and end as my tongue swirls around hers. Her taste is perfect, her jasmine scent filling my senses, lips pillowy soft, and I want to dive into them. Her mouth responds to mine in a rhythm as if I've kissed her a thousand times.

Bottomless hunger rises through me. Every taste is tantalizing. Kissing her feels like the first time I ever drank — a dizzy, heady high that's enough to make me forget everything else. But this isn't poison.

Or maybe it is and I just don't give a fuck. I need this. I need her.

I grip her harder, pressing her body to mine as the room, the palace falls away. There's just Kera in her lilac dress and all the things I've wanted to do to her since she first put her hand in mine.

And she is just as eager. She is a mirror, reflecting all my desires. She wraps her arms around me and runs her fingers through my hair, pulling me closer.

Little moans escape her throat as I gently pull on her hair. She likes it. I grip harder, and desire swells in me as she hums a sound of light pain mixed with pleasure.

The things I'm going to do to her.

We move a step closer to the bed. Her hands explore my muscles as the steel of my armor meshes against the softness of her dress. I'm going to tear both off, but a drop of hesitation suddenly hits me. This has felt inevitable since I first took her hand at the Revelry, maybe earlier, but no matter how much I desire her, I know this is a point of no return. If I lay her down, I'll never stop wanting her. And it will be a curse, because a woman like her won't end up with a monster like me.

I stand on the edge of a precipice, knowing I should turn back—a wise man would.

But fuck it.

I shift my hand so it's around her neck, and she gasps. I kiss her throat roughly, running my tongue against the hollow. She moans, and I pick her up and press her back against the wall. This is a terrible idea, but I also can't help it. I can't resist her anymore.

Her legs are bare under her lilac dress, her thighs like satin. Her hips press her panties against the bulge under my leather skirt. Desire radiates from her, and all I want is to consume her.

I kiss her as hard as she kisses me. She nips at my bottom lip, her hunger driving her. Her fingers dig into my shoulders, her legs wrapped tight around me. She tries to push my skirt aside. I'm so hard that it's all I can do to not take her right now.

No. I try to slow down, to savor this.

I release her, dropping her until she's standing in front of me. Then I get on my knees.

She did say *me first*.

Kera stares at me as I raise the skirt of her dress, then reach up and pull her panties down. She steps out of them, pliant for once. This is just about the only time she's actually listened to me. Because she's as eager as I am.

"I need you," she says.

Her legs are just far enough apart that I can put my mouth on her. So I do. I position my tongue right where she wants me.

She tries to stifle a moan, but she quickly gives up, her little cries and moans echoing in the chamber as I explore her with my tongue. She tastes like salted honey. She's perfect.

Her fingers pull at my short hair as I bring her right to the edge. I lick her clit until she's begging me to take her, until she's about to come undone. Her hands grip the wall, my shoulders, her dress.

"Please, Tor," she cries. "Please."

I could linger here until dawn, licking her and listening to her fall apart, but we both want more.

Just as I get off my knees, Kerasea drops down and stares up at me. Surprise fills my chest. The High Priestess is kneeling in front of me, her eyes filled with desire.

Her face lights with excitement as she peels down the shorts I wear under my skirt. Then she takes my hard cock in her hands. She gasps at my size and stares, greedy before she takes me in between her perfect lips.

I groan, leaning my head back as I feel her soft tongue on me. But I need to watch her. She looks up at me as she worships my cock with her hands and her mouth and if I died right now, I wouldn't complain. But as good as it feels, I still need more.

I pull Kera up to me and stroke her face.

"Take me," she says.

I smile before I roughly turn her around. Her hands hit the wall, and I lean her over, hiking up her dress. Desire is a towering inferno in my chest. I can't, I don't want to be gentle with her right now. And she doesn't want that, either. She's trembling with need. She wants to get fucked right here.

She's so wet, but I take my time parting her with my fingers first before I inch my cock inside her. As soon as I enter her, she moans, spreading her legs wider. The feel of her is otherworldly. Like reaching the skies and sinking into a velvet sea.

It's all I've wanted.

She whimpers, bracing herself against the wall, her arms shaking. "Gods, Torren." A rumble escapes my throat, but suddenly a bloody scream pierces the quiet. We both freeze, then turn toward the window.

Reality comes crashing into the room, shattering the enchantment.

"What was that?" she asks.

But we both know. That was the sound of violence.

The killer just struck again.

XLVII

Kerasea

I've had lovers before, but Torren makes me swear I haven't. My body felt lit on fire, like walking through the eternal flame—illuminated, not scorched—an addicting, powerful high.

I'd fallen into oblivion with him, but then there was that scream. A terrible, primal death knell. The cry came from outside—almost like it was right beyond this window.

Before I formed the question, I already knew it was the sound of murder from the throbbing in my head and wrists. Of all the magic I could have in my blood, mine is a connection to godless death.

Ice fills my veins as I hold still, waiting for another sound. A word. Something.

There's nothing but the silent night.

Torren and I break apart, breathing hard. He runs his hands over his face, looking shaken, vulnerable for a moment. I'm also trembling. I was lost in him, but then there was that scream. It was as painful as it was shattering.

"It sounded…it sounded like an older woman," I say.

He nods. "It did."

"Medea?" I ask.

He takes two deep breaths, his breastplate rising and falling, and then he sighs as we right ourselves, finding the clothes we removed. "I have to investigate. Go back to your chambers and bar the door. Please, Kera. I have to know you're safe in order to do my job."

The "please" is so small and pleading that my heart physically aches. I nod and smooth out my dress. The skirt is wrinkled, and I'm sure my hair is a mess, but I'll change into bedclothes in a moment anyhow.

Tor adjusts his sword and raises his chin, and just like that—he's the Praetorian again. Not the fervent lover of a moment ago but a brutal hunter.

"Ready?" he asks.

I nod.

He opens the door for me. I'm about to step around the mess and into the hall when there's a knocking sound farther down.

I freeze and exchange glances with Torren. Silently, he moves in front of me, shielding me with his body. He steps out of the room first.

"There you are," Julian says. "What are you doing in—" He stops short when I step out. I pull the door closed behind me.

"I was investigating," Torren says.

Julian looks from me to him and back again, and then he smirks. Something inside me shrivels in embarrassment, and it takes all my training not to slouch. I'm sure we both look kiss-stained and guilty.

"Mm-hmm," Julian hums. "I'm now very sorry to interrupt, Praetorian, but I heard a scream."

"I did as well," Torren says. "Let's go."

He tosses the dagger to Julian, who easily catches it. But Julian lingers, looking at me. He waits like I'll accompany them.

The Praetorian glances over his shoulder at me. "Return to your room, High Priestess. I'll take care of this."

There's the promise of violence and justice in his voice, and there's something so alluring to that. I want to follow, but just as when we were by the baths, I would be a hindrance, not a help, if I went with them.

Julian and Torren take off down the hall and disappear.

I unlock my door and take a shaking step inside. I'd lost myself so deeply in him that I allowed him to take me right there. In poor Zel's room. And then, right at the edge of true euphoria, there was that scream. That primal sound replays in my mind, haunting me. Not only was it horrific, it was…familiar.

No, it can't be what I'm thinking. *Who* I'm thinking.

I pause with my hand on the knob and shake my head at myself. There are rumors Elusian blood haunts the palace and causes madness—that is why no one stays here for longer than a week. Of course, I don't believe that, but I am starting to lose my senses. Beginning with falling for Tor.

I take off my dress and take down my hair, but I can't get in bed. I pace the floor in my slip, my head spinning. I can't resolve how good it felt to be with Tor with how terrible I feel now. That scream. That scream was so familiar that it had to be— My denial suddenly dissipates and I stop short, the truth sinking in.

The Praetorian asked me to stay in my room, but I can't just sit idle. I can't. I have to know for certain.

I throw on my velvet robe and grab a fur cloak. As I leave, I've never hoped so badly to be wrong in my life.

XLVIII.

Torren

"So...any developments you want to tell me about?" Julian smiles as we run down the marble stairs of the palace. We're sprinting, but he has enough time to raise his eyebrows at me.

A fourth person was just attacked, maybe slain, at Jubilee, and my closest friend wants nothing more than to gossip.

"Intolerable," I mutter.

But I put myself in this situation. I allowed my needs, my desires to come first. And gods, if I had to do it over again, I'd do the same. I still smell Kera's perfume on me. I still feel her in my palms.

I ball my hands into fists. I have to push what just happened to the back of my mind and leave it there. I am hunting a killer, not a lover, now.

"Does this mean you no longer suspect her, or are you debuting a new interrogation technique?" Julian asks.

"I should've drowned you in the baths," I say.

"Too late. You're stuck with me now."

Just like that, things are normal again between us—the way friends come together in the worst of times.

He laughs but then composes himself as we reach the entryway. The front doors are still ceremoniously chained, so we go toward the back of the palace. This level has a massive stone terrace overlooking the drop-off below.

We grab torches in our left hands, leaving our right free for weapons.

Anything could be a trap at Jubilee.

Julian adjusts the dagger in his hand, and then we nod to each other. I take a breath, slowing my heart. We move through the doors of the veranda as one, as if we are legionnaires again. All the memories of moving just like this in the wilderness come rushing back.

The night is cold and clear, and the moon shines on the deep white snow. I scan the ground, but there are no footprints by the doors. The area seems undisturbed, but appearances can be deceiving.

I point to the right, twice. Julian motions his head to the left, signaling he'll cover my back as I proceed east.

The cold of the knee-high snow burns my calves as I step, but pain is temporary. Discomfort makes me focus. My senses are on high alert for any sound, any movement other than Julian behind me. There's no wind—the air is completely still.

I hope the killer made the mistake of lingering; I'll settle this tonight.

A few steps later, there's something dark on the white snow. My heart rate ticks up, but I force myself to follow my training. I freeze with my hand up and then gesture to Julian. He looks to where I'm pointing, then we proceed north, with Jules still protecting my back in case this is an ambush.

I continue, step by slow step, toward the dark lump in the snow. It's a woman lying on her back. There's no doubt that she was the source of the scream. Her body is bent at unnatural angles, and blood has gathered in the snow, forming a crimson halo around her broken skull.

Someone threw her out of a window or pushed her off a balcony. And, although it is an older woman, it is not Medea.

A slight amount of relief hits my chest. The death of another senator would've triggered chaos at the conclave and would all but guarantee that I lost my position.

But who is this?

I stare up at the palace. Which room did this woman come from? The second floor is dark, but three rooms on the third floor are lit. All the chambers except Eyo's are lit on the fourth floor and all on the fifth aside from the king's bedchamber. The divining room tower lies to the east, but someone couldn't fall from there onto here—it's too far.

No, this woman fell from the palace, likely from the fourth or fifth floor. Another murder at the feet of a senator who cannot be investigated.

The injustice of it cuts deeply as I grit my teeth. The senators do as they please, even when it's murder, so long as they don't get caught. This isn't equality or freedom.

I look down at the victim. She seems familiar, but she wasn't a servant or page here—I've interviewed all of them several times now and haven't seen her. I stand still as surprise grips me.

This woman should not be here.

Where do I know her from? How did I miss an interloper at the conclave?

I kneel down and touch her wrist, fruitlessly searching for a sign of life.

I hold my breath and wait, hoping for a faint pulse, but there is nothing. She was dead upon impact—perhaps even earlier if she was stabbed. It's hard to tell, as she's wearing a black sweater and black trousers.

Julian circles around me and moves his torch toward the woman's face. Then he gasps, so startled that he nearly drops the flame.

"You know her?" I ask.

"I do…" he says slowly. "That's Mirial Bauman."

The name sounds familiar, sticking in my brain like a nettle, but I'm not sure where I've heard it before or why Julian looks like that.

"Who was she?" I ask.

"She is…was…a priestess in the temple of truth."

No.

Numbness soaks through my armor, and I shudder. Now I remember her. I have seen her scowling face in the Forum. She's been a priestess for as long as I've been alive—longer, probably. She was always at the side of Osiris Vestal, and I saw her in the gilded carriage when Kerasea arrived at Jubilee. But I was so focused on the High Priestess that I didn't think to wonder about her escort.

This woman was not supposed to be at the conclave. We have strict rules for who is and isn't allowed. Any sentry or servant who saw the priestess had a duty to report her, but no one did. So, how did she get in? And who murdered her?

My mind returns to Kera. She looked so pale after the scream, but was it because it was so jarring or because she recognized the voice?

I count windows on the third floor to find her chambers. Out of all the lights that are on, her bedroom isn't one of them. There is no chance she's asleep, so I can only assume she left.

I sigh deeply. I now have to track down the High Priestess.

XLIX

Kerasea

Zel opens the door to the divining room, and her face brightens even though she's shivering in the cold of the room. Still, she curtsies to me.

"Excellency."

I extend the fur I brought, and she immediately wraps it around herself, snuggling against the soft warmth.

"Thank you," she says.

In her eyes is also gratitude for saving her from the Praetorian. But she shouldn't thank me just yet.

"Zel, I need you to tell me who was staying in your room. Now."

Her smile fades, and she shakes her head.

She looks like she might try to deny what I already suspect, but I am in no mood for this. I stare at her the same way I stared down Torren.

"I know you were lying when we spoke before," I say. "Beyond being the conduit to the divine, I heard you talk to someone in your room at night. You lied to me, and you are fortunate that I didn't disclose it to the Praetorian, but I *will* have your honesty now. Confess before the god."

She sniffles, her eyes filling with tears, and then they spill over as she shakes. "I'm sorry! I'm so sorry for lying, High Priestess."

Zel hangs her head as she trembles. She's genuine, but it's hard to feel anything but anger. I don't have room for sympathy right now.

"Do you have any idea how dangerous it was to lie to the Senate investigator?" I ask.

She nods, but she does not, in fact, realize it. She has no idea that death would be the least of her worries.

"I know," she cries. "I didn't want to lie, but I had no choice. I swore I wouldn't tell... I..." Then her voice is choked off with tears, and her face reddens as she sobs.

I sigh my frustration and try to keep my composure.

"Tell me the name, Zel," I say. "And then I will hold your hand in the eternal flame."

She gasps, her eyes wide. She knows that if she lies to me, she'll lose that arm. It's a threat but also a promise. I can't have a servant who feels justified in hiding things from me. As soon as we return to the capital, I will have her discharged, but for now, I need the truth.

If they don't respect you, you're dead, my father used to say. *They can either love or fear you enough to respect you.*

"It was Mirial!" Zel blurts out.

I freeze. My cheeks tingle as blood drains from them. I scratch my wrist and try to breathe evenly, but that was who I thought screamed earlier.

The cup of tea on Zel's dresser fits Mirial's presence, as does the standard robe. And both would have placed Mirial in the kitchens when the Praetorian was attacked.

My stomach twists and my heart pounds as the truth hits me.

I can't be right, though. I saw Mirial leave. She only

accompanied me to Mount Ara to lecture me. She had no reason to stay.

"What was Mirial doing here?" My voice comes out as clear and even, hiding my turmoil.

Zel is all emotion, and I can't afford to be the same. I am the High Priestess, not Zel's or even Mirial's friend. I lead the Faith of millions of citizens. And I lie as part of my survival.

Zel shakes her head, still crying. "She was here to protect you. That is what she said—she asked me to hide her because this was your first conclave. She said you were in danger because of intervening in the voting and that we had to protect you."

My shoulders droop and my heart sinks. It was all for me? No, that's not possible. If Mirial was found here, however innocently, she'd be arrested at the least. Somewhere in my mind, though, I know there's no limit to what she'd do to keep me safe. She swore she would watch over me when my father was on his deathbed. And Mirial always means an oath. She would do anything to protect me.

From any danger.

"Did she throw the dagger at the Praetorian?" I ask.

"I don't know." Zel looks down and away. She doesn't rub her fingers together, but she isn't quite being honest, either.

"Place your hand in the fire, Zel, and swear you have no knowledge."

Her eyebrows knit, and her chin wobbles at my cold tone. "I think she did it—it made sense with the robe—but she didn't tell me anything. I swear."

It's the truth, and it's just as frustrating as a lie. Why would Mirial try to kill Torren? She believes that he is dangerous and lowly and that his father was a traitor...but attacking him wouldn't protect me, and Mirial is pragmatic to a fault.

Then I remember the way she silently moves—how she just appeared next to me when the sentries came into the temple. The uneasy way she looked at Torren from the carriage. She never trusted him because my father didn't.

Pieces fall into place as I grip my sleeves. Mirial could've followed me into the dark kitchens on the first night and overheard my conversation with Antinous. She could have seen the Praetorian moving Eyo's body. She could have believed the Praetorian was a real danger to me. She also could've been the one listening by the baths, as she is both silent and fast enough to elude Torren. She would have started that fire in the woodshed to hide what I can do. That I am Elusian. Because she was the one person left who knew the truth about me.

I swallow hard. All of that makes a certain amount of sense, but why keep things from me? Why not just tell me she was here at Jubilee?

"Is there anything else you are hiding from me?" I ask Zel.

She looks all around, obviously trying to think of what else she lied about. "I'd never seen that book before the Praetorian held it up. I don't think it was Mirial's, either."

No, it was all too convenient, and Mirial had no reason to poison Eyo. Well, none that I know of.

"Did Mirial talk to any of the senators while she was here?" I ask.

"Not that I saw."

An unhelpful response, but at least it's true. I'm missing something, though. This doesn't add up, and when that happens, the reason is always a lack of truth.

"The last senator I saw her talk to was Verhardt on the day of the Revelry," Zel adds.

I will myself to not react, but her statement knocks the air from my chest. This feels enormous, like it would explain everything. "Where was that?"

"Well, it was strange, really. I was coming back from the market with my mom, and I looked down Demeter Alley and I saw Mirial and Verhardt talking together. But when I stopped and looked again, they were gone."

Neither the Senate Leader nor the priestess would have had any business being on the fisherman's wharf by the Tiger River. Zel happened to see a clandestine meeting.

"Did you ask Mirial about that?" I ask.

Zel shakes her head. "No. I thought I was just seeing things, but now…I'm not sure."

"Stay here," I say. "And lock the door."

I take the key and rush out of the divining room. I have to hope that Mirial is still alive to tell me what she was doing here and why she secretly met with Verhardt on the day he died.

L

Kerasea

J ust as I reach the third floor, someone grabs me. My heart leaps, but I suppress a scream because I know it's Torren just from his scent. Still…he has a dagger at my throat.

He immediately releases me and breathes out a frustrated sigh.

"Son of a jackal, Kerasea. Is it so hard to follow a simple instruction?"

Anger oozes from his voice, but he lets the dagger drop to his side. As he does, his hand shakes slightly.

"I had to check on Zel after I heard that scream," I say.

The second I say the word "scream," he looks away.

He exhales. "Very well."

That wasn't the reaction I expected. I stare at him, but he doesn't meet my eye. What was that? Guilt? Sadness?

The edges of his eyebrows rise, and the set of his mouth is so grave, so different from when I saw him last. I think I already know the reason—I just hope I'm wrong.

"I need to speak with you," he says.

I swallow hard but nod. He gestures down the hall, and we walk to my bedroom. I hold my breath and have to remember to release it as we head inside.

When he shuts the door behind us, he's slow to turn.

Finally, he does.

There's deep conflict scrawled on his face—whatever this is, he doesn't want to say it, but he has to. I've seen this exact look many times at the temple when someone is about to confess something terrible. I brace myself, tightening my stomach and squaring my shoulders.

"Kerasea, take a seat, please," he says.

I remain standing, staring at him, but reluctantly I back up until I'm sitting on the edge of the bed. I hold on to the bedpost with my hand.

"There is no easy way for you to hear what I'm about to say," he starts. "So I will just speak plainly."

My heart thuds because somehow I already know the truth— Mirial is the one who screamed, and Tor is about to confirm it. But I wait for the axe to drop, still holding on to the shred of hope that I am wrong. That even if Mirial, the only person who really knew me, was attacked, she survived.

Because my heart can't bear the alternative.

He draws a deep breath, his armor rising, then closes his eyes for a long blink before opening them. "When I investigated the source of the scream we heard, I found a body on the terrace. It was Mirial Bauman."

He speaks gently, but his words are razor-sharp and cut to my core.

My face goes numb, blood draining out of my cheeks. It was silly to think I could brace myself for this. It's worse, so much worse for a thread of hope to snap. Mirial is dead. She was there for my first steps in the temple, my first words, my first pimple, my first heartbreak. My father trusted her with my very life, and so did I.

I'm trembling, numb, too shocked to even cry, grief a palpable thing in my veins.

According to Zel, she was here to protect me from these vipers. But why didn't Mirial tell me she was here? Why did she secretly meet with Verhardt?

My heart drops at the thought that she might've been capable of murder, but no matter what the answers are, I have to know the whole truth about my friend.

And I must discover who killed her.

A single tear rolls down my cheek, and I wipe it away.

"Did you…catch the person who did this?" I ask.

Torren sighs. "I didn't. And I am so very sorry."

Frustration and deadly fury waft off him, even though he had no duty to protect someone who snuck into the conclave. I feel the same urge as I did before—to help, to disclose that I am Elusian and the magic in my blood can provide us with answers, but I can't tell him. Torren is attracted to me, as much as I am to him, but even with what we just did, I can't reveal myself. With my father and Mirial dead, there's no one left who I can trust. No one else can ever know the truth about me. But there is one thing I can do.

"Can you…can you bring me her body?" I ask.

His brow furrows. "Her body?"

"I want to see her and I…I have to divine whether she jumped, Torren. She was…troubled. Perhaps there is no one to catch."

I hate having to lie about her, but she would've understood.

Torren closes his eyes and presses his lips together—the thought of suicide obviously not crossing his mind because it's so unlikely. But as it is still a logical possibility, he nods.

"I can. But, Kera, her body… She fell from a great distance. You understand that there was significant damage. She will not look—"

He thinks I'm concerned with the trappings of godless death. I can't think of anything that bothers me less. I have far greater concerns than gore, but it's kind of him to think about how I'd react. These little unexpected moments crack my defenses around him and meld my heart to his.

"She was like a mother to me," I say. This time I don't have to lie. "I just want some time alone with her—to say goodbye."

He swallows and sighs. "I can give you that much."

Tor reaches out and rests a hand on my shoulder, now a man again, not just the Praetorian. His warm palm takes the chill away. He hesitates, then he reaches up and strokes my cheek with the back of his fingers. His touch is firm, but also surprisingly gentle. I want to lean into his hand. I want to fall into his embrace again and let him take some of this pain away. But I hold still. I can't have him, no matter how much I want him. It's too dangerous. Mirial's death is a stark reminder of how I can never be truly close to anyone again.

He lets his hand fall away, and it drops to his side.

"I'm very sorry, Kera. May the Underworld receive her."

It's far more respect than Mirial would've given him. My heart flutters and my muscles ache to take his hand, but there's no room for that. Not now, not ever. I cannot be entangled with someone as perceptive as Torren. No matter what I desire, there are things that simply can't be.

Not in this life.

"Thank you, Torren," I say.

His eyes meet mine, searching, but I look away. He draws a sharp breath, the rejection landing.

"I'll bring her to the tower." He turns and leaves without another word.

My shoulders drop, the pain in my chest immense, but I keep my chin high. I did what I had to do. I'll do whatever I need to in order to survive.

LI

Kerasea

Torren keeps his word and brings Mirial's body to the divining room, carrying her up the ten flights of stairs. It's nearly midnight by the time she's resting on the altar, wrapped in bedsheets. She looks so much smaller than she was in life, but death diminishes us all.

Zel sits stock-still in the corner as I stand at the altar in my ceremonial robe. Once Torren left my room, I changed again, because he'd expect me to be in temple robes. But now I have to figure out how to get rid of Zel, since I can't have her or anyone else in here for this.

At least Torren believes I am about to cut Mirial open—so he won't ask further questions about why I need privacy. It was a solid cover for an egregious error.

"Will you grant me a truce for an hour and not arrest her?" I ask, pointing to Zel.

He nods.

"Return to your chambers, Zel. Bathe and grab bedding along with things you need to remain here for the duration. I'll bring you back shortly."

"Yes, Excellency. Thank you, Excellency." She looks from me to Torren and then flees, giving the Praetorian a wide berth.

Alone with him once more, I wait for him to leave. Yet there's a part of me that wants him to stay.

"I can come back to move the body when you are done," he says, lingering.

I shake my head. "That won't be necessary. I'll burn her with the eternal flame."

Lines appear on his brow. The brazier is, of course, not nearly large enough for a human corpse, but he has seen me summon the god and manipulate the eternal flame. There is logic and then there is the divine. He'll believe I can burn her remains.

He nods and then gives me a short bow before exiting the divining room. There's no time to worry about the strain between us and no room to feel regret for the confusion and pain in his eyes.

Just as when we were children, I was left with no choice but to hurt him. I wish it weren't this way, but wishes are pointless in this world. I've wished my whole life to be something different than what I am, yet I've remained the same.

I lock the door and then wait, estimating the time it will take for him to leave the tower. Then I slowly unwrap the sheets. The ones around Mirial's head are wet, soaked in dark blood and viscera. Her skull must have split from the impact of the fall.

A thousand lies on the one who pushed her.

But I am the one who is truly cursed. By blood and by birth. By what I'm about to do.

I bite the inside of my cheek. This is such a remarkably foolish thing. Of all the acts I shouldn't do at Jubilee, this is at the top of the list. If Mirial were alive, she'd tell me to leave right now.

But she is dead and I am out of options.

I have to know what happened. The murdered senators, even

Antinous, were one thing; this is another. Mirial was my friend, like a mother to me, but more than that, she was a pillar of the Faith. Someone believed they could get away with killing a priest of my temple. It is my duty to stop them. I believe this is worth the risk.

I just hope I'm right.

"God of truth, forgive your humble servant for her lies," I say, bowing my head. "And forgive me for using your holy place for my own means. I have nowhere else to turn than into your arms."

I lower my head in prayer. I hope my god will accept me polluting this sacred space with a call to another. But truth and death walk hand in hand. There must be an understanding, or at least shared indifference to mankind.

I finish unwrapping her head and sigh. Poor Mirial. Looking at her like this, her eyes wide open in fear, I know there isn't a chance this was accidental. Someone murdered her.

Yet this close to a dead body, it's hard to think about anything other than the pull of godless death.

There is a distinct call in me from an ancient, primordial power. One cold and usually silent but just as ever present and knowing as the god of truth. Perhaps more so.

Death covers Mirial like a shadow. My body hums as if there's music, but there is no one playing. It's the magic in my blood swirling and surging, begging for release. My pulse beats until it makes my skin painful at my neck and wrists—the life points being the natural draw for death. There is only one relief.

I take the sickle knife and cut a shallow line on my left wrist, careful not to hit the veins that throb. There's pain, but also the absence of it. I've wondered if all Elusians felt this same urge, but there was no one to ask. It wasn't until I saw the fresco in the banquet room that I realized all of my bloodline felt this way.

Their history remains, but Elusian teachings are long gone, destroyed during the Crimson Night. My father told me to deny any pull of magic, to turn away no matter what the pain or consequence.

Kera, never, my father said when he finally admitted my adoption. *Any time will be one too many and you will be found, tortured, and executed. You must be Kerasea Vestal, and only her.*

But as blood wells on my wrist, I have to be something else—the last Elusian. For Mirial.

I raise my bleeding wrist above Mirial's mouth. Every move I make is on instinct, but my motions feel as natural as a bird leaving the nest.

And I have done this once before. So at least I am prepared for the impending horrors.

The moment my blood hits her lips, an inky black substance begins to pour out from around Mirial's corpse. It smells like rot and festering wounds, but it is godless death rising through her to answer my call.

Mirial gasps, her chest convulsing.

It's anathema to me, turning my friend into a conduit, but she's not alive—not really. My blood can't resurrect anyone. This is either death itself or Mirial answering from beyond the River of Death. I can't be sure which.

"My dearest one," I say. "Who killed you?"

It's hard to get the question out as the tendrils of death wrap around me. The black substance feels like barbed vines and fanged snakes constricting around my limbs. It's both solid and smoke, real and imagined, but it fills the room and converges on me, wanting more.

Death always wants life.

I shudder from the smell and the chill. The touch of death is so cold, it's scalding and so hungry, it's stomach-turning. I try to move away, but it's hopeless. Even in my robes, I'm freezing as death covers me. Screams of agony begin, and I am not sure if everyone can hear this or just me—it's why I needed Torren out of the tower.

My vision starts to fade. I can't tell if it's the black substance or just the death grip that is now choking my throat and chest. I claw at my neck but there is nothing—just my skin and robes. It's a futile attempt—death can't be held at bay or pushed aside as it comes for me, but my primal response is to fight.

I try to breathe, to focus only on Mirial, her back arching and her limbs moving in the sick dance of death throes. I did this for a purpose. I disturbed her eternal rest so that I would know the truth and be able to avenge her murder. I need answers. I have to stay conscious.

But my hold is slipping. It took guided practice to commune with the god of truth, to handle the weight of the divine, and this is something else entirely.

Death is far too strong. The pressure is so immense that no matter how I try, the world goes dark. I'm barely aware that I am falling until I hit the ground.

And then there's nothing.

I wake up on the stone floor of the divining room. Breathless, I stare up at the twinkling stars through the oculus of the domed roof. I'm alive…I think. I hazard moving my limbs. It's painful, but my arms and legs rise as I command them.

I'm not sure how long I was unconscious. A minute, maybe, though it could have been hours. But it doesn't feel like it was very long, even if my body aches from my scalp to my soles.

Stumbling to my feet, I'm dizzy but otherwise whole. There's no remnant of the inky-black substance that had poured out around me. The divining room looks as it always does—white altar, purple eternal flame.

Death comes and goes without a trace.

I wobble and place my hands on the cold altar to brace myself as the horizon slants. My wrist is still bleeding, red drops falling on the white stone. The surface is empty aside from the sickle knife and bloodied sheets in the center. Death fully took Mirial's body.

The same happened last time.

But this was all for nothing. I lost consciousness before Mirial could answer.

I grit my teeth at my failure, my heart pounding and head throbbing. I subjected her body, her memory to all of that for naught. In truth, I don't know what happens to her corpse now, or if I disturbed the entire Underworld. I don't know what the ramifications will be, but I was willing to pay the unknown price. I subjected myself to the waking nightmare of death and risked being discovered for nothing.

All because I wasn't strong enough.

I hang my head, but then catch a streak of red in my vision. Raising my chin, I finally notice the wall in front of me. There is one word written in Mirial's handwriting. The fresh blood drips down the stone.

MEDEA

LII.

Torren

I t is one in the morning, and Kerasea is in my bedchamber. She is
not, however, in my arms. No, she's kept her distance, pacing in
front of me for the last five minutes as I sit on the edge of my bed.

It is an understatement to say that something is off about her.
One of her priestesses just died—by her own hand or, more likely,
by a murderer—but somehow that doesn't feel like the issue. What
more could there be? A feeling of wrongness sinks its claws into me,
tearing me apart.

"Kerasea, what do you want to tell me?" I ask.

She stops, her eyes wide, as if she forgot I was present. Then she
runs her hands down her long hair. When she shifts her arm, there's
a bandage visible on her left wrist. It's bloody, and it wasn't there
before. She must've cut herself while taking out Mirial's liver, but
the fact that it's her wrist is odd. It's almost as if it was on purpose—

"I need to say something." She sighs.

Nothing else comes out.

"Just say it, then." I speak in a gentle tone as I wonder what could be rending her speechless.

She shakes her head and presses her lips together. Then she slaps her hands down at her sides. "I can't."

Yet she's here. If she truly didn't want me to know, she would've stayed in her bedchamber. I thought perhaps this was about us, a speech about how our kiss was a mistake, but that's not it, either. She wants me to know a fact, but she doesn't want to be the one to tell me. Truth is fighting with self-preservation.

"You found something." It's a guess, but an educated one.

She stops pacing and drops her head into a nod.

"You want to be truthful, but you can't tell me because...you're afraid of the consequences?"

Another guess, but it makes her pause, so there is some validity to it. Still, other than confessing to murder, the High Priestess wouldn't face consequences for nearly anything. So what has her so wound up?

"The issue is that I can't reveal how I know, and you'll ask," Kerasea says. "You'll ask because you're a good investigator."

She stares at me, her green eyes earnest. The strangeness of this makes the hair on my arms stand. I shake off the chill.

"All right," I say. "In that case, I won't ask. You have my word."

She blinks, but the tension eases in her shoulders.

"Senator Medea murdered Mirial."

I stare, and by the time I blink, my eyes feel dry. "Shock" isn't the right word for what I feel. "Sucker punched" is more accurate. I allow myself a moment before I speak. Whatever I'd thought she might say, it was not an accusation of murder against Senator Medea.

Medea was one of the killers who formed the republic. Many suspect that she poisoned her patron brother long ago, leaving her in sole power of a storied family. She is as clever as she is ruthless and no doubt capable of pushing a priestess off a balcony, so it makes logical sense, though I'll have to think on what motive she'd have. Would war be enough?

The wrongness, of course, is why can't Kerasea reveal her source?

It feels like I walked into a trap by promising not to ask. She didn't have to tell me anything, so what does she stand to gain from this?

Nothing. Medea isn't her enemy. In fact, she is friendly to Kerasea. So if there's nothing to gain from the lie, it is likely the truth.

"All right," I say. "But you know I cannot investigate a senator without the Council lifting *un exorum*. And the Senate will demand some manner of proof if you accuse Medea."

Kerasea nods. "I know. Proof is the heart of the issue." She begins pacing again. "Mirial was murdered, and that much I can swear to. If I say I witnessed it, that would be enough, but…"

"I would know you are lying." The words fly out of me before I even think them through.

She stops, spreads her hands apart, and exhales.

That is the real issue and why she's here. She is willing to swear falsely that she witnessed Medea push Mirial off her balcony. The Senate would accept that as a credible accusation. I would be able to search for evidence and, if I find anything, use pressure on Medea— that is, unless I admit that the High Priestess could not have seen the murder because I was with her at the time.

The wind is knocked from my chest as I realize the choice she's put in front of me. I can pretend I don't know she is lying in order to catch a murderer. Or I can refuse false evidence and potentially allow a killer to walk free. Which is better? Which is more just?

Without Kerasea swearing falsely, Medea will not face any consequences—that much is undeniable. And she could very well be behind the senate murders as well. Something sticks about the idea, some glances and smiles. Nothing more than a gut instinct, but that shouldn't be ignored.

Only, *how* does Kerasea know? She doesn't *suspect* that Medea killed Mirial. This isn't someone spewing random accusations. She is as certain as I've ever seen an accuser. The High Priestess would hold up swearing before her god. She has nothing to fear, as she is nearly untouchable. Then again, other people around her are not.

It could have been Zel.

Kerasea spoke to her servant when she was bringing her back to the tower. If Zel witnessed the murder, Kerasea would believe her, but a servant child would not be viewed as credible by the Senate. By saying that she saw the murder herself, Kerasea would not only get justice for her priestess, but she could protect the girl, and I've seen how far she is willing to go to do that.

"Sleep on it, please," Kerasea says. "At dawn, tell me your response. I'll understand either way."

I glance at the night clock. That's around six hours from now.

She gives me a lingering look and then turns to leave.

"Kerasea," I say, standing. She pauses and meets my eye.

There are so many secrets, so many lies, so many things unsaid between us. I want her. I want her away from me. I want to protect her. I want to hurt her.

"I swear on the gods, if I find you out of your chambers again tonight, I will kill you myself," I murmur.

It wasn't what I was going to say.

She shrugs. "I accept your terms, Praetorian."

I walk her out, and we silently pad to her room. She unlocks the door and swings it open, then lights the nearest lamp. When I look inside, no one is in there. She is safe.

I move to close her door, and she glances at me again over her shoulder. For just a second, there is an expression of vulnerability, of a need for help, and then it vanishes and she starts to move her bureau.

At least she is finally following directions.

I return to my room, sit on my bed, and run a hand down my face. What do I do now?

My armor shines in the corner as if it is winking at me. And perhaps it *is* mocking me. I became Praetorian half to avenge my family, to clear my name. And the other half was to have the power to administer justice, the way Hadrian did to that sentry. I never anticipated these types of moral dilemmas, and that was incredibly naive, as my position is rife with them. Instead of the black and white

I expected, veritas is all shades of gray.

I know what my father would have done. He was a firmly moral man—his honor is ultimately what got him killed. He would have refused false testimony. He would have stuck to the truth even if it meant that Medea walked free.

But I am very much not my father.

I believe in the republic, in the rule of law, and in protecting the Senate—I am just more flexible in my means. But what is Kerasea actually asking me to do? Nothing. She wants me to say nothing. Is staying silent in the face of a lie wrong if it aids me in my goals? If it catches someone so powerful that they are above the law?

Is there even such a concept as the "right thing to do" in Pryor?

No matter how I debate this in my mind, in my heart, I already have an answer.

I snuff my candle and lie back on the bed. Sometimes I wonder if my father would be proud or ashamed of who I've become, but that's a hypothetical. He's dead—a victim of the corrupt Verity Guild, all of whom met their untimely demise. And I cannot live for ghosts and memories. All I can do is be what I am.

A monster who got away with multiple murders.

So, I suppose the better question is, who do I want to be?

LIII.

Kerasea

As I peel back the covers on my bed, I doubt I'll get a wink of sleep. So much happened today. I haven't even begun to process Mirial's loss, losing myself with Torren, or that someone planted evidence in Zel's room and set fire to the woodshed. I don't know if Medea was behind the other murders, too, or solely Mirial's death, but the likelihood of having two separate murderers in one palace is slim.

For just a moment, I allow myself the white-hot rage that comes with acknowledging everything Medea has taken from me. I thought she was being kind to me, bringing another woman in power under her wing, when truly, that was never her intention.

But as I lie down, exhaustion overtakes the anger. It's not drowsiness—not exactly. It feels like I'm being pulled from this realm.

I'm asleep as soon as my head touches the pillow.

When I open my eyes, I'm in the temple of truth. Familiarity washes over me, but as I look around, it's not the temple as I know it. I'm not in the grand apartments but someone else's chambers—yet it feels as if it's my own. Somewhere in my mind, I know that a commotion just woke me. I rise from bed, but I am not me.

I am Mirial Bauman, twenty years ago.

Mirial's fear and knowledge fill me—this isn't a dream, not exactly; it's a memory, passed to me from godless death. That is the only explanation for how I know that it's the Crimson Night and that I am a priestess, the middle daughter of a merchant family. I love to sleep with my window open, not only for the breeze but to catch stray secrets.

Hushed voices make me hurry out of my room. I don my robe but leave my feet bare despite the chill of the spring night. Bare feet are better for staying silent.

Something is happening in the temple and I have to protect the Faith, protect *him*.

I slip into the shadows on soundless steps. Overlooked my entire life, I'm well accustomed to moving without being noticed. I pass the empty divining room and then, as I enter the Inner Hall, I find the High Priest speaking to a common woman. They talk in low tones, standing near the feet of the god of truth.

I was correct—something is amiss. The temple closes at dusk. There is no reason for a commoner to be here in the middle of the night.

Creeping nearer, I get a better look at the woman. I keep hidden behind a pillar, but I can see that it's not just a woman but a wet nurse with a child in her arms. I wrinkle my nose. Why is a servant speaking to Osiris Vestal?

"Sanctuary, please, High Priest," the woman says. The desperation in her voice and on her round face is obvious, but if she is asking for sanctuary on this night, she is either Elusian or, more likely, a sympathizer.

I wait for Osiris to reject her out of hand, but he doesn't. His good heart is preventing him from tossing her onto the street where she belongs. But this isn't the time for mercy. We cannot put the temple in jeopardy.

"Cut her down," I say, stepping out of the darkness. "This is trouble we don't need. Not on this night."

Osiris Vestal turns to me, handsome always with brown hair so dark, it's nearly black. But his brow is troubled as he looks from me to the wet nurse. Frustration fills my chest that he doesn't immediately side with me, but he is the great leader of our Faith, and I am not. I defer to him in all things.

The nurse holds the baby forward. The child is around a year old, I think, maybe a year and a half. I am not certain, as I've never had nor wanted children of my own.

"She is the last heir of the king and so young that she has no recorded name."

The Elusians lost many babies as infants, so the naming ceremony was performed only after the child reached two years old.

Osiris glances at me for counsel. I shake my head, but I know he has a profound weakness for babies. His wife died in childbirth, and the newborn she produced died three days later—a scrawny, sickly thing. It was ultimately a kindness, as that boy would never have been worthy of being his heir. Yet, Osiris's broken heart never recovered.

The nurse, of course, seizes on his hesitation and obvious kindness.

"Please. This child is only a baby—bright and innocent. I have nursed her from her first breath. She is not evil. She is not corrupted by them. Look at her."

I scowl at the drooling thing, although she is, admittedly, beautiful, with ebony hair and large emerald eyes.

One glance and Osiris is charmed. But my counsel was wise. We should eliminate both of them. The last heir of the king can only bring ruin to the temple and the Faith.

Yet, encouraged by our silence, the nurse places the child down. The baby is able to walk in that jerky, uncoordinated way of toddlers.

"We cannot intervene in the political matters of Pryor," I say.

Osiris finally takes his teal eyes off the baby and sighs. "We will not be given the option to remain neutral. Verhardt has already asked the temple to support the Council, and I have agreed." Then he looks at the nurse with a frown. "I'm sorry. We cannot give sanctuary to you or to her."

Just as he finishes speaking, the woman begins to blubber, her chin wobbling, but I raise my head. This is the right decision. It is the only choice to safeguard him and the temple during this tumultuous time.

My thoughts and the nurse's whines are cut off by a sudden crash. The statue of the god of truth sits with a bronze brazier in the right hand. Normally. The brazier containing the eternal flame just fell, clanging onto the marble floor.

My mouth falls open. That brazier is not unstable in the least, and it was untouched, high above our heads in the hand of the god.

The three of us stare, awestruck, as the chief guard of the temple comes running into the Inner Hall. He looks at us and hesitates with his hand on his sword. His brow is so furrowed that his scar puckers. With a flick of his wrist, Osiris sends him back to his position.

"The god," Osiris says, dropping to his knees.

I sign my respect with my fingers to my mouth as I quickly kneel. The peasant woman also cowers before the divine.

There is no clearer sign from a deity. I have never once seen that brazier so much as tip, even in an earthquake. The god of truth has spoken in favor of this little child. Why, I have no idea, but it is not my place to question the divine.

She is god-chosen.

The brazier is on its side, the eternal flame spilling out—the fire never dying. The girl child walks toward it. I'm the only one who notices as Osiris closes his eyes, whispering prayers to the god, and the nurse is still busy sobbing.

I draw a sharp breath as the baby nears the flame. The wet nurse looks up and gasps. Osiris stops praying.

The child is about to be burned alive.

The three of us watch from our knees, all too stunned to move. The baby is so close to the flame of truth that she can nearly reach out and touch it. This makes no logical sense. She should have been scorched, repelled by the intense heat, yet she is not.

I look at Osiris, but he seems more curious than worried. He continues to recite his prayer with his eyes open, but my limbs twitch, itching to move the girl away from the fire.

I suppose I've already started to care. Curious how something so small can pull so hard at the heart.

The baby continues in her uneven steps, entranced by the flame like a moth. But rather than being singed, she toddles right to the edge of the fire, and then inside it.

I gasp, getting to my feet, and I am not alone in my shock. The nurse stands slack-jawed, and even the High Priest is agape.

The baby stands inside the eternal flame as if it is her mother's arms and not a fire so hot it would burn a disbeliever to ash. Even the most practiced priests barely hazard a hand into the fire. Osiris has the most control I have ever seen, but he can't do anything like this.

"The god," he says.

I sign my respect again, penitent for my initial skepticism. This baby is truly blessed. Elusian or not, she was brought here as a gift to the temple, to us, to all of Pryor. She will raise the Faith to greatness.

Once out of the fire, the girl walks to Osiris as if nothing has happened. He has moved to the other edge of the flame and crouched down to be at her level. He stares at her with awe. When she reaches his arms, he picks her up like she's his own child. And somehow, I know she will be.

"We will keep her," he says.

I open my mouth. I want to disagree, because if the Senate discovers us harboring the last Elusian, they will treat it like a declaration of holy war and kill us all. But the girl is obviously chosen by our god, and Osiris has made up his mind. He has already started to love this child. There is more affection on his face now than I have seen in twenty years. Including for myself.

I purse my lips.

"Thank you, High Priest. A million thanks to your great name," the nurse says. Tears well in her eyes. "We call her—"

Osiris raises a hand and cuts her off. He will decide a name for the child, not some servant.

The High Priest strolls out of the Inner Hall, snuggling the baby in his arms and cooing to her. As I watch him, there's a stirring in my chest—happiness, I think. I can't help but love seeing him like this any more than I can help loving him. It is a one-sided affair, as I have never burdened him with my feelings. Our duty is to the Faith first and foremost. Yet he has completely forgotten the danger we are in in favor of the child.

"But the woman now knows…everything," I whisper.

The High Priest shakes his head as if he's waking up. He looks straight ahead and then nods. I exhale, relieved. We can't have a nursemaid with this kind of knowledge, and Osiris finally realizes it.

As we pass the chief guard, Osiris draws a line over his own throat with his thumb. And then he returns to bouncing the child and smiling.

I look over my shoulder. The nurse screams as she's dragged away by her shawl. Good. She will be dealt with. No one, other than us, will know where this child came from or who she really is. The baby looks enough like Osiris that he will be able to pass her off as his own. He will give her his name. And I will do whatever is necessary to protect her. I'll give my life to protect this secret.

The woman screams a final time—a bloodcurdling sound.

Osiris doesn't look back, and neither do I.

LIV.

Torren

Aknock on my door has me on my feet in the early dawn. It has to be Kera—I already heard her stirring and moving her bureau. She is awaiting my decision. After a fairly sleepless night, I am ready to give her my answer.

I open the door, disappointed to find Julian leaning on my doorframe.

"You look just terrible," he says.

I rub my face. "For the life of me, I can't understand how you don't get beaten more often."

Julian smirks. "Oh, that's easy—they're terrified of what you'd do." Then he stands straighter as his eyes narrow on me. "What's wrong? I got your message, but you look surprised to see me."

That's right. When I couldn't sleep, I slipped a note under his door to see me once he awoke, but I'd forgotten about that. Sleep deprivation is making me sloppy.

I've made up my mind, but we still have things to discuss. I gesture for him to come inside, and then I shut the door. Normally, I'd talk to him in the baths, but I don't want to risk leaving Kera unprotected.

"Kerasea is going to accuse Medea of the murder of Mirial Bauman," I say.

A variety of expressions crosses Julian's face as his mouth opens. Then he closes it.

"All right."

I blink. That was it? That's his full response? "I feel as though you're underreacting to this piece of information."

Julian shrugs. "Maybe, but whoever killed her was probably someone powerful, which means one of the senators, and there are only five of them. Medea is vicious and certainly capable of murder. But Kera saw this from…here?"

His hazel eyes move around.

That was the other reason I wanted to speak with Julian before Kerasea accused Medea. He saw us together right after the scream.

"From the tower," I say. "Her servant girl witnessed Medea pushing Mirial from the balcony."

Julian raises his eyebrows. "Is that where the girl is now?"

"Yes, Kerasea had her stay there."

"Because you know she'll have to—"

A floorboard creaks out in the hallway, and Julian cuts himself off mid-sentence. He moves his head just enough that I know he heard it, too. Someone was standing right outside my door.

Son of a jackal. The walls have ears here, and I knew that.

I stride past him and fling open the door. I look out, but there is no one in the hall.

Fuck.

I'm too sleep-deprived. We should've had this conversation in the baths or the tower. But what's done is done. Now I have to assume the worst person heard us. Kerasea and I will have to come up with a new plan—quickly.

Failure sits heavy in my chest, but I knock on her door. I have to tell her.

One second goes by. Two. Only silence greets me.

Panic puts its icy hands on my heart as I stare at her wooden door. There are only two reasons she wouldn't answer.

I bang my fist, knocking three times, hoping she's asleep even though I know she isn't.

I hold my breath. There is still nothing, and I know she wouldn't have left without me—she's terrible at following orders, but she needed my decision before the conclave.

Julian comes up beside me as I slip the skeleton key out of my armor and into the door. My hand shakes, but as I turn the knob, the door was already unlocked. I push it open, bracing myself for blood and wounds. To find her mutilated body.

There's nothing. I race into her en suite, but there's no one in here. I search the floor, the wardrobe, the balcony—nothing. No blood trail. Her things are all here and orderly, but she is gone.

Her sheets are rumpled but empty.

"Go down to the conclave like everything is normal. I'll find her," I say.

I take off running to the only place I think she'd go.

LV

Kerasea

I don the heavy gold necklace of the High Priestess in the rose light of early dawn. I sigh, exhaustion causing pain between my shoulder blades. Walking in Mirial's memories was less restful than staying awake—not that I had a choice in the matter. Death invaded my mind.

In Mirial's remembrance, I felt both trapped and free, myself and her. It was unlike any dream I've had before—more like the vision I saw in the library's fresco.

Whatever it was, it was undeniably a result of mingling my blood with hers. I'm just not sure why it didn't happen before.

I shiver. I have to hope that the shared memory was the only repercussion from summoning godless death a second time.

Not that it was a small price to pay.

The truth about my adoption sits heavier on my chest than the necklace. I knew I was never the only liar in the temple—I just didn't know the extent of my father's half-truths. By walking in Mirial's memory, I felt her unrequited love for my father, her initial disdain for me, and how desperately she wanted to murder the woman who saved me.

And that part—the whole existence of that woman, I was never told. My father went to his pyre keeping her murder a secret.

I'll never know that woman's name or her story. I'll also never know why she spared me and secreted me away. I have my life thanks to someone I can't even honor.

I thought I would finally hear my given name—to at least know that much about my past—but with one motion, my father silenced the truth. I was unsurprised. He was exceptionally good at that.

Around four years ago, my father finally admitted that I was adopted—mostly because I'd already figured it out. Of course, his tale was far different than the memory I walked in. My father spoke of being awoken on the Crimson Night by a baby arriving at the temple. He focused on how I was chosen by the god of truth and how I stepped right into the eternal flame. He neglected, however, to mention that they had considered killing me or that he ordered the murder of my nurse to keep my identity concealed. But those were minor details.

I curl my hands in fists. My story was nothing more than an inconvenient truth. The life of a single commoner rarely matters to the powerful.

But it matters to me.

And now the life of one commoner is going to change the Senate. Mirial wasn't noble—she was the daughter of a merchant, like many of the priests in Pryor. But through the temple, her life mattered. I will be able to seek justice for her.

If Torren allows it.

I glance at the wall that separates us, wondering if he has made up his mind, then I finish readying myself for the conclave. The wide gold bangles cover my wrists and bandage, and I style my hair in a simple braid.

I've just tied the end of my hair when there's a sharp, shooting pain in my left arm. I draw a noisy breath and turn the bangle, thinking it caught on my wound, but the pain is much deeper than a pinch. I breathe through my clenched teeth, as it feels like someone is shoving a blade in between the bones of my wrist. Then I remove the bangle. There's no blade, but there is fresh blood on the white bandage I just changed.

What is this?

As I stare, my blood is stirring, rushing mostly to my left wrist, but why? I'm nowhere near a dead body. Yet the magic in me is swirling, ready and begging for release. Death is calling me, but that doesn't make sense—I call death, not the other way around. Did I open a channel last night in the divining room?

The thought is horrifying, but then I wince, lurching forward as the pain intensifies. I cradle my wrist to my abdomen as the agony becomes so intense that my vision turns white. Another burst of pain makes me stumble, my wrist pulled toward the door.

I look down at my arm and furrow my brow, forgetting the pain in favor of confusion. When I move in the direction of the door, the pain lessens. In any other direction, including staying still, it returns with a vengeance.

It takes only a moment for me to accept that I'm being led somewhere. Somewhere out of this chamber.

When I open the door, the pain subsides. But I stop to try to lock it and the sharp, stabbing feeling returns twofold.

Stairs. I need to get to the stairs.

I walk a step, then break into a run, propelled by an invisible force and by the pain in my arm.

I reach the stairway. When I start climbing, the pain lessens to a dull ache. But what does death want from me? Is this a connection to Mirial? Is she making me seek out Senator Medea?

No. I pass the fifth floor, headed for the tower. Death propels me upward. I have to continue, but why? There is no corpse up there anymore. There's no one except for…Zel.

Zel is up there.

No.

No, no, no. I sprint up the stairs of my own volition. My lungs burn, the pain now solely in my chest, not my wrist.

Please not Zel. She is only a child.

The gold on me weighs me down, but I run until I reach the temple door. A side stitch is embedded like a knife in my waist, but I keep going because the door is ajar. It should be shut and locked. I shut and locked it last night.

I push the door fully open, and there is Zel. She is still breathing, her chest rising and falling rapidly, but I don't feel any relief, because Eyo's sentry, Lucius Calais, stands behind her. He holds a dagger to her throat with one hand, his other grabbing at her skirts. It takes a single moment to realize I interrupted whatever he was about to do to her.

Zel's eyes are wide, and she's going to scream. There's a terrible glint in Calais's eye. Now that he can't exercise his physical power over her, he's going to settle for the pleasure of killing her in front of me.

How am I going to stop him?

Zel is on the other side of the room, and I have no weapon on me.

Fool! Why didn't I grab a blade? She's going to die now, and there's nothing I can do.

My stomach twists as bile rises in my throat. I have a moment, just one, to react. Half a heartbeat squeezes in my chest as she screams, the pitch high and haunting. My blood drips, trickling from my left wrist into my palm.

I dip my right fingers in my blood. Without even thinking about it, I sign in the air in a cutting motion. The same way I saw my father sign across his neck.

In a burst of inky blackness, death comes for Lucius Calais. Blood splatters Zel's back and hair as his neck is sliced apart. Then blood pours out of his body like a fountain as his head is cleaved from his shoulders, cut cleanly in the direction I just signed.

I stand, stunned. I hadn't even thought I could do that. But it wasn't thought—it was all instinct.

Victory and horror flow through me, but as he falls, Calais retains enough of a grip that his dagger slits Zel's throat.

No!

I rush forward and catch her as she collapses. But I was too late. Too slow. Crimson gushes from the wound on her neck—her life spilling out.

I try to stanch the bleeding, pressing my hands on her throat, but I know it's hopeless. My blood can't heal like the old king. I don't have that power. No one does. Not even the most skilled healer could help her now.

All I can do is hold her as she chokes on her own blood.

We crumple to the floor, Zel's body across my lap as I cradle her. I keep one hand on her neck, but I grip her hand with my other, trying to be some kind of hollow comfort. She tries to speak as she stares into my eyes, but all that comes out is a gurgling sound. Pure fear widens her eyes, her expression begging for help that can't come.

And then there is nothing. Her brown eyes stay open, but they no longer see. Her hand falls limp out of mine.

When the light leaves her eyes, all I feel is rage. Consuming, deadly fury hits, my heartbeat roaring in my ears. My hands curl holding her as I look at Calais's skull, his mouth open in shock.

I'm sorry I killed him. I regret giving him the charity of a fast death. I should've tortured him until living became worse than dying. He murdered her. He knew he would die, but in his very last moments, he chose to kill a fucking child. And I couldn't stop him. I can't stop any of these vipers as they slither and strike at will.

Rage bursts beneath my skin, the scream building in my throat. This time I don't swallow it down; I let it out. My scream rings and echoes around the divining room. I scream until I don't have any breath left.

The purple of the eternal flame draws my attention. The fire roars with righteous anger, the blaze rising in a column ten feet into the air. I stare and realize it's not just my rage, but the god's. A servant's blood was spilled in a holy place, and the god of truth riots.

Enough of these lies and liars.

Come to me.

I move my fingers and call the eternal flame. It spills out of the brazier like water and then surrounds me the way it did when I was a child. I bathe in the familiar glow and hold Zel's body tightly in my arms. The remains of Lucius Calais catch fire. His blood and clothes burn first, but then his body, his face is incinerated. The smell of charred flesh fills the air, and when he's finally gone, I look past him.

That's when I notice the Praetorian standing in the open doorway.

LVI

Torren

I don't understand what I'm seeing. I freeze and then shield my eyes, because Kerasea is surrounded by a purple bonfire so bright that it hurts to look at her. The heat radiating out is scorching, even from the doorway.

I raced here, worried she was in danger, thinking I could help, which now seems foolish. But I heard a scream. There was just a pool of blood, and I thought Lucius Calais was lying on the ground in two pieces. Now there's only Kerasea cradling her servant girl. She and Zel sit unburned in the middle of the flame.

Kerasea picks her head up, and her eyes meet mine.

With a wave of her hand, she makes the fire retreat. The eternal flame flees until it sits calmly in the brazier next to the altar. I look around, but everything in the tower is normal, as if nothing happened.

Yet Kerasea and Zel are covered in blood.

"Kerasea," I say, breathless. "Are you all right?"

I ask the question, but I already know she's unharmed. Her scream was one of anger, of mourning, not of physical pain.

Awe and fear mingle in my chest. I want to take a knee to her, but this is all impossible.

How could any of this have happened?

The High Priestess stares straight ahead, slowly rocking the girl in her lap. Kerasea's white robe is soaked in blood. There's splatter on her neck and on her golden collar. Her hands drip crimson onto the stone floor, but the blood isn't hers. Zel's chest is covered, all of it stemming from a deep wound on her neck.

"They killed a child," Kerasea says. "I was too late."

There's no emotion in her voice, and she's not looking at me. She's just staring into the distance.

I have seen men after battle look like this, wandering with grave wounds and speaking matter-of-factly as they search for their own body parts. There's a level of atrocity where the mind shuts down.

I take a step closer, ready to own my part in this.

"I was speaking to Julian and someone overheard us—I think it was Calais. I was careless, and I deeply regret it."

Kerasea's green eyes finally focus on me, and she tilts her head. "No. You didn't do anything wrong. Sentries follow orders, and he planned to murder her. Medea is going to suffer for this."

Again, she is not speculating. She is certain that Medea ordered the murder of her servant.

The High Priestess gently lays Zel's body down, and then she rises from the floor. She gives the girl a mournful stare before stepping away.

"I'm ready."

The most powerful woman in the republic pushes away her shock and raises her blood-speckled chin. I have no doubt that she is prepared to accuse Senator Medea, come what may.

"I accept your terms," I say.

She nods. She knows that means I will stay silent as she falsely swears. But I don't think she cares much anymore. No, from that hollow look on her face, she doesn't give a fuck about consequences at all.

We take the stairs back into the palace. I pause as we reach the landing for the third floor.

"I'll wait while you bathe and change," I say.

She blinks, and her brow furrows. "I'm not going to change."

I raise my eyebrows.

She gestures to the blood covering her. "Let them see what she's done."

All right then.

I can't say I know who or even what Kerasea is right now. There's no fear, no emotion in her. She barely seems present, but she is sharp as a sabine and poised to attack.

We arrive on the first floor and proceed directly to the throne room.

To say she causes a stir with her arrival is an understatement. The sentries posted outside the doors gasp. A senate page drops a scroll, and it falls to the floor with a *clang*. Another faints with a sigh. It's audible because the room has been struck silent. The senators all stop where they are standing, frozen in horror. Julian rises from behind his desk, his eyes wide.

The blood-covered High Priestess of the temple of truth walks to the center of the room and comes to a graceful stop in front of the Council.

"I accuse Senator Medea of murder under *lex religio*," she says.

I will myself not to react and remain at attention. I suppose that solves how we were going to broach the accusation. Priests are protected by the law that she just cited—even from the Senate.

Another of the senate pages faints, but Kerasea stares only at Medea. The senator sits at the table with her hands folded.

"I decline and object," Medea says.

I observe her expressions, her tone. Medea is completely calm, unfazed, and wholly guilty.

Kerasea stares.

Terrance clears his throat. "We will, of course, have to vote upon—"

It's a valiant effort to gain control of the room, but Terrance stops speaking as Kerasea raises her left hand and looks at him with pure disdain. This is not the girl they could intimidate or cajole. Her stare is enough to silence the Senate Leader.

Then she refocuses her attention on Medea. Kerasea breathes out a laugh, and the corner of her lips rises. It's not a smile so much as a terrifying sneer. Without breaking eye contact, she wipes her bloody hand over her left wrist—the one she accidentally cut last night—and then she strokes the lapis on her robe.

"I call upon the god of truth to enter this room."

The moment Kerasea lifts her right hand, the air shifts above us. Everyone stares up at the ornate ceiling as darkness descends on the room. The morning sun ceases to shine through the wall of windows. All the candles and lamps are extinguished as one.

I grab my temples as intense pressure makes my head and shoulders ache. Kerasea stands still as everyone else clutches their heads, bows under the weight, or winces, their faces contorting.

"I swear on the holy name of the god of truth that Senator Medea is a murderer and she did, at this very conclave, cause blood to be spilled, including that of Priestess Mirial Bauman."

Kerasea lowers her hand to her shoulder, and daylight partially returns. The pressure lessens in my temples, but not completely. It's enough that I can focus on the High Priestess as she extends her arm and points to Medea.

The moment she does, the senator falls out of her chair and collapses to her knees with a scream. Kerasea turns her hand, and Medea lowers her head to the marble floor. Divine might is forcing the senator to move as if she is a puppet on a string.

I have never seen a priest have this ability. Pryor has not seen someone channel this kind of power since there were Elusians. But Kera is not a magic blood.

She couldn't be. They are all dead.

"Kerasea! High Priestess! Relent. We accept the accusation," Terrance says. Terror makes his voice shake as he clasps his hands together. Gone is his sniffing and haughty disdain.

Suh and Paolo nod, apparently becoming aware of their own mortality. Foreau is slow to react but eventually assents. Medea, however, doesn't move. I don't think she can.

The High Priestess has won, but I don't know that she hears it. She is so focused on vengeance, so thoroughly connected to her god that she is barely a person right now. Unbridled rage lights her face, her eyes aglow with the divine.

As I look from her to Medea, I realize Kerasea is channeling the weight of the god into the senator. The High Priestess might split Medea's skull open in front of us. And if she does, she will be executed for murder.

In the republic, even the High Priestess's power has limits.

I move closer to her.

"High Priestess!" Paolo calls. He holds his own head but kneels next to Medea in an attempt to shield her. "Stop this, please!"

Suh clasps his hands in the air and nods vigorously in agreement, his jowls shaking. Terrance pales, suddenly impotent in front of real power.

Medea tries to cover her head with both arms crossed over her hair. Her forehead is pressed onto the floor. But Kerasea doesn't move.

"Admit what you have done," she says.

Medea doesn't speak, but I'm not certain she can.

The only person sitting still is Foreau. He winces at the table, but mostly he's taking in the whole scene like it's an amusing play. But this is life-and-death—Medea's, but most importantly, Kerasea's.

I have to act and find a way to make her relent.

I step closer to the High Priestess, then reach out and take her left hand.

As soon as our fingers touch, she breaks her stare from Medea and looks at me. I brace myself, worried she'll strike at me with a weapon I can't defend against, but she just tilts her head, puzzled.

"Enough now," I say, keeping my voice calm and measured. "You have triumphed. The Senate has agreed to an investigation. I will search for evidence—and I *will* find it."

They didn't explicitly say this, but that is the standard when lifting *un exorum*.

Kerasea blinks hard and shakes her head, as if she is just waking up. The candles and oil lamps flare back to life, and the sun returns in the throne room.

Everyone peers upward, cautious and tentative, as if the ceiling may come crashing down on them.

Kerasea has done it—accused Medea of murder and lifted *un exorum*.

But as Foreau and Terrance stare at the High Priestess, an unsettling feeling hits my chest. She has won but also marked herself as more powerful than the Council. That makes her a target for their ambitions as well as their retribution.

Today will not be the end of this.

LVII

Kerasea

I was going to murder Medea in front of the entire Council — what's left of them, anyhow. Torren was able to stop me, and though I'm not sure how he was able to break my connection to the divine, I'm glad he did.

Julian and Senator Paolo help Medea off the ground. Once she's seated, Julian gives her a glass of water, but it sits on the table, as she can barely keep her head up. I wonder why the Praetorian isn't detaining her, but I look down and realize that he's still holding my hand. Our fingers are woven together like lace.

But both of my hands and most of my robe are covered in blood.

Zel's blood.

I shake my head.

It's almost like I was asleep, like walking in Mirial's memory.

What have I become? And what did I just connect to?

My heart hammers in my chest as the events rush through my mind. The sharp, shooting pain in my wrist. The horror of catching

Calais with Zel. I watched him kill her. I saw her try to cling to life. I held her as she died, her eyes pleading for help. All of that is clear. Everything after is a bit hazy.

Chills careen down my spine, cold like the touch of death. I lost myself to rage.

The throne room begins to spin as I stare at the blood on my robe, my pulse throbbing erratically. I was able to murder Lucius Calais with only my blood.

All the times my father told me that I wasn't *really* Elusian seem ridiculous when I am, in fact, and have always been a magic blood.

But now that I have used my power, my connection to death is growing stronger. I can't be certain what answered my blood call.

Was it truth or death?

I sway to the beating of my pulse. I could've killed Medea in front of them all. I *wanted* to. Something in my blood begged for hers. And just like with walking in a memory, I didn't have full control.

How long until everyone figures out what I am?

I pant and try to stay present, but my face tingles and my stomach turns.

"Sentry Lucius Calais is dead," I say.

I blink hard as Suh and Foreau turn my way; the others are still focused on Medea.

"The god of truth struck him down as he killed my servant in the divining room. He violated a holy place, and his memory should be stricken."

My voice sounds strange in my ears, just above a whisper. I barely feel the floor beneath my feet.

My heart thumps and my vision goes in and out. Then the horizon tilts sideways.

"May the truth be revealed," I add.

It's the last words I speak before everything goes dark.

LVIII.

Torren

Kerasea faints, and I catch her in my arms.

"Julian, send word to the priests of the god of protection: the conclave has concluded," I say. "Everyone will leave today."

Before anyone can react, Julian nods and walks out of the throne room.

"We will convene a special session in the Senate Hall for the remainder of the resolutions, but the status quo pends until then." Terrance gathers his toga, but he speaks in the quietest volume I've ever heard from him.

My own reappointment, along with the rest of the laws, will wait until later this year. That is fine, as I have greater concerns.

"Everyone is to remain in this room," I say. "Senator Medea, you are under arrest by order of the Praetorian on behalf of the Senate Council. Disobey at your peril."

I scoop up Kera in my arms and carry her. Her head dips back and she's fully unconscious, but I still notice the gazes of the senators as I walk out of the room. Between taking her hand and caring for her now, I have announced that we have a connection. Dread pools in my stomach. This relationship will have repercussions—I'm certain of it. But I have to see her to safety now, regardless of the consequences.

"No one is to go in or out," I say to the two sentries standing guard. "On pain of death."

"Yes, Praetorian," they say.

They both salute, even though it means that if I find anyone out of the throne room, I will lay the blame on them and summarily execute them.

I carry Kerasea up to my bedchamber and then shift her weight so I can open my door. She's still stained in blood, but she looks so different from the priestess who could've killed a senator moments ago.

I lay her down on my bed and brush aside a piece of her hair. There's no possibility she's Elusian. She is the daughter of Osiris Vestal; she looks just like the High Priest. It's simply the aura of their palace intruding on my thoughts. That's all.

I look up from her face and spot Julian in the doorway.

He shouldn't be here.

"I thought I gave you a command," I say, standing straight.

"Which I followed," he replies. "I sent two house servants down the mountain. I thought you'd need my assistance here more than me playing messenger."

He's right. I do. Julian is the only one I can trust.

"Watch her for me," I order. "Stand guard and kill anyone who tries to enter."

His eyes search mine, but he nods. "Yes, Praetorian."

If Julian is surprised by my command, he doesn't show it. He's serious for once, but I suppose everyone was chastened by the High Priestess's display of raw power.

With Kerasea now secured, I can begin my search of Medea's chambers. I need to find evidence to corroborate Kerasea's accusation or all of this will be for nothing. Because she accused a senator, I need both testimony and evidence to convince the Council to convene the Verity Guild.

Medea chose the fifth-floor room once belonging to the king's favorite wife. It is the grandest guest chamber in Jubilee aside from the king's. No one stays in that bedchamber, as everyone claims the room is still steeped in his blood magic.

I'm starting to believe that's true.

Medea's sentry took the room of the king's first son, and her page took the chambers of the second heir. None of the king's early children or wives had his same healing magic, so they all died hundreds of years ago.

I enter Medea's lavish bedroom with my skeleton key. The walls are white brocade with gilding on every inch of molding. The floors are laid with expensive marble. Despite the opulence, the most striking features are the floor-to-ceiling windows looking out at the mountainous landscape.

Unlike the chaos of Zel's room, this chamber is neat and tidy. There are double doors that lead to a balcony. I decide to start at the scene of the crime. I turn the carved ivory handle to the glass-and-wood door. There are footprints in the snow, which means someone was out here, but those alone aren't evidence.

I search every square inch of the balcony, but there is no blood splatter, no clues to be found. As Mirial was pushed, it's not surprising, only disappointing.

While I'm at the balustrade, I crane my neck to the east, but I can't see the tower from here. An unsettling feeling grips me—a hint of doubt—but I dismiss it. Just because I can't see the tower from the balcony doesn't mean the opposite is true.

I step inside and begin a meticulous search of Medea's room and the massive en suite. There is a granite tub large enough for ten people and a mirrored dressing area encrusted in ivory and jewels. But there are no hidden weapons in the bathroom—nothing out of the ordinary at all.

I search the wardrobe. Like every benefactress, Medea has

an array of clothes and a chest of jewelry that could feed a dozen Northside families for years. But inequality is not what I'm looking for. I turn over every drawer and search under and inside every piece of furniture in the room, but there is nothing. No robes, no letters, nothing to link her to Mirial's death.

And without evidence, she will go free. As free as whoever poisoned Eyo and eviscerated Verhardt.

I have to think she was responsible for their deaths, as two killers at Jubilee is unlikely, but where is the evidence?

I breathe out a sigh of frustration, but I force myself to remain calm and focus on just the crime at hand. Criminals, especially those who have never faced consequences, are sloppy by nature. There should be something in here. Something she missed. And if I find evidence she pushed Mirial, I will be able to protect the Council if she was also behind the senate murders.

But perhaps I started in the wrong place. Medea is probably too clever to keep anything in her own chambers.

I search her sentry's and page's rooms. I work quickly but methodically, looking in all the usual and unusual hiding spots.

In total, I spend two hours tossing all three of the chambers, yet I come up empty-handed.

I raise my chin and try to shore up my reserve, reminding myself I'm doing this for Kera now.

If Zel were still alive, I'd be able to use her testimony, but she was conveniently murdered before Kerasea could accuse Medea.

I stop cold. Calais could have been conspiring with the senator. He was likely the one listening outside my door, and then he'd have reason to murder Zel. Calais had access to Eyo—he easily could have poisoned him. He was on duty when Antinous was killed, but drowning a man takes minutes. And he was at the Revelry party the night Verhardt was murdered. As a sentry, he could have escorted the Senate Leader to the altar of peace.

It fits, but I still need the evidence.

I return to Medea's room. There has to be something here—

something I missed. I feel it in my bones.

Her dismantled writing desk catches my eye. I've already pulled out every drawer, checked behind them, and found nothing. Nothing from Mirial, not a paper out of place, although right now everything litters the floor. But I check again.

Once I've gone through everything twice, I stop searching and sigh. These people have remained in power *because* they don't make sloppy mistakes. I've always known how difficult it is to bring down the elite in Pryor, and Medea is at the very top.

The late-morning mountain sun is nearly blinding as it pours through the windows. The gilding glows, and even though I'm empty-handed, I know my time is up. The senators won't tolerate being locked in for much longer. I will have to go down to the Council and admit that I found nothing.

A thought enters my mind. I could take something of Mirial's from Zel's room and claim I found it here. Medea would object, but no one would know that I planted the evidence.

I shake it off. *I* would know.

No matter how tempting it is, fabricating evidence isn't just. And I promised myself once I became Praetorian, I would do things the right way.

I stare at the wood floor, nauseated by the fact that I had even considered it, but then notice that something is off about the notepad on the ground. It's the same kind as is in all of our rooms. It's blank, but as the sun catches the paper, I see there's an indentation from the last note written on here. I pick up the notepad, and when I tilt it just a little more, I can read it.

Mirial,

See me before you leave

M

I clutch the pad so hard that I almost crush it, but this is it. My heart drums, victory coursing through my veins. This is what I was looking for. Medea not only knew that the priestess was at Jubilee, but she called her to this room. Implied in the note is that Medea was the last to see her alive. When I combine that with Kerasea's accusation, it is enough to charge Senator Medea with murder under *lex religio*.

And I will be able to see Kerasea's eyes sparkle like diamonds when I present the evidence.

I stride past the open wardrobe and come to an abrupt halt. *Diamonds*. I didn't check Medea's jewelry because I didn't think I'd find evidence in necklaces and jewels. But suddenly, I remember turning Verhardt's wrist. The emerald ring on his little finger was how we identified him, but his other ring was missing.

My heart pounds and my mouth goes dry as I open the lid of the chest. I look down.

There, on a small velvet pillow, is the diamond ring of the republic.

It was Medea this entire time.

LIX

Kerasea

I wake up to sunlight pouring onto my face, but I'm not in my own bed. I'm not even in my room in Jubilee Palace. These sheets smell like snow and sandalwood.

I sit up with a start, and the room spins. I clutch my head as I fall back onto the pillow.

"You're all right. You're safe," Julian says from the doorway.

I look around and realize I'm in Torren's bedchamber. Bloody lies, how did I get here? My head throbs, and then I realize that I must have fainted in the throne room.

"Torren carried you here and posted me to guard you, Excellency," Julian says.

I look over because there's new reverence in his eyes and his tone. Instead of his normal humor, he's serious.

"Where is he now?" I ask.

"Searching for evidence against Medea. You haven't been asleep long—maybe an hour."

I nod. At least the sleep was dreamless. But then I look down and notice the blood all over me. I cringe at the sight.

"I'm sure you'd like to bathe and change. The conclave has ended, and we are all leaving soon," Julian says.

"Thank you, Commander," I say. As usual, I'm grateful for his kindness.

I rise from the bed, but slowly because it feels like my body was beaten. Every joint aches down to my bones. Julian rushes in and offers me his arm. I take it, and we walk to my room.

"I'll be just outside your door," he says.

I smile, close the door, and undress. I'm surprised there aren't bruises on my skin. Blood soaked through my shift, so I throw it into the fire. I want to burn the ceremonial robe as well, but there are sacred lapis stones inside, so I roll it into a ball as the water warms up.

It takes two baths to fully scrub Zel's blood from my body. I wrap my wrist, pin back my wet hair, and then don simple riding clothes. Once I'm done, I open my bedroom door to see Julian turn and smile.

He escorts me to the throne room. Two sentries stand at the door. They both sign with their fingers to their lips and bow low to me as we enter.

I smile, though unease grips me. I'm not their commander. They should've saluted Julian, not me. But calling the god in front of them has put me above their chain of command, because the thing Pryor respects the most is power.

My fingertips grow icy. Religious fervor can be just as dangerous as the truth. More so.

Julian and I wait in the doorway as the senators speak. Torren stands at attention in front of the table. Ease and hope fill me at the sight of him.

But something is wrong—his jaw is clenched.

"While the evidence the Praetorian presented is compelling and troubling, ultimately all Senator Medea stands accused of is the murder of a commoner," Suh says. "Tullanium is inappropriate."

Torren found evidence and asked to bring Medea to jail. My heart quickens. Not only did he carry me to his bed and safeguard me, but he will bring a senator to justice.

"Is there not room in Tullanium for Medea?" Foreau asks. "The note from her hand to the victim along with the High Priestess's testimony is evidence enough for detainment before trial. And her being in the possession of the diamond ring of the republic minimally shows her involvement in Verhardt's death."

The diamond ring of the republic? The one Verhardt wore?

Medea masterminded all of this.

I clutch Julian's arm, feeling faint again, but I don't dare look in Medea's direction. I can't risk what my anger will summon.

Terrance sniffs in annoyance. "The ring is not evidence of her involvement when there is no witness testimony, and Medea fervently denies having it in her possession. Tullanium is simply not the place for a senator awaiting trial. We, of course, can have her post a substantial bond, but we should believe the word of our colleague. Do you agree, Paolo?"

I stare at Senator Paolo. Reasonable and part of the new guard, he should agree with Foreau. But Paolo is focused on his ring, avoiding eye contact.

"Agreed," he says.

"On a three-to-one basis, Medea shall post a five-thousand-gold-bullion bond and will be remanded to her villa in the capital following our departure from Jubilee," Terrance says. "She is to remain there until the Verity Guild tribunal convenes following the trial of Trajan Lowe. That brings all matters to a close for this conclave."

I step into the throne room. "Just a moment, Senator. Sentry Calais murdered my servant in cold blood." All eyes turn to me, including Torren's. "I want his memory and his name stricken."

No one speaks. Fear emanates from the Council—as well it should.

"He, of course, committed a great offense to you, Excellency,"

Suh says, bowing his head. "But the murder of a servant does not warrant striking a memory and removing nobility from a bloodline."

"I can't think of something that is less noble than molesting and murdering a defenseless girl," I say. "I'm sure Senator Eyo would've agreed."

Suh flushes, and Paolo shifts uncomfortably in his seat.

"Although this is not proper procedure for a complaint of this nature, I see no objection to compensating you for your loss," Terrance says.

"Compensation?" I repeat.

Terrance nods vigorously, though his white hair doesn't move. "I believe the sum of twenty gold bullions will be an adequate recovery for your servant's services."

Her services.

If I hadn't killed Calais, that is all he would have had to pay for murdering Zel in front of me. Her death is considered an offense to property because he was noble and she was part of the servant class.

Twenty gold pieces for the life of a fourteen-year-old girl. That is all she was worth to them.

I should've brought the ceiling down.

I curl my hand, my bandage tight around my wrist. Rage bubbles inside me and, with it, a hunger for pain, for blood. This Council should not exist. But I catch Torren shaking his head slightly. I have to remain calm, because that is what is expected of me, but more so this connection to death is now stronger than it ever has been. I need to stay controlled and concealed. I've known that my entire life, but I lost control at Jubilee.

"Of course," I say. "That is more than adequate."

Terrance and Suh stand, but I catch the stare of Medea. Torren is placing handcuffs on her, yet from the gleam in her eye, you'd think she won.

LX

Kerasea

My carriage rolls through the city gates of the capital, past the gentle splendor of the Southside villas. I'm seated alone as I return home. Mirial is dead. Zel is dead. And a coin purse sits on the bench next to me. I wrinkle my nose in disgust and push the velvet bag farther away.

Senator Terrance's page handed me twenty gold bullions before we left Jubilee. Zel will never fall in love, never have children of her own, never see fifteen. But this is considered just compensation.

Her murdered body is tied to the back of this carriage, wrapped in my ruined robe. Later tonight, I will burn her and say my goodbyes to the girl who squeezed my hand when I was being lectured, who quietly fixed my makeup to hide my sleeplessness. Meanwhile, Medea is in her villa atop one of the hills in the capital. A viper back in her spacious burrow.

A scream builds in my throat from the unfairness of it all, but I exhale. She will stand trial. Torren and I will be able to convict her. There will finally be a type of justice.

The carriage rolls to a stop in front of the temple of truth. I take a deep breath, sitting back in my seat. I don the placid mask of High Priestess. Not only will I have to pretend as per usual, I will now have to tell Zel's parents that they lost their eldest daughter, as well as inform the priests and acolytes that Mirial was murdered. I have been dreading this moment since I left Mount Ara, but it is time. This is my duty. They all deserve to hear the truth from me—especially Zel's parents.

I step out of the carriage and climb the stairs of the temple. As the sun hits the horizon, I turn and look at the Forum. The Senate Hall is aglow in the dying light of the setting sun. They say the Elusians were corrupt and immoral, oppressive and unjust. I'm not sure how they were worse than the Council, though.

As I pass through the bronze temple doors, I enter the familiar embrace of home. I inhale the eucalyptus scent as the priests, acolytes, and servants stand in the Great Hall waiting to greet me. The braziers are lit, clearly illuminating all the familiar faces.

I bless each person by name, but I stop in front of Zel's parents.

"Please see me in my chambers," I say.

They both bow.

I accept the welcome by the rest of the servants and nod to the chief temple guard. It's hard to keep my expression placid, as I now know what he did on the Crimson Night. But I'm sure he barely remembers it. Another body. Just another dead servant in Pryor.

I walk down the corridors to my quarters, but as usual, even in my own rooms, I'm not alone. One of my chambermaids waits to serve me, but it's not Zel. It never will be again.

As soon as I step inside, the maid kneels and removes my riding boots. My bare feet have just touched the floor when there is a knock on my door. I already know that it's Zel's parents.

"Enter," I say.

Her mother and father step inside on hesitant feet. Zel inherited her wide brown eyes from her mother and her father's thick, curly hair. Looking at the two of them, I can piece her together, and it makes my heart break once more.

"Excellency," they say simultaneously. They bow and sign with their fingers to their lips.

I close my eyes for a long blink, dismiss my chambermaid, and then I begin. "I regret to say that I have the most grievous news to tell you both."

The husband and wife exchange worried glances. Zel's mother holds her skirts so tight that her knuckles whiten, but she waits patiently. Surely she noticed that her daughter did not arrive with me. She must at least suspect that something is awry. I search for words to make this easier, but nothing can soften a death blow.

I draw a breath. "Zel has crossed to the Underworld. While we were at Jubilee, her life was taken. Your daughter died simply because I failed to keep her safe, and for that I can never form an apology worthy of your ears or make amends. I don't pretend to understand how you feel, but do know that I loved her, too. I grieve with you. We will honor her tonight with funeral rites and praise her memory, but I don't expect that it will be nearly enough."

Zel's mother closes her eyes, and her father bows his head. "May the Underworld receive her," he says.

"May she navigate the River of Death to the shores of eternal peace," I recite.

I mean it.

The quiet of truth descends on the chamber as they attempt to process the loss. I hold still and wait, ready to answer their questions, though I dread them.

"You said...you said her life was taken," her mother says. "Do you know who killed her?"

Her father frowns. I suppose he doesn't want to know, but it is now my duty to tell her.

"Lucius Calais, a nobleman and sentry."

They exchange sad glances. They know that his elite status means that he won't face any consequences. And he would not have, but for what happened.

"He is dead by my—" I begin, and then I catch myself. "By the will of the god of truth, he was killed for shedding blood in a holy place. He was struck down, but it was not in time to save Zel. She died quickly in my arms."

Tears stream down her mother's face, and pain radiates through my chest. I have replayed those last moments a dozen times. If only I'd acted faster, responded to the call of my blood sooner, she would still be alive.

In the end, this was my fault.

"That is all we can ask," her father says. "Thank you, Excellency."

"A million thanks be to your great name," her mother says.

I stare. They're thanking me? My stomach roils at their gratitude, but I maintain my composure.

"The Senate has offered recompense." I swallow my disgust for their coin and for Zel's parents thanking me when I cost their daughter her life.

I hand the bag of gold to her father. "It is not nearly enough, but please take this with my sincere condolences."

"Excellency, you are too magnanimous," he says with a deep bow. Her mother also curtsies.

The worst part is they are genuinely moved. I failed horribly as a shepherd. I allowed one of my flock to be eaten by a wolf. They were given mere gold for the life of their firstborn, and they are thanking me.

Because another noble would have kept the coins. Because another priest would've let him walk free.

I curl my hands in fists. I can't stand this a moment longer.

"If you'll excuse me," I say. "There are many matters that need my attention as we prepare for tonight."

"Of course," her father says. "Thank you, Great One."

They both bow again, then take each other's hands as they leave, and I remember finding my fingers woven with Torren's. He might be the only one who understands what I am feeling. I'm livid at my failure, at the power imbalance throughout Pryor, at the senseless murder and now being thanked. Somehow, I know he'd understand.

I want to see him—it's startling how strong the urge is to go to him—but unlike Zel's parents, I will never be able to trust him. I'll never be able to accept solace from a man who would persecute me to the ends of the world if he really knew me.

I call the chambermaid back into my room. I need to prepare for Zel's funeral rites.

LXI.

Torren

I t's well into the evening when I return to the barracks with an expensive bottle of sparkling wine and a gold laurel wreath. I set both on the counter. Perhaps Hadrian will take this bottle instead of the vessel. Although given the reason for the award, perhaps I should just smash it in the sink.

"Take the commendation, Tor," Julian says, again reading my thoughts.

We are both dressed in our finest armor, having been called to the altar of peace an hour ago. This wine was given to me as a gift, along with a laurel wreath for my investigation.

Little could have felt more wrong than accepting the awards from three remaining senators. Foreau was absent; the rest are dead or under arrest.

And I, first and foremost, am the Senate Protector.

"I can't let this go, Jules," I say. "Why would they publicly thank me? Verhardt, Eyo, and Antinous are dead. Medea is arrested. Don't you find it unusual for them to reward me?" I tip the bottle and then leave it on the counter.

Julian's brow wrinkles. "No. They are pleased with the result—they all got what they wanted."

I sigh and pinch the bridge of my nose. With Eyo's body having burned, the Council has decided that no further inquiry is proper. No one will ever be able to say for certain whether it was poison or an allergic fit and, therefore, there was no murder. To them, the only murders to solve were the ones already brought before them—the murder of Verhardt, which we have a suspect for, and the murder of Mirial, who was a commoner, and thus I have done my job. Paolo and Terrance even hinted at my reappointment. No one mentioned finding the diamond ring of the republic in Medea's possession because it is not enough evidence without testimony.

"Do you not recall? You solved the murders." Julian smiles.

My friend is also back to being deeply unserious.

I suppose nothing really changes in Pryor.

"Yes, Medea is now suffering the indignity of being confined solely to her city villa instead of her thousand-acre estate in her province."

Julian parts his hands. "She is under house arrest, Torren. Some houses are grander than others." Then he sighs. "What is really bothering you? Do I even want to know?"

Terrance and Suh have already floated the idea of Medea paying a sizable tribute to the temple instead of facing any real consequence. Without Kerasea terrifying them, they have returned to their normal indifference. They want all the murders swept under the rug and to move on with their own schemes and ambitions.

But something is off in all of this. I know there is information that would pull everything together and make sense of the timing and the chosen victims. One fact sits right at the edge of my knowledge, but I just can't reach it.

"Everything." I crash onto the sofa.

Most of all, Kerasea's testimony itself gnaws at my mind.

Before we left Jubilee, I returned to the divining room. I wrapped Zel's body and brought it down, but not before I leaned out the tower window in the direction of the palace. There was no possible way Zel saw Medea's balcony. Not during the day and especially not at night, which makes that a fabrication. I was going to confront Kerasea, but then I remembered that she never said Zel was her source — that was *my* theory. But if not her...then who?

The other oddity in the room was that the remains of Calais were completely gone. Because Kerasea and Zel sat unburned in the center of an enormous flame, I hadn't noticed at the time, but there should have been ash and fragments of bone along with teeth. I've never known fire to fully consume a body, so what happened to the remains? And how did he wind up with his head sliced off cleanly? There was no weapon in the room aside from a dagger.

I shudder. All of it was too similar to how Verhardt was decapitated, but Kerasea wasn't responsible for that crime. I've already accepted that as true.

Perhaps the answer is simple: she was able to divine that Medea committed the murder from the god of truth. But then why hide it when she showed her power in the throne room? It has to be something else, something she wouldn't say, but she swore on her god that it was true.

Maybe the thought I had in Jubilee was correct. If she were Elusian...

"Torren," Julian says. "Leave everything else alone. Accept the win."

I press my lips together.

He reaches out and puts a hand on my shoulder. "You're not going to do that, are you?"

"Probably not."

He sighs, but turns to leave. "Then at least get some rest. Late morning tomorrow, the Council will announce Terrance as Senate

Leader and there will be the funerary processions for Verhardt and Antinous. You'll need your strength for those."

With that, he shuts the door, leaving me in peace. I lean my head back. Tomorrow will be all fake mourning and ceremony. Julian is right. I need sleep or I'll never be able to handle the cries of professional mourners.

Alone in my apartments, I remove my chest armor and set it on the cushion beside me. Then I stand and take off my shirt and leather skirt. With the weight removed, I realize that Julian is right. The public announcements, day of mourning, and funerals will put to rest any question of the murders. Why can't I just accept that?

Guilt, maybe. Perhaps I've always wanted them to discover who I really am. Getting away with murder is a punishment in and of itself.

I've just removed my shin guards when there's a knock on my door. Julian must've forgotten something.

I throw open the door, but it's not him. Kerasea stands in front of me in a beige cloak with her eyes wide.

"You're not Julian," I say. I feel the cool air on my bare chest as blood rushes to my cheeks.

"Not last time I checked, no," she says slowly.

"Come in."

The last thing I need is other sentries seeing the High Priestess here while I stand in my underwear. It would fuel gossip for a week in the capital. And now that we're back home, I'm painfully aware of our positions. In Jubilee, I could lie to myself because she was next door. In the capital, she's a Southside elite and the High Priestess. I'm a man from the Northside who clawed his way to Praetorian.

Kerasea slowly nods and steps inside.

I close the door behind her, and when I turn, I see the apartment as she must—clean but sparse and, overall, shabby. The ceiling paint is cracked, as are some of the floor tiles. I have never been self-conscious about my home, even when Julian pokes fun at it, but having someone like her here is different. I was offered Villa de Armas—the home of the Praetorian—but there is nothing that could compel me to take it. Not after the screams that echoed there.

"Did you need something?" I ask, rubbing the back of my neck. "I was just about to get ready for bed."

"Oh, I…I'm sorry," she says. "It's late. I should go."

It's ten at night. Undoubtedly, she should leave. But now I have to know why she is here.

She takes a step toward the door, and I put out my hand. She stills, two feet from my palm.

"Kerasea, why did you come?"

She smiles, but then her eyes become glassy, and she sniffles. "I don't know. I… We burned Zel tonight and I just…I couldn't stand being at the temple and I thought…" She stares at the floor and then shakes her head. "I'm sorry. Now that I've said it aloud, I see how this is not your problem. I'm really very sorry to disturb you."

She takes another step toward the door, and I splay my fingers, my arm still out. I know exactly what she's feeling. She is sad, tired, frustrated, and seeking solace.

And she came to me.

"The Senate thanked me tonight, publicly commended me," I say.

She narrows one eye and then clears her expression. "Well, your investigation found the evidence…"

"You know as well as I do that I didn't deserve a laurel wreath," I say.

She stares at the floor. "I know the feeling of undeserved praise. Who thanked you?"

"Terrance, Suh, and Paolo."

"Not Foreau?"

I shake my head. "He was notably absent, but he said he was returning to the fourth province."

As she stands here, I realize that I wanted to confer with her.

I missed her already.

It's then that I notice we are far too close to each other. Her cloak looks soft, as soft as her lips.

My hand moves like it has a will of its own. I reach out and touch the edge of her cloak. It is as soft as a lamb. I want to peel it off her, but then I remember how she backed away from my touch, my efforts to console her. I force myself to let go and drop my hand. My fingers ache to feel her again, and I curl them in fists.

She breathes out, her chest rapidly rising and falling. Kerasea stares straight ahead, and then her expression hardens into resolve. I hold still as she takes a tiny step closer to me and then another until she's inches from me. Kera stares up into my eyes, and then she stands on her toes.

Joy fills my chest, and I lean down and close the distance between us.

LXII.

Kerasea

I thought Torren was about to kiss me, but instead, he tips my chin up with his thumb.

"What do you want, Kera?"

He's so close that our breath mingles. He smells like snow and sandalwood, and his nearness makes it hard for me to form a coherent thought. But he waits patiently.

What do I want? I didn't come here for this, but now it's difficult to think of anything else. I came here because I thought he'd understand how I felt. Because I wanted to be near him again. Because I missed him. And because I wanted to finish what we started.

"You," I say. "I want you."

His pupils dilate, a flash of pleasure on his face before his lips mash against mine. He wraps his arms around me, pressing me against the hardness of his chest. He's all ridges and cuts, lines and muscle, but his touch is gentle...until it's not.

With one motion, he unhooks my cloak, and it falls to the floor.

I'm wearing a simple white dress beneath it. He gazes down my body, his eyes adoring, and then he picks me up. My sandals slide off my feet, and I'm weightless as he carries me into his bedroom.

I thought he'd fling me onto his mattress or pin me to the wall again, but instead, he gently places me down next to his bed. The tiles are cold on my bare soles, the room fairly sparse but lived in.

So this is where the Praetorian sleeps. There's a simple double bed, a single nightstand, and a wooden dresser. Everything in here is well cared for, including a full bookcase. There was one in his living room as well with poetry, history, science, and maths. The spines are worn but the bindings well kept. He studies and teaches himself. There's something endearing about that.

As Praetorian, he has a villa on the Southside, but I'd already heard he never uses it. He chooses to stay in these two rooms in the barracks.

We stand beside his bed, and he leans down and kisses me again. My body hums, but it's not blood magic—it's something else. The bottom of my stomach flips from his kiss, and all I want is more. I wait, impatient, but he takes his time. His hands barely graze my breasts as desire builds inside me.

He kisses me until I'm breathless. I try to take his underwear down and he stops my hands. Then he looks me in the eye.

"Don't rush, Kera," he whispers. "We have all night."

This thing between us, whatever it is, swirls and crashes like waves. The throbbing between my legs is intolerable. I want this. I don't care what the fallout will be.

"Take all of me," I say.

His full lips curl into a wicked smile as he grabs me and turns me around. With my back to his chest, he doesn't hike up my dress. Instead, he takes my hairpins out, dropping them to the floor one by one until my ebony locks cascade around me. It's so intimate. So different from last time. Then he kisses the side of my neck, his tongue making me shiver as he unties my dress.

In seconds, I'm undone.

Torren's rough hands gently slip the straps off my shoulders, and then he lets my dress fall to my waist. The bodice holds at my hips until he guides it down to my ankles. Like him, I'm now left in my undergarments—a white chemise and panties.

I'm exposed, but I've never felt this safe.

He pushes on my hip, wordlessly asking me to face him again. I comply. His eyes drink me in, and then he lifts me up and we careen onto the bed. We land with him over me, the heat of his body radiating into my bare skin. The weight of him feels divine as he presses me into the soft bed.

"Kera," he murmurs.

Even the way he says my name is intoxicating.

He's already hard, his underwear straining, but he takes his time. Actually, he's moving painfully slowly, sliding his hands under my chemise. He cups my breasts, his thumbs grazing my nipples. His touch sends waves of pleasure through me, but I want more.

Finally, he peels down my chemise and kisses a line across my collarbone and then down. Deliciously down. My nipples strain toward his mouth, my back arching as his tongue flicks against them. Little bursts of pain and pleasure hit my spine as he nips, his white teeth biting gently. I moan, and he presses a finger to my lips.

"These walls are thin," he says.

"Do they think you're a virgin?" I smile.

A serious expression wrinkles his brow as he shakes his head. "I don't bring anyone here."

I'm trying to absorb that when he strokes my cheek.

"And your moans are only for me," he says.

Something in my core melts at his words, and desire flashes in his eyes. Still fondling my breasts, he begins to kiss the line down the center of my stomach. Then he gets to my panties. He looks up and smiles before he tugs them off me.

When my panties are on the floor, he sits back and admires me.

"Gods, you're perfect," he says.

Heat rises into my face, but the desire to watch him is so strong that I don't look away. He runs his hand from my ankle along the inside of my calf and then up my inner thigh. I part my legs to give him more access, remembering the pleasure from his tongue. He groans, adoration in his eyes. He leans down and then begins to kiss the very top of my inner thigh. I raise my hips, shamelessly begging for more. Then he dips between my legs.

I gasp as his tongue hits the very sensitive parts of me. His tongue is so soft and gentle as he teases my lips, my clit. I move my hips and run my hands through his hair, but he won't be rushed.

"Impatient little priestess," he murmurs.

"Please, Tor."

He glances up, all mischief in his eyes. Then I see the ceiling and I gasp. My back arches as his tongue finds exactly where I need him again. I grab his pillow and bite into it to try to keep quiet.

But he's trying to make me scream. Wicked man. He works his tongue in firm strokes as I tense, both wanting more and not knowing what to do with this feeling. He grips my hips, holding me in place, leaving me no choice but to submit as he licks me again and again.

Waves of pleasure crest, make me quiver. I rest my legs on his shoulders as tension builds and builds. I claw the pillow, the sheets, trying to hold myself together, but it feels like I'm falling apart.

Then he moves his hand between my legs. I'm already so wet that his finger slides inside me. Then another parts me, filling me, as he continues to lick my clit in maddening strokes. The pleasure is too much for me to take. I shudder, shaking.

"Please," I whimper.

"Come for me," he says. "Now. Give me all of you."

He puts his mouth on me again, and pleasure rises until my muscles are so taut that I feel like they'll snap. And then I jump over the edge. It's an eruption and a collapse at the same time. My vision goes white as I come, moaning his name into the pillow.

He keeps licking, claiming me, as I shudder with aftershocks. It's not until I go limp that he sits back, admiring me.

I try to catch my breath as my face tingles. I've never been so satisfied and yet still so hungry. Tor is also breathing hard, but he's in no rush. Maybe I am impatient, but I can't wait any longer.

I lean forward and push on his underwear. I know that I can't do a thing on this bed that he doesn't allow, but there's something freeing in him having full control.

Slowly, he takes down his underwear, exposing his large, thick cock. Bottomless desire like I've never felt hits me, and I want to consume him the way he just did to me, but he gently pushes back on my shoulders.

I land on the bed, my eyes wide in surprise.

"I need to feel you," he says, lying over me.

He runs his hands along my curves, and I wrap my arms and legs around him. And then he guides his cock into me.

He's so thick that my eyes widen as he slowly pushes inside me while kissing my neck. I gasp, the sensation incredible as he enters me. This is what we started. What I craved. He gives me time to adjust to every inch, to want more of him, and then he pushes deeper.

But I've never been filled this way before. I've had sex and I've enjoyed it, but nothing like this.

"Gods, Kera," he says in my ear as he pushes deeper inside me. I dig my nails into his back.

Torren keeps his eyes on mine as I open to take him. Then he turns, picking me up so I land straddling him. He sits up and kisses my breasts, my mouth as I start to ride him.

Despite his arms wrapped around me, he doesn't move my body. On top of him, I can control how much and how deep I take him. I start slowly, but he groans in pleasure when I take more. It's as intoxicating a sound as it is a feeling. Every time I pull back, my hips moving up, I miss the sensation of his cock filling me. I just want more. I ride deeper until eventually I'm taking all of him.

A deep moan escapes my lips from how good he feels. He smiles and kisses me, and it's like I can feel him straight from my mouth to my core. His hips move with mine like we've done this a hundred times before. Yet his eyes constantly search my face, reading me, giving me what I want. He's so large, so good, that it's an embarrassingly short time before I start feeling the same buildup of passion, but greater this time. An earthquake compared to a tremor.

I tense as he finds just the right rhythm. He grips my hair, and I throw my head back, grinding against him. Nothing, no sensation has ever felt this good. And then his hips shift and it feels even better.

"Give everything to me," he says. "Now. I want all of you."

He puts his palm over my mouth as I begin to come. The orgasm rips through me as if it will split me in two. My toes curling, my fingers gripping his shoulders, I lose myself completely. I forget where I am, even who I am. I'm just his.

"You're mine," he whispers in my ear.

A second wave crashes through me, the euphoria nearly unbearable. Like the first time communing with a god—pain, pleasure, a heady high. Then I fall against his chest, exhausted, but still wanting more. I want him to feel the same. I need to watch him lose himself the same way.

He lays me down again, moving me like I weigh less than a feather. Then he pins my hands above my head, careful to avoid the bandage on my wrist. I feel how much he needs to possess me. The need for control is radiating from him.

"I need you, Tor," I say.

His eyes smile. With his other hand, he guides his cock into me again.

I lean my head back, enjoying how he fills me. He's still so hard, so strong. He could take whatever he wanted, but he keeps looking for permission. I didn't expect him to be so gentle, so giving. He moves his hips, watching me. But I want him to lose control, too.

"Take what you want," I say.

He groans and moves faster, deeper. "Kera."

I hold his shoulders as he pushes harder. I can't help but moan. He presses his lips to mine, but he's breathing hard, pleasure building in him.

And in me.

A kind of greed I've never felt before has me shifting my hips up to meet him. He notices, like he notices everything.

"I need you," I say. "Make me yours."

"Mine," he groans.

A sound like a growl mixed with a groan rumbles in my ear. He comes so hard, I can feel it filling me, triggering little ripples of pleasure inside of me.

Torren lies back, breathing hard. Sweat shines on his brow and he strokes my hair, then he pulls me into him. Not to have me, but to hold me. I rest against his chest, but it's hard to ignore how much I still want more.

"I'm not done with you," he says, stroking my cheek.

A hunger from deep inside me stirs, and I whimper. He smiles and presses his lips to my forehead.

"Rest—for now."

LXIII.

Kerasea

I'm still euphoric the third time Torren pushes himself to the brink, biting my bottom lip. He moans my name, and it's like music.

"Give me everything," he says. "Come again for me."

I'm a little sore and very exhausted, but I've also never felt so alive. He can now work my body like an instrument he's mastered. He turns me over so I'm facing the bed, and then he reaches down. He strokes my clit in circles while thrusting into me. His cock is so good that I'm biting the sheets, moaning into the bed.

We find each other's rhythm once more and then crest a wave of pleasure together. He fills me and I pulse around his cock until we both go limp.

He kisses my shoulder, and then we fall back, sweating and breathing hard. I lie on my side, and he mirrors me so we face each other. His hand is on my hip, the other playing with my hair.

He strokes my face, a sleepy smile on his kiss-swollen lips. My eyelids are heavy and so are his. All I want to do is fall asleep entangled with him. I lower my eyelids, but then the night clock chimes three. With those chimes, reality creeps back in. I become aware that I'm the High Priestess in the Praetorian's bed. In the barracks where a hundred other sentries sleep. I have to leave before the sun rises. We have duties, responsibilities.

"I should return to the temple," I say.

Torren pulls me closer to him and kisses my forehead. "Stay."

I know I have to go, but I can stay for just a little while longer.

The next thing I know, I'm falling asleep.

Only, this isn't sleep. I fall out of reality into the pull of godless death. Maybe Mirial has another memory to show me. Maybe she'll help me figure out why Medea killed her.

But when I come to, the next memory I walk in isn't hers at all.

LXIV.

Torren

Kerasea lies next to me, and sleep pulls at my eyelids. I breathe in her rose oil scent and a strange feeling covers me.

Contentment.

I'm just content.

Tomorrow is a problem for another day. Tomorrow, we have to be Praetorian and High Priestess again. There will be the announcement and funeral processions, and then we'll have to both sit on the Verity Guild as we try the most important cases in the republic, including Medea's. While we may not ever be able to prove that she was behind the murders of Verhardt and Eyo, she will be convicted of murder under *lex religio*. She will lose her seat on the Council, and I will be able to keep the new Senate safe.

That is all, and it will have to be enough, because there is a set of laws for the elite and an entirely different set for everyone else.

But that is all for another day. Tonight, Kera and I are just a woman and a man.

She's fast asleep and I kiss her forehead, then I close my eyes.

I fall into deep sleep with her in my arms. As I fade, I have one thought: I've never wanted more than what I have right now.

LXV.

Kerasea

I stand on the stone terrace of the Senate Hall, the crowd around me perfumed and richer than I've even dreamed. The men have been noble for centuries, their mistresses the finest I've seen. I can't have any of them. Not yet, anyhow.

It takes a moment for me to orient myself into this already occurred memory. I feel the same sense of being myself and not, trapped in a decided outcome, yet free to observe through the eyes of someone else.

But I am not Mirial.

As I look at the elite around me, I feel an unfamiliar sense of entitlement along with simmering anger. I deserve everything; I'm owed it. Yet I don't have it. The Calais family was only made noble twenty-five years ago, our lousy ancestors failing us at every turn.

Revulsion fills me as I realize who I am. I am walking not in the memories of my friend but of Sentry Lucius Calais. I don't know why this is happening—I didn't use his body to commune with godless death. But then I remember that I did use my blood to spill his in the tower. Our blood mingled when I beheaded him, and this is my punishment. I have to walk in his thoughts.

I feel how much he covets and yet hates everything around him, and I can't escape it. I experience it, seeping through me as if it's my own emotion.

I stand near elites from the second province, all dressed for the Revelry. Eyo's fine little mistress wears a silver string gown that leaves nothing to the imagination. They've been together for a month, and while she's not the most stunning girl here, she opens her legs and her mouth on command. I've watched them through the keyhole before and have thought about putting her on her knees for me — to experience some of what he has — but I need to be patient. When I have his villa, I'll have her, too. Better than her. Maybe I'll make the High Priestess mine.

She's talking to Eyo and wearing a gold dress where I can see her tits, nearly down to her slit. When I am the senator from the second province, I'll taste that slit. A little poison in Eyo's goblet and I will be voted into his seat, and then I'll be equal to her. Greater. I'll have everything I want, including her.

Kerasea suddenly walks away from him. His play to bed her must have failed. He seems annoyed as he returns, but his mistress tempts him, licking her lips and whispering in his ear. He's not any better-looking than I am — I'm younger and more muscular — but these women climb into his bed for his status. They'll act the same way for me soon.

"I have to piss," I say as I watch the High Priestess leave.

Eyo glances at me. "Well don't do it here."

Everyone laughs like he's hilarious, and he kisses his mistress. He'll probably bend her over this balcony railing before the night ends.

Anger boils inside me, but I can't act on it. Not until the second day of the conclave. Medea's instructions were crystal clear, and the she-wolf must be obeyed. Her promises are as real as her threats. She elevated my father after he poisoned her twin brother. Father stayed loyal, and she rewarded him. It's that easy.

I bow to Eyo and smile, knowing that he has only days to live.

Now that I've been excused, I can follow Kerasea. I turn to leave, but the Praetorian is far ahead of me, stalking her. I was told he'd hunt her down, but no one has been killed yet. He must just want her for himself.

I take the corridor toward the latrines, but I stop in my tracks as there are whispered voices near the bathroom. I take a left and slide out of sight. Leaning against the wall, I strain to pick up the sounds. The hushed tones signal a secret—something worth knowing.

"Remember, not a drop of blood, and you must plant the knife," Medea says. I'd know her voice anywhere.

"It will be done," a man responds. I'm not sure who it is.

"To the end of the Verity Guild," Medea says.

"To the future, my love," he replies.

Footsteps come in my direction, and I slip inside the doorway to one of the senate offices. If anyone turns their head fully, they'll spot me. I wait with my heart pounding as Medea passes. She doesn't turn. I exhale. I wait another moment, and then I go to the latrines.

As I piss, I realize she is having someone killed tonight.

I wonder who.

I gasp and wake with a start. I'm not in my own chambers—I'm in Tor's bed. He lies sleeping peacefully beside me, his arm around me. I move to wake him. Something important just happened, something crucial. It sits at the tip of my tongue, but I'm too exhausted to remember what it was. I'm so groggy that I immediately fall back to sleep.

LXVI.

Torren

I'm awoken from dead sleep by someone knocking on my door.
Worried, I turn and look at the sun clock. It's nine in the morning.
I slow my heart. I didn't oversleep.

Wait, what is happening? I went to bed with Kera beside me.

I reach out, but there's nothing but a rough cotton bedsheet. She's
gone.

With a sigh, I sit up. I knew she had to leave and so it shouldn't
hurt. But it does. She crept out like I was a shameful secret.

I hang my head, but when I raise my chin, there's Kera standing
by the dresser, tying her dress back on. She smiles, stunning in the
morning light, and my heart leaps in my chest. She's here.

But then her smile fades. "I need to talk to you."

She probably needs to find a discreet way to leave now that it's
morning and someone is at the door. I don't blame her. The Verity
Guild will be convening tomorrow, and we will sit beside each other
as we hear Trajan Lowe's case. So we need to—

I take a breath as everything crystallizes, my heart hammering.

That was the missing piece—the reason Medea struck this time, at this conclave. This was the knowledge just at the edge of my mind. Medea was after the Verity Guild because we will hear the treason case of her nephew. Trajan Lowe was caught raising a private army, but nothing goes on in her province without her knowing it. Now I see that those soldiers were actually for Senator Medea.

The incursion, the senators were important to the killer, but not for the reasons I thought.

With Verhardt and Eyo dead, she'd have the majority vote for a declaration of war, but Kerasea and I were still a problem. Even in a war, the tribunals proceed—they had to during a war that lasted one hundred years. She had the same dilemma I have experienced: how to topple elites of Pryor when they are so protected.

I would be naturally reappointed...unless I failed to keep the Senate safe, unless I failed as Praetorian. Each time someone died, Medea was in favor of allowing me to investigate because she knew she could keep me from the information I needed, thereby making the case for getting me dismissed for incompetence.

And that is also the reason she framed Kerasea—because she had no other method to remove the High Priestess from the Verity Guild. Priestess Mirial must have been conspiring with Medea, perhaps because she wrongly thought she could protect Kerasea or maybe it was ambition to take her seat on the tribunal, but then Medea tied up the loose end.

I'm right. I know I am. I just need the proof.

I am just about to tell Kera when the knocking turns to banging on the door. "Praetorian!"

I slip out of bed and throw my pants on. "Stay here. I'll handle it," I say.

"But—"

"I have things to discuss with you, too, but let me get rid of this first."

Kera gnaws on her lip but nods.

The knocking continues, but I pause to kiss Kera on her shoulder.

I close the door to the bedroom and then open the front door. Julian stands there in his formal armor.

"We need to talk," Julian says at the same moment I blurt, "I figured it out."

It's then I notice how pale and uncharacteristically somber Julian appears this morning as he rubs his knuckles.

"What happened?" I ask.

"Chief Justice Probus is dead," he says.

With both Kera and me still in our positions, Medea must've had Probus killed. Ever resourceful, she picked a different target. Only, how did she do that while confined to her villa?

Julian partially covers his mouth with his hand.

"What is it?" I ask.

He sighs. "I am here to place you and Kerasea under arrest."

THE END FOR NOW

Acknowledgments

Thank you to the brilliant Liz Pelletier for being the most incredible editor, champion, and publisher there is. None of this happens without you, and I'm so blessed to continue to work with you on our fourth (!) title. Special thanks to Mary Lindsey and Stacy Abrams for your amazing edits and support.

Thank you, everyone at Red Tower, for your tireless efforts in shaping my series. Thank you to the amazing edit team of Madison Pelletier, Rae Swain, and Hannah Lindsey. Thank you to the incredible art team of Bree Archer, Elizabeth Turner Stokes, and Britt Marczak. Thank you to Curtis Svehlak, Justine Bylo, and Molly Majumder in production. And thank you to the fantastic publicity and marketing team, including: Victoria Chew, Melanie Smith, Meredith Johnson, Heather Riccio, Cai Cramer, Lindsey Staub, and Hannah Li-Paz. And thank you to Nicole Resciniti and the entire team at Penguin Michael Joseph for bringing this series worldwide.

Many thanks to my agents, Lauren Spieller and Hannah Morgan Teachout, for your notes, guidance, and support!

Thank you to my four children, who inspire and delight me. I am blessed to call you my family. Thank you to my mother for instilling hard work and dedication and leading by example. With every page, I hope to make you and Dad proud. Thank you to my sister, aunt, and cousins for your excitement and love.

Thank you to my friends, who've been there for me through the highs and lows of this wild author ride, especially Karen McManus, Alexa Martin, Sabina Khan, Matt Weintraub, Susan Thibault, and my incredible sprinting buddy, Carissa Broadbent. Thank you to my Red Tower siblings, especially Abigail Owen, Hannah Nicole Maehrer, Rachel Van Dyken, Rachel Howzell Hall, Cecy Robson, Geneva Lee, Kyla Linde, and Jade Presley for the laughs and brilliant insights. Every event has been even better because of you!

Thank you to all the influencers, booksellers, reviewers, and most of all readers for making me an international bestseller!

Last, but most importantly, thank you to John Coryea. I cannot write love without feeling it. Thank you for enduring this long storm by my side. You gave me a hand to hold and my heart a home. I love you today and tomorrow and tomorrow and tomorrow.